THE
PROPOSAL

ALSO BY S.E. Lynes

Valentina
Mother
The Pact

THE
PROPOSAL
S. E. LYNES

bookouture

Published by Bookouture in 2018

An imprint of StoryFire Ltd.

Carmelite House
50 Victoria Embankment
London EC4Y 0DZ

www.bookouture.com

ISBN: 978-1-78681-517-0
eBook ISBN: 978-1-78681-516-3

We seem normal only to those who don't know us very well.

Alain de Botton

CHAPTER ONE

PIPPA GATES: PRIVATE JOURNAL

The first thing you should know, dear reader, is that I am dead.

Not now, writing this, here at the farm, obviously. But if you're reading these words, then the most likely reason is that this journal has been published posthumously. If that's the case, it means that the events at Cairn Farm have made it into the press. Excerpts from this very document may well have graced the various rags and broadsheets, or been read aloud in breathless gushes by some excited TV reporter. I suppose parts of what I'm about to recount are likely to have been presented in more sober, respectful tones, as evidence at the inquest.

So if you've followed all the coverage in the media and are now reading this private account, I'm guessing you're after the inside track on what I imagine will have been called the Wiltshire Murders. You want the truth, the whole truth and nothing but the truth, so help you God.

Readers – or, dare I say, fans of my books – will also be aware that I am romantic novelist Pippa Gates. If you were interested enough to flick through any interviews I might have done, or perhaps caught me on the radio, you'll have gleaned that I used to be an English teacher and that I lived in a suburb of south London before moving out here, to Cairn Farm, Wiltshire. You might think, perhaps, after all your reading, that you know a little about me.

But let me tell you right here, my friend: you know almost *nothing*.

Still, none of that matters now. Not the version of events out there in the public domain, not my social-media feed, which I cannot access currently for reasons I will explain later; not even my new book, which I may of course never finish. Only this matters. The secret journal that I started at my desk just moments ago, this private account that will become – indeed *has* become, if you are reading it – public. In a world of alternative stories and fake news, *this* journal is the one, the only truth.

You see, as Pippa Gates, I would never be able to publish the kind of material I intend to include here, because my books are love stories, life-affirming novels designed to make people feel good, not ill or troubled for days afterwards. My books don't contain strong swearing or violence or sinister presences in the dead of night. They are optimistic. They bring joy. *Pushing Up Daisy*, the one I'm working on just now, will be no exception. It would be unfair to my readers to do otherwise.

This other story, well, this one is different.

A straightforward happy ending will not, I fear, be possible. As I have said, if you're reading this, then my sorry tale has most probably ended in my own demise. For the fans of puns among you, you might say I've bought the farm.

So much for endings. Beginnings are another matter. *Pushing Up Daisy* begins with the arrival of octogenarian Daisy Philips at the Grange retirement home, where she finds herself reunited with her teenage sweetheart, Bing. Their break-up was acrimonious, and they have not seen each other in fifty years…

My real-life tale, an altogether darker, not to mention *murderous* affair, begins, thinking about it now, with that stalwart of stories the world over: a knock at the door.

It was a Thursday near the end of term. June, back when I was still teaching at St Matthew's Comprehensive and hating every moment of it. On Thursdays, I had 10J immediately after lunch, and they were nothing short of hideous on an almost-bearable day, but this was the scrawny end of a particularly thin week. Plus, I'd had a Tinder date the night before that had finished up in a late bar off Tottenham Court Road and a vague memory of some man with a shiny bottom lip whose name I can't bring to mind right now bundling me into an Uber, having, I presume, somehow got my address out of me. In those days, my address was of no interest to anyone. In those days, I didn't live in fear of my life. In those days, I barely cared about my life, to be honest. In fact, my life, for want of a more elegant word, sucked, and the only way out of it that I could see – and this is really embarrassing – was by writing a bestseller.

Yep. That was my plan. Up there with the lottery win, the knight in shining armour and the hidden treasure at the bottom of the garden.

To say I was hanging by a thread that fateful Thursday is an understatement. To make it worse, my great Plan A – you know, the one where I write the bestseller? – was hardly coming along nicely, as it were. In fact, it was not coming along at all. I know, I know. And you're right. Why didn't I just get the flip on with it? You'd think, wouldn't you, that, considering I'd put all my hopes for escaping my tedious reality in the follow-up to my heroically failed first novel, I would have been working towards actually writing it and, oh, I don't know, trying to make it half decent this time. But alas, no, I was not. I had reached the very eve of my third deadline extension. My new idea had to be nailed to the page and sent to my editor by the following morning or my contract would be terminated. Which was fair enough. My editor, Jackie, had been beyond patient, especially given the utter bomb that was my first book. But still I had nothing. Nada. Diddly squat.

So, yes, all that was weighing on my decidedly fuzzy mind when one of the boys in 10J lit a joint in the classroom and the final straw fell on this rather grumpy camel's back. You might even say I got the hump (sorry).

You can, I'm sure, appreciate why, by the time I got home, I was in need of a large glass of something chilled. The dreaded day job, the all-day hangover, the shady memory of yet another date with yet another perfectly nice bloke who had made about as much of an impression on me as a hand plunged into a sack of lentils… well, thank God I had poured a drink, frankly, because at 4.45 p.m., my phone buzzed, as I had absolutely known it would whilst simultaneously denying that this would ever happen. On the screen I read the name I had known would be there in bold white letters: Jackie West; saw the familiar face of my editor smiling up at me, a picture taken during a lunch many months ago when she'd thought I could actually deliver. Yes, I had anticipated this call, and yet somehow not prepared for it. What? Don't shake your head and frown. We've all done it, haven't we? And what better place to admit to it than here in the safety of my private journal?

Anyway, I fixed a smile to my own face, squared my shoulders and pushed my thumb to the green circle.

'Jackie,' I said, infusing the word with a level of pleasure more suited to hearing from the organisers of the National Lottery on rollover week.

'Hi, Pippa. How're you getting on?' Subtext: *Please don't make me fire you.*

'Good. Really good, actually.' I'd wandered into the hall and now leant into the mirror, my attention taken momentarily by a sliver of shadow on my top lip. Was that a whisker? I wondered. Jesus. What fresh hell was this? I was only thirty-four.

'Pippa?'

'Yes, still here, sorry. You've just caught me at my desk.' I meandered back into the living room, where on the coffee table my laptop gaped, open as an oyster, hoping for pearls. I drained the last of the bottle into my glass. 'I was just finishing my outline.'

'Good, good. We said tomorrow, didn't we, so good – that's good.'

Despite the stress pain in my chest, I said nothing.

'So,' she said. 'Listen, when do—'

'Tomorrow morning,' I interrupted. 'I've already written half of Chapter One. I just need to tweak it, have one last look, and then…' I made myself stop.

'OK, cool. Great. Well, listen, I'm off home soon anyway, so send it as late as you like tonight. Literally midnight is fine, because I'll still have it first thing, all right?'

'Sure,' I said, thinking that *literally midnight* was at best optimistic. *Three a.m.* was more likely. Let's face it, *not at all* was looking favourite. 'I'll have it to you at some point this evening, guaranteed.'

Guaranteed.

It's always hard to know which was the first domino, so to speak, but looking back, they fell like this: bad date, bad hangover, bad day, large wine, call from editor, me blurting out ridiculous promise, me getting into borderline psychotic state with stress at the thought of my dream turning to dust, me opening the door.

And the whole surreal story followed from there.

By seven o'clock, I'd been staring at the blank screen for an hour. I'd tried to call my best mate, Marlena, but she'd been too busy with her kids and her slob of a husband, as per. I'd drunk more wine, eaten a packet of Kettle Chips (one of my five a day because potatoes) and had a long shower. I'd googled every millimetre of celebrity gossip in the hope of finding a troubled love life to mine for dramatic gold. I'd run through the entire teaching staff at St Matthew's looking for a suitable template for a romantic lead: Science Kevin was possible if I lengthened his trousers and put him in better shoes; French Jean-Pierre had nice eyes and a good name, but I'd once seen him dance at a Christmas drinks and hadn't been able to scrub the scorch marks of that image out of my mind; and Geography Dave was – well, no… just no. I'd rummaged through my own back catalogue: all the dates I'd had over the last two years, the Tinders, the Guardian Soulmates, the date-me dot coms; even cast my mind back to before I met Bill. But nothing.

What about the news if you're looking for inspiration? I hear you cry. Plenty of stories in there, surely? Well, that's the thing. I'm not really a current affairs kind of gal. Not a great fan of factual information per se. The news is always, by definition, awful, and there's never anything I personally can do about someone else's war, the latest mass shooting, or some food that I've been blithely munching for the last thirty-four years that is now apparently carcinogenic. But this is how desperate I was: I had resorted to reading the news. And reminding myself why I never do.

Too much reality, thank you very much.

I was pretty much at the end of my incredibly frayed rope, not to mention the Pinot Noir – the last dregs of the white had long since travelled down red lane – and was segueing into my second packet of Kettle Chips when, as they say, there was a knock at the door.

This wasn't due to any dramatic staples – my doorbell had actually recently died and I had no clue how to replace the battery, but let's suppose I'd engineered the event myself.

Reader, there was a knock at the door.

'Who the hell is that?' I asked no one at all, dashing into the hallway. I have no idea why I rushed in this way, because at 7 p.m. it was only ever going to be a canvassing politician, a charity worker looking for a monthly direct debit or a door-to-door salesman.

And sure enough, I opened the door to a cadaverous man with a painfully prominent Adam's apple and greasy, slicked-back grey hair, deep grooves scoring his forehead and the empty folds of once fuller cheeks bracketing his thin lips. He looked to be in his mid fifties. An old green parka (in June) hung from his skinny shoulders, stone-washed jeans sagged around his legs and his trainers, which in a past life had been white, were frankly unspeakable. In front of him he held the obligatory tray of cleaning products. I fought to stop my face from betraying the fact that with every fibre of my being I wished I'd pretended to be out.

'Good evening,' he said with the strained cheer of the desperate. 'I'm sorry to disturb you but my name is Ryan Marks. I'm just trying to get back on my feet and wondered if you'd be interested in any household cleaning products at all?'

Blog post: PippaGatesAuthor
#thiswritinglife
Find me on:
Instagram: @GatesPip
Twitter: @PipGatesWrites
Facebook: Pippa Gates Author

Tonight, here at Cairn Farm, Mrs Danvers is making a chicken casserole, perfect for the winter's evening chill. After an unseasonably warm autumn – soft ground, bacterial bugs proliferating in the temperate air – finally this morning brought longed-for flakes of snow to the Wiltshire hedgerows, nettles glittering with frost at the edges of the fields. What better way to start my blog than with the dawning of a new season, ushered in – with some panache, I must say – by the hibernal beauty of ice! Ice has the power to transform, doesn't it? Take those humble nettles, for example – venomous, yes, but one sprinkle of the old magic rime and this stinging weed becomes the most innocent sugared confection. Ah yes, for me, Jack Frost's handiwork is enough to conjure aromas of mulled wine and log fires, visions of Fair Isle sweaters and Aran socks, and I feel my entire body fill with a tingly thermal glow.

I love winter.

As it was such a crisp blue morning, Mrs D and I walked up to the top field to visit the commemorative cairn after which we renamed this crumbly old pile of bricks we call home. You can see a picture of it, actually, on today's Instagram post. Difficult to see the scale – it could be any old lump of pebbles – but

I'd say it's no higher than a chair seat or a large dog, and the stones are about the size of a fist. Anyway, that's where we walked after breakfast, to stretch our legs before I settle to my desk. Which is what I must do right now!

Word count target today is three thousand.

Reader, I shall report back!

CHAPTER TWO

Privacy affords a writer so much freedom, I'm discovering. Here in my office at Cairn Farm, the snow falling in soft flakes outside my window, it is only the thought that no one will ever read this that is permitting me to let it all hang out in ways I never thought myself capable of. I admit that this is not a diary as such, so in that sense I am writing for someone – for you, that is. So you could argue that it's not private, not really. But the thing is, while, yes, I'm talking to you, in a sense, I know even as I type the words that you won't really 'hear' me, so to speak – at least, not until anything I have to say can no longer embarrass, incriminate or condemn me. I am beyond judgement. I am beyond the grave. And it is from this hypothetical place that I must continue my story: Ryan, the ex-con, was standing on my doorstep, wasn't he? With his terrible clothes and his tray of godawful tat, asking if I would like to buy something, relying on the power of my bleeding-heart liberal guilt to propel me back indoors for my purse, to solve the world's inequalities with a wave of a ten-pound note.

After a moment, he sniffed, then looked away, his jaw a fallen L under his greyish skin. He sniffed again, looked back at me. At the bottom of his cleft chin, a scrappy afterthought of a beard hung on for dear life.

'I can talk you through everything if you like.' The trace of a Cockney accent, the vowels fighting for brevity, the 'th' battling not to become 'f'. His eyes were small and blue and almost defiantly direct.

'Let me get my purse.'

I closed the door with care – I'm keen for you to know that I did at least do this, even though I know it won't stop you judging me later – and went to fetch some cash. Irritation flared in my chest, as is so often the way when you're interrupted from a task you weren't getting on with in the first place. *How dare this person stop me from procrastinating?* That was the gist. Really, I'd prefer to give these guys a tenner and tell them to keep their crap. But I do recognise that, as with many things in life, you have to buy into the pretence: he was a salesman, and I was a customer paying good money for quality wares brought here to my home. We do this every day of our lives, do we not? *How are you? I'm fine *pushes fingernails through palm of hand*. Everything OK with your meal? Absolutely delicious, thank you *nudges dried-out chicken breast under limp lettuce leaf*. Happy with your haircut? Love it! *drops tip into jar, goes home and runs head under tap, cries, wonders about paper bag with eyeholes*.*

Now, I don't know if I'm remembering this rightly, and I may be trying to make more excuses for why the evening turned out as it did, but I know that when I opened the door again, Ryan Marks's blue eyes were the first thing I saw. They were, I thought, the colour of ink dropped in water. It was a shame about the rest of him.

'So, I've got a tenner,' I said. A lie. I'd stopped off on the way home and withdrawn two hundred pounds from the cashpoint. It was the only way I could keep track of my finances, back when I really had to – card-touch payment is a disaster for someone like me; my salary would have lasted a week. But I was hardly going to advertise cash in the house to him, was I?

'That's perfectly all right,' he said. 'I'm sure I can find something for such a lovely round figure.' He met my eye and gave a kind of half-sneer.

Was that an innuendo? And what of the East End accent battling to break through those effortful consonants? Was he trying to climb up, put distance between himself and some seamy past, something squalid and shameful he wanted to leave behind?

'Just give me anything,' I said.

'If you like, I can talk you through this fine range of top-quality cleaning wares and you can decide.' He threw his hand across the tray with a voila gesture, both words and action laced with a certain waggishness, a precarious, conspiratorial mischief.

'Have you sold much tonight?' I caught myself leaning on the door jamb, wishing I'd taken off my Ugg boots before answering the door, removed my old cardigan, plucked out that bloody whisker.

He parted his meagre lips to reveal a set of crooked, brownish teeth. A smoker, possibly, or a coffee addict.

'Thing is with products of this quality,' he said, 'they practically sell themselves.' His tone was soft, his accent no more than a lilt. Perhaps there had been not a climb but a fall – from elegant beginnings, from privilege. White-collar crime? Possibly. Fraud? Maybe. Tax evasion? 'I should wait on the street and sound a horn,' he rattled on, leaning in. 'Wait for the crowds to come running.'

I laughed, surprised by his apparent wit.

He smoothed a hand over his lank, oily hair – three silver rings of Celtic design, one on his pinky finger, one on the middle and one on the index. I caught a whiff of patchouli, of cheap soap, but also something earthier, something lived-in, almost fungal. His nails were long and square, the tips a preternatural white.

'Now this' – from the tray he picked up what I could only call in that moment an *item* made of lime-green plastic – 'I can't *imagine* surviving without.'

'Me neither.' I took it from him. 'What the hell is it?'

Another thin-lipped smile, amusement bending his scraggy eyebrows. 'It's an iPhone holder, which, wait for it, you hang on the door handle. Be it a kitchen-cupboard door or wardrobe or whatever, you hang this little baby up…' He reached forward and took it deftly from my hands. Another second and he had slipped it from its cellophane sleeve and was holding it up like evidence. 'You slide your phone in there, see.' He mimed slotting the phone into its lurid holder. 'Nice and easy, in it slips. When you want it, you just slip it out.' He drew it out, pushed it back in. 'In, out. In. Out. There you go. And you hang it up like this.' He grinned, a little manically, and hung it from his forefinger. 'Hands-free set, see, so you can get on with… well, whatever it is you want to get on with that requires two hands.'

I couldn't tell if he was playing with me or not. His face was earnest, but I was fighting not to hear double entendres in everything he said.

'I had no idea I needed one of those,' I replied simply.

'That's the thing about need,' he said. 'You can't identify it until you know what it is, and you don't know what it is until you find it.'

'I suppose you're right.' My fingertips hovered over my mouth, something I do in moments of self-consciousness.

He, by contrast, showed nothing of the sort. He put one horrid trainer on my front step. 'Glad I came now, aren't you? You need me in your life and you don't even realise it. What's your name, by the way?'

'Pippa. What's… oh, it's Ryan, isn't it? Sorry. You did say.' I realised I had only glanced at his card. He could have been anyone, anyone at all. I made myself meet his eye, and he returned my gaze without flinching.

'If you don't mind my saying,' I said, 'you don't really fit the usual profile.'

He gave a grave nod but didn't seem offended. In fact he threw his eyes left and right playfully, then dipped towards me. 'That's because the others are all petty criminals, whereas I… am actually a murderer.' His face remained deadpan for a moment before he pointed at me and broke into a gutsy, hoarse smoker's laugh. In the dank cavern of his mouth, a gold tooth shone. 'Only joking.'

'I know,' I said, laughing along. Of course I knew he was joking; what did he take me for, an idiot?

'No, seriously.' He straightened up, took his foot off the threshold and returned it to the front path. 'I'm trying to get my life back together just like all the others. It's nice when people give us the time of day, when they treat us like human beings. It makes a difference.'

'What happened to you?' I said. 'Sorry, ignore that. None of my business.'

He shook his head – *don't worry* – and stared momentarily at his feet. The soles of his trainers lolled away from the leather, like filthy tongues. 'Long story. But it's not what happened to me, it's what I did, Pip. My fault, I take full responsibility. But I built myself up once and I'll do it again. I've learnt.' He looked up, his eyes no less blue in the falling light. 'I've paid.'

He had paid. He had paid and yet here he was, still paying – through the disdainful looks and the doors closed in his face, the job opportunities no doubt gone forever. I felt my eyes prick.

'What will you do now?'

He shrugged. 'I think I might be the only carpenter with a degree in English literature, but there you are. Advantages of Her Majesty's finest accommodation for you.'

I opened the door a little wider. My toes breached the brass brink of my house.

'I—'

'What do you do?' he interrupted. 'Sorry, you were going to say something.'

'Not at all, I'm a… I'm… I'm a writer.' Not strictly true. I was a comprehensive school teacher who wasn't very good at keeping order in the classroom; I was a serial dater who had managed to write one crap novel that hadn't sold. Did I stop to wonder why I'd preferred to tell him what, at best, I almost was, instead of the lesser truth? I was trying to impress him, obviously – I see that now. But why? I suppose, despite my revulsion, my quiet fear of him, I still hoped he'd find me interesting.

He rested an arm against the wall of the house. 'What kind of writer?'

'Novels.' Novels plural. What a fraud, what a joke.

He shifted the angle of his head, as if to adjust to a sudden change in the light. 'I love books. Used to read tons inside. Cormac McCarthy, Ian McEwan. I like the older stuff too – Dickens. I like Iris Murdoch, Daphne du Maurier.'

'I love du Maurier,' I said. '*Rebecca* particularly.'

'Oh yes, great book. And might I have heard of your work?'

I laughed, embarrassed, as if I'd just described myself as a painter and now, hearing mention of Rembrandt and Picasso, found myself having to explain that I decorated houses for a living.

'I'm not exactly in that league,' I said. 'I wrote a book called *Fight for Your Love*, but you won't have... I mean, it's probably more aimed at... although a man could read it, I suppose. It's about a boxer who... I'll shut up.'

I wished he'd stop smiling after everything I said.

'*Fight for Your Love.*' He gave a kind of bow. 'I'll make sure I buy that as soon as I save my pennies.'

I held up a finger. 'Wait here.' This time I didn't close the door. Go ahead, tut. Mutter to yourself something along the lines of *Oh, for goodness' sake, who does that?* I'll answer that for you: me. I do. I did.

I ran to the living room, pulled a paperback copy from my stash and dashed back to find Ryan in my hallway, the front door closed behind him.

I had not heard the door shut. And I think that was the first time I felt the burning sensation beneath my skin: that fine layer, like an allergic reaction, a spice, a poison.

'Oh,' I said.

He threw up his hands. 'I was just trying to keep out the cold. I thought if you saw the door shut you'd think I'd gone. Sorry, I shouldn't have come in like that.' He opened the door and stepped out again.

I followed him to the doorstep and handed him the book. It wasn't cold out. There had been no reason for him to come in, nor to close the front door.

'I'll take an iPhone holder,' I said curtly and held out the book. 'And you can take this.'

'An exchange?'

'No, I'll pay for the holder thing too.'

He coughed into his hand and lifted his gaze to meet mine. 'Look, I'm sorry I came into your house. I'm still getting used to being out. It was inappropriate. I'm sorry.'

His eyes sank at the corners. I softened.

'That's all right,' I said. 'But I still insist on paying. The book is… it's a gift. I mean, you don't have to have it. Gosh, that's probably presumptuous of me. You probably don't even want—'

'If you wrote it, I want to read it. Will you sign it? I have a pen.' He dug in the inside pocket of his tatty coat and pulled out a silver fountain pen. 'I'd love you to sign it. Can you put "For Ryan"?'

'Of course.'

The pen was like him: incongruous. Perhaps he'd stolen it. I didn't care. He wasn't like any man I had ever spoken to.

'Actually,' he added, just as I was about to inscribe his name, 'could you put, "To my darling. We belong together. Love from Pippa"?'

'What?'

He chuckled, gruff and low. 'I know it sounds weird, but it's just a joke, for the others at the hostel, you know? Please? Go on, it'll wind them right up, with you being a famous author and all that.'

'I… I'm hardly…'

'Hey, listen, don't if you don't want to. Just thought I'd spin them a yarn when I get back, that's all. Just sign it, that'll do. Forget it, sorry. Not doing very well, am I?'

'No, it's OK. You're OK, don't worry.'

I felt bad for him. I wrote what he'd asked for, signed my name and returned the book. There was a fumble then over the pen; our fingers touched. I fought the urge to dash and wash my hands and instead rubbed them on my leggings as discreetly as I could. When I looked up, I saw that his eyes had darkened. They reflected the sky, I realised, and as the day had faded, they too had changed: a higher concentration of ink to water.

'Goodbye then,' he said, plucking the crisp ten-pound note from my fingers and handing over the plastic abomination that I would put straight into the trash. 'It was great meeting you, Pippa. You're… well, you're different.'

I felt myself blush. *So are you*, I thought. *So are you.*

'Good luck, Ryan,' I called after him.

He ambled down the path, his shoulders narrow as a child's coat hanger, his jeans loose as sacks. The gate squeaked. He glanced down, then back at me. 'You need some WD-40 on that hinge. And your bell needs a new battery.' A sparse grin, a wave.

'I'll get onto it. Bye.'

Safe inside, I leant back against the front door, closed my eyes and gave a long sigh.

'Who are you?' I muttered to no one. 'What's your story, eh?'

Really, though. What *was* his story? Where was he from? What had his childhood been like? Had he worn the corners off his privileged accent in order to escape a pummelling in the nick? Or had he consciously set about improving his elocution while he served his time, alone in his prison cell, determined to make a new start? Was he the pearl or was he the grit? Who the hell was Ryan Marks and what was his story? What *on earth* was his story?

A second later, I had thrown open the door and was running down my front path.

'Ryan,' I called after him. 'Ryan!'

He was already next door, his finger hovering over their doorbell. He turned, frowned at me in apparent amusement. 'Pippa Gates, famous author. Miss me already?'

He started back down my neighbour's front path, towards where I stood on the pavement, anxious as a child waiting for Father to come home.

'I know we belong together,' he said, grinning. 'Just didn't realise you meant right now.'

My chest burned. The fire spread again under my skin. 'I…'

'You want another phone holder? I could give you three for two.'

'No, I…'

'Magic screen wipes? Fluorescent pink e-cloth?'

'No.' I shook my head. 'I was wondering… how much would it cost to buy the entire tray?'

His brows came together, made deep dimples.

'What, all of it?' he said. 'Your house must be a real mess.'

'I mean it,' I said, almost laughing with the sheer terror of what I was about to do – what I was by then powerless to stop myself from doing. 'How much for the lot?'

He was standing close to me now. Around us, the faint amber glow of the street lamps brightened against the oncoming dusk. I could smell the musty charity-shop whiff of his clothes, a body dried with a damp towel, tobacco too, and that cheap institutional soap. He was clean – scrubbed, actually – but still I fought the urge to put my sleeve over my nose. I did not move away from him even though instinct told me to run – to run and never look back.

He bit his bottom lip with his appalling teeth and surveyed his tray of tat. 'About two hundred quid? Something like that?'

My heart pounded. I knew I would have to speak quickly. I fixed his now penetrating blue-black eyes with mine. 'Ryan… I have a kind of proposal for you…'

Blog post: PippaGatesAuthor
#thiswritinglife
Find me on:
Instagram: @GatesPip
Twitter: @PipGatesWrites
Facebook: Pippa Gates Author

Not much to report other than a healthy word count, thanks to Mrs Danvers and a very strict timetable: breakfast at seven, walk around the grounds, elevenses at 10.45 a.m., cup of tea at midday, lunch at one, cup of tea and biscuit at four, finish work at six, aperitif at seven, dinner at eight. Those of you who follow me on Instagram will have seen yesterday's pictures of FULL SNOW COVERAGE – ta-dah! Cairn Farm's upper field is a thick white pelt. Actually, we are in talks with a local farmer who wants to rent it out for his sheep. Of all the things I thought I'd have in life, ovine tenants is not one!

If you saw my Instagram yesterday, you may also have seen the rather fabulous birthday cake that Mrs D made for me. Honestly, I had no idea. I'm used to the aroma of baked goods wafting around the place, but I never expected such a cake. All the way into Bath to the kitchen shop to pick up the coloured icing! When I saw it was a book-shaped cake, my heart melted, of course, but when I realised that there were actual words from *Framed by Love* piped across the pages in black icing, well... I don't mind admitting to shedding a few tears.

That's devotion. I am a lucky, lucky girl.

I am also a girl on a deadline, my friends. I'm writing a chapter that flashes back to Daisy and Bing's first date – an afternoon-tea dance in Weston-super-Mare, under the watchful eye of Daisy's aunt Bertha, a kind of Nanny McPhee meets Miss Trunchbull. So I shall say ta-ta for now and speak to you in a couple of days, when I hope to report significant progress on *Pushing Up Daisy.*

CHAPTER THREE

This is what, my third journal entry? I have to say, I'm thoroughly enjoying it. Mrs Danvers would doubtless disapprove of me taking time out from my book, but sometimes you need a break from the creative work, and it's far too cold to be outdoors for long. Besides, it's doing me good to set down the events that led me here, to Cairn Farm, to this desk, this writing life. Thinking about the night that Ryan arrived at my home, I can see that that proposal was the start of it all. Not the bad day, not the deadline, not the dire need to escape a life that was killing me, but my action. My proposal. I take responsibility. That's what this journal is partly about, I suppose: that most painful yet therapeutic of processes: taking a look at your life and taking responsibility for the choices that made it what it is.

'A proposal?' Ryan said, his black stare brutal.

'Yes,' I replied. 'I… Look, this is going to sound strange, so I'll just come out with it. If I buy all your stuff, all of it, if I give you two hundred quid, cash, will you come into my house, right now, this evening, and tell me your life story?'

He looked first towards one end of the street, then the other.

'Sorry,' he said. 'Just scanning for the joke squad and their hidden cameras.'

'I'm serious,' I said. 'I need a story. In fact, I'm bloody desperate for one. If I don't come up with one tonight, the life I want is over before it's even properly started. And you have a story to tell, Ryan. I'm pretty sure of it. It's not… it's not your cleaning products I'm buying, it's your life. Will you sell it to me?'

'You want my life?'

'Your past, your story, whatever. Where you come from, what you came from, who you are… how you ended up in prison. I'll need all of it. Ugly details, the lot. They're what make a story true. And – this is important – once you've told it, it would be mine. I would own it. And as such, I would have the right to change and shape it as I need. But even if I do change it, if it does make it into print, if you ever read it, there will be things that you'll recognise. I mean, I'll change names and places, but there'll be little details and events that you'll know came from you. You have to be aware of that before you agree. It's… it feels unethical otherwise.'

I made myself look at him. He was grinning at me with something like wonder.

'All right,' he said, winking. 'You're on.'

I should not have let him in, of that there is no doubt. I didn't know him, and I had no idea of his crime. But I've never really been one for doing what I should, and yes, I've been in some scrapes. Nothing horrific, nothing I haven't been able to handle. Marlena would have told you differently, but she's never done anything even remotely risky. She's never taken drugs or hitched a lift on her own in a foreign country or woken up in a strange bed not knowing whether she's had sex with the man or woman (or both) lying next to her.

Anyway, this isn't Marlena's journal. It's mine.

Ryan surveyed the kitchen quite openly. I followed his gaze – wondered if the room was for him a burglar's paradise or simply the last word in luxury. I didn't see my place as luxurious, obviously. I wonder whether anyone, at whatever level, ever finds their own place to be so. Maybe even the Queen only notices the thinning tread on the Axminster, the beginnings of tarnish on the silverware; maybe, to her, Buckingham Palace is simply *home*.

Home, I thought, with a pang. A secure roof over one's head. That was surely the biggest luxury of all. My throat thickened.

'You have good taste,' he said, nodding in apparent approval. 'We used to get those interiors magazines inside sometimes and some of those houses are incredible. I should know, I've been in a fair few.' He paused, smiled. 'The houses, I mean, not the magazines.'

I returned his smile, to acknowledge his little joke.

'It's only IKEA,' I said, which, looking back, was about as sensitive as… well, as putting lifestyle mags in a prison. 'You should see my friend Marlena's place,' I prattled on like a fool. 'She works for the glossies, and her house looks like she's lifted it right out of the features pages. She's had two kitchen updates in the time I've had one. Honestly, it's incredible.'

He said nothing. He was looking out of the French windows at the garden, and I thought perhaps he'd seen a fox or a squirrel. I really had to stop talking.

'She lives nearby, actually,' I said, not stopping, nowhere near stopping. 'Next road down from this one. We live at the exact same house number, would you believe. Except on her road the houses are bigger. This is a small Victorian; hers is a large. She has a wider hallway, wider rooms, you know? They say even twenty centimetres can make a difference.' Oh, dear God, stop. I was nervous. Or maybe I was trying to communicate that help would be at hand should I need it. It had just dawned on me that when he'd said he'd seen the inside of a fair few of those designer houses, he hadn't meant as a guest at a cocktail party.

'I like your forsythia,' he said.

'My what?'

'The yellow shrub? Named after William Forsyth, royal head gardener and founding member of the Royal Horticultural Society. And if I'm not mistaken, a distant relative of Sir Bruce.'

'Bruce Forsyth?' I said. 'You're having me on.'

'I'm not,' he replied, no trace of amusement in his voice. 'And that's a witch hazel, the old hamamelis, isn't it?'

'I have no idea,' I said, wondering at what point he'd swallowed a gardening manual. 'Not much of a horticulturist.'

He turned to face me. 'Ah, you can take a whore to culture…'

'… but you can't make her think,' I finished, on safer ground. 'Dorothy Parker?'

'I believe so.'

So the two of us were sparring now, were we? Like black-and-white movie stars itching for a tap dance. My face became hot. 'Er… would you like a drink?'

'I shouldn't really. I'll have tea, though, if it's not too much trouble.'

Such perfect manners. I wished he'd said yes to a *drink* drink, my nerves jangling as they were. But alcohol was probably not a good idea. Certainly not more alcohol, in my case – I could already feel the beginnings of a withdrawal headache.

'Your apple tree needs a prune,' he said, sparing me any more Latin, thank God. 'The beds need turning over and that shed is on a bit of a lean, isn't it?'

'I guess so.' I put the kettle on. 'Listen, do you mind if I fetch my notebook?'

'Of course not. Do what you need to do.'

I dashed to the living room. There was an inch of red left in the bottle, so I put the neck to my lips and drained it. My notebook was beside the computer; I picked it up along with my phone. Thinking that I should probably tell someone about the rather rash move I'd made, I texted Marlena.

Hopefully got a story! Cleaning-product door-to-door guy in my kitchen about to tell me his!

She replied within seconds: *The creepy ex-con he was just here r u mad*

Never one for punctuation, Marlena. I guess she spent her days punctuating other people's copy; perhaps she'd run out of commas and semicolons.

I texted back: *He's nice. Don't worry. Got to go!*

Omg u r a nightmare he cd be a psychopath text if any trouble u mad cow

Mooooo!

Enough with the banter, I thought as I sent my silly reply. I needed to focus. I only had Ryan for an hour or two, and I had to make sure I didn't waste the two hundred quid I'd promised him. I switched off the phone and pocketed it before going to join him in the kitchen. He had taken his coat off and was standing next to the counter, his back to me, looking at something on my iPad. As I got closer, I realised with a tightening in my chest that he'd opened Amazon and was reading the blurb for *Fight for Your Love.*

'Don't read the reviews,' I said, persuading myself to be flattered rather than unnerved. 'They're atrocious.'

He didn't turn to look at me. 'You're right, it's probably less highbrow than I'm used to, but it looks good. Kid from the wrong side of the tracks finds redemption through love and mends his ways. About a boxer, you said?'

'I don't really know much about boxing.' I was trying not to be offended by *less highbrow* even though I knew it was perfectly true. 'But I do know about love. Sorry, that sounds wrong; I mean romance or whatever. I write love stories.'

'Ah, the world needs love stories.' He did turn then and gave me a sad smile. A lock of shiny hair fell from his ponytail and curled against his cheek. His gaze darkened, became strange. 'The world would be a better place with more love in it, if you ask me.'

'That's exactly what I think.'

The admission, the solemnity of it, felt too intimate, especially after all the verbal fencing. Insides flaring, skin prickling, I turned away, busied myself with the tea. His presence in the domestic confines of my house was too big. The way he spoke was too direct, too close, too honest, somehow, for someone who had only moments ago been invited in. I was not used to honesty. I was not used to any of it.

That physical change came again – something chemical poured into me, settled in a layer between skin and flesh. An irritant, spread finely, smouldering.

I was afraid, I realised. I should ask him to leave.

'Do you take sugar? Milk?' I asked.

'One, please,' he said, and, 'yes,' and, 'thank you, Pippa.'

The strength had gone from my hands. The cups landed heavily on the counter. I would tell him I'd changed my mind, I thought. Or that I felt ill. But I didn't say anything. Why? Honestly? Because I didn't want to be rude. Because it would have been *embarrassing*. For both of us. Many a first date had I sat through for this reason alone.

But this was not a first date.

I took the tea over to where he was sitting, on one of the two high stools where Bill used to sit. Where Bill had been sitting, in fact, when I had read his sexy phone messages to another woman aloud to him and asked him to enlighten me.

I slid Ryan's mug across to him and took the other stool, putting the counter top between us. He was staring at me; I felt his eyes through my clothes, that feeling again beneath my skin like a bright, flaming film. I wondered whether my heartbeat was audible to both of us, like a rumbling stomach, or whether I alone could hear it.

'Where's your coat?' I said.

'Oh, I hung it up in that little cupboard under the stairs.'

When? When had he done this?

'It's so tidy,' he said, looking around him. 'I feel like I'm making the place messy just by being here.'

This close, I could smell stale tobacco, stronger than out on the street, the thick floral scent, the smell of pride. I spread my fingers over my mouth so that I could breathe instead the apple washing-up liquid with which I'd washed my hands a moment ago.

'I did a blitz about an hour before you came.' I said. 'My house is only tidy when I'm supposed to be writing. If I was supposed to be cleaning, I'd probably write. Honestly, what I need is someone to chain me to the desk and stand over me until I've done my word count.'

'Psychology's a bitch. We eat more when we're on a diet. Drink more when we're abstaining. And when we're trying to be celibate, we end up thinking about nothing but sex.' He paused. I dropped my gaze while the highly inappropriate last remark dissolved between us. His sweater was grey, thin, with holes near the hem, possibly due to the brass buckle on his black leather belt. Before I could change tack, he added, 'And do you have love in your life, Pippa?'

Heat climbed up my face. 'I'm divorced.'

Ryan said nothing. I realised he was waiting for me to look up, and when I did, I had the impression he'd been watching me all the while, still as a sphinx. I was fiddling with the buttons on my cardigan. I made myself stop.

'I mean, it's not for want of trying,' I went on when he still didn't speak. 'I go on dates. I get offers but…

'But you never meet anyone who understands you?' he said. 'Or who you think could understand you if they knew you better? Or… let's see… you never dare reveal yourself enough to find out if someone understands you or not?'

Feeling myself flush, I scanned the room as a rock climber scans the cliff face for a handhold. I found a picture of Marlena and me that I had attached to the fridge. I should switch my phone back on, I thought, but I was too frightened to reach into my pocket – couldn't see how I could do this in front of him without appearing rude.

'Have you ever heard of *chicha de muko*?' he asked.

'Chee cha de moo cow? No? Why? What is it?'

He sat back, crossed his long, angular legs and knitted his hands over one knee. 'When I was travelling in Ecuador, I tried this weird delicacy they have there. It's basically maize. They boil it, chew it, spit it out and then put the mixture into this special urn to ferment. They bury the urn and then, a few days later, dig it up. The enzymes in the saliva catalyse the breakdown of starch in the maize and turn it into maltose. And that is *chicha*.'

'And then what?'

'They drink it.'

I grimaced. 'Gross.'

He shrugged. 'It's basically controlled rot. Like Stilton cheese. There's a Sardinian cheese that has maggots in it, literally crawling in it – *casu* something or other. Yoghurt is just milk with multiplied bacteria in it, don't forget.'

'Well I'm sorry, but it sounds disgusting.'

'Ah, disgust. The last emotion you acquire.' He smiled, his teeth like wood in the evening gloom. 'It seems atavistic, but it's actually a cultural construct that becomes hardwired into your brain over time.'

'Are you winding me up?'

'Disgust is a mirror,' he continued, as if I hadn't spoken. 'It reflects us back to ourselves. It's fundamentally an emotional protest against death. Think about a road accident. Crowds gather to look, don't they? They express disgust at the blood and guts and what have you, even though that's why they looked in the first place.'

Christ. He hadn't swallowed a gardening manual in prison, he'd swallowed a dictionary followed by an encyclopedia, washed down with a bluffer's guide to evolution, and was clearly keen to let me know. Perhaps it was a side effect of having only recently been released – a kind of arrested development, a smart-arse phase that you pass through in your late teens and early twenties, when you think you're the first person ever to have gained an education.

'All sounds a bit mad to me,' I said by way of polite dismissal. I would not be drawn into a battle of wits.

Unfazed, he sipped his tea. 'Oh, we're all mad.'

Despite myself, I took the bait. 'We're all mad? So what's that, another *theory*?' He'd evidently swallowed a psychiatry journal too. Joy. Perhaps he was about to give me a mini tutorial on Freud.

'If you like,' he said, shrugging again like a man with stiff shoulders. 'You're mad, I'm mad. It's a very useful thing to know, Pippa Gates.'

'In what way?'

He reached forward and took my hand in his, palm up, as if for a reading. His fingers were dry and warm, but the scratch of his long nails gave me the creeps. 'Let's say if I want to find out, for example, if you and I really belong together…'

'Right.' My chest constricted. I took a deep breath.

'Right, so. Rather than me asking you what your star sign is or whether you like Steely Dan or Maria Callas, I'd ask you… Pippa Gates, in what way are you mad?'

I stared at my hand in his as if it were no longer mine at all but that of a waxwork or a doll or a shop dummy. 'I…'

'And you would have the right to ask me in return, Ryan, in what way are *you* mad?'

'And would you answer?'

'I would. Would you?'

'Yes.'

He held my gaze. I saw his pupils dilate, saw myself in them as if through a telescope held the wrong way round. I withdrew my hand.

'I don't like Steely Dan,' I said.

'And I'm Taurus,' he fired back. 'But you've got other questions for me, haven't you, Pippa Gates?'

Two, three. Testing.

This is my testimony. On this sunny and marvellous day, this most marvellous of days, I am speaking into this… Ah, fuck it, that sounds shit.

One, two. Two, three.

This is my testimony. If you find this and you're listening, please return, complete with tape, to the address on the sticker. Thank you.

This is my… I hereby report, by way of testimony… Fuck. It.

Two, three.

I have found the person. Yes…

I have found her. I hereby chart our relationship so that one day, when we are together, we can listen and be thankful.

My record of events begins yesterday evening, between the hours of 7 p.m. and approximately 11.30 p.m., when I met my other half. Please note that I don't use that term lightly, in its commonplace and rather trivial usage denoting the ball-and-chain or her indoors or any of those dismissive and, I would say, rather derogatory terms. No. I mean what I say in its most literal sense. I am half. She is half. Together, and only together, we are whole. We are equal yet different. She is the piece that I have searched for all my life. It sounds grandiose, but that's the way it is. She slots into me and I into her with a resounding and perfect click.

This is my testimony. I've said that. I'll cut that later if I can find something to edit this on, transfer it into a digital audio file, maybe, once I get back on my feet. Amazing what you can nick from a second-hand shop. Boots are harder to pilfer unless, like me, you have the brass neck to put them on your feet, leave your smelly old trainers on the shelf and just walk out. Anyway, I was looking for a recording device of some sort and I found one, so that's good. These things are probably obsolete now, so I don't suppose anyone would have wanted it anyway, and if they did, tough shit.

All property is theft.

I didn't steal this out of greed. I've only ever stolen out of need. And I need now to record the moment my life changed. It is fundamental that I do this. It is an historic event that cannot go undocumented. It is seismic. This is no facile hyperbole in a cheap, inflated, fake world. I'm telling you it as it was. She opened the door and the earth shifted on its tectonic plates. A crack appeared in its crust. Nothing was or would be the same. Blades of grass trembled. The sky darkened momentarily, I swear, like a light bulb in a power surge.

We spoke. In those first few exchanges, I knew. I knew beyond doubt. Connection: a circuit completed, a light that shines.

Actually, that's two electricity metaphors. I'll cut one out later. Where was I? Oh yeah, and then, oh, and then, the hours... the hours, the hours, the glorious hours.

Yesterday evening, a lifetime ago.

Yesterday evening, the most important of my life.

She is my soulmate. Everything she is... is everything.

We belong together.

She knows it, on some level.

She has only to admit it.

Blog post: PippaGatesAuthor
#thiswritinglife
Find me on:
Instagram: @GatesPip
Twitter: @PipGatesWrites
Facebook: Pippa Gates Author

Yesterday evening we wrapped up super-warm and took a trip out to Blagdon Lake, at the northern edge of the Mendip Hills. Ever the tour guide and mine of information, Mrs Danvers was keen to inform me that the lake is actually man-made. It was created by the Bristol Waterworks Company, now simply Bristol Water, back at the end of the nineteenth century, and was designed by Charles Hawksley. There was something about the pumping station, which I'll confess I missed – not a great one for factual information; more of a fiction girl, myself. Anyway, we saw the fishing lodge and looked at a couple of the original steam engines in the visitor centre.

As we wandered around the lake, Mrs D suggested we might try trout fishing one day.

'That sounds like fun,' I said. 'I've always fancied a Barbour jacket, and now that I live in the country, it seems a shame not to buy the appropriate attire. Hunter wellies? Perhaps a tweed cap?'

I was off on one! But I was excited. It's just one more part of how wonderful it is to be living here in the country now, away from the smoke and the crowds. Really, I am blessed, and as soon as I got back, I popped the new pics on to Instagram,

Twitter and my Facebook page. These days it's important for an author to have a strong online presence. It's important to be seen as a person living life to the full and to have a platform to communicate with readers. Once I pick up Frieda, for example, in a few weeks' time, I'm going to make sure I post as many pictures as I can of her irresistible puppy cuteness. Oh my goodness, I cannot wait! Some of my readers will no doubt ask for my address so they can send hand-knitted doggy jumpers, or some home-made dog biscuits. My agent will send them on care of Mrs Danvers.

Mrs Danvers, in case you haven't twigged, is a nickname. She was the fictional housekeeper in the famous novel *Rebecca*, by Daphne du Maurier. For those of you who haven't read the book, Mrs Danvers attended to her mistress's every need, and was fiercely and jealously protective, even of her memory. Nothing could equal that kind of devotion, where love meets proprietorial obsession in the most exquisite way. If that's not love, what is? To think that I thought I knew all about love, but no, not at all. Mrs Danvers has illuminated me on that subject.

Quite redefined it, actually.

CHAPTER FOUR

When I met Ryan, I had been divorced for two years. Bill, my ex, had gifted me the house when he left to live with his girlfriend of eight months that I didn't know about. It was the least he could do, he said, and I agreed. He could throw in the car, I suggested, and the furniture, and a modest monthly payment by way of compensation, and we'd call it quits. He said OK. As Marlena never tired of telling me, Bill was a good man. And by good, I mean put-a-rope-around-my-neck-now-and-save-me-from-this-mind-melting-tedium good.

With Bill out of my hair, I spent my evenings and weekends prepping classes, marking essays and working on my first book, *Fight for Your Love.* This was of course when I wasn't running the gauntlet of various dating apps and websites in a self-motivated state of supreme optimism laced with utter dread. I would meet up with men, sometimes women – let's get that out of the way before we start – and stagger home in the wee small hours, invariably texting Marlena some variation of:

Just pulled a total hottie. Bit dark coming home tbh, hopefully no rapists on Barnes Common tonight. Catch up soon! :-)

Another conquest and on a school night! In dodgy minicab. If you don't hear from me tomorrow I've been strangled and left for dead. Check the Thames! xxx

Staggering home at 3 a.m. Morning-after pill for me, I think, naughty strumpet! :-)

Whatever.

She would reply at 7 a.m. the next day with a variation on: *Ffs not again Pip are you all right text and let me know you got back ok*

I would leave it until mid-morning to reply, sometimes even until lunch, by which time there would be two or three more messages, possibly a missed call.

'Pip?' Marlie's voice, tremulous and strained. 'Pip, can you just call me?'

'Hi, Pip? Can you call or text or something?'

'Pip? Pippa? It's Marlie. Look, can you get in touch before I call the police?'

When she next saw me, her face would be all frowning exasperation. But it did her good, there in her safe little life. Through me, she actually got to live a little for a change, if only vicariously. Sometimes, if I'd cut a date short on account of his wearing the wrong shoes or the wrong clothes or making the wrong jokes, et cetera, I would call her while I walked home from the station and she would stay on the line until I got home safe.

'Night, babe,' I would coo, slotting my key into the front-door lock. 'Thanks for talking me home.'

'Night night, nutter. Love you.'

'Love you too, hon.'

Sometimes, on the rare occasion when I managed to insert a sharp knife beneath her shell and prise her away from the wet rock of her family, we would get hammered on two-for-one cocktails in a rather sad West End bar that smelled of sweaty socks. We only went there for old times' sake. It was where we'd first got pissed together, when we were both stuck in dead-end post-grad jobs in a tourist attraction off Leicester Square. This was before we shared a flat in Vauxhall, before she got an internship at *Good Housekeeping* and I did a PGCE, before she met Steve the Peeve. Since my divorce, our nights out would invariably finish with me crying into her shoulder at the end of the evening, a fact that makes me cross with myself even now.

'Why have you got everything, Marlie?' I would wail. 'What's wrong with me?'

She would hold me in her arms and mutter into my ear, 'I only have what you didn't want, hon.'

I would have been too inebriated to pick up on the fag end of patience in her voice. The kind of tone that you apply to a drunk on the street who has lost their belongings and is sitting on the kerb with a dazed expression and a can of Special Brew. You speak firmly and kindly, but inside you have no respect for them. Inside you're thinking: *what a mess*.

I can't believe I ever gave Marlena that power.

'Steve would never be enough for you, Pip,' she would say as she guided me home. 'He likes curry and he has an Xbox, for God's sake. And Zane and Zoe would drive you bonkers.'

And yes, reader, as I type this, I am indeed rolling my eyes at the cutesy alliterative name choices, not to mention the self-conscious trendiness of 'Zane'. London wannabes at their worst. You see? You know me quite well already.

Me, yes. Back to me. Look at me – look at the *state* of me. The tears coursing down the burgeoning thread veins on my cheeks. 'I love your kids, Marlie,' I'm protesting. 'I'd love a guy like Steve – I would. Guys like Steve never go for girls like—'

But by then I've vomited into someone's front garden.

Marlena links my arm so that I don't fall over.

'You've had loads of guys,' she says. 'You had Jake, and what about Tom? And that absolute honey, Jonathan? What was his problem? Oh yeah, he sold insurance. That wasn't fabulous enough for you, was it? You want a rock star with a pension plan, you do, and last time I checked, they're pretty thin on the ground. And kids spoil the romance, remember? You said that, Pip. You. Now, lift up your foot.'

By now she's bundling me into the house and wrestling me up the stairs. I sit slumped on the bed while she pulls my dress over my head, takes off my shoes, eases me back and arranges me into the recovery position.

'Rest now.' She towers over my crumpled form. I view her with one open eye. 'I'll give you a call in the morning.'

Once, a few years ago, as she pushed me down, I clamped my arms around her and tried to pull her with me.

'Stay,' I whispered into her soft, perfumed neck. 'Come on, it'll be nice.'

'Stop it, Pip.' She wriggled out of my embrace. 'Don't be silly.'

What humiliated me most was the gentle way she extricated herself. I can remember looking into her brown eyes and seeing not panic or desire but sympathy, only sympathy.

We never mentioned my little pass. I bet she thought I'd lost the memory of it amongst the evening's destroyed brain cells. I hadn't. I don't think I ever will. I loved her, you see. Always did, no matter what happened… but I can't think about that. Not now, not yet. I do wonder sometimes – did she stand over me after I'd passed out? Did she watch me as, mouth open, black eye make-up skidding across the pillowcase, I slid into oblivion? Did she stand and watch – and judge?

But I was not crazy. I was unhappy.

That was before I met Ryan. With Ryan came the real crazy.

Blog post: PippaGatesAuthor
#thiswritinglife
Find me on:
Instagram: @GatesPip
Twitter: @PipGatesWrites
Facebook: Pippa Gates Author

My goodness, it was chilly today! I think it's going to be a white Christmas, but Mrs D and I are keen to explore the local area and we won't let something as trivial as the cold put us off! So this morning we went to see the Cherhill White Horse. It's amazing – hard to do it justice with a phone camera. There's so much chalk! Two thirds of Wiltshire lies on the stuff. It stretches from the Dorset Downs in the west to Dover in the east apparently. You'll have heard of Salisbury Plain, I'm sure, and, well, after this morning's educational endeavours, I can tell you that Salisbury Plain is the largest area of chalk in the whole of Wiltshire. I didn't even really know what chalk actually was, but Mrs D informed me that it's a soft white porous limestone. In all my years at the blackboard, I never thought about that. And between the chalk areas lie these clay valleys and vales, the largest of which is Avon, which cuts diagonally through Bradford-on-Avon and into Bath and Bristol. Mrs D told me a whole lot more, but I can't remember all of it. I had, if I'm honest, tuned out. I was wondering if Bing and Daisy had ever seen the White Horse, and that perhaps I would take them to see it, give them a picnic and a picnic blanket.

'Maybe,' I said to Mrs Danvers as we came home in the car, 'this is where they could fall in love.'

'Who?'

'Daisy and Bing, silly!'

'Good idea. Huge fertility symbol.'

I laughed. Ah yes, the white stallion kicking against the green hillside – *there* is where Bing and Daisy first fall in love, before things go wrong, before they are separated by circumstance and misunderstanding and years – so many years. The moment. Can we pinpoint it? Can you remember when and where you were when you fell in love with your significant other? How did you know it had happened? Did you feel it? How did it feel? That. I need to capture that.

CHAPTER FIVE

Writing about Ryan, about that night, is intense, even now. It cramps my fingers, hurts my eyes, makes my chest tighten. I find I have to get up at intervals, walk about, change the subject, if only in my head. Even now, the memory of meeting him, of inviting him into my home, feels surreal. It was a momentous event – I know that now. And momentous events, be they good or bad, catapult us from our core, leave us floating, weightless, lost. It's funny how, sometimes, we don't see their enormity until much later, and yet at other times we predict enormity or momentousness or whatever you want to call it when, actually, it isn't there. Like when my first book, *Fight for Your Love*, found a publisher. This is *momentous*, I thought. This is *life-changing*. This is *it*! I would give up the classroom, stop drinking – well, stop drinking so much – and buy a beautiful rural retreat where I would live out my dream and write full-time. My perfectly crumbling ramshackle-yet-charming red-brick abode would be furnished and decorated with impeccable taste, like Marlena's house – all designer paint, shades like Elephant's Sandal and Sparrow's Armpit and Monkey's Toenail, and White Company throws that my teacher's salary could never afford, and quirky glassware picked up, oh, y'know, just from flea markets round and about. In between attending book launches, giving literary talks and accepting awards, flat of hand pressed to chest, eyelashes lowered in modesty, I would meet the love of my life.

But it was not momentous or life-changing. *Fight for Your Love* was not the success I'd hoped for. In fact, it was not a success at all.

'It's great!' Marlena said.

But I heard the exclamation mark. I bloody heard it. She pitched her voice a semitone too high when she said it, you see, and I knew immediately that she thought it stank. Too much of a realist for my kind of work, Marlena. She and Steve had what I'd call a practical approach to love. I know for a fact that he used to use the loo while she was taking a bath – I'm talking sitting, not standing – and that his party trick after a few lagers and a chicken bhuna was to belch the first few bars of the Rolling Stones' 'Satisfaction'. In what world is that acceptable? In what world is that *romantic*? Not mine.

And in all the time I knew Marlena – and it was a long time before we fell out – Steve *never* ordered vintage champagne just because it was Tuesday. He never brought home a rescue puppy with a ribbon tied in a bow around the soft folds of its neck just to cheer her up. He never took her breakfast in bed with a flower in a little white vase on the tray and a card with a simple yet exquisite and completely spontaneous and original and witty-without-being-smartass declaration of love just because it was their fifth weekend together or she'd sniffled and he'd worried she might be getting a cold. He never gave her a foot massage. He never brought her flowers. He never sang her love songs. He never just called to say he loved her.

It was no wonder Marlena didn't think much of the book.

The problem was, the reviewers didn't either. One called it 'hopelessly lacking in realism, an insult to the world of boxing', another said it was 'written as if by a twelve-year-old', and another suggested I throw away my laptop and 'never trouble the literary world again'. One said, 'I haven't received this product yet so I'm giving it one star.' But I'm only telling you this last because even I laughed at that one.

You will have gathered by now that I wasn't able to hand in my resignation while gleefully studying the cow-of-a-head-teacher's face as she laced together a smile from the tortured strands of dismay and, most importantly, soul-excoriating envy. I wasn't even able to go part-time, not on a few thousand copies sold, ten of which had been bought by my mother for her book club. That's a joke – my mother's dead; she committed suicide when I was six, but I'm not going into that now, possibly not ever, so don't hold your breath. And clearly, I did not get invited to attend any book launches or give any talks. I did not sit on any panels. I did not win any awards. And the love of my life, whoever that was, proved conspicuous by his or her absence.

With Ryan, however, came a new story, and with it, new hope. He was born in 1971, he told me. That made him forty-seven or so, younger than I'd thought but still thirteen years older than me.

'But I didn't leave home until 1975,' he said, sitting at my kitchen bar, mug in hand, apparently at ease. 'That's to say, I didn't leave the *house* until I was four.'

Barely had my pen touched the page when I lifted it off again. 'You didn't leave your own home until you were four years old?'

He pressed his lips tight before going on. 'I was four years old when a neighbour heard me through the air vent at the bottom of the house and called the police. The police rescued me and my sister, Baby, from the cellar. She was two. She died soon after.'

'Oh my God, Ryan. That's terrible. That's…' There were no words – why was I even trying to find them? I made myself face him. It would be an insult not to look at him.

He gave a costive scowl but remained still: straight-backed and poised on the stool.

'If it's all right with you, Pippa,' he said after a moment, his voice low and a little stern, 'I'll stick to the facts. I don't need a counselling session, and I'm not agreeing to make some sort of confession here. But I'm happy to give you what you asked me for,

which is my story, as well as I'm able to tell it. Once I've done that,
you can do what you want with it. You're paying for it; it will be
yours. But I don't need you to give me advice or feel sorry for me.'

'Of course,' I said quietly, a little chastened. He was right. He
did not need my sympathy. Who was I to offer it? He did not need
me to add my own observations or pretend that I could in any way
relate to what he was telling me. *Be quiet and take notes* – this was
my only job now. How anything he was about to tell me could
be woven into a love story by the morning, I had no idea. But he
had not promised to fall in with my creative needs, only to tell
me about his life. Naïvely, I had assumed that he would tell me
something useful. But like a robber who discovers he cannot sell
what he has stolen, I could hardly complain to the shop owner
that the loot would not make me a profit.

'Carry on.' Seizing a moment of courage, I reached into my
pocket for my phone and laid it on the table. 'I'm listening.'

He cleared his throat, shifted on his stool.

'I was hospitalised,' he said. 'I was badly dehydrated, under-
weight. My bones were weak. My language had not developed as
it should have. I was given intensive literacy lessons, psychiatric
treatment, physiotherapy, you name it.' He sipped his tea, then
put his mug carefully on the counter, as if to place it exactly where
it had been before.

I realised I was holding my breath and blew it out. 'What
happened to your parents?'

'They'd been arrested and would eventually be put away on
several different counts of chronic child abuse. They'll never get
out. I have no idea whether they're still alive. I can't remember very
much about that time, Pippa, I'm sorry. The details of my parents'
sentencing I learned only later. I was very young. That time, for
me, is just a series of faces, images, voices. People were kind. They
were curious. There was a lady who had glasses on a chain, another
I remember with a clipboard. Impressions, mostly. Smells of the

particular hospital cleaning products they used. Shame I didn't do then what I do now, eh? I would have made a killing.'

Neither of us laughed. I returned his smile but said nothing. What he was telling me had the fantastical warp of horror, but it was true. I felt like I was floating, that I had understood him at the level of language, but that the meaning of what he was telling me would take longer to absorb.

'I learned to walk, to run. I was given a special diet, as much ice cream as I wanted. I went bananas over it, gave myself brain freeze every time. Well, you can imagine.'

I could not. The pen pressed hard against the top knuckle of my middle finger.

'And then about a year after that, I was housed with a family in a village in Sussex. He was a vicar, and she was, well, she was a vicar's wife in the old-fashioned way. The two of them worked hard for the church and the community and that sort of thing. Constant baking. Jam-making. Those little checked squares of material you put on the jars. I used to help her with the labels. By then I could read and write, and I loved to do that. I still love that.'

He stopped.

'Are you all right?' I asked. 'Would you like more tea? Are you hungry? I have… well, sod all actually.'

'Would you have anything stronger?'

'Oh, yes.' I slid from my stool and fetched a bottle of plonk from the iron wine rack that Bill's cousin had given us for a wedding present.

I poured a large glass for Ryan. I knew I shouldn't drink any more, especially with an ex-con in the house, but I was in deep now and the old destructive tendencies were reaching up the walls like vines. I poured myself a glass, as large as his.

So what if he kills me?

I actually remember having that thought. Don't get me wrong, I'd had similar thoughts before. Sometimes, when I was driving, I'd get this overwhelming urge to accelerate, to go faster and faster until I ploughed into a wall, just to see what happened; when chopping vegetables, the temptation would come from nowhere to drive the knife into my chest. That kind of thing. So when I imagined Ryan wrapping his bony hands around my neck and tightening his grip, I have no shame in admitting, here in the privacy of these pages, that the idea, the heady wildness of it, thrilled me to my core.

'Cheers.' The direct way he'd looked at me earlier was back. 'Here's to you, Pippa Gates. You are a very unusual woman.' He took a deep slug and closed his eyes, a small and private ecstasy.

I looked away, embarrassed at the sight. Since I'd arrived home, I'd drunk more than an entire bottle without stopping once to think about how it tasted or how much it cost. Only a moment ago, I had referred to this wine in my head as *plonk from the rack*, where it had nestled among at least another seven bottles. But to him it was a rare treat.

'Are you sure you're not hungry?' I asked, glancing towards the fridge. Marlena and I stared back, arms around each other, grinning. We had been younger then. Things had been simpler. 'I think I have some eggs.'

He shook his head. 'Tell you what. I'll tell you the rest and then I'll make you the best omelette you've ever had in your life. How about that?'

There was no way that was going to happen.

'All right,' I said. 'Sounds good.'

I had known him less than an hour and I had given him wine and agreed to let him cook me dinner. But I was not crazy. I maintain that even now. I was unhappy and desperate for a story. Yes, Ryan Marks scared me. Yes, he was overfamiliar and inappropriate. Yes, his presence was at moments downright menacing. But I wasn't bored. I was so many, many miles from bored.

He told me then about the string of foster parents, the nomadic life of an abused orphan who could not settle.

'The problem was that I had difficulty bonding,' he said. 'I had difficulty knowing right from wrong. I was too… different.'

'In what way?'

'I would tie girls up in the playground and push grass into their mouths, that kind of thing.'

'All boys do that, don't they?'

'Not the way I did it.'

A silence. I rode it out.

'I didn't know how to behave,' he said after a moment. 'I guess I'd been tied up myself. My mother used to make me eat stuff I didn't want to. My sister was the only person I'd ever known, and I only knew her until I was four.'

'Baby? Did she have a name?'

'She was called Tanya. But I called her Baby. My parents called her Baby. They called me Boy.'

I closed my eyes.

'It gets better,' he said with a lightness he might or might not have felt.

'You don't have to protect me, you know. I can handle it.'

He picked up the bottle and topped me up – poured another full glass for himself. 'I know that. As I said, you're unusual, Pippa. You're different.'

I laughed it off, but again that burning half-terror flashed slick beneath my skin. 'As in weird, you mean?'

'As in the things you want and don't want.'

The presumptuous intimacy of the statement was breathtaking. The *arrogance* of it.

'The things I want and don't want?' I said, despite myself, falling into his little trap once again.

He leant towards me, rested his forearm on the table. I moved back. My breath caught, came out ragged. I didn't want him to answer; I was desperate to hear what he had to say.

'You don't want a steady guy who'll pay the mortgage,' he said, making a steeple of his long fingers, his knuckles swollen knots in spindly twigs. 'You don't want a guy who'll buy you what you asked for for your birthday, who'll take you to a posh restaurant on Valentine's Day, buy you flowers after every argument. You don't want someone who signs up to the box-ticking life of doing everything because it's someone else's idea of how we should live – wine clubs and tennis clubs and private members' clubs. An annual foreign holiday in an exotic location and golf at weekends and friends for dinner every Saturday and riding lessons for the kids.'

'I like nice restaurants,' I countered. 'And who doesn't like getting what they want for their birthday?' I thought of Bill – how I'd always told him exactly what I wanted and how, every year, I felt familiar disappointment crush my soul flat when he bought me exactly that. 'I'd love to have the time and money to play tennis. I like flowers. I really like flowers.'

He shook his head. 'You like them. But you don't want them, not really.'

'You don't know that; you don't know—'

He unlocked his gnarled fingers and pointed at me. 'You don't want kids.'

I threw up my hands. 'Fair play. I don't. From what I've observed, children are the... well, they're the death of love, aren't they?'

'Real life is the death of love, if you want to look at it like that.'

I shrugged, a show of an indifference I didn't feel.

'That's why my stories take you to the beginning of love and no further.' I sat forward, warming to my theme. 'I mean, think about it. The most beautiful love story ever written is *Romeo and Juliet*. Why? Because it ends before either can disappoint the other. Because it ends, amidst love's glorious beginning, in death.'

He gave a slow nod, his smile keeping pace. 'So you don't want happily ever after.'

'Don't be ridiculous. Of course I do. I do... absolutely... it's just...'

'You see?' He drank and again placed his glass carefully, so carefully, back on the worktop. 'That's my question, Pippa. Do you know what you want? Do you know what you *need*?'

'I...'

My heart beat faster. My skin tingled. I glanced towards the back door, tried to remember if I'd unlocked it. I didn't think so; why would I? I could manoeuvre myself over there if I was clever, but I wouldn't have time to turn the key and get out. I could not outrun him if I did. My mobile phone sat on the worktop. But it was still off.

I drank, deeply. In protest, a pain throbbed in my head. My mouth ached – the tannins, possibly. I suspected my lips had gone black. It was better to keep him talking. Give the illusion that I was not afraid, that this was mere conversation. To do anything else now was, could be, suicide.

'Marlena says I'm never happy,' I said – a concession. 'She says I set impossible standards.'

His smile was smug, irritating. 'You've not found what you want, that's all. And you can't ask for it if you don't know what it is.' He leant back and cocked his head to one side, looking at me quizzically, as a scientist might study an unexpected chemical reaction. 'You have a cultural construct of what you think you want, but you don't actually want it, and it's setting up this confusion within you. If you're going to find the words to ask for what you want, you're going to have to figure out what it is.'

'Oh for God's sake.' I stood, so quickly that the stool fell back and crashed to the floor. My face raged hot. I pressed my hands to my cheeks to cool them. 'You've read a lot of books, Ryan, is what I think. Good for you. With your Latin plant names and your theories and your… your *vocabulary*. You think you're tying me up in knots, don't you? You think you're… I don't know… some kind of mystic or something, that you can see into my soul or my head or… But you don't know me. You've only known me half an hour, an hour tops. I might know perfectly well what I want. I might know exactly.' It was only as the last words left my mouth that I realised I was no longer pretending to enter into the discussion. I *had* entered into it, and I was outraged.

He, by contrast, didn't move. Only shook his head, his mouth pressed into a flat, conceited line.

'You don't, Pippa,' he said. 'You don't have a single clue.'

Audio excerpt #2

Two, three. Two, two. Right.

It's noisy in the dorm, so I've come outside. Said I needed a smoke. I'm probably picking up the trains on the tape, but short of cancelling them… Actually, the hostel looks quite impressive in the dark. More gothic. A big red-brick monolith job, wide-bore pipes running round the room perimeters. Old boiler. Maximum inefficiency. The windows are loose; the air blasts through in icy gusts. Heating set to freeze in winter, burn in summer. I offered to fit a thermostat, offered to have a look at the windows too, but the caretaker's a testy bugger.

I've just had a listen back to the first bit I recorded and I can hear that I was on quite a high. It's a trip, meeting your future. A fix. She knew what she was doing, coming on to me. Women can be like that. All perfume and coy smiles and then when you make a move, they throw up their hands, as if they haven't understood what you were both doing, as if you're the brute. They don't take responsibility. She wanted me. I could see it in her eyes. Why else would she sign what we both knew was a contract? Why give her book to me as a gift? She was giving me part of herself. Like a down payment, a promise to give me the rest later – she knew that; I knew that. I mean, look at the facts: no sooner had she signed herself over to me than she was running after me, asking me to do the same. Come in, *she said.* I want your life story. *What she meant was,* I want you.

And I want her. Body and soul. Heart and mind. Material goods are of no interest to me, beyond my practical needs. I don't give a monkey's chuff about some archaic notion of dowries or properties or advantageous matches. And whilst the physical body has its comforts and attractions, and I can say with all certainty that I prefer the female of the species, I'm not particularly motivated by the pleasures of the flesh either. Don't get me wrong – she is a very attractive woman; she knows it and she uses it to her advantage. For all that she wraps it up in the whole wacky bob with the red streak and the quirky fringe, the bovver boots I saw in the hallway, she's fooling no one. But this is a meeting of minds. The cerebral leads; something instinctive, something visceral follows. Women are slower to admit to these things. And if it's time she needs, then time she will get. I have to play this carefully. I don't want her taking fright. I don't want to end up back inside. I'm not going back in there, no way.

I will never, ever go back inside.

CHAPTER SIX

In an attempt to wrest back control, I picked up the chair and sat back down.

'Let's agree to differ,' I said, ignoring the self-satisfied smirk on his face.

Whatever I had initiated, I would now finish, and finish without riling him or letting him think he had riled me. I would set my face to neutral. Whatever he said, no matter what, I would not react, at least not externally. This was business. He had no intention of hurting me. He was fresh out of jail and in thrall to his new-found education, thrilling at the effect of his cheap theories aimed at decoding and derailing someone above him on the social ladder, excited at proving himself intellectually to someone who had thought him nothing but an ex-con.

That was all. He was not a murderer. He was not dangerous. Just a prat.

I picked up my pen. 'Why don't you tell me the rest of your story?'

And he did. I fought to keep my face impassive. He had asked me not to counsel him. Now, albeit tacitly, I was asking him to back off with his little theories about me and my life and what I did and did not want. The words clambered across the pages. My flaming fear of him, about what he could or might do to me, abated a little – to embers. Here was our transaction. I had offered him money for his story; he had thought he could come into my home and tell me mine. I had communicated to him that no, he could not. I had told him to give me what I'd asked for, what I was paying for, and only that, thank you very much.

My main worry shifted its centre, to what would happen later, when I'd taken the dictation of his life and had no further use for him. Half of me was filled with the fear that he would not leave; half of me burned with the knowledge that once he did, my life would never be the same. I didn't know in what way I thought my life would change. I could not even anticipate what the night itself would bring. And the prospect of that unknown was terrifying; it was more exciting than anything I could remember.

'When I was twelve,' he said, 'I was placed with my great-aunt.' It had got towards 8.30 p.m. by then, maybe 9 p.m. Ryan's was not a presence that had me looking at my watch.

'Where was that?' I asked, by now scribbling like a journalist.

'It doesn't matter where – pick any old place, a place you know. Auntie Doreen took good care of me. I was still a tearaway, but she gave me that thing we were talking about earlier.'

When he said no more, I looked up.

'Love,' he said, and smiled sadly.

I tapped the pen to my teeth. 'Oh yes,' I said. 'Love.'

'She lived in a small flat near the bus station. She was my mother's sister, but my mother was obviously in the nick. Auntie Reenie had never had kids. She'd been jilted at the altar and never met anyone after that – or never wanted to, I don't know.' He paused. 'It's OK when you're in your… what are you, Pippa? Your thirties?'

I nodded.

'It's OK when you're your age, but when you get older, when you hit fifty or sixty, if you've got no one, things start to get tough. They were tougher still back then. These were less enlightened times, don't forget. My auntie never got invited to parties or to dinners. No woman would have gone to the pub on her own at that time.' He leant forward, and when I looked up again, to see why he'd stopped, he was staring at me as if waiting for me to meet his eye before adding, 'There was no Tinder or Guardian Soulmates or anything like that.'

I glanced at my phone. Had he looked at it? Had he switched it on and scrolled back through Marlena's messages and found something relating to my dating habits? Why else would he mention those two dating sites specifically? A shiver passed through me. I straightened the pages of my notebook in an attempt to regain control.

'So you lived with—'

'The other thing about my Auntie Reenie,' he interrupted, oblivious, 'was that she'd always wanted kids. So when she got me, she was delighted. Well, you know, who wouldn't be?' He gave a brief *humph* at his own humorous aside. 'She was in her fifties by then, but she looked late sixties. A hard life can do that to you, you know. It can age you.'

I nodded. Yes, I had put Ryan in his mid fifties when he was in fact a decade younger.

'So,' I said. 'Life got better?'

'For a time.' He was getting to the end of his second glass of wine. I wondered if he'd help himself to yet another. 'As I said, I was a tearaway, always in trouble at school for fighting. I was hardly *in* school, to be honest. I'm sure you could write the rest of my story without me having to tell you.'

I shook my head. 'I don't think so. I had a very boring childhood, I'm happy to say.' I would not tell him about my childhood, no way. Finding my mother's lifeless body when I was six was something I'd only ever told Bill and Marlie about.

'I bet you were a daddy's girl, weren't you? Little princess?'

I glanced at him to gauge his tone, but his face was open, not cynical. The shadows under his eyes were dark; fine red lines ran through the whites of his eyes. I could do this. I could talk to him without falling into a trap.

I cleared my throat. 'I was an only child. And yes, I got all the dollies and the *Cinderella* video.'

'And I bet they never said no to you, did they?'

I laughed and narrowed my eyes at him. 'Not often, no.'

He too laughed. 'I bet you were waited on hand and foot. Did they bring you hot chocolate in bed, put your little electric blanket on for you? Did you have a television in your room?'

Spot on, but oh how ignorant he was even so, how little he understood that even devotion such as this could turn to ash. The burning sensation came again. I shot him a placatory look, as if to say: *you win*. 'It's not my fault they doted on me.'

'I'm not saying it is. But I bet no one measured up to your daddy, did they?'

Smart move. Aiming an educated guess at the most probable Achilles heel; well, I would not wince, and I would not limp, not while he was watching.

'I thought Bill did,' I said, deflecting, but my voice was small. 'My ex. He was very adoring, you know? He brought me breakfast in bed on a tray, with a flower in a little vase. I mean, he did that because I told him to, so I suppose I was still disappointed, but… on our first anniversary he took me to Paris. We saw a show at the Moulin Rouge…'

'But?'

'But again, that was my idea,' I said. 'I'd shouted it at him in an argument – *why don't you ever take me to Paris?* And then, eventually, he stopped.'

'Stopped what?'

'Doing whatever I asked. He said he'd surprise me instead. But his surprises were straight out of the book of the bleeding obvious, you know? A necklace with a diamond pendant on our wedding anniversary. Twelve red roses and dinner for two at a chic restaurant on Valentine's Day. We'd be sitting there with a thousand other couples, all of us forced into someone else's idea of what romance is, all of us stilted and silently disenchanted.'

Reader, I can hear you. You're smiling away there in your self-satisfaction, thinking: *ah yes, that's what he just said about her and what she did and didn't want.* Well don't worry, it wasn't lost on me, and, yes, I was furious with myself, at a loss as to how I had let myself say so much when only moments earlier I had vowed to say nothing.

'You agree with Marlena, don't you?' I asked, hating myself for asking even before I phrased the question, if that makes sense. What did I care about his opinion of me? 'You think I'm impossible.'

He pushed out his bottom lip and shook his head.

'It doesn't matter what I think,' he said, and I thought then that it did – it absolutely did. I was about to interrupt when he spoke again. 'But no, I don't think that. You're unusual. You're demanding, perhaps. Because you don't know what you need, Pippa. Or maybe you do but you don't dare say it, even to yourself.' He reached over the bar and brushed his finger against my cheek, then leant back and shrugged, as if that was a perfectly casual remark to make, as if touching my cheek was a normal thing to do, as if the combination of these things wasn't as intimate as a hand beneath my clothes. 'A lot of women I've met, they think they know what they need, but they don't. And sometimes I have to show them.'

Sometimes I have to show them. I wondered what the hell that meant but wasn't about to ask. The by-now-familiar fire of alarm flashed under my skin. I can't say that it was pleasant. I can't say it was *un*pleasant. If you'd asked me at that moment how I was feeling, I think the best I could have done would have been to say: *I am frightened, yes, but I am alive.*

I picked up my notebook, fumbled, pressed it flat for the second or maybe third time. 'So your aunt was glad to have you.'

Through purple-stained teeth, he grinned.

'My aunt,' he said strangely, slowly, like someone on an acid trip. 'Good old Auntie Reenie. She never said no to me. Never. She would make me cups of tea and take them to me in bed. She cooked me beans on toast, fish fingers and beans, egg, chips and beans. She was very versatile with beans.'

'Reminds me of the Monty Python Spam sketch,' I said, and was, perversely, delighted when he sniggered and replied, 'Except with beans.'

'Speaking of which, I've had two bags of crisps for my dinner. Would you like to eat something?'

He shook his head. 'A little hunger is a good thing, Pippa. Builds the anticipation.'

A little hunger. Anticipation. In response, my stomach gurgled. I drank the rest of my wine, convinced I could hear my own pulse inside my head. My head spun. I reached for the bottle, but he had already lifted it – was pouring me another glass, then one for himself. The bottle emptied.

'I can't remember the last time I drank red wine,' he said softly, holding it up to the bright kitchen light so that it lit up like a ruby in the sun. 'It's so… it's so fucking delicious.'

My eyes filled. I slid off my stool and dimmed the kitchen downlighters.

'Wow,' he said. 'Mood lighting.'

'Just getting to the age where I need a more forgiving wattage.'

'Or maybe you just need to embrace your imperfections.' He drank, set the glass back on the counter. Holding my gaze, he smirked and raised his eyebrows. 'So, if you had to guess what came next, what would you say?'

'In your story? Erm, let me see. Drugs? Shoplifting?'

'Kerching. Exacto. You read the news.'

'Oh God, I don't. What on earth would I want to do that for? There's enough reality at my comp for anyone, frankly…' I stopped. 'Sorry. That was clumsy. It's in my mind not to say anything insensitive – it always makes me worse. I don't mean to compare my school or my situation with your… with…'

'Hey, we're all like that.' He waved my words away. 'I once took some biscuits to a friend of mine who'd lost his fingers in a factory accident. I bought chocolate fucking fingers; he thought I was taking the piss.'

We both laughed – properly this time – like hyenas.

'But you're right,' he said. 'It was only weed at first, and nicking the odd thing, like a bike pump or a Mars bar or something like that. But then my Auntie Reenie died when I was sixteen and I got taken into care, and at that point it all went badly wrong.'

'That was rotten luck.'

He shrugged, pushed out his bottom lip. 'They say there's no such thing as luck, don't they? But I think most successful lives are a mixture of good decisions and good luck and unsuccessful lives are the opposite – bad decisions and pure bad luck.'

He told me about the home. The crackle of plastic beneath striped flannelette sheets, the smell of bleach and boiled cabbage. He told me about the night terrors, the fear that stayed with him through every waking moment. As he spoke, the feline vowels of his Cockney accent bled through. I fell silent, scribbled notes, underlined details that I knew would bring my novel to life: the mouse he trained to lick butter from his fingers; Peg, the boy with one leg shorter than the other; the thin strawberry jam in which no one had ever found a piece of fruit.

No one would accuse me of writing something unrealistic this time. This time, I would answer my critics with hard, gritty facts, with details that could only have come from having *lived it*.

'So that went on for a couple of years. Down and down. Dodgy geezers, dodgy birds.'

'Like who? Can you describe a few?'

'Yeah, let's see.' He ran through a few colourful acquaintances. A prostitute who died of an overdose at twenty-nine; an old bird called Lena who used to sing in the clubs until one of her boyfriends found her with another of her boyfriends behind a pub and slashed her throat. A dealer called Joe who was bad, bad news. He stopped, exhaled.

'But you turned yourself around,' I said.

'I did.'

And I took his blackened smile for pride.

Blog post: PippaGatesAuthor
#thiswritinglife
Find me on:
Instagram: @GatesPip
Twitter: @PipGatesWrites
Facebook: Pippa Gates Author

Some of you might have seen the fabulous pics of the beach yesterday. It was meant to be a morning-only jaunt, to give me the afternoon to write, but the sea air was so fresh and Mrs Danvers made me laugh so much by shouting *ozones, get those ozones*, while looking out to sea, and then of course the smell of fish and chips reached us on the breeze and that was it. Like Bisto kids, we followed our noses and ended up in this cute beachside café, and all thoughts of *Pushing Up Daisy* blew away. In fact, those of you who follow me on Instagram will have seen the Herculean portion I posted yesterday, complete with mushy peas, and I would like to report that yes, reader, I ate the lot!

Sea air gives you such an appetite.

Life out here is saner, healthier. Purer.

CHAPTER SEVEN

Ryan talked and talked. Words poured out of him. At a certain point, I'm not sure when, we opened a second bottle. My eyelids became heavy, my eyeballs dry. His lips and gums were the colour of blackcurrants, and I wondered if mine were too. The black mouth, together with his crooked wooden-looking teeth and oily tied-back hair, his gauntness and the dark shadows under his eyes, made him look vampiric. I tried not to think about Marlena, who had probably tried to call me more than once by now. She would be worried about me.

Well, let her worry.

The young Ryan had worked his way up from an apprentice-ship in a small window firm in Feltham and eventually had the courage to go it alone. Tools, a van, investments paid for with borrowed money.

'I worked in the clients' gardens mostly,' he said. 'I slept in the van and took showers at the local leisure centre, which is where I got into swimming.'

He pulled his sweater over his head, releasing a strong gust of that awful soap, the trace of those damp, musty towels, cheap talcum powder or deodorant, possibly. His T-shirt rode up. Beneath it, his carved stomach, the tail of some inked creature disappearing into his jeans. The T-shirt had worn to a transparent shroud, somewhere between cream, grey and fawn, a rash of holes at the hem. But more than these things, what caught my eye were the hand-drawn crosses on his wrists, and the track marks on his inner arms, a crude join-the-dots up to the crook of his elbow.

I looked down at my notes. *Swimming*, I wrote. Yes, it was swimming that had given him that torso. Hard physical work, not enough to eat and probably the drug habit. If he didn't want to talk about that, I would not ask. I would leave it out of my notes, and out of the story. If I had not seen his arm, I might have added an addiction, for colour, but not now. Now it felt like a violation.

Fending off the temptation to grab a painkiller for my throbbing head, I forced myself to focus. 'So, you lived in your van? That must have been tough.'

'It was all right. Kept the tools safe, anyway. Tell you what, when they break in and find a madman in his pants holding a crowbar, they do one quick enough. One guy actually screamed like a chimp. Must have thought I was an axe murderer or something.'

I realised he had told me this story to make me laugh, which I did. And I thought about the thousand times I'd feigned laughter over some dull guy's comedy of errors, how they'd once mistranslated the menu and ordered the squid's balls or whatever by mistake, how they'd locked themselves out of their hotel room, naked, after a midnight stumble into what they thought was the en suite – *the look on the receptionist's face!* What larks, harr-de-harr. Yawn.

'The main problem was presenting myself to the clients,' he went on. 'I used to buy packs of white T-shirts. If a client needed a quote, I'd go into a café or something and have a good wash at the sink, then I'd change into a brand-new T and go. Then, when I got my own business unit, I fitted a basic shower myself, bought a suit from a charity shop to wear for pricing up the jobs. I was basically passing myself off as successful for years before I actually was. But the weird thing was, I became successful doing it.'

'Fake it till you make it,' I said, scribbling the word *pride* on my notepad.

'Indeed.' He smiled, his eyes unfocused, as if he were lost in a reverie of some kind.

'Someone special?' I asked.

He blinked, looked at me. 'Ah, no, I was remembering those days, that's all.'

'And what was it about them that would make you smile like that?'

He shook his head but could not keep the smile from his grape-dyed lips. 'You don't want to know.'

But I did – I absolutely did. 'That's why you're here, isn't it? To tell me everything.' I found his eyes with mine, saw a flicker of defiance there, of surrender.

'I was a very bad boy,' he said. 'I… I fooled around. A lot.'

'With… what, as in… with the clients?'

He sipped his wine, replaced the base of his glass precisely inside the ring it had made on the counter top. 'There are a lot of bored wives out there, Pippa. A lot of lonely women. They've got money, they're bored out of their minds and… and frustrated, if you know what I mean.' He raised his arms over his head and knitted his hands behind it. Again his T-shirt rose up; his belt buckle caught the light. 'I told myself I was helping them with that. But I wasn't. Not really. I was taking advantage.'

'So let me get this straight. You would go and fit their windows, then fit them up with… with a shag?'

He gave a smoky laugh. 'Other way round. The… the bedroom came first, but yes, that was the idea.'

I clapped my hand over my mouth, unable to stifle a chuckle. 'That's outrageous.'

'I know.' He leant forward and plucked the pen from my fingers. He turned the notepad upside down and wrote: *BUT I'M A REFORMED CHARACTER, MISS. I PROMISE.*

Still laughing, I grabbed the pen and pad from him and wrote: *OI. THAT'S VANDALISM.*

'Sorry, miss.' He threw up his hands. 'I'll be on my best behaviour from now on. I'm near the end anyway now. I lost everything quite soon after that.'

The laughter stopped.

After perhaps a minute, he began to talk again. My stomach growled, my head ached, but I wrote frantically, keeping pace as he finished his story. Ideas pinged off at tangents, ways in which I would transform these raw facts and shape them into fiction. I would call the story *The Window Maker*, or maybe add a pun – *A Framework for Love* – or…

He had slept with a great many women. I imagined him cleaner, in a T-shirt that was white, thick and new, not a grubby, nondescript sludge-coloured piece of near-rag. I saw him younger, smoother, with washed hair, shorter nails, whiter teeth. But still, he would have been a bit of rough. A real suburban Oliver Mellors to the Lady Chatterleys of south London.

The business flourished. The women were experts at emptying their often-absent husbands' bank accounts for the purpose of never-ending refurbishments, designer clothing, extortionate cosmetic treatments. He told me how, once they'd used him for one window repair, they found that the whole house needed to be refitted.

'I bet they did,' I said, and we laughed in our little conspiracy.

'But that was when, as they say, disaster struck.'

'Oh no,' I said. *Oh yes*, I thought. Disaster was great for my story. No one wants to hear about things going well, do they?

Scribble, scribble. Jot, jot.

It turned out that Joe, the dealer he'd mentioned earlier, had put up the money for Ryan's business. But now he was now calling it in. With interest. Ryan pleaded for an extension. I imagined the scene – some disused warehouse, concrete floor, rafters. But Joe was hard, hardened, and didn't want to know. He gave Ryan three months to pay it back or there would be consequences. I heard him say it – *consequences* – heard the quasi-pirate voice I'd already given him in my head, saw the scar he didn't yet have skitter across his cheek.

Three months passed. Ryan had only a third of the cash. And one afternoon, while he was out quoting for a job, two of Joe's heavies came into the workshop and locked the door behind them.

'By this time,' he said, 'I'd employed a young apprentice. Joe's men put his hand into a vice, poor kid. Removed the top of his little finger and put it in an envelope wrapped up in a note.'

My heart raced. This was story gold. 'What did it say?'

'"One month".'

'Wow. So, what… was that in cut-out newspaper letters?'

He shrugged. 'If you want. The lad never came back. And that's when I got the call from this woman who lived in an enormous house in Strawberry Hill. Wanted her windows doing. When I got there, she was wearing a dress with flowers on it and she smelled… she smelled incredible. She made me coffee in her big shiny kitchen – not Nescafé, you know what I mean? She gave me the good stuff.'

Good stuff, I wrote. Lavazza, maybe, or Illy, or perhaps some hand-ground beans from a local coffee shop…

'And then?'

'And then?' He raised his eyebrows, smirking all the while. 'She looks at me. "Isabelle recommended you very highly," she says. I knew straight off what was going on. I remembered Isabelle. I remembered her very well. She was the one who'd asked me to come and check the windows in the bedroom. She said she thought the catch was sticking.'

'Ah.' I bit down on my bottom lip, which was entirely anaesthetised by red wine. 'The old sticky catch, eh? Classic.'

'So, she asks me to quote for sashes throughout. The job was too big, really, for me, but I was sweating on getting this money together, and I thought if I asked her for a deposit I could give that straight to Joe and explain that the rest would come in soon, guaranteed. If I took on another lad, maybe two, and we worked round the clock, I reckoned I could do it.

'Anyway, she leaves me the run of the house to measure up. Six bedrooms, three bathrooms, all marble, gold fittings, the lot. The carpets were so thick and soft, and I remember thinking, this is what it feels like to be rich, to have carpets like this and to be able to walk on them barefoot.'

He met my eyes, his gaze black. I realised that outside it had gone dark.

'And then I found this little box room on the second floor,' he said, his voice lowering, as if to entice me towards the kernel of the story. Sure enough, I leant into him, pulled by an invisible twine. 'The walls were painted yellow. Mint-condition cot, little wardrobe with stencils of animals and all that crap on the doors. Everything pristine but no pictures or anything, and I thought, hang on, there's no photos in *any* of these rooms. Usually, in those houses, they have those big professional family shots hanging on the walls, you know?'

I nodded, scribbling. Marlie had one – an enormous studio portrait in black and white of her and Steve and the kids that hung in the hallway for all to see. I couldn't stand it.

'But there was nothing like that, not even a little photo on the mantelpiece so far as I can remember.'

'Weird.'

'Weird, yeah. So anyway, there was this wooden chest at the foot of the cot. Little brass key in the lock. I opened it. I don't really know why, to be honest. Maybe I was curious to see whether they'd put baby clothes in there or something.'

'And had they?'

He shook his head. 'It was full of...'

I leant further in. We were no more than a few inches apart. 'Full of what?'

He dipped towards me, our foreheads almost touching.

'Banknotes,' he whispered. 'There must have been about two hundred G in there, maybe double that.' By now, his Cockney accent had taken over entirely: *musta bin, fulla bank nowts, two andrid G.*

'Whoa,' I said. 'G? Is that thousand?'

He nodded. 'And I knew that whatever it was her husband did, it was not on the level. White-collar crime. Something majorly dodgy.'

'Oh my God.' My hand ached. This was beyond gold. It was diamond-encrusted platinum with a side cluster of emeralds. We were heading for a climax, I could feel it – the story demanded it. And he was about to deliver. 'So what?' I said. 'You stole it?'

'I would only ever steal out of need, Pip. You gotta know that. But it was like someone had sent it to me from heaven or something. Like a sign, you know?'

Desperate, I scrawled, my hand aching. *Sign from heaven.*

'So I went downstairs. She – the woman – was in the kitchen. She'd changed into this silk robe thing with lotus flowers on it, and I could tell she had nothing on underneath, and I thought, uh-oh, here we go.'

Holy shit. The page rubbed against the side of my frantically scribbling hand.

'I told her I'd have the job priced up by the next day. I was about to go, but she was right there in front of me, and before I knew it we were kissing and then we were on the kitchen bar and… well, yeah. I'm sure I don't need to spell it out.'

'Wow. You really were popular, weren't you?' I stopped writing, glanced up at him.

He cocked his head and smiled. 'I was.'

I looked back at my notes, flustered. He had given me enough detail to make sure I imagined the rest. Was he trying to turn me on in some way? Was he getting off on it? How gross. How pathetic. The kitchen spun. I pressed my hand to my forehead.

'You need to eat,' he said. 'And don't worry. Like I said, I'm a reformed character.' He was out of his seat. He had opened the fridge door. The white light made hollows of his eyes. 'You weren't joking, were you? You really don't have any food.'

'I have eggs.' I glanced again towards the back door. It would take five seconds to get to it. Another twenty to unlock it. The best way to run was down the side return and pray to God I hadn't locked the gate.

'Got 'em.'

I turned back. He was standing by the stove, an egg pinched between the thumb and forefinger of each hand. 'How do you like your eggs, madam?'

'Unfertilised, preferably,' I quipped.

He smiled. Couldn't stop himself, ha.

'Good crack,' he replied.

'Ah, touché.' I bowed. 'Eggsellent.'

He shook his head. 'Enough. No more egg gags.'

'Well, no, we don't want to over—'

'Don't say it.'

'All right.' I saluted. I actually saluted. 'No references to puddings or the overegging thereof from me, I promise.'

He grinned. 'Couldn't help yourself, could you? Now don't move.'

I couldn't have moved even if I'd wanted to. I couldn't move, and I couldn't ask him to leave.

He started opening cupboards, delving inside them, rummaging around. He stopped, stood abruptly and crossed over to the sink; washed his hands with washing-up liquid, twice, rubbing between his fingers like a surgeon, and shook them before drying them on some kitchen roll. Face set in concentration, from another cupboard he grabbed a Pyrex bowl; from the cutlery drawer the hand whisk; from the spice rack salt, pepper; the fridge again, the last drops of a single pint of milk. He cut the mould off a piece of cheese I couldn't remember buying.

As he worked, he finished his story. I wrote, my handwriting less legible with every word.

The woman had led him upstairs. They had made love again in the bed she shared with her husband. She told him that her husband was away on business and that she felt sure Ryan would need to check her measurements regularly over the next few days. The roll in the hay became a passionate affair. But all the while he knew he had to get the cash from the trunk.

The following week, he received another note from Joe. It said only: *Two weeks*.

That night, he returned to see his Lady Chatterley. They slept together and then, in the wee small hours and with the excuse of having to rise early, he left her sleeping. He had brought a large backpack with him, filled with blank sheets of paper, which he had left outside the front door. He crept out, retrieved it and stole into the box room. He switched as much of the money as he could for the blank sheets, making sure to place a layer of real money on top so that the crime would not be discovered immediately. Then silently he closed the chest, wiped it down with his T-shirt and crept down the stairs.

'And just as I got to the front door,' he said, pouring the omelette mixture, which hit the base of the frying pan in a sizzling rush, 'her husband goes and walks in.'

'No!'

'Oh yes.'

'Oh my God. What the hell did you do?' I wanted, I realised, for him to succeed, to get away and keep the money. I wondered if I could write it so that my reader would feel that too.

'We fought.'

The fight was vicious. The other guy had risen from the dirty business of street crime and fist fights into a life of golf clubs and fine champagne, but he could still handle himself in a brawl. Hearing the fracas, Lady Chatterley woke up.

'She had to call the cops,' he said. 'I get that. She told them I'd come to quote for windows the day before but that she had no idea what I was doing in her house. She had to say that. He would have killed her otherwise. And of course, I had a bag full of money. I may as well have been wearing a stripy top and an eye mask, carrying a brown sack marked SWAG over my back.'

I giggled. 'So you were found guilty?'

'Yeah. Got sent down for aggravated burglary. And because of my colourful youth, let's say, they imposed the maximum sentence. Bob's your uncle, Fanny's your aunt…' He slid a golden omelette the size of a vinyl album onto a large white plate. He cut the omelette in two, put one half on my plate and one half on his, then raised his almost-empty glass and chinked it against mine. 'Here I am.'

'Here you are.'

'And now,' he said, 'you have my life.'

Blog post: PippaGatesAuthor
#thiswritinglife
Find me on:
Instagram: @GatesPip
Twitter: @PipGatesWrites
Facebook: Pippa Gates Author

Out here, nature is a constant source of wonder. The three picture windows in the living room are an ever-changing triptych, a living art installation dedicated to the seasons. I can scarcely believe I survived all those years in the city. Today we have snow, which is just beautiful. I swear it would make even the ugliest landscape look like a Christmas card!

When I first moved here, the snow used to scare me. The first time it snowed, poor Bobby from Wilson's Stores had to come and dig me out! Up the long drive he came in his pickup, all kitted out with snow chains, of course. And wearing nothing more than jeans and a quilted jacket – no scarf, no hat, no designer winter gear like the men I know back in the city.

'This is so kind of you,' I said, stamping my feet, blowing into my hands. I had, typically, come outside inadequately clothed.

But he was already shovelling the snow, his shoulders broad beneath the fabric of his jacket.

'Two sugars and a splash of milk,' he said. He paused for a moment, leant on the huge shovel and grinned with his lovely creamy teeth. 'My fee is a decent cup of coffee.'

It's hard to think of anything bad happening to Bobby. I really do hope he has gone travelling and that it isn't something more sinister. Perhaps he couldn't bring himself to tell his fiancée face to face and intends to contact her once he's put some miles between himself and Wiltshire. I hope that's what he's done.

I hope he's OK.

CHAPTER EIGHT

'Well?' Ryan was watching me, his own first mouthful hovering fluffy and golden on his fork.

'It's the best omelette I've ever eaten.'

'Told you.' His expression was the very image of self-satisfaction, a face you'd never tire of slapping.

While we ate, we talked. Well, I talked – about my life, my job. About Bill, a little. He asked about my parents. My mother had died when I was six, I told him simply.

'How?'

'She just did,' I replied, wondering why I could not bring myself to say it was none of his business. 'And my father moved to Thailand when I was eighteen.'

'How do you feel about that?'

I shrugged. 'Fine.' Still I did not look at him.

'You mentioned your mate? The one who lives nearby?'

'Marlie? Yes, we've been friends for years.'

I told him about Marlena, about our decade-long friendship, her family, her job, her house.

'Sounds like she has the perfect life,' he said, scrutinising me, twitching like an eagle. 'You sound almost jealous.'

'God, no!' I shook my head. 'Not in the slightest. She has to put up with Steve. He's a slob, an absolute slob. I could never tolerate a man like that, no way.'

'I imagine not.' He lifted the plates. A moment later, they were in the dishwasher, the counter top wiped clean. There was no sign of the Pyrex dish or the frying pan. He must have washed them, dried them and put them away already. He drew a packet of tobacco from his back pocket and began to roll a cigarette. I read the time upside down from his watch: after 10.30 p.m. He had to go. I had to get him to go.

He wandered over to the back door and turned the key. 'Shouldn't keep the key in the lock, you know.'

'I know that.'

'Do you mind if I smoke in the garden?'

'Sure,' I said.

Smoking was a post-ritual activity, wasn't it? A punctuation of sorts. That was good. Afterwards, I could ask him to leave without embarrassment. I *would* ask him to leave.

'Roll one for me, will you?' I said.

Yes, we would smoke and then I would clap my hands in a jovial fashion and say it had been nice to meet him but I had work in the morning, et cetera, pay him his two hundred pounds and show him out.

But that's not what happened.

'Thanks so much for your story,' I said, stepping outside and letting him light my cigarette. 'I'm quite drunk, I'm afraid, but I've written it all down. Just have to give the bones of it to my editor before I go to bed. You've saved my life!'

The tip of his cigarette glowed in the dark.

'So how long do you think you'll be selling door to door?' I asked, his silence bothering me.

'Not long,' he said. 'Staying clean and well clothed enough for job interviews is the main problem. I know I look terrible, by the way. And I know I don't smell great either, just in case you think I don't know that. The soap at the hostel is horrible. I'd be better off with washing-up liquid.'

My face flared hot. I was glad of the darkness. And then I remembered...

'Actually, I have some men's clothes,' I said. 'My ex's. He left them behind because they were too small for him. Too contented, you see. He developed a paunch.'

Nothing. And then, after a moment: 'That's kind, but that's not what I meant.'

'I know it isn't. Why would you drop hints for clothes to a single woman? Unless there's something you're not telling me? I mean, I can throw in some French knickers if that's your thing. Although they're not my ex-husband's, obviously.'

Smoke shot from his nostrils, betraying his amusement.

'I mean, it's not much,' I continued, my head reeling from the rush of nicotine. 'But there are some shirts, a couple of suits, I think. Not designer or anything, but decent, you know, and some shoes... What size feet are you?'

'Nine.'

I threw down my cigarette. 'Perfect. And you're about Bill's height, just a lot slimmer. Look, wait here. They're in the loft. Just give me five minutes.'

By now, you'll be thinking, *Oh for God's sake, she left him unsupervised in her kitchen?* Like when you watch a crime series and they're all flashing torches in the dark warehouse and you're shouting at the television, *Switch the flipping light on, you idiot.* But I was drunk, frankly. And I thought if he was going to do anything, he'd have done it by then.

But no, that's not it. That would imply that I felt safe. And at no point did I think I was safe. This is hard to admit, even here. What I felt was something beyond safety or fear, something that was feeding the very roots of me, sending signals through my sap.

I didn't *care*.

That's as near as I can get to it.

I didn't care how much danger I was in.

I didn't care whether I lived or died.

This – this was the nucleus of a feeling that had not left me in all the time he had been in my house.

Of course, my own private adrenalin ride may have sprung from the fact that, deeper still, I *did* feel safe, safe enough to fantasise that I was not. Because, let's face it, at the time, all I knew, or thought I knew, was that he'd been inside for aggravated burglary with, it seemed to me, some pretty extenuating circumstances.

Oh, I don't know. Psychology's a bitch. Short of hypnosis, I'll probably never know what I really felt, and God knows, I'll be dead before anyone explains it to me.

I ran up the stairs, panting by the time I reached the top. The loft hatch was in the bathroom ceiling. I dislodged the trapdoor, hauled down the collapsible stepladder and climbed up. Blind, I felt around, pawing at air until… there… the cord. I pulled it, and the bulb blinked on. See? I'm not a complete nut.

I ducked, shuffled my way through the bin bags and boxes and tennis racquets. I really needed a clear-out soon – there was more crap in here than a blocked toilet at a pop festival. Bill's clothes were in a transparent plastic box. They were probably unfashionable by now, but beggars couldn't—

I stopped myself. He was *not* a beggar. He was a man, a rather scruffy man, admittedly, but a man nonetheless, trying – no, *working* – to get back on his feet. But… now I was trapped in the loft – he had only to slide the hatch cover over and he could bolt it shut. He could keep me captive and no one— No, that was ridiculous. The first thing the police would do would be to investigate the house. If Marlie didn't hear from me by midnight, she'd come over or call the police, and she knew Ryan was here. He would be arrested in moments.

Calm down, crazy lady.

The box was at the back of the loft space, gritty with breeze-block crumbs. I wiped them away with my sleeve and lugged it back to the hatch, wondering how the hell I would get it down. I would empty it up here, I decided, throw the clothes down into the bathroom.

But as I got to the square opening, I saw him. He was looking up at me, and I had the feeling that I had known this, that he would be there, before I even saw him.

'Hi,' he said. 'Thought you might need a hand.'

He was upstairs. In my house. In my *bathroom*. I felt for my phone. It was not in my back pocket. I had taken it out, must have done, but when?

'Thanks,' I said, a dull and quickening thud in my heart, a prickle of sweat at my hairline and, yes, that slick burning layer beneath my skin.

I slid the box over the lip of the hatch, lowered it until I felt the weight transfer, felt it leave my hands and land in his.

'Got it,' he said.

I had to get him back downstairs. I had to get him out of my house.

'Listen,' I said as I climbed down. 'I'll just shove the whole lot in a bin bag and you can pick and choose when you get ho— back to the—

My foot landed on lino. When I turned round, my nose was almost touching his chest. The smell of stale tobacco was stronger, with base notes of day-old sweat and that earthy smell again, moist and fertile.

'Lead on,' I said, with fake cheer, gesturing towards the door.

'Actually.' He nodded to the loo. 'Would you mind?'

The urge to shout *Leave!* coursed through me, but I could hardly stop him from using the bathroom. He was a human being. And nothing he had done had been threatening. Not in any overt sense. It was, in all probability, my own prejudice, that of an educated middle-class woman who had been brought up in material comfort. Yes, it was *prejudice* that made my heart hammer, sent trickles of sweat down my back, formed that searing membrane under my skin.

'Go for it.' I held out my arms for the box.

'It's OK. I'll carry it down when I come.'

'All right.'

'Thank you, Pippa,' he said, with a quiet humility that was new.

At the bathroom door, I stopped.

'Listen, what shall I call the man in my story?' I asked him. 'I think you should name him.'

He pushed out his bottom lip and nodded, slowly, as if to say, *That seems fair*.

'Gary,' he said. 'Gary Hughes.'

'All right.'

In the kitchen, I found my phone on the breakfast bar. I switched it on and left it on the worktop to boot up. I took off my shoes, ran silently back up to my bedroom and snatched the cash from my bedside table. As I returned downstairs, I heard the sound of running water coming from the bathroom. He must be washing his hands, I thought. He would be down soon.

He had to leave. I had to get him out.

Back in the kitchen, I sat on a high stool. Stood up. Ran the cloth over the already clean worktop. Still he didn't come down. I paced into the hall, put the cash on top of the tray of cleaning products. No, I would give the money to him in his hand – that would be kinder. I listened at the bottom of the stairs. I couldn't hear the water running anymore, but nor could I hear any footsteps, no creaks or thuds. I was breathing heavily, I realised, as if I'd sprinted a mile, my skin lined with white heat, my forehead damp. I returned to the kitchen, found an envelope and put the cash inside. That was more dignified, more discreet. Counting cash into his open palm risked making both of us feel cheap. And I didn't want to offend him. I took out a biro and scribbled, *For Ryan, with thanks.* That made the whole transaction classier. For some reason, now that it was over, something about it felt seedy and wrong, as if I had stolen something from him – something I had no right to take.

My phone had booted up. Five missed calls and three messages, all from Marlena.

20.32: *Please tell me that man has left by now*

21.47: *Pip pls answer I'm getting worried just text ok or something so I know you're ok*

23.03: *Pip that's it this is insane I'm coming over*

I checked my watch: 23.04.

The house was silent. More silent than usual for the fact of him in it but not making a sound. I sat on the bar stool, ear cocked like an animal about to exit the burrow. Nothing. Where was he?

A cough echoed on the bathroom walls.

I let out a stifled breath. The bathroom door handle clicked. Footsteps on the landing, the heavy tread of a man. I was glad to hear it. The hot flash spread under my skin. While he was here, I would not be able to relax. Once he left, I would be alone. The silence a moment ago had been a premonition of the loneliness I was about to feel. I had to get him out. He could have taken a razor from the bathroom cabinet and could right now be readying himself to swing around the base of the banister and— My heart pounded. Sweat salty on my top lip. He was a stranger. He was a man. Men overpowered women. That was why I raced home from the station at night, why I half died of fright every time I grabbed a minicab, why my pulse ran wild whenever I followed some guy I barely knew back to his flat.

Heart thumping, chest tight, I grabbed the envelope and squeezed it in my fist. Fingertips to the handle of the cutlery drawer, I pictured the carving knife in its protective sheath. The light darkened, a fraction of a shade. I looked up to find him standing in the doorway, backlit by the hall light, in shadow. He had changed into some of Bill's clothes: a black T-shirt, hoody and jeans. His hair was wet. Even from a metre or so away I could smell the grapefruit scent of my shower gel, my brand of washing powder on the clothes. His feet were white and bare. The pain in my head surged. I had the impression my brow was protruding over my eyes. Had he taken a shower in my house?

My mouth must have dropped open because his expression shifted. He looked from me down to himself and plucked at the fresh T-shirt with his fingertips.

'I put the rest of the clothes into the holdall,' he said.

'What holdall?'

'There was a Puma sports bag in the box. Is that OK?'

'Yeah. Yeah, sure. I didn't even know it was there.'

A moment passed.

'I… I had a shower,' he said.

I shoved my phone in my back pocket, took a step towards him and held out the envelope. 'It's all there. You can take the clothes. And the bag. And your cleaning stuff – I don't want it, no offence. And thanks for the story.'

He took the cash and pushed it into the front pocket of the loose jeans, threw up his hands and shook his head.

'Look,' he said. 'I get it. I'm sorry. I'm sorry, all right? I shouldn't have used your shower. I've had a little too much to drink and your bathroom was so clean. The temptation was too much. The shower was right there… all those soaps and those lovely dry towels, and I just – I guess I just cracked.'

'That's OK,' I managed. I would wash the towels, clean the bathroom from top to bottom. I didn't care if he'd nicked all my toiletries, used my most private space. I had to get him to leave.

He turned and walked along the hallway towards the front door. Another half a metre and he would be out, out of my life forever. 'Can I at least put some shoes on?'

'Sure,' I said, my voice no more than a croak. Even now, he could turn. It was almost midnight. No one would hear me scream. Even if Marlena did call the police, it would be too late.

I followed close behind him, my throat tight. He held up his hands once again, as if I had a gun to his back. Despite my desperation, part of me felt guilty at the way I was behaving after the perfectly civilised evening we'd had. How familiar it was, this feeling, like the way I always felt after sex with a stranger. No sooner had I got what I'd been after than he was nothing to me and I wanted him gone.

At the pile of stuff in the hall, he stopped. He did not crouch to take hold of it. He did not reach for his shoes. His bony shoulders straightened. He turned, slowly. His left foot lifted a little.

I closed my eyes. A second. Another second, his breath in my face – toothpaste over tobacco, wine, earth. I opened my eyes to the blurred edges of him, vague hollows, white ridges.

'I think we both know what's happened here tonight,' he murmured. The heat of him, the crisp smell of freshly laundered clothes…

'Ryan…'

'You can deny it if you like, Pippa, but you know and I know that we made a deal, and you can't – you can't just throw me out like this.'

I stepped back, pictured the kitchen knife in its sleeve in the cutlery drawer, my phone, Marlena. 'I… I'm not sure I… I don't know what you mean. You've given me your story and I've given you two hundred pounds. That's the deal. It's all there. I don't mind if you count it. I won't be offended.'

'Not the money, Pippa. You *know* I don't mean the money.' He closed the gap between us, his eyes narrow and mean, his gaping lower lip wet, his gums purple and black.

'Not the…' My words were little more than a rasp. I tried to stand my ground but was too afraid. I retreated another step, felt the wall hit my back.

'You wrote it. In your book.' He stepped towards me, closing the distance between us to nothing. His mouth was at my ear, the graze of his teeth, the wall hard against my shoulder blades. 'You wrote, "To my darling. We belong together. Love from Pippa". Didn't you? Didn't you? Then you chased after me. Down the street, you ran after me. You made the proposal.'

I couldn't move. 'I didn't mean—'

'You signed it, Pippa.' His lips brushed my earlobe. 'You wanted me.'

'The book was a gift,' I whispered. 'I wanted your story. That's all.'

'And I gave it to you. It's yours. My life is yours.' He brought his face round and fixed his bloodshot eyes on mine. The flickers of flippancy, of sorrow, of regret were all gone. I saw in his eyes what I had not seen until now: madness.

'Ryan.' My chest heaved. My eyes stung. 'Honestly. I have no idea what you're talking about.'

'Oh, you do, Pippa. You do, you do, you do.'

'You're… you're not well.'

'Do you mean mad? Is that what you mean? If it is, then yes, Pippa, my love, I am mad. More, much more than you know. But so are you.'

'I'm not mad. I'm not…'

We were both whispering – a warped enactment of a couple trying to have a private argument in a crowded room.

He drew his rough, knotted knuckle down my cheek. 'I tell you what's going to happen now, Pippa. Pip. I'm going to stay here. In the morning, we can start our life together. It'll be strange at first, but we'll work at it. We'll make it work, and it *will* work because, like you said, we belong together. Like you wrote in your gift. Don't you see?'

Every cell of me filled with white heat.

'Please go,' I sobbed. 'I'm sorry. I'm so sorry if you've got the wrong impression. But you need to leave.'

'Oh, Pippa. Pippa, my love.' He ran his clean thumb across my mouth. 'You're lying. You've been lying for a long, long time, so long you don't even know you're doing it.'

'I'm not lying, I'm not—'

'You didn't know what you wanted because you hadn't found it. But now you have. Now you know what you want. I can see it in your eyes, could see it the moment you opened your front door. That's when we found each other, my love.' He brushed the tip of his nose against my neck, pressed his mouth to my ear and murmured, 'This began when you opened your door.'

Tears ran down my neck. Soaked into the fabric of my T-shirt.

'Ryan. Please stop. Please. You have to go.'

'Come on,' he said softly, closing his hand gently around my throat. 'Let's go upstairs.'

The squeak of my gate hinge reached us.

'Lies, Pip,' he whispered urgently. 'Lying is for others, not you. Lying's for the boys and girls who give you what you don't want…' On he went, spitting words, faster and faster, a tirade of venom vomiting out.

Footsteps on my front path.

'Lying is for when you eat your minute steak,' he hissed, his toxic outpouring gathering feverish momentum, 'your hand-rolled sushi, your al dente farfalle, and pretend not to wonder whether he's going to pick up the bill, whether he's going to pretend he's a gentleman for long enough to…' I closed my eyes against his frantic invective, his saliva speckling my burning skin like fine rain.

A loud rapping on the glass of the front door. Over his square shoulder I saw a familiar outline.

'Marlie!'

He pressed himself against me. The ridge of his hip bones, the hard plate of his chest. The smell of my perfume on the skin of his neck. 'Lies, Pippa. It's how you keep going. It's how you survive. But we can do more than survive. We can live. Stay with me, Pippa.'

'Pippa? Pip?' The clank of the letter box, then Marlie's voice, louder now, frantic. 'Oh my God! Get off her! I'm calling the police! I'm calling the police right now! Get off her. I'm calling them.'

He stood back. I closed my eyes. His hand left my neck. When I opened my eyes, he was opening the door.

'Who are you?' His low voice brimmed with threat. 'Who the hell are you?'

'I bought ten J-cloths off you about four hours ago.' Marlena's voice trembled. Her phone was clamped to her ear. 'I'm already through to the police. Yes, hello, police?'

I watched, motionless. Calmly he took the phone from her hand and pushed his thumb to it.

'This has nothing to do with you.' He handed it back to her. 'Pippa invited me in, all right? She invited me. We talked. We had dinner. I was just saying goodbye. This is none of your business, OK?' He stepped towards her; her mouth fell open. 'None of your fucking business.'

'Ryan.' I managed to pull myself away from the wall. His tray, the sports bag of Bill's clothes on top, lay between us on the floor. 'She won't do anything. Just leave her. Leave us alone. Take your stuff and go and we won't call the police, all right?'

He turned away from Marlie. Without speaking, without looking at me, he dropped to his haunches, lifted the tray and the bag. He stood, pulled back his shoulders. In the dim of the hallway, his stark white feet were childlike, vulnerable. He glanced up at me, something like sorrow in his eyes.

'You need to stop lying to yourself, Pip.'

I had recovered a little, though my heart still pounded.

'Get help, Ryan,' I said, drying my face with my sleeve. 'I'm sorry if you misunderstood, but don't ever come back here, all right? If you do, I'll call the police and you'll end up back inside. Don't make me do that. It's in your head, Ryan, it's all in your—'

But he had turned away from me and was walking out of my house. He barged past Marlena, shaking his head in apparent disgust, and strode down the front path. Marlena was staring at me, her eyes wild.

'Don't call the police,' I said.

'I'm calling the police.'

'I said don't, Marlie. Listen to me, will you? Just once in your life listen to what I say. Don't call the police.'

'All right.' She put her phone in her pocket. 'All right.'

She held out her arms and came towards me. I pushed past her and ran into the front garden. At the gate, I stared into the darkness. The white soles of Ryan Marks's feet were all that I could see: one, then the other, smaller and smaller. Until he was gone.

Audio Excerpt #3

Two, three. Testing.

Our meeting was interrupted, and that's a shame, but I've resolved to write her a letter and post it in the old-fashioned way. Women find that kind of thing charming. I read that in a magazine while I was inside; those things are full of tips.

I think… I think if I could have stayed, she would have seen everything much more clearly. She is, more than anything, confused.

But her overprotective friend couldn't stop herself from interfering, and so now I suppose I'll have to win her round over time. As I said, the old-fashioned way. I don't mind. She's worth the wait. What's regrettable is that we'd already become so close when her friend blew us apart. OK, so we didn't consummate our union, but our conversation was more intense than mere sex. It had its own foreplay and its own rhythm, its climax and its mellow, exhausted afterwards. I know she understood that. We even smoked a cigarette afterwards in the garden, like lovers. She knew what that meant. Why else would she have asked me to roll her one if not because she understood the subtext of the act? Consolidation, that's what it was. We were cementing our bond. We had achieved greater intimacy in those few hours than most couples do in a lifetime of marriage.

I've been looking for that kind of connection all my life. Now I've found it and it feels… it feels electric. I think, despite herself, she accepts that we're all mad, that it's just a question of whether we admit it to ourselves or not. My parents' insanities were gloriously and uniquely compatible. What they had was rare. It was just that the world didn't understand them. No one understood them. They shared a vision, and I appreciate that now. They were ahead of their time. Cases like mine are coming to light with increasing frequency. If you're still listening to this recording, you'll be nodding in agreement. You'd have to have been living on the moon not to notice. There was that guy in Germany, wasn't there, and only recently the thirteen in the US. The whole cellar thing is catching on. Not as a conventional way of living, obviously, I don't mean that. But as an alternative.

Equality and diversity. Each to his own. Live and let live. What two people find acceptable is for them alone, isn't it? Who is anyone else to judge?

But in this age of public life for all, the wise will show the world only what it understands. The trick is to reflect back to the world what it wants to see, a version of itself. And to keep what it doesn't want to see, what it does not understand, private.

CHAPTER NINE

'Are you all right?' Marlena was waiting for me in the hall.

'Yes.' I stepped back inside, closed the front door, checked it had locked.

She went ahead into the kitchen. 'I'll put the kettle on.'

'You don't need to stay,' I said, following her. 'I'm fine.'

She gave a brief, bitter-sounding laugh but did not turn round. 'Looks like it.'

'Honestly, Marlie, I'm fine. He'd got the wrong end of the stick, that's all. It was probably my fault. He was about to leave.'

She banged the mugs onto the work surface and turned to me. Her face was pure incredulity.

'Are you drunk or mad?' she said. 'Or both? I mean, I've just got here to find you pinned up against the wall by a criminal, stinking of wine and…'

She went on for a bit, but I tuned out. I was thinking, yes, I'm drunk, and yes, actually, possibly a bit fruit loop. I wondered in what way Marlena was at risk of losing her marbles, what were her little mental black spots, her chinks, her hairline cracks. None, probably, knowing her. She probably never even got as far as irrational. Her parents had named her – approximately – after the song 'Marlene on the Wall' by Suzanne Vega, in turn named after a poster of Marlene Dietrich. Marlene Dietrich never lost her shit. All she had to do was watch from the wall with her mocking smile.

'… you've got to start taking responsibility,' Marlie was saying. 'Your behaviour is… well, it's irresponsible. It's dangerous.'

'Don't judge me,' I said.

'I'm not! I'm worried about you, that's all.'

'Well don't be. I don't need you to worry about me, and I don't need you to look after me.'

She frowned, shook her head. 'Pippa? You were being strangled by a criminal.'

'I wasn't being strangled! He had his hand on my neck, that's all.'

'He could have… he could have raped you.' This she whispered, as if perhaps I should feel ashamed.

'So what do you want me to do, stay at home on my own all the time? Buy a habit and join a convent, singing "The hills are alive…"? Anyone could rape anyone, Marlie! Any of the guys I go on dates with, any man who follows me from the station at night, any male teacher at the school… The caretaker, he's a bloke, the man at the supermarket checkout, the man in the off-licence… That's just reality. That's called being a woman. It's called being a single woman who doesn't have the luxury of a husband to pick her up and drop her off and know when she's supposed to be home.'

Marlena closed her eyes a moment and made a great show of exhaling. 'Now you're being ridiculous. You know what I mean. You can't go inviting ex-cons into your house, not when you're here on your own. Or any guy who calls at your door, for that matter. I mean, who does that? Did you even check his badge? Anything could have happened to you if I hadn't got here. What the hell are you on, inviting him in?' She had raised her voice. A cheer went off inside me. Next stop, full-blown wobbly. I hoped so. It would be so great to see her lose it. Just once.

'Don't be so dramatic,' I said. 'These guys are just trying to get back on their feet. They're not murderers, for God's sake.'

'How do you know that?' she shouted. 'What's the matter with you? We should be calling the police.'

'Why?' I scoffed. I mimed making a phone call. 'Er, yeah, hello, Officer, yeah, a man was in my house and he made me an omelette and had a shower.'

'You let him have a shower?' Eyes popping.

'Don't look at me like I let him wank on my bed sheets. The showers at the hostel are awful so I said he could use mine.'

'Have you checked your bathroom?'

'No! What for – boxes of ammunition? Human traffic?'

She floundered. 'I… I just think you need to stop being so bloody reckless.'

'Said the woman with the perfect life.'

'Oh no, no, no. Don't do that.' How quiet she had become. *You've all gone quiet down the front, tra la la.* 'My life isn't perfect and you know it.'

'Why isn't it? Which bit? Which millimetre of it? Eh? And do not give me Zane's dyslexia or honest to God I'll scream.'

Her face creased, as if she'd stubbed her toe. She looked out of the window, then back towards me. 'Why are you being like this? I love you, Pip. You're my best friend. You know things aren't always perfect with me. They're not perfect with anyone. Most of us are just muddling through, getting it wrong, saying sorry, getting it wrong again, but do you know what, we stick with it! We don't throw a fit when the roses aren't the right shade of pink.'

'I don't do that.'

'You bloody do. Steve doesn't do half the things Bill did for you. He busted his guts for you. Honestly, whenever I spoke to him, he seemed to be worrying about what he'd done wrong this time and what he might do wrong the next. He was exhausted with it, Pip. No wonder he…' She sighed. Her hands closed into fists.

A silent beat followed. My head throbbed.

'No wonder he what?' I asked, my voice low.

'Nothing.'

'No wonder he went for cliché number one and shagged his secretary, you mean? No wonder he chose to turn everything we had to shit? Are you seriously saying it was my fault?'

The air had thinned. I noticed her pyjama bottoms, her coat thrown over the top. She had no make-up on. She had clearly been in bed. With Steve. All warm and cosy and loved and safe. Marlena on the wall, recording the rise and fall of her fucked-up, febrile friend.

'I'm going to go,' she said, walking with purpose out of the kitchen.

I made no move to stop her. I did not call her name as she marched down the hall, did not tell her to come back as she undid the catch, did not cry *Wait!* as she stepped out. The door closed behind her with a bang.

I stared after her a moment, listening to her clipped, resentful footsteps, before bending slowly forward and pressing my cheek to the cold counter top.

'Fuck.'

My best friend had just saved me from something unspeakable. My response? To defend him, lie for him and attack her. Bravo, Pippa. Good work. Take an advanced certificate in how to lose friends and alienate people, why don't you?

Shock. I was in shock. I would call her first thing in the morning and apologise. And then she could apologise to me for telling me I was somehow to blame for my broken marriage. Last time I checked, Bill was the one who couldn't keep it in his trousers. And if I couldn't keep it in mine anymore, well, that was his fault.

I straightened up, rubbed my face, my gums, which were numb. I fetched two paracetamols from the cupboard and downed them with cold water. I refilled the glass and drank that down too.

Still breathing heavily, I ran a third glass of water and returned to where I had started this whole surreal evening: to the living room, to my computer, to the blank screen. I sat down and typed:

Framed by Love by Pippa Gates: synopsis
    Gary Hughes never had it easy. Born on the wrong
side of the tracks, his life…

Each sentence led on from the next with a fluidity such that there were moments when I wondered whether some spirit form was guiding my hand. I barely consulted my notes. Everything was in my head, ready to go, as if I were taking dictation. All the alterations and adaptations I had noted mentally as Ryan was speaking appeared to have been branded into my subconscious. In my version of his story, the hero has never been locked in a cellar. That was too dark, too much. This hero did his time for petty theft and learnt his trade inside. Once out, qualified as a carpenter and determined to go straight, he gets work, does it well and eventually goes it alone – only with a little help from the drug-dealing villain from the old days. The threat of the revolving door hangs over poor Gary. One false move and he's back inside.

I used the van, painted it black, wrote *G. Hughes Windows* across the side in white cursive hand… a little truth, a little lie, and so on: hand into sleeve, bunch of flowers, saw the woman in half, pull the rabbit from the hat.

The client is… the client is a divorcee; no, better, a widow. She calls Gary when a window is smashed in an attempted burglary. She is vulnerable! She is alone! But there is no seduction attempt by her. *Framed by Love's* main character is a gigolo, but likeable, an opportunist. He seduces her, takes advantage of her loneliness. *Oh, the nights, Gary, the nights are the worst!* The sex scenes are red hot. What begins as a fling becomes a passionate affair: mismatched lovers buffeted by strong emotions neither can control.

She is older than him, yes, and wealthy. He comes from nothing. Perhaps, according to the traditions of romantic fiction, they don't like each other at first. Perhaps she has another suitor, someone on paper more appropriate but who can never give her what she really needs. Maybe. She has never known real love; her late husband was cold and ungenerous, physically and emotionally. She gives Gary security, a home. She gives him elocution lessons – a bit of *Pygmalion*, why not? Ryan was so well spoken, after all – a conscious effort on his part to better himself, for sure. Gary wants to better himself too. She helps him. In return he gives her love, satisfaction. Intimacy.

But then – zowee! – he discovers the cash in the trunk! The evidence of a baby she never had. He can give her that baby, he knows he can, virile so-and-so that he is. But old habits die hard, and with the loan shark on his back… He has no choice. He is in fear for his very life! One night, while she sleeps, he takes the cash and is about to leave forever when he realises he can't. He loves her. He can't steal from her. He is a reformed character! He puts the money back. Meanwhile, it turns out that the woman put the money there to test him, but only because she's insecure and can't believe someone as wonderful as Gary could truly love her. She tells him this when he confesses everything to her and asks for her forgiveness. She pays off the loan shark and asks him to marry her. He says yes.

An hour later, I sat back from the screen and reread my last line: *This is a story about one man's struggle to escape the chains of his past, and about the redemptive power of love.*

I had written it so quickly, it was full of typos and missing punctuation. I would have to comb through and correct it, but here was the core. There are only seven stories in the world. If you're an avid reader, you might know that. This was a Cinderella story, I thought. The classic rags-to-riches tale. But this time a poor, defenceless man is saved by a handsome princess, as it were.

Cool.

I changed a few details, made the female character a self-made businesswoman rather than a woman whose husband had earned the big bucks. She was active in the community, a pillar of society. She would need a strong name... Petra, that meant rock, I was pretty sure; yes, Petra Stark. Perfect. I made the loan shark, who I'd decided was a Brazilian gangster called Gil, much fiercer. To the scar on his cheek I added a few neck tattoos and a knuckleduster ring in the shape of a fanged snake. I toyed with a third nipple – with the idea of one, I mean, ha! But no, too James Bond villain, too silly to be scary. I downgraded Gary's promiscuity as I felt it made him less sympathetic. I made him charming, a real lover of women. His teenage sweetheart had died, I decided. Of a drug overdose. I was thinking of Ryan's obvious former drug addiction and wanted to add a note of tragedy that would endear Gary to the reader without making his real-life counterpart uncomfortable. Ryan, I knew, would read the book the moment it came out.

So a rich but loveless slightly older woman and a damaged man trying to make good in a tough world. Both these characters were in need of love. Aren't we all? Love is the answer – always. If I believed that then, dear reader, I believe it more than ever now.

The next morning, sunglasses bolted to face, riding waves of nausea and armed with a box of paracetamol, two cans of fat Coke and some flaccid croissants from the corner shop, I called Marlena. She didn't pick up. She was busy, I told myself. She would call me back. As I entered the school gates, I checked my emails and was delighted to see that Jackie, my editor, had replied at 8.40 a.m. My email was probably the first one she'd read!

Hey Pippa,

This looks amazing. It's classic and has some real heart. Go for it. I know you'll do a great job.

Well done for getting back in the saddle.

J x

I punched the air and returned my phone to my bag. I felt truly dreadful but consoled myself with the fact that whatever punishment this red-wine-and-fag hangover had in store for me, I could relax in the knowledge that after so long in the frozen wastes of writer's block, I now had another book in the offing. And this time it would be based on something genuine, a life that was real.

A life I now owned.

That evening, I picked up a microwave meal for one, which included a special offer on a bottle of white, both of which I took to my desk. Words flowed, just as they had the previous evening, eased no doubt by the miraculous effects of that classiest of hairs of the dog: Pinot Grigio.

This time the characters came alive. They spoke to one another, moved, thought. They negotiated their world like clay figures manipulated by the gods. Well, by me. Further and further they pulled me in, showed me who they were. I didn't look at Amazon, not even once; I didn't google holiday destinations or idyllic country cottages for sale or revolutionary tights that stayed put. I didn't get sucked into any celebrity gossip. I didn't even scroll through Facebook or Instagram or Twitter until anxious nausea overtook me. I left my dating sites alone.

I would be celibate, I decided, at least until the first draft was complete.

The following morning I tried Marlena again, but again, no reply. I didn't leave a message. I was pretty sure Zane had football on Saturdays, and Zoe had ballet. The phone would be in her bag. She and Peeve would probably be having some puke-worthy couple's coffee somewhere, though God only knew what she found to say to him. So no, she wouldn't have heard her phone. Or she was ignoring my calls. Well even if she was, she wouldn't be cross for long. We'd been friends for a long time.

I made a black tea – no milk – and swung on the fridge door. Nothing, beyond a bottle of black nail varnish, some months-old tikka masala paste that I couldn't be bothered to inspect for embryonic green fuzz, and some Branston pickle from who knew when. The cupboards weren't offering me much either, not unless I fancied eating pasta quills with the aforementioned pickle… or paste. So no food. No food whatsoever.

I checked the back door. It was locked. I removed the key and put it in the cutlery drawer, wishing I'd asked Ryan to leave me a cheeky cigarette. After a brief hesitation, I returned to the cutlery drawer and retrieved the key, opened the back door and found my half-smoked roll-up on the patio.

'Ah, there you are!' I picked it up, blew on it. Not too bad. It hadn't rained since Thursday.

What? Oh, stop it with the *you didn't, did you?* I did, all right? But two puffs in and I almost vomited. I threw it down and crushed it into the flagstone with my monkey boot. In the garden that backed onto mine I could hear children playing, the soft inflection of their nonsense imaginary game scripts. How different it was by day out here to how it had been two nights ago. Two different worlds, almost, the light and the dark, co-existing. The sun hurt my eyes; I went back inside.

In the kitchen, I checked my phone. Nothing. No missed calls, no messages. I wondered what Marlie was up to. I wondered whether Ryan had made it back to his hostel, whether he was thinking about Thursday night. Thank God he had gone without a struggle. Thank *God*.

I decided to run through the park and call in at the supermarket on the way back. Before you go thinking I'm an exercise nut, I'll reassure you that I'm not. If I tell you I run regularly, what I mean is that every six months, a strange burst of adrenalin hits and the need to move at speed overtakes me. I run a long way on these occasions, my body suspended in a state of shock. It's only when I return home that I realise that everything hurts.

I returned home from my exercise-and-grocery-shop multitask special laden with, among other healthy 'treats', sugar-free muesli and almond milk, which I ate standing up at the bar and thinking: *Check me out, eating muesli with almond milk like Elle Macpherson or some shit.* This was followed by sourdough toast and honey – *Butter? Of course not! I laugh in the face of dairy!* Oh, how blissfully hoodwinked I was by my own delusion that this was how I would live my life from then on. I showered and dressed joyfully, and it was only when I got back to my computer that I realised it was only 9.30 a.m. On a weekend. Unheard of.

I was officially a high-functioning power person.

Again the words came, row upon row. The heebie-jeebies subsided. Marlena and I would be all right; Ryan had gone, was out of my life forever. He'd got the message. I'd had a close shave. But everything was OK now.

Several hours later, without so much as a whisper of a Hobnob breakout, I paused instead for a sensible lunch. Carrot and coriander soup and some crusty bread – yes, wheat, but one day at a time, sweet Jesus. I even used a bowl and a plate, *and* cutlery, like a grown-up who eats actual meals instead of crisps. All this while I read through my morning's work, making serious little *mm-mm* noises – a bit like a late-night culture-show presenter listening to an avant-garde art-house director spout on about the influence of bottle tops on the theatre of the absurd. Or something.

My work was a little thin, but the bones of it were there.

I went back into the kitchen to dump my crockery in the sink – Rome wasn't built in a day, dear reader, back off. On the way back, I noticed an envelope on the mat. It didn't look like a bill or a circular – too square, and the paper was a creamy colour, not white. I picked it up.

Ms P. K. Gates was all it said on the front – the hand looping, romantic. Fountain pen, not biro. Whoever it was knew my middle name, Katherine, or at least my initial. On the back of the envelope was an address in Twickenham. Inside was a matching piece of writing paper, the same rather flamboyant handwriting. With a prescient churning in my stomach, I read:

Dear Pip,

I'm sorry I left on such poor terms on Thursday evening. Your friend interrupted us at a bad moment and I thought it best to go.

I meant what I said, and I think by now you will have admitted to yourself what you started when you gave me your book, made your proposal and invited me into your house. I'm enjoying the book, by the way. I like your voice and feel like you are here with me, reading to me.

I just wanted to reiterate and confirm what you wrote and signed in your dedication: that we belong together. I sense that you have since pulled back from that, and I understand that meeting one's true destiny can be terrifying. Perhaps it is only because I have been deprived of liberty that I am not as afraid of it as the average person. To live an authentic life is one of the toughest things we can choose to do. When I agree with you that we belong together, I don't mean this in a threatening way; it is simply a statement of fact. You deal in fiction, that is true, but I think you know that fiction belongs on the page, not in real life. It is time to end the lies that have held you back for so long.

Thank you again for the clothes and the shoes. They will tide me over until my financial position becomes more secure.

When you're ready to contact me, I am at Quaker House, the address on the back of the envelope. Or you can call me on the number below. Even ex-cons have mobiles these days. What's the world coming to, eh?

See you soon – *à bientôt*.

Yours,

Ryan

The letter shook in my hands, words jumping. My body filled with heat, cold, heat once again. In a daze I went into the living room and sat down slowly, so slowly, as if lowering myself onto a bed of nails. Forcing myself to focus, I read the page for a second time. The tone was so reasonable, if a little formal, the content so unimaginably mad. The triumph of the morning drained from me and was replaced with a grim feeling, like a boulder in my gut.

I had my story, yes, but at what cost?

A stranger, a potentially dangerous stranger, now had my address and believed that I had signed some kind of contract obligating me to him. He had been into my house and, I had to admit, into my head. He knew my middle name, and I had no idea how.

That feeling, the slick burning oil all over me, came again then at the mere thought of him. It was my body's memory of him. It *was* him, his essence, there where I could neither scratch it out nor scrub it away. A tattoo, inked black beneath my skin.

But he was delusional. He had concocted a fantasy of us as two souls destined for each other, a true love match across the most impossible boundaries. It was like a warped version of something I would write. But I knew the difference between fact and fiction; it was Ryan who did not. Classic projection.

I attempted to train my emotional response, to divert fear towards sympathy. The poor misguided man. There were mental-health difficulties here. He meant no harm. He was clever, very clever, but had lost or perhaps never had any grip on nuance, the ability to read another person and understand how they responded to you.

Or perhaps he had simply fallen in love with me. It happened. Always tricky to extricate oneself from some lovesick admirer's all-too-obvious crush – it was why I preferred one-night stands. Sarah at work was already showing signs of neediness after no more than half a dozen drunken Friday-night liaisons and would probably have to go. Yes, perhaps he had simply fallen for me, hard. In that case, he was only as deluded as Romeo when he pined over Rosaline. Mismatched lovers did overcome all odds, yes, but only if both felt the same: Romeo and Juliet, not Rosaline. A sinister and physically repulsive criminal and a middle-class school teacher whose idea of danger was crisps for dinner would never happen for real – I knew that. But I almost admired his belief in this whole two-people-who-belong-together-love-at-first-sight stuff, as if such a phenomenon actually existed outside of stories, especially given his eagerness to show himself to be worldly-wise. Cynical, even. Having been locked away with only books for reference, he had become educated, yes, but had lost all sense of how these things really worked outside the prison walls. Despite his haggard appearance, he was a little boy, really, a little boy released suddenly and shockingly into a world he did not understand.

But the world had to believe in star-crossed lovers, and in love against all odds, or we were lost, weren't we? Without that kind of love, there was no romance. And without romance, there was no beauty, no life worth living.

What was I going to do?

Blog post: PippaGatesAuthor
#thiswritinglife
Find me on:
Instagram: @GatesPip
Twitter: @PipGatesWrites
Facebook: Pippa Gates Author

Pushing Up Daisy is coming along a treat. Daisy is starting to soften in her attitude towards Bing as she replays memories of their love story from all those years ago. Bing was the greatest dancer long before Sister Sledge ever said how, what or indeed wow, although I can't say more without giving it away, and if there's one thing I can't stand, it's a spoiler! I've reached forty-five thousand words and that's largely thanks to Mrs D making sure I stay here at my desk from dawn until dusk! I always used to joke that what I needed was a wife, and now, of course, I have one! Honestly, my every need is met. I hit my desk by nine after breakfast, pause for coffee and a light accompaniment such as a home-baked scone at 10.45 a.m. precisely, a refreshing cup of tea at midday before lunch, which I eat alone at my desk on the dot of 1 p.m. I use the time productively – to read through what I have written so far that morning. Social media is for the evenings – that's when I catch up on Twitter and Instagram and Facebook. There's no screen time at all once we've had dinner. Evenings are strictly reserved for television, reading and downtime.

It's like a writers' retreat here. Except it's my life!

No wonder I never knuckled down before. I hated rules, found all forms of constraint offensive to my personal sense of freedom. So for those of you out there struggling to find the discipline to do whatever it is you're striving to do, I do understand and I do sympathise. And of course, not everyone is waited on hand and foot as I am, I absolutely get that too! But if I could reach out to you for a moment and share something that Mrs D once explained to me, it would be this: if you give a child a ball to kick next to a busy road, the child cannot play for fear of the ball escaping into the traffic. If instead you build walls around the child, he is free to kick the ball in the safety of his courtyard. In that sense, he is free within his prison. Do you see? A certain confinement is the *right* kind of freedom.

Mrs Danvers has helped me to see that.

CHAPTER TEN

I tried to put Ryan's letter out of my mind and worked solidly on his literary alter ego there in my manuscript. I gave him Ryan's eyes, his sense of humour, his way of making a steeple with his hands.

I ate regular, nutritious meals all weekend. On Sunday, late afternoon, I ironed the clothes that I'd laundered the previous day while taking a writing break. As the steam hissed over the panels and seams of my work attire, I smiled at the thought that Ryan would approve of my new-found discipline. I can't impress upon you enough, dear reader, how out of character all of this was for me. I was turning over a new leaf, as they say. Ryan had given me my work. My work had given me focus. Focus had given me discipline. My life was slotting into place.

I felt... wholesome.

On Monday I taught four periods, and where usually I would have wasted my frees flirting with Sarah or Jean Pierre, I used my time to catch up on marking and prep for the following day. I stayed behind at school to finish all I had to do so that I could devote the entire evening to writing. I had written four chapters and planned to write a fifth if I could. I still hadn't heard from Marlena and was starting to feel my willingness to apologise diminish. I had been in shock when we argued, and it was she, not I, who had said the most hurtful things. I owed her an apology, yes, but she owed me one too. I decided not to call her again. I had tried three times. The ball was in her court.

As for Ryan's letter, I would ignore it. Simple. He would soon get the message.

I headed out of the school gates at around 5 p.m. There were only three cars left in the car park and silently I congratulated myself on my professional diligence. I hadn't given out a single detention that day. Frankly, in my head, I was halfway to my OBE acceptance speech.

I was searching my handbag for my car key when I saw Bill standing at the edge of the car park just shy of the school gates. But it was not Bill. He was much thinner, a little taller and he was staring at me in a way Bill never had: his eyes blazing with murderous intent.

Ryan.

Pretending I hadn't recognised him, I dug around with increasing urgency: one purse, one lidless fluffy lip salve, one dead phone, a tampon that had made a bolt for it and would have to go in the bin… Where the hell was… my key – there, yes!

No, that was my house key. It dropped to the ground. I bent to pick it up.

'Pippa Gates, author.'

Bill's tan brogues at the edge of my vision. Ryan looming over me as if he had teleported, though of course in my panic I had let precious seconds pass. I stood up, took a step back.

'Ryan,' I said.

'Fancy seeing you here.'

He had the same scrubbed appearance, the same carbolic smell. Bill's too-large T-shirt, jeans and suit jacket had an almost stylish drape on him. The look was not wholly successful, however. The shoulder pads of the jacket dipped a little at the edges where his own shoulders were not wide enough to hold them up. Bill's old brogues, which on Bill had looked if not chic then at least on trend, looked like Mr Men shoes on Ryan.

'I work here,' I said.

'So I see.' He looked towards the school, then back to me, something haughty in his gaze. 'Didn't realise this was your school.'

'Well it is.' I smiled. Why did I do that? Why do you think? Because smiling is the automatic response of women to everything, even incipient danger. Because from the moment we are born we are conditioned to grin like ninnies in the face of every human interaction, no matter how disconcerting. Certainly I had been. From my mother's oppressive nosiness and blisteringly scathing commentaries as depression rampaged through her nervous system, to my father's switch from present and funny and affectionate to cold and devastatingly absent. I think I even smiled when he wrote to tell me he was now living in Thailand, biting my teeth together as I read his letter, pressing them into my gums as my heart broke.

'Ryan,' I said as pleasantly as I could. 'What are you doing here?'

'I was taking a walk.' He returned my smile. His eyes no longer registered anything sinister; rather flippancy, a kind of mocking mischief. 'I like to walk; it's a pastime of mine. I thought I recognised your car.'

'How would you know it was mine?'

He shrugged but said nothing more. I tried to think if my car had been parked outside my house the night he came. I couldn't remember – it was possible. Had I told him which school I taught at? Again, possible.

Instinctively I looked about me, towards the playing fields, but there were no hockey or football matches going on, no late students wandering out after an extracurricular club. I returned my gaze to him. Where I had seen a trace of imperiousness, now I saw only the crazed glimmer of something less controlled.

'I'm off home,' I said, unlocking the car in a showy display of finality.

'You can give me a lift to Twickenham,' he replied brightly. 'I can let you have my review of your book on the way.'

'I…'

But he was already rounding the front of the car. I watched him, frozen. He was opening the passenger-side door, and still I watched. He was in the passenger seat.

The fire I by now associated with him and all thoughts of him seared along the underside of my skin. Again I cast my eyes towards the school. It was 5 p.m., not at all late, but there was no one around – no one at all.

I could say I wasn't going home after all. But that wouldn't work. And I couldn't manhandle him out of my car. I could tell him to get out, but that would be confrontational, and I didn't want to find out what happened when he lost his temper. It would be safer to drive him to where he wanted to go and let him pontificate on the literary merit – or lack thereof – of my debut novel. As when he had been in my kitchen, the most prudent option was to do whatever he wanted.

I got in. I would drop him at his hostel. I would keep the conversation light. I would wait until he was out of the car then tell him that I wanted him to leave me alone. If he became aggressive, I would remind him of the conditions of his licence – I didn't know what they were, but I assumed that stalking women was a no-no.

'Quaker House,' he said.

'Up past the station, is that right? The big red-brick building after the lights?'

'Very good,' he said. Supercilious bastard.

I started the engine.

He opened the glove compartment and pushed it shut. 'You got my letter?'

'Yes, thank you.' I pulled out of the car park, scanning the pavement, the houses. Not a soul. I lived in a bloody ghost town and was only noticing it now.

'I thought you might reply.'

'I've been busy. I'm writing again. My editor liked the idea.'

He pushed out his bottom lip in apparent satisfaction. 'What have you called it?'

'*Framed by Love*. For now.'

'Good title. Very punny.'

I said nothing.

'So I read *Fight for Your Love*,' he said after a moment, opening the glove compartment again and closing it again with a click. My teeth clenched; my jaw muscle flexed.

'Oh yes?' I hit the first set of lights. Five more minutes, ten max, and he would be out of my car and out of my life. He could give me his little lecture and then it would all be over. I had been right – all he wanted was to share his erudite opinion. He wanted to show off. Lucky me.

'You have a good style,' he said with authority, as if he were in some way qualified to judge me and my writing, arrogant twat. 'You have a great turn of phrase. There were some nice metaphors in there, some cute observations. I can tell you've read a lot of Shakespeare. But I can see what the critics meant. It does lack authenticity. There were a few bits that made me laugh out loud, to be honest, Pippa. And not in a good way, I'm afraid.'

'I can't actually remember asking you for your opinion.'

He laughed. 'For a writer, you have a very limited awareness of the many little emotional contracts we make without words.'

'Another theory,' I said. 'Emotional contracts, did you say? How fascinating.'

'You know what I'm talking about. Don't pretend you don't. Come up from the sea of lies, just for a moment. Come up and breathe with me, come on.'

My knuckles whitened on the steering wheel.

'Yes, emotional contracts, Pippa. Like, say, if you suggest a cup of coffee in a café with someone, you agree to share something more than the coffee, don't you? *Let's take a moment to get to know each other*, you're saying, *but not so long that if we don't like each other it will become embarrassing to both of us later.* Of course, these are not the words you use; all you say is, *Would you like a cup of coffee?*

I said nothing, was aware of my nostrils flaring, the tightness of my jaw.

'*Come to dinner,*' he went on. 'Now there you're effectively presenting them with a metaphorical document. If they agree to enter into the contract and attend your dinner party, they're effectively signing up to becoming more than your casual acquaintance. If they reciprocate, another little contract is made: they are in receipt of your more than casual acquaintanceship and would like to extend the terms. In time, dinner here, dinner there; if that goes on, the contract becomes binding, something trickier to renege on. You become *friends.*'

I gave an ostentatious yawn.

'Come on, Pip,' he said, though his tone was amused. 'We both know you're not bored, and we both know you know exactly what I mean. It's me that's been inside, not you. When you gave me that book, you were asking me to read it and give you my opinion. More than that, you were asking for my approval and admiration. Tell me that's not true and I'll get out of the car right now.'

'The car is moving,' I said, and then, when he said nothing, 'The book was a gift. Nothing more.'

'If you like…' He shrugged. I caught the movement in my peripheral vision and felt my insides ignite.

We hit the high street. Outside a pub, a dishevelled woman with no teeth and broken veins shook her fist at passers-by. On the bench a little further on, a man – her boyfriend, perhaps – slumped in his filthy mackintosh, clutching an empty paper cup. Ryan was still talking.

'… and when you signed your name, you knew exactly what you were doing. Hiding in plain sight, Pippa. Many a true word and all that.'

'Oh look, we're almost here. At your *hostel*.' I emphasised the word, like a snob. I drove through the lights, pulled into the car park. I didn't turn to look at him. Instead, I stared out of the windscreen at the red bricks of the building, my knuckles still white on the steering wheel. He could easily murder me, I thought. He could strangle me right here, leave me in this car and walk away whistling.

'Listen, Ryan,' I said. 'I would chat to you for a bit longer, but I really have to get back. I'm on a deadline, and it's not easy with a full-time job.'

He made no move to unclip his seat belt. Instead, he sighed heavily.

'Ryan,' I said. 'It was nice meeting you. And I am glad you liked the book. The next one will be more authentic and that's largely thanks to you. It was good to meet you. Goodbye now.'

He unclipped his belt and looked at his watch. 'So, what are we, Monday? I'll hear from you before the end of the week, I'm sure.'

Before I had time to process the words, he had already kissed my cheek and thrust himself out of the car. The passenger door slammed shut.

'You won't,' I called out, redundantly, to the dead smell of cheap soap, to the receding figure of Ryan Marks walking slowly towards the hostel, my ex-husband's clothes draping loosely across his back.

Back at home, jangling, I googled Ryan Marks. I was still seething – at his arrogance, his presumption. He didn't know me. He didn't know anything about me. Is there anything worse than someone who thinks they have you all figured out?

So.

Ryan Marks… a plumber in Newcastle.

Ryan Mark Electrics… a shop selling bulbs and electrical equipment in Barrow-in-Furness

Ryan Markman… a plumber in Widnes. There was a Facebook profile picture – not at all bad. Married, though. For now.

Marks and Weston… a firm of solicitors in Sheen.

'Bollocks.'

Clearly his window business had not been registered under his name. Perhaps he'd never put it online. He said he'd been inside for… had he said how long? I couldn't remember. What I had been expecting was a newspaper article, I realised, articulating the thought to myself only then. Some grainy black-and-white shot of a man under a blanket being hustled into the Old Bailey. Ridiculous. His misdemeanours were hardly crimes of the century. It was no wonder there was no digital footprint. The man had no status.

He was a lowlife.

He was nothing.

But I had signed my book to him. And I had been pleased when he said he liked it, pissed off beyond belief when he criticised it. I did owe him my new idea. I should dedicate the second book to him. It would be the right thing to do. He would feel acknowledged. I could satisfy his ego without indulging his fantasy.

I fried an egg and ate it with some toast while I read through what I had written over the weekend.

There were a few bits that made me laugh out loud, to be honest, Pippa. And not in a good way, I'm afraid.

You have a great turn of phrase.

It wasn't as good as I'd hoped, but I steeled myself not to go back and change it. I should plough on, keep moving forward. It had to be good. I had to write something that would impress Ryan enough to wipe that smug grin off his horrid skinny face. My fingers pressed the keys.

You have a good style. There were some nice metaphors in there, some cute observations.

His long, knotted fingers, his blue-black eyes as the light faded. The glow of his cigarette in the dark.

I wanted to call Marlena but couldn't. Pride stopped me, I think. It was always me. Always me who suggested we hook up, go for a drink, catch a film. What would happen if I never suggested anything again? Our friendship would dwindle. She didn't need me like I needed her.

But still. I did need her.

I decided on a text instead.

Hey, I wrote. *I've been trying to say sorry about the other night but can't get hold of you. Thanks for coming over xx*

I would not admit that I had been in danger. I would not let her think she'd saved me. I would not tell her she had been right.

She replied within seconds. *I'm sorry too but you need to be more careful I worry about you xx*

Anger flared up inside me, so quickly it must have been there already, glowing. I sent back the simple close-out of female friendships everywhere: *X*

The phone rang. At the sight of Marlena's face on the screen, I smiled.

'So, have you recovered?' she asked.

An immediate flash of irritation. 'I'm fine. Honestly, Marlie, he really was leaving. I think you got the wrong end of the stick, that's all. He sent a note, actually, to say thanks. He's a nice guy. He just got a bit inappropriate, nothing more.'

'Pip, he had you pinned up against the wall.'

'Hardly pinned.' I laughed.

'He's an ex-con and now he's sending you notes?'

'Ex.' I fought to keep my voice level. 'Bill is my *ex*-husband. That means he's not my husband anymore. Ryan is an *ex*-con. That means—'

'All right, I get it. He's paid his debt to society. But seriously? You can't go inviting strangers into your house, please tell me you get that.'

'I invite strangers into my house all the time, Marlie. I go to their houses too. You can't run an FBI investigation into everyone

you meet, you know. It's called dating. It's what you do when you
didn't meet your husband when you were in your teens, or when
your ex-husband was a two-timing shit. I date! I have casual sex
too, all right? I have a *lot* of casual sex. I have a master's degree
in oversharing with strangers. I've found an app that's stripped
away all the bullshit and got it down to *Is this person in my radius
and do I want to shag them or not?* Do I swipe left or right? It's not
ideal, but it's useful, and I know you find it difficult to get your
head around it, but these are the qualifications you acquire when
you don't have your cosy married suburban life all figured out.'

'Don't, Pip, I—'

'No, Marlie. You have no idea what it's like for me. I want love
the same as you do. I want sex the same as you do. I'm only in my
thirties, not ready for the knacker's yard quite yet.'

There was a pause.

'I get it,' she said after a moment. 'I mean, I don't get it. But
I do get it. I can imagine it. I mean, for me, sex is just one more
thing I have to do once the bins are out and before I'm allowed
to go to sleep.'

An olive branch. We both laughed.

'And I'm sorry for what I said about Bill. About, you know…
I didn't mean it like that.'

'I know you didn't.' Hmm.

'Just promise me you'll be careful, all right? I don't want
anything bad to happen to you; I'm allowed to worry about that,
aren't I?'

'Yes,' I said. 'I suppose so. But you're not my mother.'

'No.' She hesitated. 'But I am your best friend. Whether you
like it or not.'

Another pause. Like a rest on a steep flight of stairs, a moment
to catch a breath, to wait for strength to return to your legs. Guilt
washed over me. It had been wrong of me to use my mother to
score points like that.

'I have to go,' I said. 'I'm writing.'

I rang off, faced the screen. But no words came. Ryan, Marlena. Marlena, Ryan. Why were relationships so fucking complicated? Why was the world so fucking complicated? *You're not my mother.* Where had that come from? Immediately, the image of my mother rose up as it always did whenever I thought of her, the one I had not managed to replace with a happier, more idyllic image: her sprawled on her bed, her hair greasy against her pink scalp, her arm over the side as if reaching for something. Life, possibly.

The cursor winked at the end of my last paragraph. Waited.

I picked up my iPhone. My thumb hovered over the Tinder app. There was a guy I'd had a few exchanges with… ah, there he was: Matthew. He hadn't put too many selfies up, didn't look like he was standing in a hole on the group shot, didn't use cute spellings or overload on the emojis. Didn't smile with his teeth; that was a worry. But he was nearby. And his sense of humour, on the evidence so far, wasn't completely tragic.

Bored, I wrote. *Fancy meeting up later?*

Monday night. He would, I hoped, realise I wasn't after a dinner date. I wasn't after any kind of date at all.

Ryan would surely disapprove.

Testing, two, three.

Good.

So.

*Goodbye, Ryan, she said. It was quite… endearing,
I suppose. The lack of conviction in her voice. About as
convincing as a school teacher who can't control her pupils.
Boy, would it have hit a nerve if I'd said that to her directly.
That would've pissed her right off, but she would've loved it
too, of course.*

*That one of your theories, Ryan? Read that in a book,
did you, Ryan?*

*I have to stop myself from smiling when she calls me that.
She knows my real name, of course she does, but, like her
connection to me, she's not yet ready to acknowledge it. She will
be. She will be, all right. She will 'discover' my name when
and only when she's ready. And that little eureka moment
will precede the much greater one: her final acceptance of
what binds the two of us irrevocably and for ever. But I'll
get on to that.*

*Because now I'm warming right up to my subject. Good job
too, it's fucking freezing out here. I can see my breath and I'm
not even smoking. Can't record and smoke at the same time.*
En même temps. *Must keep up my French; I'm forgetting it
already. Where was I? Oh yes, so here's the thing – why let me
into her car? Why stare at me from the school car park when
I was simply passing by, having a stroll, minding my own*

business? Why watch me? I didn't know it was her school. She never told me, never gave me the name of it, just said it was local, that she'd walk there if she didn't have to carry exercise books. My appearance there was a coincidence.

But the thing is… I'm cynical about coincidences. Seems to me that when two people are tied by that delicate thread, silken and sticky as a spider's dragline, with that incredible tensile strength, that same miraculous ductility, its invisible yet undeniable presence means that no matter where they are, no matter what they're doing or who they're with, the other is always in their thoughts, informing their actions in myriad ways so that, yes, by chance, their worlds collide in these unexpected and seemingly serendipitous moments.

Except there is no chance. There is no coincidence, no serendipity. There is only what I was getting to earlier, that which binds us irrevocably and for ever but which for the moment she is too frightened to accept. That all-consuming, single most terrifying, omnipotent thing: love.

CHAPTER ELEVEN

Pippa? Yeah, Matthew? Yeah. Hi. Hi.

The bar was an artisan microbrewery next to a perfectly good pub, but it was Matthew's choice so I went along with it. In the flesh – always a minefield with internet dating – he was taller than I thought he'd be, taller than me, crucially, which was not difficult but a relief nonetheless, and he didn't lunge at me or anything awkward like that, but nor did he look at the floor or mumble. All in all, a promising start.

Inside, the decor was *derelict recherché*, if that's a thing – furniture improvised from pallets and blocks of wood, bare bulbs on long black flexes casting a warm and expensive sepia glow over brick walls and a concrete floor, a clientele who were young, trendy and successful – or at least pretending to be. Huge effort to achieve effortlessness. Ryan would have called the whole place a lie.

But that was OK. What we were about to do was a lie. We were about to pretend that after a couple of hours we knew each other well enough to have sex, or that we felt intense animal attraction such that we didn't care how well we knew each other.

'They do craft beer here,' Matthew said with an eager smile. 'It's quite nice.'

We'd found seats: two cubes of concrete with thin cushions on top.

'I'll have a pint of whatever you think.' I smiled back, relieved that Matthew's teeth were normal, that he didn't lisp, that he wasn't wearing sports trainers – God, I hate that. His quiff was blonder than in the photographs, his beard thicker, in line with the fashion for masculine authenticity, pipes, unicycles and what-have-you. All in all, he wasn't bad. Attractive, even.

I wondered what was wrong with him, caught the thought, directed it back to myself: what was wrong with *me*? Gave myself a stern warning: do *not* share this shit.

A moment later he returned holding two glasses of beer.

'They don't do pints,' he said, setting them down. 'These are schooners, apparently. It's two thirds of a pint. And they don't do lager either, as such. This is a blonde ale. If you don't like it, I can change it, no problem.'

I was glad of his ability to make an executive decision, and of his good-humoured sardonic response to the pretentious non-metric measures. I took a sip of my schooner. Probably cost a tenner a pop… or should that be a guinea?

'Tastes strong,' I said.

'The guy described it as crisp, hoppy and citrusy. It's called Don Pedro.'

'Is that ironic?'

'No idea. But it is strong, though, you're right. Nearly seven per cent.'

Good, I thought. It would do the trick.

'Delicious.' I downed half. Or was that a third – who knew? Who cared?

He sat down on the block-with-cushion opposite, drank deeply as I had.

'So,' he said, putting down his glass and rubbing his hands together. 'Come here often?'

I smiled in polite acknowledgement of his wry use of the age-old chat-up line. 'Actually, no. Never been here before in my life.'

He looked around him, mouth a non-committal flat line, as if looking for someone he might know. I wondered whether he'd brought others here, whether he'd taken a mental inventory of my appearance as I had his, perhaps found it wanting with regard to my rather favourable profile pic.

'I've been here once or twice,' he said. 'I came here the other week before a gig.'

Ah. We were going to talk music tastes, how nice. Clearly confident about his own, he was too experienced, too serial a dater, to ask the direct question. Over time, he'd come up with a way of making it no more than chit-chat between two people who knew each other much, much better than we did.

'Oh yeah?' I obliged. 'What did you go and see?'

'The Allergies.'

I had never heard of them, which was I suppose the idea. In the world of the metropolitan sophisticate, when searching for something to impress chicks like me, chicks who wore their hair asymmetrical, their fringe short, their lippy matt, a borderline geeky interest in indie music took the place of a nice car with an engine suspiciously high on horsepower.

'Any good?' I said.

'Really good actually. What kind of bands are you into?'

Tempted as I was to list One Direction and Little Mix among my favourites – a joke with and for myself only – I decided to behave, mention in passing groups I had heard on Radio 6 Music without getting too esoteric: The xx, Foster the People, nothing to frighten the horses. These conversations, I had found, could spiral into competition so easily and, wanting to flatter his male ego perhaps, it seemed politic to concede expert status to him.

And so we talked music, since *shall we go somewhere and get our rocks off* was, even I could see, a little too direct so soon in the proceedings.

'I listen to a lot of vintage stuff,' I said, by way of conversational development. 'Led Zeppelin, Bowie, Patti Smith.' I didn't really, I just mentioned the ones he would want to hear – a hunch based on his predilection for bands named after unfortunate averse physical reactions. I wasn't going to get him into bed with Ed Sheeran or Adele now, was I? And at least he hadn't asked what my star sign was.

Is that unfair? It is, isn't it? Matthew was perfectly fine, more than fine, and all I wanted was sex, don't forget, not a life partner. He was a website designer. Lived near me but not so near as to mean embarrassing encounters in Tesco in the coming days. We talked about Tinder.

'I'm not looking for a relationship,' he said.

No shit, I did not reply, telling him instead, 'No, that's fine. I prefer no strings just at the moment.'

We left that there.

'Actually, I have kind of a friend with benefits at work,' he said after a moment as the bar door opened, letting in a cigarette-smoke-tinged blast of cold air. 'It's just a weekend thing, but recently she's intimated that she wants more, so I'm trying to cool it all down.'

I thought of Sarah at work.

'Yes,' I said, avoiding gender specifics – see earlier frightening-horses note. 'I have a similar set-up.'

We laughed then about some disastrous encounters we'd had. He told me that one woman had burst into tears an hour into their first meeting and said she was still hurting over an ex.

'Nightmare,' I offered, thinking that this might have been me a year earlier, those early forays into the wilds of the dating jungle when I was still raw with the pain of rejection and betrayal. I had not cried on a date, but Lord, I had been near.

I was tempted to tell him about a guy I'd brought home whose bedroom performance seemed to involve working his way through the entire Kama Sutra as though it was a Haynes manual, a set of techniques that gave the act a kind of clinical, detached quality, like floor gymnastics or dressage or, of course, fixing a car. But I didn't. I felt we were not quite at that point yet, and hey, I didn't want him ending up with performance anxiety – that would be cutting my nose off, would it not?

Instead, I bought another round: two more two thirds of a pint, sheesh. The barman had a whole ale-pouring-as-art thing going on. He wore a butcher's pinny (*sans* blood; let us thank God for small mercies) and a tiny paisley bow tie. I stared at the bow tie, transfixed, thinking about the no-strings evening ahead. We would have to cut ourselves loose, Matthew and I. And alcohol was the sharpest knife available.

I signalled to the barman. 'Can I also get two shots of…' I could hardly ask for Bacardi, could I? 'Erm… bourbon?'

'Sure.'

A couple of the men I had dated had offered me weed, a few MDMA, and one cocaine. The MDMA had given me at least an approximation of euphoria, something akin to affection, or love, or lust; cocaine had made me feel stressed, and the blow had sent me to sleep. The bourbon, the barman was explaining, was not brewed on the premises but by a wonderful Dutch couple… I nodded, tuned out. The little-known-ness made it better, clearly. Were we all of us looking for an unknown brand, I wondered, an unknown bourbon, a hidden tattoo, a secret past, a harmful habit – something that might give our safe little lives some authenticity, a point of interest, some sort of key to stop us slipping into the mind-melting waters of the everyday – becoming just another brick in the wall?

I set the tray of drinks down before Matthew, who was staring at his phone. He put it back in his pocket and raised his eyebrows at the shot glasses.

'Chasers,' I said.

'Nice.' He lifted one, knocked it back.

Good boy, I thought. Get it down you.

By eleven, we were suitably pissed – pissed enough. He didn't hesitate when it came to his round, and, showing perfect etiquette, returned with more bourbon chasers. The possibility of throwing a sickie the next day loomed – all part of the fabric of the invincibility cloak that five or six units wraps around you.

'Should we get an Uber back to yours?' I said.

He threw out his hands. 'Listen, any chance we can go to yours? It's just, my flatmate is in and he's… well, he's… and the flat's a real mess.'

Perhaps Matthew was married. It was possible; it's always possible. But that was not my concern nor my responsibility. Still, I preferred to go back to their place. I liked to have control over when I got the hell out: normally in the wee small hours, before we had to enter into the excruciating business of waking up and pretending we were pleased to see each other – or that we knew each other at all.

Still, beggars…

'You'll have to be out early,' I said. 'I leave for work at eight.'

'Deal.'

He pounced while we were still in the cab. His mouth wasn't too wet, thankfully, only one teeth clash, tongue not testing any gag reflexes, and he kept his hands at my waist with a coyness that was almost touching. I kissed him back, to be polite, but was not drunk enough to be unselfconscious in front of the third party at the wheel. I backed away, took his hand and gave it a squeeze: *wait*. He seemed to understand, choosing to put his hand on my thigh but without sliding it upwards. I thought of Ryan, of how he had informed me in that almost well-spoken and invulnerable way of his that he and I were a couple now and always. That made this a spot of light adultery then. The idea gave me a small thrill.

In the hallway, Matthew kissed me again before the front door had closed. I wondered if he'd seen this in a film and noted to himself that women love urgency. Perhaps he was seeking to make me feel irresistible. His whiskers tickled my nose and his tongue reached into my mouth too quickly and too far. I didn't protest – hard to protest when your mouth is full, after all, and sometimes you just had to let them get on with it. I wasn't there to give lessons.

'Let's go upstairs,' I said, taking his hand. I was worried that his penchant for screen passion might convince him that doing it on the kitchen worktop might be a good idea, and frankly, I wasn't sure the Corian would stand it.

A bed would suffice. A bed had covers to hide under and was perfectly adequate for what would no doubt be a standard session of what we are encouraged to call lovemaking.

Ryan appeared again in my mind's eye.

Lovemaking? he jeered. *Really, Pippa?*

'Shut up,' I said.

'What?' Matthew was looking at me. We were at the top of the stairs.

'Nothing,' I said. 'Sorry. Come on.' I led him into the bedroom.

He kissed me again. Another teeth clash, whoops. I would have to encourage him towards other parts of my body, I thought, unsure how much longer I could stand his clumsiness. We were still standing up. I couldn't figure out how to get him to slow down, to stop kissing me, to sit on the side of the bed. I unbuttoned his shirt and pulled it over his head. He gripped my waist and tried to kiss me again. He missed, his lips landed on my eye. He kissed the other eye then, as if this was what he had meant to do all along. He held my face in both his hands – face-cup alert – and kissed my nose, my cheeks, my chin and, finally, my mouth.

It was, if nothing else, sweet.

We took off one another's outer clothes with as much expertise and spontaneity as we could manage. I was glad I'd had a shower and changed into matching underwear, not to mention run a razor over the important parts. I reached for the duvet and threw it back, climbed into bed and pulled the cover over me. Once hidden, I unfastened my bra. Too many clasp fumbles over the years had taught me that it was easier that way. I wriggled out of my pants and saw he was doing the same. He was covered in fine blonde hairs and freckles and his skin was soft. He had the beginnings of a beer belly but his shoulders and thighs were muscular. Five-a-side football at weekends, I thought. Or a gym membership, though not an exercise addict. Liked a beer. Did he sign up for wine-tasting courses, I wondered, or aspire to one day be a member of a private club? Had he shown enough irony about the microbrewery, and if not, would that one day translate into a life spent ticking boxes, using the word *entertain* to describe having people who weren't really friends over for formal dinner parties?

What did I care? This wasn't marriage.

He kissed my neck softly, over and over, and yes, that was nice. He worked his way down to my breasts, as bedroom etiquette demanded – it didn't do to rush to the main event. I tried to run my hands through his sticky hair, gave up, tickled his neck instead while making the appropriate noises. He kissed my belly and then, perhaps not brave enough to go lower, returned to my lips. We kissed. I fought the urge to ask him why – why kiss at all? I was not his girlfriend, after all. What did he think this was?

'Do you have protection?' he said, coming up for air.

'Sure, yeah. Hold on.' I reached into the bedside cabinet. 'Here.'

Moments later, we were in motion. It didn't last too long and it wasn't too short either. It was... adequate and, after what had preceded it, less intimate. I was grateful he'd used the hole intended for the purpose, so to speak, and not attempted anything more ambitious. For anyone long out of the dating game, I can tell you that pornography has a lot to answer for. He came, I didn't, but that was usual, and I didn't know him well enough to ask him for anything more.

But it was human contact. It was warmth. It was the time-worn comfort of flesh on flesh, hearts beating if not as one then at least as two in close proximity. And in those few moments – before our bodies broke their warm embrace, before comforting became cloying, before afterglow became sweat – I closed my eyes and yes, I felt, if only by the most infinitesimal of margins, a little less alone.

We lay back on the pillows. I gave a sigh, as if out of breath, which I was not.

'That was great,' he said.

'Yes. Lovely.'

Lies, I thought. All lies.

Two a.m. My mouth had dried to a husk. I fetched a glass of water from the bathroom and stood in the bedroom doorway, surveying Sleeping Beauty. Light from the street lamp outside my window bathed his open mouth, his hair pushed tall into a stale, waxy cockscomb.

A stranger.

I unhooked my dressing gown from the back of the door and put it on, then crept over to the bed.

'Are you awake?' I said. 'Matthew?'

He didn't stir. I reached out a tentative hand and shook him. 'Hello?'

He opened one eye and grunted, turned on to his back and gave a sleepy smile. He held out his arms, apparently up for round two.

'Ah,' I said. 'I... actually I need you to go.'

He blinked both eyes open and frowned, as well he might. He checked his watch, which was still on his wrist. 'But it's two in the morning.'

'I know. And I'm sorry. I just... I just can't sleep with someone else in the bed and I've got to teach tomorrow and... I'm sorry, I just need you to leave.' I turned away and left the bedroom. 'I'll book you an Uber,' I called from the landing. 'My treat.'

I padded downstairs, pulling my dressing gown tight around me. My phone was in the kitchen, I was pretty sure. I'd left it there to charge.

It was. I picked it up and saw immediately the green text box on the screen, number unknown.

Get rid of him, it said. *He is beneath you.*

Blog post: PippaGatesAuthor
#thiswritinglife
Find me on:
Instagram: @GatesPip
Twitter: @PipGatesWrites
Facebook: Pippa Gates Author

When I first moved out here, I didn't have a blog, and it seems a shame not to have those first days on record: the first forays into country life, the panic upon realising that, no, I couldn't pop to the corner shop at 8 p.m., that whatever it was I didn't have, I would have to do without. Do without! The very idea! And of course, during those wobbly early days and weeks there was no Mrs Danvers yet.

Thank goodness for Wilson's Stores, and for Bobby, who was kind enough to sell me some coffee even though he was closing.

I don't go to Wilson's anymore, not after Bobby's disappearance, but I do still like a nice coffee. Mrs D always brings a *café au lait* to my desk at 10.45 a.m. sharp, and I know that for the rest of my time on this earth my every need will be met with a devotion I could never have dreamed of.

I am blessed!

But it's hi ho, hi ho from me. Off to work I go. *Pushing Up Daisy* (working title only, folks) will not write itself! So away I go to spend a few hours at the Grange Retirement Home in Weston-super-Mare with Daisy and Bing… Will they put aside their old grudges in time to rekindle the young love they once had?

Well now, that would be telling.

CHAPTER TWELVE

The number was unknown, sure, but I knew who'd sent the text, obviously. Ryan must have taken my number the night he was here. He must have sneaked a look at my contacts when I was making tea or when I'd gone to the loo or something.

Casting my mind back, I remembered how he'd hung up his coat in the cupboard under the stairs without me seeing him do it. How he'd stepped into my hallway and closed the door behind him mere seconds after meeting me, when all I'd done was pop into the living room for a copy of my book. But Ryan had a Cheshire Cat quality to him. One minute he was there, the next not, then there he was again, grinning, paws folded under his chin.

Once Matthew's cab was out of sight, I returned to the kitchen, all fired up to send Ryan a message he wouldn't forget in a hurry. He'd said he would never return to prison, appeared to have a deep, visceral horror of the mere thought. One call to the police and he would be back inside before you could say harassment. Yes, I would threaten him with the police, and then I would delete the messages and block his number.

But there was already another message on the screen.

Well done. You saw sense. You are one step further towards enlightenment.

I swivelled around, my eyes darting across the kitchen, the hall. I ran to the front door and checked it. It was locked. I ran back into the kitchen and opened the cutlery drawer where I kept my spare set of keys. They were still there.

But had I put them in the compartment with the nutcracker and the bottle opener?

I could have sworn I kept them with the miscellaneous bits and pieces: the nail varnish, the chewed pencils and the emergency lighter. I should get an alarm, I thought. A fake one, even, just some tin box to stick up on the outside wall.

On instinct, I grabbed the carving knife and ran to the French windows. The handle gave under my grip. Christ, they were open – they'd been open all evening while I'd been out. Had they? I bit my thumb, tore off a thick white strip of nail. *Think, Pippa.*

I had come home from school. I had gone to my desk but had not been able to settle. I had locked the French windows and put the key in the… oh, but no, I had then returned and unlocked the door to smoke the scabby dog-end of shame. Clearly I had been antsy after seeing Ryan, after the strained conversation with Marlie. My response then had been to seek some company, that much was clear to me now. It was possible I'd been searching for safety in a number greater than one.

I stared at the phone, the incandescent film I now associated with Ryan spread under my skin like toxic oil. An allergic reaction. To him, to the very thought of him. I saved his number under RM so that, should he dare text me again, I would know immediately that it was him. If he should ring, I would know better than to answer it.

I have no need of enlightenment, thank you, I wrote.

I pressed send. My breath caught, my lungs emptied. Breathing out the panic, I ran a glass of water and drank it down. Nothing was clear, nothing was solid, nothing was certain. I breathed in, held it, breathed out, told myself to identify three things I knew, any three. One: the water was cold. Two, wherever he was right now, Ryan Marks could see the house. Three, he would text back within—

The phone bleeped.

You need time. Falling off the wagon is to be expected. You will see the light, don't despair. It is in the work itself that you'll find inspiration, Pip, nowhere else. But for now, as you wish, I will step back. I am receding as we speak. Goodnight, my love. Sweet dreams.

I growled at the phone, switched it off and, possessed by a burst of energy, ran out into the back garden.

On the lawn, I turned a slow circle, surveyed the houses to the back, to each side, all in darkness. Beyond the back gardens, in one of the houses in the next street, a dim pink light glowed. I squinted, tried to see if I could make out a figure looking out. A shadow, tall but utterly still. A cabinet or something, not a human being. Even the foxes were quiet tonight. There is something about being awake in a residential street when everyone else is asleep. By day, you feel yourself surrounded, crowded out, wedged in by other people, by their noises and their smells, their trash and their building work, their professional routines, their lawn-mowing, their arguments and laughter and semi-private rituals, and yet, in those dark suburban silences in the dead of night, when you stand in the garden in your dressing gown, the empty ache of another human being still inside you, all you really feel is the howling, crushing solitude of it all: this life, how lonely, how fucking lonely you really are.

'Ryan?' I called into that dark suburban night. 'Ryan, are you there?'

AUDIO EXCERPT #5

Two. Two.

It's... let's see... a little after 4 a.m. and I'm having a smoke in the hostel car park before I hit the hay. Nothing too heavy, just a few crumbled leaves of some well mellow stuff my mate got me from a guy in Feltham. It's been noisy in the hostel tonight for some reason, so I got out and went for a wander. I like to walk. I walk whenever I can, everywhere. Not your country strolls or your riverside rambles, no, I like the pavement. I like the loose embrace of buildings, the discreet containment. After so long inside, I guess I get the jitters if a space is too open. I keep away from the main road when I can.

Once I'd crossed the bridge, I went the back way, up by the college, by the railway track. I can walk for hours. There's a fascination for me in putting one foot in front of the other and just continuing that process, knowing that I don't have to turn ninety degrees every hundred metres or whatever. My first prison was a former castle. In the yard, there was one patch of sunlight, no more than about two metres square. The lads used to huddle together in this one yellow square on the tarmac. It was the only bit of warmth in the whole place. There'd be fifty of us, trying to escape the cold hand of the shade, following that light as it made its way around. You could set your watch by it – the yard was one big sundial, a tarmac testament to time passing, day by long day.

I did my days. I did my time. Now, I walk, sometimes by night. By day, I walk some more, catch up on the sunlight I missed.

It's four in the morning. She had some bloke back to her place, crazy lost girl. As if that's going to fill the empty space where love should be. Where I should be. I am the only one who can fill that void. I am the only one who can shine light into that yard. She knows it. I know she knows it. She tells me to leave her alone, that she'll call the police. Fair enough. I respect that. I don't think she will, but I can't take that chance. Another thing I've learnt, along with all the rest, is how to wait. I can wait like I can walk – forever if that's what it takes. She'll come to her senses. For now, there's no use risking the police. I have to play this thing right. If I engage too closely with the target, so to speak, I'll blow the whole operation. I have to keep my tread light. Just enough, not too much, so that even if she wants to call the police, she'll have nothing of any consequence to show them. I have the book she signed as proof that this is reciprocal. And the one she's writing. It's all about me.

All her thoughts are on me.

Me.

CHAPTER THIRTEEN

Ryan did not contact me, at least not for a while.

Still, I checked my horizons every time I left the house, every time I finished school, went anywhere at all. After the moment of doubt with my spare keys, I feared, irrationally, that he'd steal my car, ransack my house. Marlena's keys were on that fob too. He could have stolen them while I was at work, made copies, returned them, easy as pie for a man like him. Each time I got into the car, I checked the back seat. What was I expecting? Him, sitting there with a gun? Nothing so defined as that. An item of his clothing, perhaps, a scuff on the upholstery.

Once, I found dried mud on the floor, in the footwell of the passenger seat. I let out a cry, my breath ragged within seconds. I kicked at it, then took out the foot mat altogether and beat and shook it like a lunatic. That was so him. A sign, too subtle to report without appearing insane, but a sign all the same, of him, of him having been inside my private space and left a trace, on purpose, to spook me. I talked to myself, there in the car, on my own. It was probably from the time I'd given him a lift. I had not checked the footwell until that moment. There had perhaps always been something there, like a bag of groceries or my handbag or… or a stack of books. The mud might have come from Sarah's shoes. I always drove her to my place on a Friday. She may have had reason to cross the school field at break or something. Whatever.

Once home, every day, I toured the house, opened wardrobes, looked under beds. There was nothing, and as those first weeks turned into months, as the memory of him in my house, in my car, the evidence or not of him in my private life began to fade, I began to believe that he had done what I'd asked and moved on. What a relief, I told myself, as I stared out of the front window of my house, looking for him. What a relief, I said, as I stood in the garden late at night, listening for him, as I sniffed the damp air and wondered if I could smell his tobacco. What a relief.

Perhaps chastened – literally – by the thought of Ryan keeping a secret vigil, I returned to my writing with the diligence of a… well, of a nun, to be frank. I stuck to my after-school routine: a light supper, two hours' work every evening. I went on two further dates but did not return home with either of them, nor did I invite them into my home. I was not convinced that Ryan wouldn't somehow know, but that was not what stopped me; what stopped me was that I simply could not be bothered to see them through. They seemed… bland, beige, the conversations all the same, the ritual as predictable as tea and biscuits.

And so, a hermit during the week, on Fridays I went out, sometimes with my colleagues, sometimes with Sarah, who, after a brief spell of clinginess, was happy to leave in the dead of night without making a big thing of it. If that surprises you, all I will say is that the trick with these arrangements is to find someone as lonely as yourself. Sarah, lovely as she was, excreted loneliness from every pore, and to paraphrase Alan Bennett, *If you're in the desert dying of thirst, you don't stop to think about whether you prefer Evian or Perrier.* We take what we can get. We drink what is offered. We find company, or peace, or some sweet human warmth, where we can. And for the moment, men were too fucking complicated.

But back to me as paragon. I was enjoying that.

In those months, I bought wholesome food and managed most of the time to eat it. Kettle Chips and Pringles, I conceded, could not be eaten in moderation. One opened them with that idea in mind but inevitably wolfed the entire packet within an indecent matter of minutes and waited for the self-loathing to kick in. There was no other way. And so I stopped buying them. And although cooking was never my forte nor my interest – it was always Bill's thing – I bought a cookery book, an actual hardback, with a smiling peach-skinned woman on the front. I became mistress of the chicken-breast-with-something-inside-it school of cuisine, taking said breasts and filling them – euphorically, as suggested by the photograph – with pesto and Parma ham, taking this recipe as my point of departure and going off piste with a devil-may-care attitude, straying into outlandish culinary woodland such as... oh, such as chicken breast with chorizo; chicken breast with thinly sliced mushrooms; chicken breast with... well, I'll leave space for you here: add what you want, knock yourself out. These gourmet offerings I consumed with a bag of salad (so simple, so quick!) and a baked potato (so fat-free, so healthy!). And, I have to tell you, I threw on that Malden salt with a flourish worthy of Jamie fricking Oliver.

Reader, I even drank water.

I drank wine obviously, don't panic. But I also drank water.

My complexion improved. I have no idea if I lost or gained weight, since I had given the scales to my ex-husband, informing him with malice that he should maybe start using them. It seemed, however, that my skirt buttoned easier, that my trousers didn't bunch up quite so readily in my... well, you know where I mean.

My mood stabilised. My energy levels improved. My manuscript grew.

I reached thirty thousand words. Forty. Fifty. Whilst I had changed many details about his life – locations, ages, hair colours – Ryan was always my reference point. The name Gary Hughes was my gift to him, a more meaningful form of thanks than mere money for his story. You'll think that's mad, to think of the man who had abused my trust after I'd invited him into my home, but that's the way it was. It helped to keep the main character rooted in reality. After all, that's why I had asked him in, wasn't it? To steal his life, to create something authentic. Sometimes, writing, I felt him so close by that I would look up from my desk and expect to see him there on the sofa, his lean legs crossed, his long, knotted fingers cradled on his thin lap. I wondered if he was still selling door to door, or if he had found a job somewhere by now. Sometimes I would catch a whiff of patchouli and whatever oil, or grease, he had in his hair. In such moments, I would fetch the air freshener and spray it all over the house. I would look out of the front window to see if he was there on the street, or stand on the back lawn and call his name. To silence.

My internet dating dwindled to nothing.

Sarah came over less and less, and then... not.

'You're only interested in me on Fridays,' she said that last time, removing my hand from her cheek, putting her empty wine glass on my coffee table. 'The rest of the week, it's like I don't exist.'

'I'm sorry you feel that way,' I said, in the way of sorry-not-sorry merchants the world over. But inside, I was thinking: *Shut up and come upstairs, will you? Why can't we ditch the bullshit and be lonely-not-lonely just for an hour?*

I did not check Guardian Soulmates, did not contact anyone on Tinder, did not even raise a flirtatious eyebrow when a new, young and extremely attractive male maths teacher replaced Sarah, who was so upset with me that she got a job in a boys' school in Twickenham. I did not contact Marlena and she did not contact me.

This was what it meant to be successful and focused, I realised: no love life, no social life, no children, no friends.

No distractions.

No strings and no one to pull them.

No chaos.

*

By the end of the winter term, I had finished the first draft and decided to leave it in a drawer for the two weeks of the festive period so that I could better see any mistakes and areas for development once I returned to it in the new year. I used the holiday to get ahead with my teaching prep, with the intention of dedicating as much spare time as I could to editing and redrafting *Framed by Love* once the spring term began.

Every morning, I checked the post for letters from Ryan. He was always my first thought when I switched on my phone in the morning. This, I reasoned, was because I was writing his life. But nothing came – no cards, no texts, no Facebook friend requests. I was tempted to text him and see if he was all right. Indeed, I did write those texts, but that way lay danger, I was certain. Whatever mental-health issues he had, they were not my responsibility.

On the first day of the holidays, Marlena invited me for Christmas dinner, as she had done every year (if you discount the years I spent with Bill; God knows I do) since I first told her about my mother and father. You know by now that my mother took her own life when I was a child, and I may have mentioned that my father moved to Thailand when I was eighteen, and though I have never said this to Marlie, I will say it here with utter frankness: I would have preferred it if he'd died. His death I could have spoken about. His death I could have mourned. His abandonment of me when I had barely stepped into adulthood I could not, could never admit to, much less forgive.

I would like to say I spent the holidays reading literary essays and serious novels, but the reality is that I spent most of my time watching three television programmes at once whilst looking at but not commenting on other people's perfect lives on Facebook and Instagram. Old habits threatened. Crisps made a comeback. Wine was back in fashion. The Tinder app had been opened but remained, as yet, unswiped.

On Christmas Day, after a morning spent eating dry-roasted peanuts, drinking Prosecco and orange juice, and unwrapping my one present – actually, this took approximately thirty seconds; the gift in question was a pair of leopard-print beetle crushers that I'd ordered for myself and wrapped in some *Ho Bloody Ho* paper that I'd found hilarious the year before but which hadn't even raised a smile when I pulled it from the cupboard under the stairs – I presented myself at Marlena's house at 2 p.m.

As well as gift vouchers for the kids, I took a bottle of pink Moët & Chandon, which had been on offer in Tesco – a snip at thirty quid – a potted hyacinth and a box of Thornton's chocolates. I rang the doorbell and stood on the doorstep fighting a sudden and unexpected attack of what felt like exam nerves. It was cold out, admittedly, but that wasn't the reason my teeth were chattering. It wasn't that we hadn't made up after our horrible argument; we had. But where usually I would have seen her for a few drunken catch-ups over the last couple of months, I hadn't seen her at all. Neither one of us had suggested meeting up, not even for a coffee at the weekend. Which is to say, I hadn't suggested it. And because *I* hadn't suggested it, it had not happened.

Marlena opened the door. Beneath a duck-egg-blue linen apron, a midnight-blue dress floated its sleeves down to her elbows, and her dirty-blonde hair was piled on top of her head in a lazy, half-tumbling chignon. She had made up her big brown eyes with dark eyeshadow and applied a warm, plum-coloured lipstick, and her skin was flushed with the heat of the kitchen. At the sight of her, I could not help but catch my breath.

'Pippa!' Her eyes filled up, and I felt mine go the same way. Before I could say anything, she had reached forward and was pulling me into her arms. After so long on my own, I could not deny how good it was to be held, and having been teetering on the verge of tears, I plummeted over the side, falling prey to the most self-pitying thought imaginable: Marlena was, perhaps, the only person on this earth who loved me. And, no perhaps about it, she was the only person on this earth that I truly loved.

How easily I had forgotten.

'It's good to see you,' she said into my shoulder.

'You too,' I just about managed into her neck.

Wiping away the tears, I followed her inside to the open-plan kitchen/living space where Steve and Zoe and Zane were playing on some interactive computer game or other. Marlena's parents were sitting on the sofa, watching in amusement and drinking the old person's aperitif: tea. Much whooping and laughter. The smell of turkey roasting under bacon rashers. My mouth watered, following where my eyes had led.

'Pippa's here,' Marlie announced. 'She's brought you two prezzies, you lucky pair.'

Steve and the kids called hello but didn't really take too much notice. No need to thank me for the vouchers, I didn't say, and wondered then how happy Steve was about me being included in their Christmas dinner now that the kids were older and age-appropriate company for him. Marlena's invitation had come later than usual. Perhaps she had left it in the hope that I would have found something or someone else. Someone who would fly away with me to a hot country and drink cocktails by the pool until all the mince pies and carols and bonhomie stuff was over.

'Can I do anything to help?' I asked. She had her back to me, whisking something in a pan.

'There's some Prosecco in the fridge door. Just getting these lumps out of the gravy. You know where the glasses are, babe. Excuse me.' She put her hands to her mouth, loudhailer style. 'Steve! Ste-eve! What are you drinking?'

He looked over, momentarily distracted from whatever aliens they were fighting, virtual racetrack they were driving, whatever.

'If you're having fizz I'll have some of that,' he hollered, apparently seeing no need to leave his game and fix the drinks himself.

'Your mum and dad?' I asked.

She shook her head. 'God, no. They might have a sweet sherry in a bit, crazy bastards.'

I smiled, poured the Prosecco, then went over to hand Steve's glass to him.

'Cheers,' he said, without taking his eyes from the screen.

I put his drink on the coffee table, glancing at the alien space war, to which he was so glued, raging on the screen. Small things, I thought, leaving him to it.

Back in the kitchen, Marlie was lifting the gargantuan turkey out of the oven. She basted it, returned it and blew at her damp fringe. The table was already set, I noticed, and wondered if she'd done this too.

'So, how's you?' she asked, clinking her glass against mine.

'Good, yeah. I've finished my first draft.'

Her face opened in surprise. 'That's amazing! That's quick, isn't it?'

'It is. Merry Christmas.'

We drank, both of us downing half a glass.

'Thanks for bringing posh champagne, by the way,' she said. 'We'll open that with dinner.'

'No, save it,' I said. 'For you and Steve sometime.' Or for us, I thought but didn't say.

'Actually, Steve's got a lovely Malbec...'

And so we continued in that vein – small and easy talk, nothing difficult or showy, an expedient intimacy not faked but decided upon for safety's sake. When the meal was ready, I helped take in the loaded serving dishes and called everyone to the table. The glazed caramel hump of the turkey took pride of place in the centre, in front of Steve's usual chair. In a moment, he would carve and we would all tell him what a great job he'd done. Marlena's thanks would be added as an afterthought, no doubt, the second clause in a two-clause toast: *Merry Christmas, everyone. Here's to the chef.*

Her mum and dad made their careful way to the table; Steve chased the kids, who squealed and ran to their chairs.

'Hey, did you ever see that ex-con again?' Marlie asked as we made to sit down. 'Is that the story you used in the end?'

'I saw him once. Gave him a lift home one day. Not seen him since. Yes. It's his story.'

'Won't he have copyright on it or something?'

'Nah. I've changed a lot. He has no claim on it.'

'Am I in it?'

'Yeah,' I said. 'You're the murder victim.'

We laughed and I felt us drop another millimetre towards how we had been before our fight. Several glasses ahead of her as I was, I began to relax.

'You're doing a great job with that turkey, Steve.' Marlie's mum was looking at him as if he were not a forty-something bloke with a paunch but an actual, living god.

He placed a thick slab of breast on her plate. 'Trick is to use a sharp knife.'

I stood and held up my glass. 'Here's to the chef,' I said. 'Marlie's been slaving away for hours in that kitchen.'

I looked round for Marlie, but she'd disappeared. She returned then, holding the salt grinder in one hand and a red envelope in the other.

'Someone knows you're here,' she said, handing me the envelope. 'Found this on the doormat.'

Blog post: PippaGatesAuthor
#thiswritinglife
Find me on:
Instagram: @GatesPip
Twitter: @PipGatesWrites
Facebook: Pippa Gates Author

Alas, the snow has melted, returning green to the fields after week of white, grey to the gravel chippings outside my office window. The snow inevitably put me in mind of Bobby Wilson, and now that it's gone, I cannot help but make the connection with him too being gone. In the local paper, there are still appeals for information, even though it's been weeks. There's no sign of his motorbike, no trace of his phone. No one saw him on the day he disappeared. I wonder when they'll stop looking. He was a restless soul, a traveller and a dreamer. Everyone who knew him said that. Even I, who only spoke to him properly the day he cleared the snow from my drive, can remember so clearly how he talked and talked of his wanderlust. His fiancée, Tessa, wasn't happy about it, apparently. They say she wanted to get married. Poor Tessa.

Lost romance, thwarted love, a man gone missing, leaving his fiancée to wonder, always wonder what became of him. That fiancée was Daisy, waiting for Bing at the church, dressed in white, her arm linked through her father's, her expectant smile fading by the minute, all confidence, all hope draining away

On my desk, there is a perfect porcelain figurine of a couple ballroom dancing. For me they are Daisy and Bing, and I often look at this statuette when inspiration falters. They are as one, lost in the harmony of music only they can hear. They are shiny, their glazes pastel cream, baby blue, baby pink. A trace of gold outline on the hem of the woman's skirt is evidence of years passing, rubbing away what once was. They were in the window of a charity shop in Bath, the result of someone's house clearance, no doubt. No one wants ornaments like this anymore.

I imagine that house, that life. It could have been Bing and Daisy's home, why not? They might have lived there had Bing not jilted her at the altar. In that other life, he turned up at the church, best suit, carnation in his lapel, Sunday shoes on his feet, and they married. They bought a flat, then moved to that house when Daisy was pregnant with their first child. The child was born there, a boy. Bing bought her this statuette as a gift, to remind her that she would always be his darling, his dancing girl. They had two more children, two girls. These children became adults, had children of their own, eventually grandchildren. Bing and Daisy returned to dancing in their retirement. They won medals, trophies. Dancing kept them fit. They lived to see their first two great-grandchildren born. But then Bing passed away peacefully in his sleep, and soon afterwards Daisy died from a bout of pneumonia; or perhaps, to be fanciful, a broken heart.

And now the house is sold, and once the children have taken what they want for remembrance, the rest – furniture, glassware, knick-knacks – is scooped up by a clearance company. The porcelain dancers – Bing and Daisy – end up in the charity shop. They are dancing a foxtrot in the window when Mrs D walks past and sees them and thinks of me and how this gift will make me smile and spur me on to write.

I have a responsibility to them now, these dancing lovers. That's the way it works. You can't just create people and leave them to fend for themselves. You make a contract with them the moment you commit them to the page. You have to nurture them. You have to believe in them and let them live out their story. Bing and Daisy might have lived a happy, fruitful life and, here in my journal, just now, they did. Call it my gift to them, my apology.

Because that is not what I have written for them in *Pushing Up Daisy*. Bing did not turn up at the church. He was afraid. Scarred by his experiences in the trenches and believing himself not worthy of someone as wonderful as Daisy, he walked instead along the sands at Weston-super-Mare. He continued on, up the coast, finding work where he could, reaching Gloucester, Wales… becoming a drifter. Many years later, he met another woman and married her instead. They settled in South Wales, had children, two boys. He never loved his wife, but he was kind to her and she to him. Any feelings of regret in the dead of night were his punishment for letting Daisy down all those years before. As for Daisy? She too married, but her story went less well. There were no children, and after her husband's death, she found shocking pictures of muscle-bound men in a shoebox beneath a loose floorboard in the bedroom. Her husband left her well provided for, but no amount of financial security could mend her broken heart.

And then, and then…

And then years, so many years, later, there she is in the retirement home and who should walk into the residents' lounge but the man who stood her up all those years ago. Bing. Her love, her darling. They are both in their early eighties. They are old, so old. They have lost so much, they have lost the life they could have had but for Bing's terrible and haunting memories of war, his inability to talk about them to anyone. Their tragedy is like so many – the failure of communication, the fear of voicing aloud that which scares us most, of never finding someone who understands. Nothing more. If only he had told her how he felt. If only she had known. Only communication and forgiveness stand between loneliness and a last chance at love.

Porcelain figures, dancing on my desk. Idly I pick them up, twist them this way and that, watch the glaze flash in the dull light. I set them back down and consider them for a long while. They are together, their choreographed poses locked for all time. To separate them I would have to smash this figurine on the concrete floor of my study. Poor Bing and Daisy. They missed out on the life they should have had, but now, in their eighties, it is my job to make that right. I, the writer, will bring them together, and just when all hope appears lost, I will let them dance again.

CHAPTER FOURTEEN

No matter what you've read about me in any news stories accompanying the publication of this journal, you must know, I *want* you to know, that I'm not heartless. That's not me at all, whatever the journalists or the police or the forensic scientists say. Cynicism and flippancy and sarcasm… they're all defence mechanisms, and not particularly evolved ones, in my humble opinion. Not to mention hopelessly transparent. Lies. Oh, how exhausting are the infinite layers of lies. It's like trying to have a sauna with all your clothes on. Easier to strip off, no matter how embarrassing, let it all hang out. When I get back on social media, I will post updates about my work in progress. I will avoid superciliousness in all its forms. I understand now that the public domain is not really for private matters. Any misery I might be suffering is mine to suffer alone. I understand that my posts should meet specific criteria: is it funny? Is it beautiful? Is it interesting? No one wants to know about the rest. No one wants real life.

I understand that, thanks to Mrs Danvers.

The other thing about the internet is its transience. As my father used to say in his rather hilarious imitation of a northern working-class person: *Today's news is tomorrow's chip papers, lass*. But that was back when I was a child, at a time when he always said things like that, always held my hand when we walked along the pavement to the sweet shop. That was at a time when I thought

I knew him, thought he loved me and would never forsake me. There are days when I still let myself think about those times and cannot for the life of me fathom how he did that – how did he hold my hand and buy me sweets and toys and tickle me until I couldn't breathe and tell me funny stories and do impressions and crawl around the lounge with a wicker basket on his head pretending to be a tiger until I screamed, giggling, for him to stop? How is all *that* reconcilable with the man who left me like a wizard in a proverbial puff of smoke when I was eighteen? How is that possible? It is not. And yet that is what he did.

My mother is no different, I suppose. When I think of my parents, the word *incompatible* comes to mind. *Irreconcilable*, perhaps. Not with each other. They were besotted. I think one of the reasons my mother was at times unkind to me was possibly because she felt, even when I was very little, some latent competition for the irresistible brown hangdog eyes of my father. So no, they were not incompatible with one another but with themselves, within themselves. My father in all his kindness and warmth; his increasing cruelty and coldness after my mother's death. My mother in all her glamour, lipstick and acid wit; her insecurity, her utter and, as it turned out, deadly fragility.

It is the disentangling I find most difficult. My mother, her long, patterned dresses, her slim waist, the indigo crushed velvet cape she wore when she went out for dinner with my father. My mother, slumped across her bed, in only her vest and pants, one arm reaching for something – perhaps the phone on the bedside table, perhaps the glass of water she never drank. Perhaps she had changed her mind. I don't know. I only know that her skin was cold under my fingertips when I tried to shake her by the shoulder. I wish I had never walked into that room, that it hadn't been me who found her, that I hadn't been just six years old. But I did, it was, I was.

'Mummy.' I whispered it, afraid I would wake her but needing badly for her to open her eyes. 'Mummy, are you asleep?'

I remember my father, sometime earlier, weeks, months maybe, crying at her in the hallway while I watched, silent, face pressed between the banister posts at the top of the stairs: 'What do you want from me, Harriet? What do you fucking want?'

'I don't know.' My mother sobbing, pulling at her blonde hair. 'I don't know, I don't know, I don't know.'

There were other scenes like that, scenes I remember only as fraught whispers behind closed doors, crescendos of angst from downstairs, all sense muffled by my pink bedroom carpet, the floorboards, the sitting-room ceiling beneath. I would lie in bed and listen and think they sounded like people talking underwater, vowels and consonants ever more frantic as they realised they were drowning.

I try not to think about those arguments, about what they meant. I try not to think about my mother. She is as shocking as my own unexpected reflection in a mirror. She is the expression caught before I have had time to compose my face: railing, boredom, impossibility. Myself.

And Peter Gates. My father. Much earlier. I am perhaps five. His arm is around me. I am cosy and small at his side while he watches football on the television. This working-class affectation was lost on me then – it's lost on me now, for that matter; one more irreconcilable thing that I cannot make fit with the fact that he and my mother met at art school, hardly an environment flush with blue collars. I never got the chance in adult life to ask him about his enthusiasm for football. But I remember the tobacco smell of him, the yeasty tang of ale from a tin; and me, still, so still, praying that he would forget I was there, breathless with tension at the loss of him whenever he reached forward to drink, lungs filling once more when he settled back into the cushions beside me and I felt the warmth of him once more. I hoped that we could stay like that forever. My father and me. My father. And then the other father, who each year that followed my mother's death stepped further away, who stopped pulling me into his arms, who never again held my hand. Who wrote to me at university from Thailand to tell me he had left the UK for the foreseeable future and to get in touch if I was ever out that way. Who left me shaking and vomiting into the small sink in the solitude of my halls of residence room, no one to rub my back, no one to hold me tight, no one to say, *there, there.*

How do I fit these men together? The latter throws a shadow of doubt so dark over the former that sometimes I struggle to see the first *him* at all. It's as if he doesn't exist. It's as if he never existed, not really, and was in fact an act. My father loved me. My father never loved me. The two statements are as contradictory as they are true. Maybe he is why I write. Maybe my books are nothing more than, a child, crying out to him: *Look at me, Daddy. Look what I did. Aren't I clever? Love me, Daddy. Love me.*

My God, I'm glad this is private. I wouldn't admit this stuff to anyone but you, and even then, only now that I'm dead. Yes, there is great liberation in death. I'm beginning to see that more clearly each day.

And I realise with my rather maudlin digression that I've left you dangling somewhat. Marlena had passed me a card, hadn't she? I was at her table on Christmas Day, trying to give her some credit, standing with my ever-emptying glass like the lone spinster aunt, and in my shaking hands was a red envelope upon which was written: *P. K. Gates, Author* in writing I recognised.

'Are you all right?' Marlena said. 'Pip?'

'Actually, would you excuse me a moment?' I made for the hall, calling behind me, 'Please eat. Don't wait for me.'

I opened the front door and looked first one way, then the other. I had expected to see no one, for him to be long gone. But there he was, at the end of the road. He wasn't walking away; he was waiting, watching the house.

'Ryan,' I shouted, rage firing in my chest.

He raised a hand in a wave, then turned and walked away, slowly, deliberately. Bastard. I ran, faster than I could remember doing in years, adrenalin pumping. I ran as I always imagined I might run at night whenever I heard footsteps behind me on the way home from the station.

'Ryan,' I called out. 'Wait!'

How dare he? How dare he bait me like this? And not even in my own home. I ran. Reached the corner, heart banging. He was ambling down the main road, a roll to his stride, a real prison gait, I thought, full of swagger and belligerence.

'Ryan!'

He stopped and turned to face me. The fire of him flashed, burned beneath my skin. He had changed, if only a little. He was dressed in better clothes – jeans and a sweater but a nice pair of jeans, a decent-quality dark-green sweatshirt and sturdy black leather lace-up boots. His cheeks seemed less caved in, his skin less grey.

I was still holding the card. 'What the hell do you think you're doing?'

He smiled. 'You said your best mate lived at the same house number on the next road across.'

I considered him a moment, wondering if he actually believed his response was in any way an answer to my question.

'What has that got to do with anything?' I was still panting, my chest tight.

'When you weren't home, I thought I'd deliver it in person. I thought you might be feeling a bit, you know, out of place, everyone playing happy families and all that. That it might be nice for you to receive a seasonal wish in front of your significant others. You know, from an admirer.'

I opened my mouth but said nothing. His hair had been cut but it was still long, almost shoulder length, and still oily-looking. He pushed at it, his silver rings catching what was left of the winter-afternoon light. 'How did you know I'd be there?'

'I didn't. I just thought you might be. And if you weren't, then I thought she'd pop it round.' He paused. I didn't believe him. 'You two haven't seen each other in ages,' he went on, 'so I thought if you hadn't made it up by Christmas it'd give her a pretext to come and visit. You can't go losing all your friends, Pippa. Sarah doesn't come over anymore either, does she? Marlena's the only one you've got left.'

The fear burned through me, an oil slick set alight, flames racing on the surface of the sea. How much of my life had he seen, watched, recorded? How easily the judgement fell from his lips.

'My life is none of your concern, Ryan. You told me you'd leave me alone.'

'And I have, haven't I? And you've been writing. Well done.'

'How do you know… Forget it, you don't know. You don't know anything about me. I'm not lonely.'

'I never said you were. You said that, just now. *Are* you lonely, Pip?'

'Don't call me Pip. Only those closest to me call me that.'

'So that's Marlena, then, yes?' He glanced behind him, as if looking for someone else, then back to me. 'Who else?'

I floundered. My hands clenched into fists. His blue eyes were pale in the grey December light, the ironic expression an offhand insult, one that stuck. On my bare arms the skin tingled. The air was freezing and I felt it bitterly then. I had run out without my coat. As for him, he had on no coat, no scarf, no hat. My temperature was dropping fast. I was trembling, with cold, with fear, with rage. I wanted to wrap my hands around his thin throat; I saw myself do it, saw my arms lock, there in front of me, my fingers claw, push his spindly Adam's apple into the repulsive loosening skin of his neck.

'It's only a card, Pip.'

A howl. My own. I clamped my mouth shut against it. I would not. I would not. I…

'Look,' I said, making myself breathe. 'I don't want to have to call the police, all right? I know what that'll mean for you. But if you don't leave me alone, I will do it, don't think I won't. So just… just stay away, all right? Stay away from me.'

He threw up his hands, smiled with that arrogant, easy charm. 'I just wanted to say happy Christmas, that's all. No crime in that. I'm not here to bother you, Pip; I'm here to wait for you. There's a difference. You've chosen celibacy, I see, which is a step in the right direction. You can't sleep with your friends and expect them not to get attached, you know.'

'What?' I stared at him, incredulous. Was that a reference to Sarah? Christ, could he see through the walls?

'You're learning to be self-sufficient,' he went on, unfazed, 'and that's important. To be part of a successful couple, you need to be a whole person.'

Fucking. Cheeky. Bastard.

'I am a whole person,' I said through gritted teeth.

'You're a person with a hole in your soul is what you are, Pip. I understand. It's a big thing to admit. I just want you to know that I'll wait. For as long as it takes.'

'Ryan?' I said. 'Fuck. Off.'

I turned and marched back in the direction of Marlena's house. At her gate, I looked back, wondering if he would still be there. He was, his legs straight, his feet apart. He didn't shrink away or look down. He simply waved, as if he'd been seeing me home safe, before disappearing behind the last of the houses. I stared after him a moment, there where he had been. The street corner: how desolate it was, how empty.

Blog post: PippaGatesAuthor
#thiswritinglife
Find me on:
Instagram: @GatesPip
Twitter: @PipGatesWrites
Facebook: Pippa Gates Author

A little later than usual to the desk today, so I'll keep this post brief. You might have seen the pictures of Mrs Danvers' handiwork if you checked my Instagram account yesterday evening. A rather magnificent soda bread and an incredible sausage plait, made with organic meat from the wonderful butcher's in the village. So creative! The ratatouille and dauphinoise potatoes I didn't post, but I can tell you that our dinner last night was highly delicious. There was chocolate mousse for dessert. We are allowed wine and pudding on Friday nights, which is not excessive, I know, but I might have to watch the calories today even so! Mrs D will have to watch them for me, I should say, since I have no hand in any of the food preparation here at Cairn Farm. Nor the laundry nor any of the household jobs for that matter. My job is to write! #luckyme

Having shared a fine bottle of Amarone with dinner, we cleared our heads this morning by taking a stroll around the farm grounds, only to find that someone or something had disturbed the commemorative cairn at the top of the upper field. Some of the stones had been scattered about, and having something of the poltergeist about it, it really did set our nerves on edge. Mrs D said it was probably a fox – that perhaps it had scented meat in the earth.

Still, the surface of the ground hadn't been disturbed, so that's something. But we must be vigilant from now on. Mrs Danvers is at this very moment installing a new secure mailbox at the end of the driveway, together with a second padlock for the gate. Anyone who wants access to our land from now on will have to call and prearrange. Or break in.

It doesn't do to lose control of one's boundaries.

CHAPTER FIFTEEN

PIPPA GATES: PRIVATE JOURNAL

I wonder whether Mrs Danvers and I are living in a fool's paradise, to coin a cliché, and whether we, or at least I, know this on some fundamental level. Maybe that's why I'm writing my private journal. This is my dying declaration, made in the certainty of oncoming death.

More of that later. First, I must tell you the conclusion of the Christmas-card encounter. I returned to Marlena's shaking and cold, and in need of a drink. At the sight of her entire family tucking into a steaming-hot Christmas lunch, pink-faced and smiling and topped off by paper crowns, I burst into tears.

'Oh God, Pip.' Marlie was out of her chair and at my side in an instant. She always loved it when I cried. Further proof, if any was needed, of how much better her life was than mine.

I shook my head, hid my face behind my hand. 'I'm fine. It's... I'm not sure. I'm probably just premenstrual or something.' A deep cough came from the table. I assumed it was Marlie's father. Men of his generation didn't like period detail, as it were, unless it was of the *Downton Abbey* variety.

'Come and sit down,' Marlie said softly. 'I've put your dinner in the oven. Sit down, that's it. I'll get it.'

I sat down, trying not to look at anyone, glancing up through my eyelashes at intervals and attempting a watery smile. I gave a weak laugh and lifted my glass.

'Cheers, everyone,' I said. 'Happy Christmas.'

They replied, a little too loudly and a little too in unison. It was all kindly meant, but I was feeling increasingly like the lunatic who came to tea. I drained my glass and slid the red envelope under my plate. There was no way I had the strength to look at it now. I should put it directly into the bin, I knew. But I also knew that I would not. Ryan was like a terrifying episode of *Doctor Who* back when I was a child. Scared half to death, I would put my hands over my face, but I could never stop myself from opening my fingers, peeping, waiting for Daleks.

In the end, I thought the best thing to do would be to catch Marlie in a quiet moment, tell her everything and ask her to sit with me while I opened the card.

I had to wait, of course. Marlena is like the local post office; there's always a bloody queue. After dinner, after *I* – not Steve, and not her kids – had helped wash up and tidy, after *I* had helped make the grandparents their coffee, after *I* had put the batteries into Zane and Zoe's new robot money boxes, oh, and after the endless games of charades and telling of jokes from Zane's *One Thousand Jokes to Tell Your Friends* (I mean, why do parents do that to themselves? Why not buy him a drum kit while you're at it, Steve, a pet rat maybe, and have done?)... finally the kids were watching television, Steve was snoring like a boar on the sofa and Marlie's mum and dad had both fallen asleep with the discretion of the elderly, faces hidden behind their hands.

'Have you got a sec?' I said, averting my eyes from the sight of Steve's open mouth, the lime-green strip of what could only be sprout lodged in his back-right molar.

'Sure,' she replied.

'Can we go somewhere...'

She picked up. 'Sure, let's go upstairs.'

I followed her into her and Steve's room, trying and failing not to see Steve's cast-off underpants, crotch *à l'air*.

Pig. How could she want that? How could she want *him*?

We sat together on her bed. I told her about Ryan dropping the note through my door after he'd been at my house, about his weird insistence that we had made some kind of contract, about him appearing at the school.

'Oh my God, Pippa,' she said, putting her arm around my shoulders. 'Why didn't you tell me? Why didn't you ring?'

I leant into her shoulder. It was rather hard and bony, but I didn't care. She smelled of cooking, of the Coco perfume she always wore.

'I guess the way we left it,' I said, 'I thought you'd be cross with me.' That was a lie. I had been cross with her. 'And anyway, it's not that bad.'

I didn't tell her about the texts, about the possibility of him taking and replacing my house key, the dried mud in the footwell, about the fact that he was obviously watching my comings and goings, possibly every day. I didn't tell her because, frankly, I didn't want to give her the satisfaction, the vicarious thrill she would inevitably feel at my poor decision-making, my chaotic emotional life.

'Look,' I said. 'It's not stalking or anything.'

'It bloody is, Pippa! What are you saying? You can't turn up at someone's place of work and get in their car without their permission. That's insane.' Her tone was increasingly indignant. I began to regret telling her any of it.

'He's not *insane*,' I said. 'He's recently out of prison, that's all. He's bound to be a bit weird at first, isn't he? Lack social graces, maybe not be attuned to nuances and boundaries and stuff? Anyway, I told him to leave me alone and he has.'

She sighed. Neither of us spoke.

'How long for?' she asked after a moment.

'Ages. Months.'

'So who sent the card?' she said.

Ah.

'Him. But again, in his mind he's just wishing me happy Christmas.'

I opened it, mostly to shut her up. It was an individual card, not one from a packet. On it was a kitsch picture of Jesus in a halo and the caption: *It's all about Me!*

I laughed – it just popped out like wind and I closed my mouth against it. I opened the card, aware of Marlie's body heat, the alcohol tinge of her breath as she read over my shoulder. The message was written in the looping hand I recognised. It looked like he'd used the fountain pen with which I had signed my book, and in his eyes my life, over to him.

Dear Pippa Gates, author extraordinaire,

Our paths being momentarily divided, I wanted to wish you merry Christmas.

I hope your new book is coming along well and that my life is proving useful to you. You seem to have become diligent of late and this is a good and necessary thing. Remember Malcolm Gladwell's ten thousand hours! *Nil sine magno labore.*

I am no longer selling door to door. I have moved into a rented flat with some guys from the hostel and have taken my first paid job, washing plates in an Italian restaurant in Chiswick. The manager believes in second chances and has already intimated that he will train me to be a waiter in the coming weeks. From there I expect to progress to house chef. I have the training, I have the talent and I have the discipline. All I have to do is keep my head down and stay clean, which I fully intend to do. I decided when we spoke that I would prefer to cook rather than make windows for a living. Food is one of life's most important joys and the careful preparation and appreciation of it what separates us from beasts. I'm glad you too are eating better, by the way.

Please be sure to let me know when your book is released. I am keen to read it. You have my number.

Tout vient à qui sait attendre…

One day yours,

Ryan Marks

The fire that had flashed within me from the moment I had seen the envelope, that had caught and spread through me on the street corner, burned hotter still. For a moment, I couldn't breathe. Neither of us spoke.

'There's nothing openly hostile,' I said eventually, when I'd got my breath back.

Marlie sighed and plucked the card from my hand. 'So why do I feel like I need a shower?'

I knew exactly why. From the playful use of my name, the phrase *momentarily divided* and all that lay beneath that, the casually patronising yet accurate analysis of my dedication to my work, the obvious continuing observation of my life and habits, the exchanging of his own news, as if we were friends. And the proverbs! *Nothing is gained without hard work* in Latin and *all good things come to those who wait* in French… Did he believe that by having them in their original language I would think him mysterious? Clever? Yes, I thought. That was what he'd wanted from the start – for me to think him clever. Which meant, surely, that he saw me that way.

'I don't think he means to be creepy,' I said. 'I think he's simply convinced that he and I have a relationship of some kind, which we don't. I *have* told him.'

'You've definitely told him? You're sure you've closed it down.'

'What's that supposed to mean?'

She shrugged, hesitated.

'What?' I insisted.

'It's just that… remember that mate of yours from teacher training college, her boyfriend? Rufus, that was his name, wasn't it? He came onto you that time, and you, you didn't exactly… I mean, you gave him your mobile number, didn't you?'

'So?'

'So he ended up texting you for a booty call, didn't he? Don't you remember? You called me about it; I can remember you reading it down the phone to me. "Nicky's away for the weekend. I need someone to help me with this." Didn't he send you a photo of his erection?'

He had indeed.

I giggled. 'So?'

Her arm left my shoulder. 'So, he wouldn't have done that, would he, if you hadn't… I mean, you don't always…'

'Don't always what?'

She shrugged. 'Close it down. Come on, Pippa, you know that.'

Another pause. A silence with lead boots. My best friend saw me as a prick tease. How very buck-passingly, slut-shamingly old-fashioned of her. How very judgemental. How very dare she.

'So you're saying that this weirdo delivering a card to my friend's house on Christmas Day is my fault? That's what you're saying, is it? You know, just so we're clear.'

She sighed and stood up, paced one way and then the other, chewed at her fingernail.

I waited. In her bedroom, the smell of another couple's life, laundry, bed. I said nothing. Far be it from me to stop her expanding on any more little judgements she had regarding me and my… behaviour.

She stopped pacing, pulled her finger from her mouth and met my eye. 'How has he got our address, Pip?'

'Erm, he hasn't. I…'

'How has he got our address?' She had raised her voice – only a little, but still.

'I don't know,' I wailed. Oh, this was such a mistake. How had we got to this? I should have taken the card home and read it later. Alone. 'He's a door-to-door salesman, for Christ's sake. He has everyone's address! He must have followed me here. Maybe he was… I don't know… maybe he was about to post the card and he saw me and… followed me. And you bought stuff from him, didn't you? He obviously remembered where you lived! But it's not you he wants, it's me. He's obsessed with me. Honestly, Marlie, you're not in any danger.'

'Oh, for fuck's sake, Pippa, when will you stop?'

'Stop what?'

'Keeping all your little irons in the fire. Letting these men think you might, you know, cave in one day if they just hang around long enough. *One day yours,* that's how he signed off. Why would he sign off like that? What did you do, tell him he had to go while keeping up the prolonged eye contact, maybe biting your bottom lip for good measure?'

'What?' Now I had raised my voice. 'What the hell do you mean by that?'

'You invited him into your kitchen, Pip! If I'm not mistaken, there were a couple of empty wine bottles on the counter when I came round, worried sick as usual. Off my head with worry, Pip! I'm always off my head with worry about you. And when you see him at your school, instead of telling him to piss off, you give him a lift in your car! Keeping him dangling, throwing him a crumb from the table. This is what you do, Pippa! Honestly, hon, you need to grow out of that shit. You're a grown woman. It's pathetic.'

I thought about Sarah. *I'm a human being,* she had said. *Not a pair of shoes you can get out of your wardrobe when you're bored of wearing the others.* I thought of Matthew, whom I had continued to text, though not to suggest meeting up. And Josh, from before Matthew, to whom I still sent memes from time to time, made vague arrangements that never materialised. There were others, too.

'I don't do that,' I said. 'I'm not like that. It's just banter, which, by the way, they're more than happy to join in with. And I was happy with Bill. It's not my fault he shagged his secretary.'

'You weren't happy with Bill! Come on, Pip! No matter what he did for you, it was never enough!'

A horrid silence fell. She had gone down this road last time. Clearly it was an opinion she held dear – too dear to let go.

I stood up, slipping the card back into its envelope. Something had been breached, something that had to do with Marlena and me, our ten-year friendship, if that was what this even was.

'Thanks,' I said coldly. 'Thanks a lot. Here's me thinking you were my friend, and all the while you're standing in judgement from the vantage point of your smug little life. I can't have this argument again, Marlie. I thought you said you were sorry, but you're not sorry at all. For the record, Bill betrayed me. He lied to me and dumped me for another woman. But that's my fault, apparently. Don't worry, I get it.'

'Pippa, I'm sorry, I didn't mean—'

'You did mean it! That's my point. I mean, who do you think you are? You think, you actually *think*, your perfect life is no more than you deserve, is that it?'

'That's not fair. No one's life is perfect. I've got every right to be frustrated with you, Pippa. It's me who has to answer your calls in the dead of night, me who has to talk you down from the ledge when it all goes wrong, run to your rescue in my fucking pyjamas. You have no idea how much it takes to keep a family going while trying to hold down a full-time job, what it feels like to never get to the end of a television programme you want to watch, to never even go for a pee without someone in there with you. I'm not smug, Pippa, that's entirely your projection – I'm just like anyone else in this life, fucking up on a daily basis, again and again no matter how hard I try not to. Do you know what I feel most of all? Tired. Fucking exhausted, but I stick at it. Steve might get on my tits ninety per cent of the time, but I don't spend my days planning what he should be doing for me then punishing him when he doesn't do it, because do you know what? He's just a human being, like we all are. Christ, he can barely pick up subtext, let alone read my mind, so don't tell me I'm smug, all right?'

'I just don't want your charity, that's all.'

'Oh my God.' She was shouting now – tears of frustration leaked from her eyes, her hands balled into fists. 'It's called friendship, Pippa. If you don't want me to come running, why call me in the first place? Why text me at two in the morning? Why tell me you've invited an ex-con into your house? No one can do anything right for you, can they? And I didn't mean it about Bill, I—'

'Yes, you did!' By now I was crying too, my face and neck hot. 'You absolutely did, you're just pissed off you let the truth slip out for once. And d'you know what? You might be right. I might set impossible standards, but one day I'll find someone to meet them and you'll be stuck waiting on Steve hand and foot and listening to him snoring and looking at his… his fucking sprouts in his teeth and his… his crusty pants on the bedroom floor, five centimetres from the damn laundry basket… so you can stick your judgement up your arse.'

I ran from the room, down the stairs and grabbed my coat from the end of the banister.

'Merry Christmas,' I shouted up to her, throwing as much petulance in as I could, before I opened the door and stumbled into the street.

Outside, I stopped, threaded my arms through my coat sleeves. I sniffed, wiped my face with the back of my hand. I looked back at the door and waited, hand to my forehead, breathless with shock. On the street, warm windows boasted Christmas trees and fake snow cornices, taunting tableaux of other people's happiness. I stared back at Marlie's house, but there was no sign of her. She wasn't going to come running down and cry after me to come back. She wasn't going to chase me down the street and take me in her arms while we sobbed our apologies. She wasn't even going to look out of the window.

I pulled my coat tight and walked away.

In the fridge was half a bottle of cheap Pinot Grigio, which at first I pressed to my lips before shaking myself and fetching a glass. In the living room, I poured a large measure and downed half. I topped up, took out Ryan's card and read it again.

Tout vient à qui sait attendre…
    One day yours,
    Ryan Marks

I had to hand it to him: the man knew exactly how to get under my skin. That flashing of heat I felt whenever I saw him or heard his voice or read his words was exactly that: him, a burning membrane beneath the epidermis, adhering to the very tissue of my being.

I pulled out my phone from my pocket and brought up his number.

Thanks for your card, I texted. *But you must realise that we are not friends. Whatever understanding you have of our relationship is all in your head. Do not contact me again. Not ever. Or I will call the police. It is only out of sympathy for you that I have not already done this. I wish you well in your life and genuinely hope you get back on your feet. All good things, Ryan. Truly. Pippa.*

I pressed send, slugged back the rest of the glass of wine, then drained the bottle into the glass.

I stared at my phone: a rolling ellipsis. That meant he was texting back. I waited. The dots vanished. He had changed his mind.

I cried out in frustration, almost threw the phone against the wall, but then the message appeared, fully formed, in a long strip.

You look well, Pippa. Hard work suits you. Dating and drinking was just an escape; meeting me has helped you to realise how dishonest you were being with yourself, and I'm happy about that. I am on your side, Pippa. I know you say you don't want contact with me, and that you'll call the police, but it's possible you're already coming to terms with the fact that what I said the night we met is true. We are two sides of the same coin, my love. I am your Ecuadorean chicha; *the maggots in your cheese, the bacteria in your yoghurt. Your evident insanity is my perfect sense. I will respect your wishes, however, until you tell me otherwise. Take care, Pip. I look forward to reading* Framed by Love. *R x PS Sorry you fell out with Marlena. I guess it's just you and me now.*

I downed my white wine, felt it launch itself at my head. I stumbled, snivelling, to the window. Outside, soft flakes of snow fell on the wet ground. They would not stick, I thought. They would not last. I dialled 999 and pressed end call, knowing as I did so that I had never intended to speak to the police in the first place.

Lies, Pippa, I thought. *You are full to the brim of lies.*

Blog post: PippaGatesAuthor
#thiswritinglife
Find me on:
Instagram: @GatesPip
Twitter: @PipGatesWrites
Facebook: Pippa Gates Author

Pushing Up Daisy #firstdraft is entering its final ten thousand words. There's still no sign of Bobby, the chap from Wilson's Stores. I wish I'd known him better. He seemed so nice, so amiable and helpful. But you can never know what's going on, can you? Even under the most benign surfaces there can lurk all sorts of darkness and subterfuge – the venomous nettle covered in frost, the earth thick with snow.

Although I'm sure that's not true of Bobby.

I'd better get on. Apologies for the super-short post but that first draft won't finish itself unless I stay chained to this desk, and the shackles are beginning to rub! Mrs D has promised home-made pesto from the basil that we bought at the farmers' market yesterday. I can smell it, actually, from down here. It's a shame you can't too.

Really, it's exquisite.

CHAPTER SIXTEEN

PIPPA GATES: PRIVATE JOURNAL

Despite our propensity for lies, the truth is a need. It will out, as they say, because it must. There are dead bodies to unearth. There is evidence to uncover. The truth is a kind of pressure – it simmers in its gasket until it reaches a certain temperature and then, of course, it blows. If none of that metaphor comes off, I apologise. I'll admit I don't actually know what a gasket is, and if I had Google to hand, I would look and check that the analogy works, but of course Mrs D doesn't let me have the internet on this computer. Suffice to say, we are approaching that night, dear reader, when with some kind of warped symmetry, there was another knock at the door.

Life/art – you couldn't write this stuff.

Except you could, obviously. You can. And I will.

I didn't see Marlie or Ryan again for a very long while. And what a while it was! Friendlessness focuses the mind. You can get so much done. Your evenings stretch before you; your weekends are endless.

And I had the most effective motivating factor known to artists the world over: fear. Fear of writing another dud was the bellows at my heels; success my finish line, its tape flickering in the sun. Commercial success would bring freedom – London house prices being what they were, I could sell up and move away, tell no one where I was going, get a much-needed fresh start. My bridges burnt, there was no more to do now than head off, knapsack on the end of my stick, to find new streets paved in gold – you get the gist. I'll stop with the metaphors, a terrible habit I really need to get out of. I resolved to write with a focus and determination I had never known before. I wrote such that I barely recognised myself. This book would be the best that I could make it. It would be an absolute cracker.

Framed by Love grew, line by line, like a scarf – whoops, there I go again. By day, I taught; by night, I built on my scrappy first draft. I was writing for my life. I was writing so that I could live without looking out of the window, without checking the back seat of my car, without calling out to a sinister and unseen presence in the dead of night.

Ryan Marks went further into hiding, but his shadow still darkened – or did it? – the pavement outside my window, his tobacco still floated – possibly – on the air, my pots and pans moved – maybe – around a kitchen that often seemed a little cleaner when I got home than when I had left for work. I could be sure about none of this. But it made sense to keep checking.

Gary Hughes, meanwhile, his literary avatar, came to full and breathing life. He serves a short prison sentence, gets out, determines never to go back. He borrows money from old neighbourhood contact scar-faced Gil, sets up his windows business.

Petra Stark, the wealthy but lonely woman, no longer an actual widow but a widow only to her husband's nefarious business interests, takes Gary to her bedroom. Hot sex ensues. Gil, the evil loan shark, looms, the embodiment of a past that Gary can never shake off. Can any of us shake off our past? No, but we can transcend it, goddammit! That gave the story a wider meaning, which was good. The reader would find something to identify with, something I would explore for them through someone else's life. After all, looking directly into your own shitty past is rubbish, isn't it? Like a Medusa's gaze, it can turn you to stone. Looking into someone else's past is much easier: a mirror to hold up to the snakes, your pain but a reflection, its power diminished.

I chained myself to my desk and wrote until my eyes stung and my shoulders ached. I wrote until my every waking thought was with them, my characters, my fictional friends and family. I gave them a happy ending, Gary and Petra. Romance requires it, yes, but so did I. I loved them, had grown to love them. In a final and shocking twist, the loan shark realises that Petra's husband swindled him years earlier and, in an act of revenge, lands *him* in it, not Gary, releasing the lovers to their happy ending. When I wrote the final scene, I cried. With happiness. For them!

I finished the final draft in February and, with a feeling of euphoria mixed with a sense of grief, handed it in to Jackie on the tenth, almost three weeks ahead of the new deadline that had been set for the end of that month.

Jackie called me a mere week later. I spent that week pacing the proverbial boards of my house, barely able to concentrate on my classes, on the television, on anything at all. I returned to dangerous old habits with such alacrity that I only came to my senses afterwards, by which point my actions had the surreal quality of a dream, the murkiness of something seen underwater. Two Tinder encounters, Monday and Thursday, back to their flats, home by three. Having no Marlena to text anymore, I avoided dark commons and alleyways, took cabs instead. Wednesday night brought a surprise reacquaintance with Sarah over a Chinese takeaway and a great deal of red wine – pleasant, soft, comforting. The remaining evenings, more red wine, drunk alone to stave off any inchoate heebie-jeebies, and many inhaled packets of Kettle Chips and Cadbury's Fruit & Nut. Not bad for one week, I say. Such frenzied bacchanalia!

I guess I had some catching up to do.

I half expected Ryan to call or send a text telling me to calm my excesses and get back to work, throw in some casual slut-shaming or pass comment on my alcohol consumption. I checked my phone regularly, expecting to see his number – so often, in fact, that you'd think that with all that raging hedonism I'd been trying to provoke a reaction.

But nothing.

So when the phone finally rang, I did think for a moment it would be him. But it wasn't.

'Pippa.' As I said, it was Jackie, her voice chirpy – gassed, as the kids at school say. 'It's brilliant.'

Every writer will tell you that those words are the sweetest they will ever hear. *It's brilliant.* A beautiful, beautiful phrase to make you dance and shout and shake it all about.

'Really?' I said. I wasn't fishing for compliments, I was simply in shock.

'Really, Pippa. It's gritty, it's real, it's got heart, soul, romance, love… it's got everything, and do you know what? The connection between Gary and Petra is so convincing, one of the most believable love stories I've read. I was crying like a baby at the end.'

To my surprise, I found that I too was crying, if not like a baby then like a grown woman who has been flattered to a state of near-distress. I was so raw, I think, in that moment. My soul had thrown its hands to the sky, it was on its knees, praying for someone, anyone, to tell me, its owner, that I had done just this one thing right. Looking back, I can see that Ryan, Marlena, my whole monastic lifestyle change – nights spent poring over words at my computer screen until the story was all I could think about, all I wanted to spend time with, all I wanted to do – had been a journey.

It had also been, I think now, a love affair.

'I'm delighted,' I said. 'I can't speak. I am so, so happy.'

The book came out in May.

And that, dear reader, was the start of the most extraordinary year and a half, give or take, of my life. A long period of time in terms of my own personal story, but one that can be potted, since all going well in life is the least interesting part, *n'est-ce pas*? So I'll nutshell it for you, in order to get to the bit where it went, to coin a vulgar yet amusing phrase, tits up.

Having just said that the words *it's brilliant* form the most heart-inflating phrase for any writer, I may have to qualify and say that they might come second only to *global bestseller*. Which, as it turned out, was to be the destiny of *Framed by Love*, and for me, as its author, the nearest I was ever going to get to watching my kid win the sack race or pick up an award at the school prize-giving evening. These things take time, however. I could not give up the day job until I was absolutely sure that I could stay afloat financially. But watching *Framed by Love* soar up the charts, I glowed with something akin to maternal pride: the book was not me but it was *of* me. I had made it, and there it was doing so well in the world, enough to make its author proud – and I never had to ask, *Oh, but is it happy?*

The royalty cheques increased, and with them my dream of telling the head teacher to stick her curriculum where the sun didn't shine. The book was optioned by Really Good Films and is, as we speak, awaiting production. I was invited to do an interview on Radio 4, to sit on the romantic-fiction panel at three separate literary festivals, even, once, on a political forum debating contemporary penal practice called 'Refusing Recidivism – Closing the Revolving Door'. Requests flooded in. *Ms Gates, can I ask, where did you find the inspiration for the character of Gary Hughes?*

Ah yes, it's interesting you should ask that question…

I didn't tell them about Ryan. It felt too much like betrayal. I told them that a friend of mine had confided in me her secret longing for the muscular young man who had fitted a slab of granite into her utility. What? No euphemism intended, honest. But yes, that always got a laugh.

My savings account fattened. During the months I'd spent writing *Framed by Love*, I'd saved more than I had since Bill left simply by not going out *at all*. Far too excited by the unexpected success, by the rave reviews, which pronounced my book 'authentic' and 'believable', I didn't settle to my desk to write a follow-up. I couldn't! I knew I needed to write another corker to capitalise on my new fan base, but every time I sat down to write, I found myself on social media instead, or answering emails from readers who had been moved by my work. It was lovely to hear from them. I wondered if Ryan had an email account yet and whether he might drop me a line or post on my author page. He didn't. The success became unsettling; I had no one to share it with. Thinking about it now, that was probably the reason why, when I wasn't on social media or enjoying the warm rays of attention, I was seeking company elsewhere. Old haunts, old flames. Old habits.

My phone stayed silent. I wasn't even sure if Marlie knew the book had come out. And if Ryan was still watching my comings and goings, he was keeping quiet.

Despite no progress – let's face it, no attempt – on a new story, the money rolled in to the extent that at last I could think about giving up teaching at that school. I knew I would have to write another book soon, but I told myself I couldn't do that unless I focused on my writing. And in order to do *that*, I would have to leave behind forever the panic and helplessness of ill-controlled classes, the burning humiliation of yet another tongue-lashing from the head, not to mention my renewed quest for dangerous liaisons in the dead of night.

But it wasn't easier finances, lack of focus or a run of bad dates that prompted me to take that final brave step to move to the country and commence life as a full-time writer. It was something else entirely, something that made my escape less of a dream and more of an urgent necessity. It was the moment I finally got my glossy interview in a mainstream national magazine, the day I knew my pithiest quotations would at last make it into large bold font alongside my smiling soft-focus photograph.

Joy! Or not, as it turned out.

The reporter who came to my home one spring morning about a year after the book had been published was young, blonde and bespectacled, and shook my hand with a zealous green eye-lock that told me she would be editor-in-chief before long. I met those green eyes with nothing more than excitement, the kind of unguarded anticipation we feel when we have no idea of what's coming.

Once we'd settled in my kitchen with our cups of coffee – at the bar where I'd had, in a galaxy far, far away, the most disturbing yet profitable conversation of my life – the usual question came up: so was the character of Gary Hughes based on anyone in particular?

I smiled patiently and trotted out my usual response. *Well, actually, no. A friend of mine was having her utility room done...*

So smug was I in my retelling of what by then had attained the status of a hoary old chestnut to be toasted on the campfire, I failed to question why a woman so possessed of professional drive and presence would not have read this answer for herself in one of my many interviews. She would, I should have known, been thorough in her research prior to interviewing me.

I let myself be lulled, dear reader. I made the classic mistake that comes with vanity. I assumed she was interested in me for my literary prowess, my success, when in fact she had another agenda entirely. She was looking for an angle.

I finished my answer. *So really, yeah, the idea started there.*

She smiled and tapped her pen to her bottom teeth.

'Thanks,' she said, and then, in a practised show of a thought having just this moment occurred, added, 'I guess I was wondering if you'd taken your inspiration from a real criminal. I had a dig around and there actually was a Gary Hughes, though the case was almost thirty years ago and it was much more violent... the rape and murder of a wealthy woman in Norfolk.' She paused, glanced at her notes, and then at me. The whites of her eyes were clear and shocking. 'There's the wealthy-woman similarity, I suppose.

And he gained a carpentry qualification in prison, I believe, so that's a similarity too. But he was a heroin addict, so I guess that's different. Anyway, he was released about eighteen months ago, under a different name obviously. Relocated, all that stuff.' She stopped, fixed me again with her determined hazel gaze.

'Is that right?' I managed. 'What a coincidence.'

She shrugged quickly and gave a brief sigh. 'Just thought you might be interested. I mean, his story's nothing like your character's. For a start, he was a really violent criminal. Really violent. Won't have come up in your research, though, I shouldn't think. No reason why it should.'

My chest rose and fell. Research. There was no research. My research was Ryan, only Ryan. I wiped my hand over my mouth, which had gone dry.

'Yes, his story is really quite different,' she was saying, and I had the sense she was enjoying herself. 'He was rescued from a cellar, can you believe, when he was a little kid.'

'A cellar?' I tried to sip my coffee but could not. There had been no mention of the cellar in the book. For all that I had paid good money for Ryan's story, the cellar was in a box with the heroin addiction, stored under things I hadn't had the heart to use.

'He was four years old when they found him, apparently,' she said, interrupting my thoughts. 'So shocking. Who would do that to a child?' She stared at me, her expression unreadable. Those eyes of hers, like a frozen, stagnant pond.

CHAPTER SEVENTEEN

The moment the journalist left, I raced to my computer. I had searched for Ryan but of course had never found him, nor had I thought to ask myself whether or not that was his real name. Idiot. Idiot, idiot, idiot. He had flashed his ID card at the door that night and I had seen it, could remember seeing it. But I had not taken it from him, not held it close enough to really look. The photo must have resembled him enough to pass as him when waved in front of a stranger's face.

Especially if that stranger didn't want to look at you – didn't, in that moment, want to *see* you. Poverty was the ultimate cover; after all, those who *have* often do not wish to look at or see those who *have not*.

But no, I was getting confused. Ryan Marks would be his new name, all perfectly legitimate, for his own protection. No wonder he hadn't existed online.

But Gary Hughes would.

Facebook, let's see. Many men of that name. None of them him. None of them anything like him. There was another link, to someone in America. Not him either.

Into the search window I added the words *Norfolk* and *murder*.

There was a link to a report in *The Telegraph*: *Gasman Killer to be Released*. No photographs, only a block of text, which, frantic by then, I skimmed: *murder of Simone Pullinger… luxurious prop-*

erty... posing as a gas engineer... sexual... brutality of the attack...
maximum sentence.

I stopped, unable to bear it. That wasn't Ryan. Gary Hughes
was not him. It could not be him. A coincidence, nothing more.
When I'd asked him to name the character, he had plucked the
name out of thin air. He might even have met Gary Hughes inside.
Yes, that would be it.

Desperate, I clicked *Images*. Nothing, nothing... and then,
looking directly out at me, those small, round, ink-blue eyes. I
clicked... the photo enlarged – dark spiky hair, the face rounder,
the mouth expressionless. But him. Him, absolutely... my God...
This report was from a front page in the local press – a crude photo
of the *Norfolk Post*, blurred, the text difficult to read, the headline
clear enough: *Gary Hughes Gets Maximum Sentence.*

'No.' I closed down the window, slammed the laptop shut. It
could not be him. It could not. I would not read it. I would not.

I opened the laptop again. Scrolled. Further down the listings,
a video... a documentary. *Panorama: How Murderers are Made.*
Beneath, a list of names that the search engine had picked up:
Sonia Pearce, Bradley Hayes, Gary Hughes.

My chest tightened. No hot slick beneath my skin. Only my
heart quickening, a small pain, like the end of a broom handle
being pressed into my sternum. And my hairline, from one moment
to the next, prickling with sweat.

I clicked on the video link. It was from a little over two years
earlier. The programme began with a grainy clip of two children
playing – a girl and a boy – then another clip showing the same
little girl sitting cross-legged on an armchair, her head cocked
to one side, her bottom lip shiny and pouting, a row of pearly
milk teeth. Soft piano music played over the top, in a minor
key, presumably to lend an ominous atmosphere. Another clip:
a desperately skinny boy with a crew cut and no T-shirt running
around a scrappy lawn with what looked like a Border collie,

taunting it with a ball. And then another little boy. This one was sitting in a hospital examination room, dressed in a hospital gown. He was having his throat examined by a doctor.

'*These children have one thing in common,*' came the voice-over as my eyes glued themselves to this final image. '*They all grew up to be murderers. We ask, what else did they have in common? How are murderers made?*'

The footage was replaced by the title sequence, a theme tune and visuals that, despite never having watched the programme, I recognised.

And you would ask me, I'm sure, if you were here: did you recognise him? Did you *know* it was him? And I would tell you without any clue as to how I would explain it that no, I did not *recognise* him, but that yes, I knew – I knew without a doubt – that it *was* him.

I didn't shout or scream. I did nothing, only sat in the hollow shell of my kitchen and watched as the unfolding images took a wrecking ball to me and my recent life.

The stories were cut together, jumping, teasing. Chronological order. I was glued to every second, wanted at every second to switch it off. I knew that I would watch it again. And again.

The first was the story of a young American girl who had suffocated the school hamster and who then, in adult life, had gone on to murder her adoptive mother and older adoptive sister by stabbing them both to death with a kitchen knife. By the end of the documentary, it transpired from her own lips, in a voice as chilling as it was innocent, that she had been sexually abused by her biological father before she had been taken into care at the age of three – the wet bottom lip, the milk teeth, the words incompatible with the image. The various agencies had not informed the adoptive parents that this had been the case. The poor couple had taken on a child with no idea what they were getting into. The adoptive father looked haggard and haunted, broken and bewildered.

The young boy with the dog had not suffered any abuse beyond weird, neglectful parenting – filthy conditions, some advanced hoarding, mental-health issues on the part of his immediate family. The clip with the dog had been filmed a few days after he had been taken into care. They'd had to shave his head because he was covered in lice. He had gone on to shoot his wife and two young children in their beds, for no apparent reason, before turning the gun on himself.

And so to Gary Hughes, whose story patched itself together in ever more horrifying clips, interspersed, of course, with the equally horrifying and downward-spiralling snippets of the other two children. Gary, who, aged four, was rescued from the basement of a semi-detached Victorian house in east London after a neighbour had heard him calling for help through the air brick. Gary, who was rehoused in Norfolk, who had never settled at school, whose issues had manifested by the age of ten in brutal attacks on his peers and the disturbing, ritualistic killing of baby starlings in their nest, tiny broken birds he had laid out and covered with a tea towel from his foster mother's kitchen. Gary, who, aged twenty-two, off his head on heroin, had brutally raped a woman at knifepoint before murdering her in her home in a village on the outskirts of Norwich after posing as a gas engineer. The case had made national news, over twenty-five years ago now.

Ryan Marks. Not Ryan Marks, but Gary Hughes. Gary, who had been sentenced to double life imprisonment, in acknowledgement of the heinous nature of his crime. There was footage of him behind bars, his face pixelated. More recent footage of him jogging around a courtyard, his face pixelated once again, but his emaciated limbs recognisable even so. The calm voice-over continued but I caught only broken words: *next year… protection… new identity… rebuild his life…*

Him again. In shadow. His voice had been slowed to a deeper pitch, but I heard the East End simmering beneath the corrected vowels and consonants all the same. My body recognised that voice – in the familiar burning of my skin.

'*Definitely.*' He was answering some unseen interviewer. A pause then, that tip of his chin. '*I'm a reformed character.*'

The credits rolled.

'My God,' I whispered, through my fingers. 'My God, my God.'

The urge to vomit came. I dashed to the bathroom. Hung over the toilet bowl, panting and spitting. Nothing. I stood, splashed my face with cold water, stared into the mirror. My eyes were black with shadow, the whites rippled with fine red threads. I leant on the sink, still panting. My legs gave way; I sat on the side of the bath.

Face in my hands, all I could see were his eyes looking into the camera, into my home, into, it seemed, my soul. But his face had been nothing but moving overlapping squares. I couldn't have seen his eyes; how could I? It was not possible.

The journalist's evidence that Gary and my fictional character were not linked other than in name was precisely the opposite: the details of the cellar, the carpentry, the similarity of the cases were his private message to me: *find me*, he was saying. This is who I am. *Sometimes I have to show them*, he had said. But did he think he was a gigolo or did he know he was a rapist? Did he believe himself a murderer or had this woman, in his eyes, got no more than she deserved?

The sister who had lived in the cellar with him, whom he had called 'Baby' and who he told me had died, possibly to incur greater sympathy, had been a complete fabrication. The anger-management issues – they had been the truth. He had spoken not of one woman but of many, all desperate for him to make love to them. There were no doubt more victims, then, hidden in the shadows of shame, afraid to ever come out.

I tried to remember exactly how he had told me this story – tried to picture his body language, whether or not he'd met my eye. It seemed to me, remembering now, that he had been more exact when he told me the early part, and that at a certain point he had become vaguer about the details. I couldn't be sure. I had been a little drunk, and perhaps he had found himself increasingly under the influence too. Had he started with the intention of telling me the truth and then deviated? Had he reached a fork in the road marked *Truth* and *Lies* and chosen the latter because the former was simply too awful to admit to? Or had he decided, quite consciously, to feed me a bucketful of bullshit because it amused him to do so?

There had been no getting his life back on track, no window business, no lonely women in the leafy suburbs of south-west London. Thinking about it, that detail he'd used about cutting off the young apprentice's finger – hadn't I seen that done in at least two movies? One of them a spoof, for Christ's sake. Talk about hackneyed – did people even do that stuff? I didn't know, and I guess that was what he was banking on. I didn't know anything about his world. Oh God, how could I have fallen for it? I was no more than an idiot, the lies no more than I deserved. There was no window maker. There was no tender rough diamond. There was only a violent criminal who, rather than working his way to success from nothing, only to be thwarted by misadventure, had worked his way from Broadmoor to an open prison in south Wales, where he had been held until a couple of years ago.

That left only the whole *we belong together* thing. He was, I saw now, trying to mess with my head. That was all it had ever been. All this time he'd been getting off on the fact that he'd clearly worked his way under my skin – in an almost tangible way. I had thought him sad, deluded. I had felt *sorry* for him. I had thought he *loved* me. But he had done nothing but play with me.

I felt sick. The truth was a bitter taste in my mouth. You could be an ex-con, but once a murderer always a murderer. You didn't get to say 'ex'; the act was too big not to define a person, surely? And I had let him into my house and let him cook me an omelette while we shared a bottle of red wine. Like friends. Like, let's face it, prospective lovers. Marlena had saved me and I had cut her out of my life. And as a consequence of that night, I had gained the career of my dreams, was about to buy the house of my dreams, enter into the life of my dreams.

But I had lost pretty much everything else.

I had to leave town. Naturally. I no longer felt safe. No locks, no amount of security could protect me from that man.

'I am a murderer,' he had joked, with his hideous sneer. 'Only joking.'

'I know,' I had replied, like an idiot.

Idiot! He had breached the boundary of my home, infringed the privacy of my bathroom, encroached upon my best friend's house. But more than this, the hot, slick oil of him had insinuated its way beneath the most intimate boundary of all: my skin.

I handed in my notice the next day. In person, of course, citing my success as the reason. And yes, I watched the head's face fall then recompose itself into a wincing smile, a real lemon-sucking special, which, despite my stress, my urgency to leave town, gave me the most profound satisfaction. A stick-that-in-your-pipe-and-smoke-it moment par excellence. The worm had turned. The underdog had finally had its day. The perennial bridesmaid had become the bride.

Once that deed was done, I had little else from which to cut loose. No husband, no custody of children at weekends. Sarah and I were no longer friends with benefits, nor even friends for that matter. The Tinder and Soulmates collective had failed to kindle even the most meagre fire, and Marlena and I hadn't spoken since that awful Christmas showdown. And Ryan? Ryan had, I presumed, disappeared into the ether and forgotten all about me. I almost texted him to see if he'd noticed his name inside the cover of *Framed by Love*. What I mean is, I knew he had noticed it and read the book. What I actually wondered about was what he'd thought and why he hadn't contacted me to tell me.

Really, though, why? Why, when I had dedicated my damn book to him, hadn't he at least called?

I won't bore you with the endless trips to Wiltshire, the chintz I had to rifle through, the stroke of luck when I found this place, Cairn Farm, formally known as Smith's Farm. Mr Smith's wife had died; he was eager to sell. There was no chain and I was in a rush.

Visions of how it would be flooded my mind the moment I stepped in and saw its darling wonky walls, its low-slung timber door jambs, the higgledy-piggledy vibrant blooms I had yet to learn the names of sprawling through its flower beds. But I had found it – me, myself – and I felt the swell of pride in my chest. I could do this. I could write my own story and live it without anyone telling me what to do and how to be.

I remember my first glimpse of the door coming off the hallway, how I had tried the handle and found it locked.

'Is this the downstairs loo?'

'Ah, no, there's no cloakroom on the ground floor.' The estate agent had glanced at the brochure. 'Let's see. You've got two small bedrooms on the second floor, four beds on the first, one en suite, one bathroom with shower, then you've got your three receptions plus your dining kitchen on this floor. That door there… is your basement. Would you like to have a look?' Obligingly he turned the brass key, and the door swung open onto the square mezzanine from which stone steps descended into blackness.

Creeped out by the dark descent, by the thought of heading down there with only me and a man in the house, I shook my head. 'I'll take your word for it. I'll probably only use it for junk anyway.'

We continued out through the back door to the gravel car park, the garage-cum-barn, the fields.

'Used to be tarmacked, all this,' the estate agent said. 'Chippings make it look a lot nicer. They've taken down the big silage tanks and the cattle sheds. I think they had plans to turn it into a campsite, but the wife passed away.' He checked his notes. 'Never get as long as you think, do you?'

'Quite,' I replied, not seeing the irony then, of course. 'I'll take it. In a bit of a rush myself.'

Take that, Ryan, I thought. *Or Gary or whatever your name is. I bet you never thought I had it in me.*

And so, in early September last year, over two years since my unwitting escape from Gary Hughes, I left my former life behind. Needless to say, I had not written a single word of a new book, had not even thought of a new idea, but there was no way I could have. No way! I had been far too busy, and besides, my publisher wouldn't fire me now – I was too successful!

On the day itself, I texted Marlena.

Sorry we haven't been in touch. Hope you're well. Just to let you know, I'm moving to the country today. I added my new address and pressed send.

She replied: *I'm sorry too good luck Pip M x*

I read it against the prick of tears in my eyes. Not *see you soon*, or *I must come and visit*, but *good luck*. That was pretty final, wasn't it?

'All done, love?' One of the removals men was standing at my door, the last box in his arms.

'Yes,' I replied, stepping out of the house, momentarily perplexed. Neither of the men smoked, but there was a definite smell of tobacco in the air.

'Love?'

I nodded. 'Sorry, yes. All done.'

I followed the removal van for a while before overtaking it on the motorway and relying on the satnav of my snazzy new 4x4. I turned into the now familiar long drive, unhooked the loose piece of pale blue frayed nylon rope – how rustic! – from the gatepost, heard the glorious popping of tyres on gravel as I drove towards my darling crumbly red-brick farmhouse. To the front, those gorgeous Georgian-style windows, the wide front door that I would barely use. Then, as I drove past the side of the house, the funny little window at the bottom that must, I thought, give onto the basement. Two chimney pots that I had quite forgotten about pointed skyward, waiting for me to send aromatic woodsmoke puffing from their terracotta spouts. Round to the back, to where the barn hid behind the main building – and parking for six cars at least – and the empty fields stretched away to the horizon.

Only four months ago; I can barely believe it. Four months is a lifetime. And, as I like to remind you, it is probably the end of mine.

This was it, I thought that day. I was free. From the school, the faceless city streets, the waste-of-space men, the pretentious bars, the complicated entanglements of unclear friendships. I could finally focus on a new idea, write my next book in peace. And Gary. Gary would never find me here.

AUDIO EXCERPT #6

Testing, one, two. Two, three.

Just getting my fucking thoughts together. I need to calm down. I need to calm the fuck down.

Bitch!

Fucking removal van outside her house and not so much as a goodbye. My own fucking fault. It's been a month since I last checked on her. I've been busy; I've let things slide. But I was busy for her. For her! Fuck!

Well, that's not going to happen again. She thinks she wants to move away, but that's just those delusions again, taking hold. Lies on lies. I don't know how she stands it. Not getting in touch when her book was published was low, though. That was fucking low. That book belongs to both of us, and she fucking knows it. An invitation to the launch wouldn't have hurt, would it? But oh no, that would have been too truthful, wouldn't it? She would've had to admit she owed half of it to me, not make up some bullshit story about some decorator and his fucking granite slab. Not even a little thank-you text. Ungrateful bitch. I know she's still got my number. It was there last time I checked her phone and that was only last month.

Did she actually think I'd just fade away? Did she imagine, what, that I wasn't keeping track? She must have known I'd read every interview, every tweet, follow her Instagram, her Facebook and all that inane bollocks. Half, if not more than half of those posts were for me – little messages, little teasers. She knows what she's doing, oh God, she's so delusional it's frightening. And she must have seen me walk by the house. She'd have to have been blind not to. She sensed me, I know she did, outside in the dark all those lonely nights while she wrote her book, smelled my cigarettes on the breeze when she stood out there in her back garden looking at the stars. The restraint, the fucking restraint it took not to step out of the shadows, but she knew I was there. She knew I was there all right.

Can't believe she's moving without telling me. I wouldn't mind but I was just working up to calling round and telling her I'd made head chef. Does she have any idea how respectful I've been, letting her write her book, letting her get on with it? She must have known I'd been in her house all those times while she was at work. She didn't call the police, though, did she?

This isn't working. I feel more stressed than when I started. My blood is fucking boiling here. I mean, who does she think gave her the story? Who does she think gave her the discipline to write it? Where is the appreciation? She owes me. She fucking owes me. I mean, what did she think, that dedicating the book to me would do what, sort me out, thanks and goodbye? A kiss-off – a fucking kiss-off. She'd have none of it without me. Fucking two hundred pounds, that's all I got, and now she's off to some big pile in the country.

Bitch. Fucking idiot self-deluded bitch. Monkeys and typewriters. Instagram and Twitter. The world's gone mad, and here am I having my mental health questioned, having to roll up for check-ups and check-ins and have a fucking statement against my name. Playing their game. It's laughable. And she… she was already mad, with all her bullshit about her process and her idea and all that. I'm her idea! I'm her fucking process. Without me she'd still be a slut with a daddy complex and a drunk and a total fucking fuck-up. Lies upon lies upon lies, when will she learn. She got her book from me. Me, no one else. The dedication's not even my real name for a start and there was no with love there was no with love and thanks no nothing about me in the acknowledgements and where was the door-to-door salesman in those interviews, eh, the mystery man who came into her house and made her laugh and made her think and brought her to life from under the anaesthetic of her mediocre little suburban existence the man who gave her the whole idea the man whose life whose fucking LIFE she stole or believed she'd stolen the man with whom she made the connection of her life? Of her LIFE. Where was he? Where the fuck was he?

I need a joint.

Two. Two, three.

Right. Start again. I've calmed down a bit. It was all provocation. I get that. I'm not stupid. She knew I'd be following all her stupid tweets, her posts, reading the book, seeing it was for me. She wrote that book for me. That book is her wish fulfilment for the two of us. That book is a letter, from her to me. She knew I'd be following her progress, and she couldn't help herself, baiting me with that handyman story. Very clever. She's practically daring me to respond so she can prove she has some sort of advantage. That's her headstrong nature; that's what I loved about her from the start. She's deliberately perverse in the way of understimulated, intellectually unrecognised artists the world over. Even now, on the back of it all, she will know she can write better and that I can help her do that. Deep down, she will know that. And all this moving operation, this charade, well, that's more of the same. The book is her peekaboo from behind the *bedroom door. The move is no more than the old 'chase me chase me' routine. I have to admire the scale. Wiltshire, the removal guy said. Not too far from Weston-super-Mare. A farmhouse, as befits her dreams.*

Well, good for her. I'm proud of her. I just needed to vent. I am proud of her. It's my fault. I should have contacted her sooner. But I wanted to make head chef. I wanted to have something to show. I wanted to impress her. It's not easy, doing what I've done. The odds were stacked, I tell you.

I nearly walked in when I saw the lorry parked outside her house. The front door was wide open – I nearly walked in and confronted her and asked her what the fuck she thought she was doing.

But it's all part of the lies. It's her compulsion – I can see that now I've calmed down a bit, now I'm back at my flat and I've got my little Dictaphone and I can formalise my thoughts. The way she works is this: what she writes, she thinks she wants. What she lives, she doesn't want. Her fiction is her fact, and vice versa. I'm pretty pleased with that deduction, to be honest. It came to me when I read Framed by Love *for the first time. Sure enough, she'd used all the bullshit I'd fed her and added more of her own. Obviously she didn't bother checking the name out – that would be typical of her, ostrich that she is. I have to say, I thought it would dawn on her when she was ready, thought she might wonder where I'd plucked that name from, but there you have it – if it's not fiction, she doesn't give a toss. It's not real, not to her. Only real if it's in a novel. Or a film or TV or whatever. She's pathetic. She'll always be pathetic without me. With me, she could be extraordinary. If she'd only relaxed to the idea of me, she would have known my name. She's written a fucking book about me, for Christ's sake. And these last two years, she hasn't spent one moment without me, without thinking about me anyway.*

And it's the same for me. While I've been getting on with it, making my way from pot washer to waiter to sous chef to head chef at Gino's, she's been my every waking thought. If we were computers, she and I, our minds would be the cloud. Whatever we're doing, our thoughts are shared, one with the other. We exist in two places, separate and together, always together. She would deny it, even now. But that book is full of me – I'm on every fucking page. I don't mean just my name. I'm in it, my essence, in the form of everything she has fantasised about me. I gave her what she wanted, the sanitised bullshit her middle-class sensibilities craved: the kid from the wrong side of the tracks, the rough diamond who knows how to be gentle, how to show a woman a good time. The sex scene is her siren's call. To me. The romance of our long-denied bond is irresistible to her, that much is obvious. The most romantic love is that which cannot be, she said that night. Romeo and Juliet. I get that. I get her. But what's more pathetic is that, even in the fantasy of her fiction, she still doesn't get it, still doesn't know what she wants. What she wants is not romance, not tenderness, not safety. She wants the opposite: cruelty, danger, fear. That's the way to her heart. I know it – and somewhere inside her, so does she.

Cruelty. Danger. Fear.

She thinks she's going to steal my story and leave me behind?

Think again, Pippa Gates. Think again.

CHAPTER EIGHTEEN

Something has just this moment dawned on me, something that has been in the back of my mind all this time as I sit here at my desk, trying to tell you my story. Because I am telling *you*. I'm not writing this for myself. I don't do Dear Diary, can't see the point. It occurs to me that if I am dead, or about to be, then you, dear reader, already know my fate. A posthumous journal is a voice from beyond the grave, is it not?

But more than that, even though we're together in this moment, you and I, you can't see me here, alive, can you?

What I mean is, you there, sitting on your train or your bus seat or curled up on your sofa or tucked up in bed with your cocoa or your cheeky tot of gin or brandy or whatever takes the edge off your own personal – I was going to say hell, but let's say reality – *you* have no sense of *me*. You have no knowledge of my physical reality. You don't know where I am or how I'm dressed or even if I *am* dressed, *oh là là*.

Not that I have any advantage. It's a perfectly parallel situation. After all, I can't see you either, can I? You could be sitting on the loo for all I know, the labours of my keyboard helping to ease your digestive tract after a day's stress-induced gut-clenching. And by the same token, you don't know where I am now – that is, where I *was* when I wrote this…

This.

THIS.

See?

And this goes for anything you read, by any writer, if you think about it: social-media post, magazine article, news report, blog, book. *Your* evening relaxation may have been *their* frenzied dawn; *your* rickety morning train ride may have risen from the blackened lamp of *their* burnt midnight oil. Whatever, you and the writer are together. You co-exist in a unique and special between-time time zone. You are then. And you are now. Except that the writer's now may have happened weeks, months, even *years* ago. That smiling photo you paused to admire while you scrolled through your favourite author's feed earlier might have been taken last year, and who knows what followed it? Gales of laughter. A kiss. A horrid argument.

The end of an affair.

Sex.

Death.

But you only see the smile, there in your now. You see the smile, but you don't see the pink dotted tongue and rogue fillings of mirth; you don't see the wet connection of smooching lips; the contortion of angry mouths, the collapse of legs the broken heart can no longer sustain.

The rolling of bed covers.

The gun.

And how, or in what state, you might ask yourself, did this writer compose the words you find before you on this page? In this now? Did she sit at her desk for hours, upright and formal as a judge, looking out occasionally towards the snow-topped pines of her country garden, or perhaps the golden sands of her beachside retreat? Or was she slouched on a knackered old couch, coffee stains on her jogging bottoms, a hedgehog of sluttish cigarette ends spiked in the ashtray, while outside rain battered the concrete slabs of her thistle-infested back yard?

The page flows. But at the end of which paragraph did she take a break – nip to the loo, say, or raid the biscuit tin or dance around the kitchen? Or perhaps you'd have her poised, possibly in silhouette, with a well-earned glass of red in hand as the sun lowers over those wintry pines, that shimmering moonlit bay. Jazz tinkles – vinyl, natch – on the turntable. Something rustic yet sophisticated simmers on the stove – no, better, the Aga – while she… she… contemplates the metaphorical possibilities of… let's see… her dog chasing a squirrel across the lawn, the pink sun sinking into the sea.

Tell me, reader: how do you see her?

How do you see *me*?

Am I sitting here right now in a silly hat? Am I biting my nails in existentialist angst, weeping for the sheer misery of my broken life? Or am I staring you in the face, meeting your eye in the simmering intensity of a moment, this moment, which spans both my now and yours, telling you that everything you're reading here is the truth?

I just hope my fans remember me – are you one? Do *you* remember me? Online, of course, you'll know me slightly, and, as I've said, even those with little or no interest in the world will have heard or read my name, if only on the front page. Even the most ignorant will know about the Wiltshire Murders. And those of you who followed me when I had access to social media will have seen that I shared elements of my life that I can't share in my books. I've posted glimpses, but never anything truly intimate – like despair, say, or frailty. Or terror.

Mrs D says that my job, my only job, is to finish my manuscript, but this journal feels more and more important, especially as we approach the dark heart of it. I only hope I have time to record everything truthfully before my death. Make no mistake. This is no attempt at exoneration. I will be condemning myself with the utmost severity. After all, as I have mentioned many times, I am dead – what do I care?

So, with two dead bodies buried in the grounds, a bomb of evidence ticking in an airport car park, another one rusting in a lake, I'd better crack on. You are about to be – indeed, you *are* – the custodian of my truth. I'm handing it over to you. Take it. Roll up. Read allabowdit. Hear the real story straight from the proverbial equine cakehole.

I realise I won't be able to record the moment of my *actual* death. That would be impossible. Think about it: tra la la la laaa writey writey write write… night fell like a blanket, stars twinkled like jewels… argh… slump… a sigh (last breath).

No.

And thinking about it, if I'm dead in your now, then here in my now, I don't know that I'm about to be, do I?

Which means that, where my imminent death is concerned, I'm writing in a state of ignorance as to how and when it will take place. And yet, if you're reading this, then my death is, *must be*, imminent and most of you will already know the circumstances. Do you see? My state of ignorance reaches all the way to your state of knowledge, like a lifeline – a deathline, ha! You have the advantage. You know that I'm dead. I'm writing this strongly suspecting but not knowing absolutely when and if I'm about to die.

I love that. I bloody love that. Almost as much as I love the fact that here I can tell the truth without fear of arrest or humiliation or scandal. I don't care, do I? I'm dead, innit? Kaput, six feet under, deceased, late, as bereft of life as the Monty Python parrot. Here I'm at liberty to tell you that my hair needs a wash, not to mention a good cut and colour. On Twitter or Instagram, if only I could access them, I might tell you in chirrupy tones that not only is my hair cleaner than a freshly bleached whistle, the cut sharper than David Bowie's cheekbones, but that Mrs D is a marvel! I might say something like: *Honestly, I don't know where I'd be without good old Mrs Danvers!*

Well, actually, I do. Living off Chinese takeaways, Kettle Chips and Cup A Soup, that's what; inhaling the occasional packet of

After Eights, the tray of Ferrero Rocher I meant to gift-recycle. Not to mention the mess of drunken nights spent looking for someone, anyone, frankly, to put their arms around me and hold me, if only for thirty seconds. But you know all that by now.

Mrs D has put an end to all that chaos, both emotional and nutritional. I used to eat nothing all day in the futile pursuit of a washboard stomach, thighs that didn't meet, a backside you could bounce coins off, et cetera, then find myself by the evening ready to snatch a frozen lasagne from an unattended meals-on-wheels van. I swear to God, late at night in those days, there were back-of-restaurant bins giving me the eye. And this ravenous state always translated, once home, into snaffling whatever fell out of the fridge first – half a can of cold baked beans, a leftover sausage that passed the sniff test, maybe a block of Cadbury's Fruit & Nut secreted in the fridge door behind the white wine... ah, the white wine – go on then, if you insist...

No such nutritional chaos now. Mrs D has trained me out of old habits.

Mrs Danvers has made me see sense.

But I must crack on. This journal is about the truth, and these frenetic flights will not get the truth onto the page. I need to tell you about Bobby. I need to gird my loins and come clean about what happened there. Oh God. This, dear reader, is where it gets tough.

I met Bobby during my first week here, when I first walked into his shop to buy coffee. He was a sign. A beautiful god-shaped sign that my life had changed for the better. I remember banging on the window of Wilson's Stores one evening, and how he waved to me from the storeroom at the back of the shop, his even, creamy teeth pretty much all that was visible of his handsome face. How he strolled over to the front of the shop and, with a teasing smile, drew back the bolts and unlocked the door.

'We're closed, you know,' he said, his flocculent chestnut hair an overgrown tangle, the shadow of fresh stubble spraying a perfect contour over his angular jaw.

'I didn't realise,' I said with a smile.

'The Closed sign,' he said, his grin lazy as he pulled the door open wider. 'That's a clue.'

'So sorry, but I've run out of coffee.'

'Well, we open again tomorrow morning, you know.'

'Ah. Yes, but seriously, if I don't have caffeine I literally won't function tomorrow. I wouldn't be able to drive here. Literally, I'd be dead at the wheel.' What a city slicker I was. I was trying to be humorous, but even so, what a princess. It makes me laugh just to think about the things I used to say.

'Well, we can't have that.'

I was already scuttling towards the shelves. 'Honestly, if I don't get my double espre—' I stopped and peered at the selection.

'Found what you want?' Bobby asked.

Oh yes, I thought. And it wasn't the coffee.

'Do you have Lavazza?' I asked.

'Nope.'

'Illy?'

'It's all there. What you see is what I've got.'

I could tell without turning around that he had not moved, could still see his white T-shirt lifted a little at one side where he'd reached up to the bolt at the top of the door, the hint of toned surfer's stomach beneath. One glance at him on my way in had been a direct gaze into the sun. Now the glorious after-image floated across the retina of my mind's eye – on its way to pay a hefty deposit into my memory bank. I pretended to flick through the coffee choices, which ranged from rank through burnt chicory to vile. I picked one and held it up.

'I'll try this one,' I said. 'Nothing ventured, eh?'

*

The week after, he came and cleared my drains for me, no euphemism intended. He stayed for coffee, which became lunch. As I said to Mrs D, later, when I had been saved, lunch was all it was ever meant to be. But I was weak then, and still prey to the social constructs that had wrecked my happiness from the start: a lovely home, a handsome man, a blissful married life – all the things that Ryan had thrust in my face and ridiculed that first time we met. And Bobby – poor, dear Bobby – promised all those things. On top of which, he was so damn adorable – open and funny, kind and sexy as hell. When he stayed on that day, we got to talk, really talk. He confided in me, told me of his wanderlust, of his fiancée Tessa's objections to his travel plans, her desire to get married and turn the shop into a tourist trap. Funny word, that: trap.

'That's a shame,' I said. He needed sympathy, that much was clear. 'I can see how much it means to you to get out into the world. And there's a whole world out there.'

'I just want one last trip,' he said. 'Get travelling out of my system before I settle down, you know?'

'You're so young,' I replied, taking his empty coffee cup from his hands with the lightest brush of my fingertips against his and placing it on the table. 'You don't need to think about settling down yet, surely? You should be free.'

'I don't think Tess sees it that way. She's keen to expand the business.'

I hesitated a moment until I realised that by business he meant the grotty little shop. Bless. I kept my poker face on.

'That seems a shame,' I offered. 'I think it's perfectly understandable to want to spread your wings. What are wings for if not for spreading?' I smiled. 'There's nothing to understand, as far as I'm concerned. But I suppose not everyone is blessed with an imagination, and Tessa sounds like more of a local, homely kind of girl.'

'It's not like I don't have plans for the shop,' he continued, even though I had not and never would have asked him to defend himself. I was happy to be his sounding board, for him to bounce off me, as it were. 'I've already put in for planning permission to build a café at the back. I'm going to use the rest of the land for a garden. I might even build a maze, or a folly, something that tourists will put on their itinerary.'

'A maze sounds incredible,' I said. 'There's one at Hampton Court, near where I used to live. You should go and see it.'

'I will,' he said, meeting my eye, a shy smile creeping over his face.

'I might even take you,' I said, 'if you're good. And listen. For what it's worth, I don't think you should give up your dreams for anyone. I'd hate to see you tied to something… or someone… just because you thought you had to honour some sort of promise.'

We ended up in bed together. What did you expect? It wasn't my fault. It just happened. We connected. He needed understanding, and I understood. I'm very good at understanding others when I put my mind to it. Reader, let's not forget that I write romance. And whilst, against romantic tradition, Bobby and I found each other attractive pretty much immediately, I still have a vested interest in how two people overcome the obstacles and find their way to one another.

Research is everything.

He left as day turned to dusk. Actually, what am I saying? It was pitch black outside by the time he finally plucked his trousers from the living-room floor. Being late summer, the sun had gone down at around seven thirty. About an hour after Bobby did.

Sorry, couldn't resist.

'I have to get back,' he said, breaking the spell. 'Tessa's cooking me dinner and I should probably grab a shower before I go over.'

'Sure,' I replied, eager to play she-who-would-never-need-anything-more-than-he-wanted-to-give. 'Off you go.'

'Can I see you again?' he asked, hovering on the doorstep.

'I don't know,' I said, fingering his jacket collar. 'You're in a serious relationship and I don't want to be the one to come between you and Teresa.'

'Tessa.'

'Of course.' I kissed him goodbye, hard, bit at his lower lip as I pulled away. It had turned cold outside and I pulled my robe tight around me. 'But we can be friends,' I said, stroking his cheek. 'You can always *visit*.'

He grinned. Ah, the way a handsome man grins – is there anything sexier, frankly, especially when it's because he's picked up the message? All those Tinder dates in boozy, darkened bars; those long Guardian Soulmate Sundays looking around museums and art galleries pretending to be interested. Bobby was the first man I had… encountered… who had held my interest for more than the initial laying-on of eyes. There was a freshness about him that came perhaps from a lack of metropolitan edge. He didn't say things for effect. He wasn't involved in some invisible competition with himself as people so often are in the city. When I asked him what music he liked, he didn't make it about how cool he was. All right, I might have preferred something more sophisticated than Robbie Williams and Kanye West, but out here, it didn't seem to matter. Not anymore.

And the sex? It was good. Really. And if I don't tell you about it here, I'm sorry. With Bobby gone, it feels wrong, even if I *am* dead.

'Goodbye, you,' he said.

'Goodbye, *you*,' I replied. 'And stop grinning like that, before I'm forced to pull you back inside.'

At the door of his truck, he turned and waved before climbing in and gunning the engine. God, he was lush. Tessa was a lucky, lucky girl.

Turned out Bobby felt the need to *visit* every afternoon. Around three or so, he would arrive on his vintage BMW motorbike and I would hear the rasp, the crackle of stone chippings outside the kitchen window. I worked on the ground floor then, which is at the back of the farm, although I wasn't writing. I hadn't had time for writing, what with the success of *Framed by Love* and the subsequent upheaval, and I couldn't seem to get back to it. I was enjoying the prolonged moment. And while it was exquisite having Bobby come to me each day, now, of course, I wish he hadn't. If we hadn't become involved, he would not have been here when, for the second time in my story, there was a knock on the door. I should have known who it was. I should have smuggled Bobby out of the front door. But I did not. And now it's too late.

Blog post: PippaGatesAuthor
#thiswritinglife
Find me on:
Instagram: @GatesPip
Twitter: @PipGatesWrites
Facebook: Pippa Gates Author

One thing, perhaps the most extraordinary thing, about life in the country is the night sky. We think we have the sky in the city, but we don't. We can't see it. It is hidden by the amber glow of street lights, car lights, office lights… all these sources of light pollution block out the majesty in a way I could not have imagined.

Since Mrs Danvers came along, I have learnt all about the constellations. I was always interested in stars, in a kind of romantic way, but not until now have I bothered to study them properly. Why? Because, as in so many other ways, I can finally see. I can see the light, you might say, and it is star-shaped and beautiful. On a clear evening, here in rural Wiltshire, there really is nothing better than a spot of stargazing!

Stonehenge is the obvious place to go, but we tend to leave that for the tourists and go instead to Cranborne Chase, an official area of outstanding natural beauty – an AONB; yes, it has an acronym, who knew? We usually head for the Larmer Tree Gardens, near Tollard Royal, the binoculars Mrs D bought in Bath round our necks – we have a pair each! Sometimes we simply head up to the back of the farm, where there are fields, as you know. We have an app on the iPad that means you need only hold it over your head and it will 'translate' the sky. Oh, the miracles of technology! In those moments of peaceful reflection, we gaze up together and challenge ourselves to identify the constellations.

'What's that one?' Mrs D will ask, pointing up.

'The North Star,' I will say, or, 'The Little Dipper,' or 'Cepheus the King.'

And we smile at our knowledge. You won't see pictures on Instagram, I'm afraid. There's no photograph can do it justice. As with so many things, what we have here has to be seen with your own eyes. If you were to visit us here at the farm, and see how things are set up, you would realise what a small part of the picture Instagram has given you.

CHAPTER NINETEEN

PIPPA GATES: PRIVATE JOURNAL

It was a little over two months after I arrived; before I started *Pushing Up Daisy*; before Mrs Danvers. I had unpacked and the farmhouse resembled a home at last. The contents of my small three-bedroom semi looked rather sparse in the new, larger space, but I liked that. The shortage of furniture seemed to me to be a statement on my new life: less unnecessary clutter, less complication. All right, so I was sleeping with a man who was engaged to a woman in the village, but that would not last. It was a fling, nothing more. Something to ease me over any initial loneliness I might feel. I sound cold, I realise. But that's only the retrospective voice, the distance that comes with a little time passing. At the time, I was very fond of Bobby and utterly excited at the prospect of his daily visits. I cared for him. And when I think about what happened, I do feel terrible, genuinely.

It was about six in the evening. Bobby wasn't seeing Tessa or whatever her name was that night, and so we had planned to have dinner together. It's amazing how even the most passionate affair soon turns its attentions to more mundane matters, such as the buying and eating of food, which wine to get, whether or not to watch a film, rom com or action or worthy subtitled job. I'm not much of a cook, as you know, but I'd bought some monkfish and some bacon for a recipe I'd seen on the BBC Good Food website. I suppose I was working on a how-hard-can-it-be basis.

I planned to commit the method to memory and then pretend I was making it up off the top of my head like they do on the cooking shows that Bill used to watch. I was trying to impress Bobby, I'll admit to that.

We hadn't got around to dinner. We were in bed, legs entwined, sticky with each other's sweat, lazing in a kind of post-coital fug.

'I've never asked you about your books,' Bobby said. Without warning, he slid his arm from beneath me and in one taut, athletic burst was out of the bed and stalking across the floorboards to the little table where I'd put a lamp and a few books for no better reason than wanting the room to look as casual yet artful as one of the homes Marlena featured in her magazine. On the pile was Hilary Mantel's *Wolf Hall*, Zadie Smith's *On Beauty* and my own *Framed by Love*. I'm not sure what I was thinking. That my book might somehow absorb the literary greatness of these other authors simply by sharing a table? Or that this was how I saw myself, as somehow belonging to their ilk, a clear case of delusions of grandeur if ever there was one.

Whatever, I wasn't looking at the books; I was trying to tear my eyes from the lean curve of Bobby's buttocks, the long, slender reach of his golden-dusted legs. He picked up my book from the table and studied it a moment, looking for all the world like a statue of the young Hippocrates. Then he turned back to me, quite abruptly – holy God – and walked slowly back to the bed. He moved no more quickly than if he'd been strolling out, fully clothed, on a warm summer's day. He was so comfortable in his own nakedness, I thought. Whereas I, thus exposed, would run for cover whenever I could, from bed to wherever my clothes happened to have landed. I even did this when I was alone.

He climbed in beside me.

'*Framed by Love* by Pippa Gates,' he read, his tone amused. He flicked through the pages. 'What's it about? Where did you get the idea? Is it based on a real person?'

I dragged myself upright, propped myself up with two pillows against the bedhead and tucked the duvet strategically under my arms. My own self-consciousness aside, I was willing to bet that my tablemates, Zadie and Hilary, would no doubt put their breasts away before discussing their work.

'You've asked three questions,' I said. 'Which one do you want me to answer?'

He grinned. 'All three.'

And so I told him pretty much everything I've told you so far. How Ryan had appeared that night on my doorstep, and everything that followed. How Ryan had become Gary. Bobby listened like a priest in a confessional, breaking his silence only to ask pertinent questions in a quiet, respectful way.

'And that's part of the reason I moved out here,' I said finally. It had taken me over half an hour to tell him.

'To escape him?'

'I suppose so, although that sounds more dramatic than it is.'

'But why didn't you call the police?'

I shrugged. 'I was going to. I would have. But when he was hassling me, the problem was that every time I thought about what it all actually amounted to, it was next to nothing. The keys being in a different drawer compartment, a bit of dried mud, the smell of his tobacco… They'd have looked at me like I was mad, a time-waster. It was me who invited him into my home, me who gave him my husband's clothes. I signed his book with an affectionate message; I gave him a lift home one time after school. What had he really done? A couple of texts and a Christmas card, nothing he couldn't shrug off in interview. He could say he was teasing, or even show them the book I'd given him and say we were involved.

'And then he stopped. I didn't see him for over a year. It was only the documentary that frightened me. That's when I made the move.'

'Did you keep the card?'

I nodded. 'It's in my bedside table.'

'What about the texts?'

'Still in my phone.'

'And did you note down the times you thought he'd been in your house?'

'There was nothing to note down. I thought I'd left the pots on the counter, and when I came home, they were in the dishwasher. Hardly enough for a blue light, is it? I wasn't even sure at the time that I'd left them there... I can be quite scatty.'

Still Bobby looked perturbed.

'You're as bad as Marlena,' I said. 'There's nothing to worry about. I mean, when I found out he was Gary Hughes, yes, that was enough to make me want to move away, but to be honest, I needed a fresh start anyway, and it seemed like the ideal solution. I wanted him out of my life, but I didn't need to call the police or anything, I don't think. If I had, they might have put him back inside, and I wouldn't have done that to him.'

'So you care for him?'

'What? No! But he'd served his time. Yes, he'd been... inappropriate, but he hadn't held a knife to my throat or anything. He was just a bit creepy, you know? And if he was puny and smelled of carbolic soap, that was hardly his fault. For all I know, he might have Asperger's or something; have some kind of difficulty relating to others. It was probably no more than that, a bit of a short circuit when it comes to social clues – you know, what you say and what you don't kind of thing.'

'And you're sure he can't find you here?'

I shrugged. 'Who can be sure of anything? But I've been here for a couple of months now and there's been no contact. No card, no text, nothing. Trust me, he would have sent a happy new home card or something. He wouldn't have been able to resist. I think he's got the message.' I pushed my hand across Bobby's chest and kissed his lovely buttery neck. 'Come on, forget it. We should be talking about something more pleasant. We should be working up an appetite before dinner.'

But Bobby was thumbing through the book. He opened it at page one.

'"Gary Hughes walked down the tree-lined suburban street, surveying the double-fronted Victorian houses, their impressive windows glowing amber in the late afternoon",' he read.

I snatched the book away, giggling. 'Stop it,' I shrieked. 'I can't bear it.'

He laughed, finally seemed to relax and tickled my waist. 'Do you want a drink?'

'Sure,' I said. 'Let's get smashed.'

Minutes later, he reappeared at the door. He was holding a tray upon which an open bottle of chilled Prosecco sweated alongside two glasses, each containing a raspberry. Ah yes, I remember thinking, he must have taken a couple of the raspberries I'd bought for dessert. Cute touch. But I was fighting disappointment. It was all a bit textbook, wasn't it? A bit clichéd?

Not much to say about the interlude that followed. We drank the fizz. We wrapped ourselves around each other and sank into bed.

'Shall I cook dinner?' he asked afterwards.

'No, it's OK, I'll do it.' A familiar melancholy landed and settled in my chest. Perhaps it was the mention of Gary. Of Ryan, as I still thought of him. Perhaps it was me, me alone, a long-suffering condition: the impulse to say *bye bye, baby* as soon as the tender aftermath had reached its inevitable end. No sooner had I possessed him than part of me – and at least this time it was only part – wanted him to go. I'm ashamed to say it now, especially now, even here, even dead.

I wanted Bobby to leave.

If only he had.

The first thing I heard was the purr of a car and the familiar crunch of gravel under tyre. This was before Mrs Danvers put the lock on the gate, obviously. But then it was before Mrs Danvers per se.

A car. A visitor, unannounced, unarranged, unexpected.

'Who's that?' Bobby asked.

'I have no idea,' I lied. I was convinced it was Teresa – or was it Tessa? Tina? – come for a showdown. Bobby's highly recognisable motorbike was parked at the back of the house. Not visible from the road, but whoever was in that car would see the gleam of those curvaceous chrome handlebars the moment they rounded the corner to the parking area at the back. We should have put the damn bike in the barn, I realised. But we'd had other things on our minds.

'Wait here,' I said.

I pulled my robe from the back of the bedroom door and stole downstairs. If it was Teresa, I would act like nothing had happened. I would tell her that Bobby had asked if he could borrow a tool – that's right, a wrench or a shovel or something – from the garage, and as far as I was concerned he was still in there. I would feign concern and say I hoped nothing bad had happened to him. I had been about to take a shower. I thought he'd gone. Then Bobby could sneak out the front way and pretend to busy himself with the hydrangeas. Or something.

From the hallway, I couldn't see out of the kitchen window, which looked out on the car-parking area, and beyond, to the fields. This was before the commemorative cairn, obviously, but we are getting nearer to that.

I crept towards the kitchen and pushed open the door. It was still light outside and I could just make out the corner of the back end of what looked like a people-carrier-type car.

So not Teresa. Unless she had a family car or had borrowed her parents' vehicle.

Could it be Marlena? No, it couldn't possibly be. That wasn't her car, and besides, Marlie wouldn't simply drive out here on a whim, would she? Not without contacting me first. She would send me an email, maybe a text; at the outside, she would call. If Marlie were to come here, it would be on the understanding that we were meeting to try to make things right between us. It would be too momentous a visit to come without calling first.

I took a step further into the kitchen, all the while holding my breath, braced against the possibility of someone looking in through the window. If it was Marlie, then she might well peer inside before grabbing hold of the old brass knocker and banging on the rather dilapidated back door. She might even go round to the front door, the one I never used.

I leant into the old back door, my cheek against the wood.

'Marlie?' I said, too quietly for anyone to hear, knowing absolutely that whoever it was on the other side, it wasn't, couldn't be her.

No sound. No footsteps. No clearing of throat, sniff, nothing. I wondered what was taking so long. All whoever it was had to do was get out of the car and walk about two metres.

'Everything all right?' Bobby had appeared behind me. Despite the dimness of the hallway, I could see that he'd pulled on his boxer shorts and T-shirt, and that his thatch of hair was gloriously tousled on his handsome, toothy head. If it was his fiancée, we were buggered.

I stepped back into the dark hall. 'I think it might be my friend Marlena, you know the one I told you about? But she never said anything about coming. I've not been in touch with her since I got here.'

'Surprise visit?'

'That would really be unlike her.'

'Do you want me to go and look?'

I was about to answer when the knock came. It was almost comical, Bobby and I cowering there in the dark hall like burglars caught red-handed trying to sneak out. Like Gary Hughes, I thought, in the version of his life that Ryan had given me.

'It's OK,' I whispered – why whisper? What reason I gave myself in that moment, I don't know. 'I'll get it.'

Oh, those final moments of freedom, how little I savoured them. How little I understood. But they were only moments. And like life, they were all too brief.

I opened the door. To Ryan. To Gary Hughes. The violent, criminally insane Gary Hughes.

'Step back,' he said.

And I don't know if I heard him say it before or after I saw the gun.

CHAPTER TWENTY

I threw my hands up and did as he asked, bumped against the solid form of Bobby.

'Nice,' said Gary, nodding sarcastically at Bobby.

'Ryan,' I began, heat flashing under my skin. I don't know why I called him Ryan; perhaps some survival instinct – if he thought I still didn't know who he really was, he might be tempted to go along with the pretence we had struck up that first night.

'Shut up,' he said. 'You've done enough talking, and I've done enough waiting, so shut the fuck up and let's get this thing started finally, shall we?'

'What thing?' My voice was no more than water. My insides aflame, a white heat, every sound and smell and sight a dream.

He laughed and shook his head. 'You are a piece of work, you know that, don't you?' He addressed Bobby then. 'And I don't know who you think you are, sunshine, Mr Hunky Local Shopkeeper, but I hope you realise you're sleeping with my fiancée.'

'She's not your fiancée, you prick,' said Bobby, his voice low and loud in my ear. 'So I suggest you take your gun and your mouth and get out of here before I call the police. Pip might not want to put you back in prison, but I have no problem with that whatsoever, mate, so if I were you, I'd leave her alone.'

Gary laughed, louder this time. 'Well, Pip, I have to say, you've got yourself a proper romantic hero there. Well done you. You couldn't write him, could you?'

'Ryan, please,' I said, trembling. 'Gary…'

His eyebrows shot up. 'Ah, so you *do* know my name? Got your little mitts on my real life story, have you? Not quite as romantic, is it?'

'Gary, I—'

He held up his free hand. 'Shush now. You see, the way I look at it, it doesn't matter whose life is whose. Fact is, I gave you *Framed by Love*.' He looked around him theatrically, as if to take in the property. But we were in the hall. It was dark. There wasn't anything to see. 'And it looks like you've done pretty well off it. So by my reckoning, half of all this must be mine.'

A strange noise escaped me, a high and quiet sigh. 'Gary, listen. If you just go, we can—'

'I thought I told you to shut up.'

I stopped, pushed my open palms towards him in a gesture that I hoped told him I'd understood.

He flicked the tip of the gun towards the kitchen door – *go in there*. The gun looked weird, bulbous, like a *Star Trek* weapon or a toy or something. I wondered if it *was* a toy, whether between us, Bobby and I could rush at him and overpower him. But we didn't. I did as I was told and stepped towards the kitchen. Bobby also moved.

'Not you, sunshine,' said Gary. 'Just her. That's it. In you go, Pip, like a good girl, and sit yourself on a chair. Not that chair, that one, over there.'

I tiptoed around the kitchen table and sat down on a chair at the far side. I could no longer see into the hall, only the dark yawn of the doorway. Gary, I knew, must be on the right towards the back door; Bobby on the left, at the foot of the stairs. I was shaking, sobbing – yes, I was scared, terrified, but no part of me could have conceived what was about to happen. Not for one moment. Even now, when I look back, and knowing that it did happen, there's still part of me that cannot believe it; cannot make sense of what should not, should never, have occurred but did.

It was no more than a second or two after I'd sat down. A thick, spitting sound, once, twice, then the thud, the searing ice burn that shot through the core of me as my body reacted to the shock of a violence my head did not yet understand. Bobby's bare foot appeared in the kitchen doorway. The angle of it made me heave. I stood, knocking the chair to the floor.

'Gary,' I managed to say, heart hammering, sweat slick on my back. 'What have you done? Have you stunned him? Is that a stun gun?'

I crept slowly around the table, whimpering, hunched. Bobby was collapsed at the bottom of the stairs, his pale legs crossed wrongly, horribly, his chin pushed into his chest, his face hidden. A dark pool spread across his blue cotton T-shirt. That could not be blood. It could not be. I dropped to my knees. And thinking about this now, remembering this moment, this image of myself floats, as if I am outside it, looking at the cowering curve of my own back. The image warps, blurs. It is not solid. I cannot hold it.

'Oh my God.' I crouched over him, pressed my hands to his stomach. 'Tell me you haven't killed him, tell me you haven't…'

From behind me came the low squeak of the back door opening. 'You'll have to help me get his bike into the barn.'

I turned to look at him: Ryan, Gary. Carpenter. Murderer. The arrogance, the superior edgy charm, had gone. In its place was only malice, and, yes, madness. He sighed and shut the door, plunging us both into shadow. He looked at me with pure disdain, as if I were something less than human, a tramp, nobody. 'Second thoughts, you need to get dressed. Quickly. Move.'

He followed me up the stairs, jabbing me in the back with the gun.

'Move,' he said, and, 'Hurry the fuck up. Come on, there's a lot to do.'

I dressed, shivering, crying, the black eye of the barrel trained on my chest. The flashing burn beneath my skin returned, spread, filled every cell. My fingers wouldn't obey me; they fumbled, put the wrong leg of my jeans on, took it off, tried again.

'Stop messing about, Pippa,' he said. 'This isn't a game. It's not a fucking book.'

'Gary.' I snivelled, sitting like a child on the bedroom floor, the task of pulling on my jeans requiring all my concentration. 'I can… I can call the police. I'll tell them I did it. We can make up a story. Come on, we're both good at that, aren't we? Stories? If we turn ourselves in now, they'll be lenient with us. Please, Gary. I'll say it was me. I'll say he was attacking me and you came in and you… you saved me. Come on, we can—'

'Just put your shoes on, will you,' he said. 'Boots. Something sturdy. Have you got strong gloves, like gardening gloves?'

'I… Maybe in the barn… I don't know.'

Once I'd pulled a sweatshirt over my head, he told me to go downstairs, followed, jabbed at my back with the gun. The weird shape was a silencer, I thought, or perhaps I only thought that later, I can't remember. It was hellish, all of it, every moment, with the cloudiness of a bad dream, the out-of-body sense that I would wake up, that this was not real, but at the same time that I could not, would never wake up. And the all-too-familiar feeling of being filled with glowing embers, beyond heat, if that makes sense. I wonder now if that's the body protecting the brain. This is how shock works, I think. It is there to save us from spontaneous combustion.

'Keys,' Gary commanded. 'To the bike.'

'Bobby leaves his keys in the ignition,' I said, though I cannot have said it loud enough, because Gary raised the gun, and a moment later I felt a hard blow across my cheek.

'Just get the fucking keys. If I want you to tell me something, I'll ask.'

He marched me, whimpering, outside. The keys *were* in the ignition; that's the way it is out here, and at the sight of them I almost wept. Bobby would never ride that bike again. He would never visit. There would be no more afternoons together hidden from the world. It was all I could do to stay upright.

Gary pressed the gun into my back as I took shaky steps to the barn, stood over me while I pulled the heavy sliding door across. When it was open, he nodded towards the back wall, where the old tin troughs were. 'Stand over there where I can see you.'

Pointing the gun at me all the while, he walked, half backward, across the gravel to the bike, climbed onto it and fired up the engine. I thought about running. I did. But it was pointless. I knew he would kill me, sparing me no more thought than he would an insect.

He drove the bike into the barn. The roar of the engine echoed in the rafters. When he turned off the engine, a horrid silence crowded in.

'We can use that old tarp for now,' he said.

I nodded, mute with fright.

He pushed me back towards the house. Inside, the sight of Bobby, collapsed at the bottom of the stairs, made me retch. I clamped my mouth tight, swallowed it down.

'Bobby,' I whispered, eyes and nose running.

Gary's voice came from behind me. 'You're going to have to help me carry him. Take the feet.'

I turned to face him. 'Where are we taking him?'

He said nothing, simply cocked his head and slipped the gun into the back of his jeans. With a pathetic scream, I dashed for the stairs. I have no idea now what I was thinking, but in that moment, my mind was as white as a page and, like a blank page, fresh out of ideas. I scrabbled past Bobby's body, got to perhaps the third or fourth step. A tightness at my shins. The lasso of Gary's sinewy arms.

'Where the fuck do you think you're going, you stupid bitch?' He dragged me back, onto the hall floor, towards the door. The stairs' edge grazed my cheek, scuffed the palms of my hands.

'All right,' I cried. 'All right!'

He rolled me onto my back and let go, his eyes black, the tips of his teeth just visible in his sneer. I could surprise him, I thought. Kick him in the balls and run. But no, he would run faster. He would overpower me in moments. He would drag me back inside and put the gun to my head and pull the trigger.

'Get up,' he said.

I made myself stand. My legs shook; my arms ached where he had dragged me like so much junk.

'Now take the feet.'

I took Bobby's bare feet in my hands. They were warm, and at the touch of them I had a vision of him coming into the bedroom, quite naked, with the tray of Prosecco, the glasses into which he had put raspberries. What a cliché, I had thought at the time. Yet another man doing romance by numbers. Why did I have these thoughts? Why was I so horrible, so bitter, so dark? What was wrong with me? We could have been happy, Bobby and me. It was only me, would only have been me that would have prevented it. Well, that and his fiancée, but he couldn't have been in love with her if he was with me, could he? But even without her, plain sailing, it would have been me that would have ruined us. It was always me, me and my secret and changing expectations, my constant and impossible disappointment. I had thought Bobby just a fling, but he was perfect. He had been perfect. And now he was dead, and it had taken his death for me to see how perfect he was.

'Stop dithering and lift, will you? I didn't ask you to give him a fucking foot massage.'

'All right, all right.'

I lifted. Gary, nearest the back door, took the bulk of the weight. Together we carried Bobby out into the parking area, up to the first field, across, up again to the upper field. We stopped often – me, hands to my knees, panting for breath. There were gates to open, and the ground was uneven and uphill. All the while, Gary scanned the darkening skies, nervous as prey.

We reached the top corner of the field and dropped Bobby's body there. Gary crouched over him, checked for breath, pressed his thumb against Bobby's wrist. A moment later, he rolled the body under the hedgerow.

'Spades,' he said. 'Have you got spades?'

I nodded. 'There's a spade in the garage. And a pick – I think it's a pick.'

He nodded. 'Go.'

I'm not going to go into the practicalities of burying a body, moment by moment. Suffice it to say, it took a long time, and never before or since can I remember my body aching as much as it did after that night. It was after one in the morning by the time we threw Bobby into the hole. The sky was black and littered with stars, stars I had gazed at with such wonder when I'd first arrived here only weeks ago. No more wonder, I thought. From now on, stars would signify only dread, and death.

On Gary's orders, I stumbled back to the farmhouse, my legs by now trembling. I was cold with dried sweat, weeping, covered in mud. And Bobby, my lovely boy, was there at the bottom of the hole.

It was only when we got back to the car park that it occurred to me that we had not shovelled the earth back over him.

But Gary was striding ahead, towards the car, towards the car that looked like a large, relatively new family car, not the kind a lone criminal would ever drive. And there was someone in the passenger seat.

CHAPTER TWENTY-ONE

'Who's in the car?' I called after him.

'Your mate,' he said casually, as if she'd come for the ride.

'Gary, what have you done?' I quickened my pace. Ran towards the car. 'Marlena,' I cried out. 'Marlie!'

I ran around to the passenger side and opened the door. Marlena was slumped, her head on her chest, as if asleep.

'Marlie!' I shook her, but she didn't stir. 'Marlie, it's me. It's Pippa, my love. Wake up, Marlie, wake up. Please wake up.' I began to sob, her head in my arms, against my muddy chest. 'Marlie, wake up, wake up. Wake up, my darling, please.'

'Come away.' Gary pushed me aside. With ease, he scooped up Marlena's body in his arms and headed towards the farmhouse. 'Come and open the door. Hurry up, woman, my arms are tired.'

Weeping uncontrollably by now, lips juddering, I ran ahead and opened the door, tried not to look at the space by the stairs where Bobby had been, the smear of blood on the floorboards.

Gary was already in the kitchen, lowering Marlie into a chair. He propped her against the chair back and stood up, then leant forward and slapped her hard across the face. She stirred, only a fraction, but I saw it and cried out with relief.

'Marlie!' I knelt at her feet. Gary took a step back and let me take her face in my hands. 'Marlena, my love. It's me. It's me, Pip.' I covered her face in kisses, stroked her cold, sweat-dampened hair. She smelled strange: of cooled sweat, grease, fear. Her eyes flickered, rolled, closed again. She groaned. Again I held her head against my chest.

'Oh, Marlie,' I said, weeping. 'I'm so sorry. I'm so sorry, my darling, darling girl.'

From behind me came Gary's soft, cynical chuckle.

'What a waste,' he said. 'Look how much you love her. You were so busy comparing yourself to her, you forgot that, didn't you? You women are all the same. You can't see each other for looking at what the other one has, what she looks like, what she can do, what you don't have, what you don't look like, what you can't do. You're all the fucking same. If you could all stop competing for one second, you could just fucking get on with it. I thought you said the world needed more love.'

I raised my head to look at him. He was still chuckling softly, shaking his head in that hateful, superior way. God, how I hated him. Fear dissolved, re-formed, galvanised into something else. My life was in ruins. I had passed through fire and emerged on the other side, unburnt. My best friend's head was in my arms – she was all that mattered. All the time I had wasted, I could have got on and loved – not just her, but others. I could have got on with it. I could have loved.

But there was no way I was going to give Gary Hughes, or whoever he was, the satisfaction.

'Spare me your fucking theories, Gary,' I spat. 'You think you've got it all worked out, don't you? With your theories, your *chicha* and your secret emotional contracts that only exist in your head. Do you think men are any different? Open your eyes, you fucking idiot. You're all just as bad. The car industry alone would collapse if it weren't for men and their fucking penis envy, you fucking prick. If you've got it so worked out, if you have all the answers, then how come I'm a globally successful author, how come Marlie has an amazing job and two beautiful children, and you, last time I checked, were selling cleaning products – which aren't worth shit, by the way – door to door? Tell me, oh wise one, what's your theory on *that*?'

He raised his hand. I flinched – I remember flinching. And then I was on the floor, the whole of the right side of my face a mass of white, numb pain. I remember that, and the fact that I was still holding Marlie's hand.

'Shut up,' he said. 'Just shut up, for once in your life, Pippa. You still don't get it, do you?'

Shivering, one hand clamped to my face, I knelt up and looked up into those black, black eyes. His face softened – an expression almost of sympathy.

'Our agreement,' he said, so softly it made my skin burn hot, that flashing fire I had felt every time I had seen him, the fire I thought I had passed through only a moment ago but which burned in me even so. 'This isn't about your boyfriend or the woman you're in love with.'

'What? Sarah? I'm not in love with her, she's just—'

'Not her! Your best friend, Pippa. Marlena.'

'Don't be ridiculous. I'm not in love with Marlena, for God's sake.'

That smug chuckle again. My God, how I wanted to punch his rotten, woody brown teeth from his thin grey face.

'You've been in love with her since you met her,' he said, his eyebrows raised, as if to explain something perfectly elementary. 'You see, Pip, this is your problem. The lies. Lies, lies, lies. All day long, all night, how do you stand it? You must be exhausted with it all. You're in love with your little friend here, you always have been, and you can't have her – you can never have her – and that pisses you off something terrible.'

I thought of the time I'd made a pass at her. Her sympathy. *Stop it, Pip. Don't be silly.*

'So you punish her.' He was standing above me as if to impart the word of the Lord, pour his wisdom upon my shame before dunking my sinner's head in the water. 'You've been trying to punish her for years, trying to make her jealous, make her worry, playing fast and loose with your safety so that she'll come running... Admit it, Pippa.'

'No, I —'

'Admit it. There's only me here, my love. No one will hear you. You see, I finally realised what was holding you back from me. All your hesitation, your cat-and-mouse bullshit. You're drowning in love for that woman, Pip. It haunts you. It informs everything you do, or it did until you met me. But even now, she's still in the way. We can't be together until she's gone. And that's what you're going to do for us. Because you hate her too, Pip. You hate her precisely because you love her. You want her, but she doesn't want you. She is the centre of your world, and no matter how many times you cry for help, how many times you say look, look, I'm in danger, no matter how many times she comes running, it will never be enough, will it? She has her family and they, not you – not you, my love – are the centre of her world. You will *never* be the centre of her world. Do you see?'

'That's not true! Your theories are all wrong, they're all mad. You're mad. You're insane...'

His amusement became open laughter now. 'Oh, I am. I'm as bonkers as they come, my darling. But so are you. So are you.' He moved towards me and I turned away from him, saw Marlie blinking, coming round.

'Marlie?' I whispered. 'Marlie, it's me. It's Pip.'

'Admit it, Pippa.' He was close behind me now. I felt the heat of him, felt his mouth at my ear. 'You're in love with your little friend here and that's precisely why you want her dead. That's what hate is. It's all it is. It's OK. There's no one here. Let it go, my love. You'll feel so much better if you do.'

I turned to him, stood slowly, met his eye. Despite myself, I had begun to cry. I hated him. I hated every cell of him. 'You don't know me,' I said, ignoring the tears as they fell. 'You're not my friend, you're not my boyfriend and you're not my priest.'

'Admit it.'

'Stop! Stop saying that.'

'Save me,' he mocked, his voice high and girlish. 'Save me, Marlie. Look, Marlie, I'm walking home alone. Marlie, look, I might get attacked. Save me, Marlie, save me.'

I thought of all the times I'd texted her at 3 a.m., how I'd gone back to strangers' houses, how I'd left at all hours of the morning and texted her, how I'd called her from the station at midnight so she could talk me home. Why? Why call? Was it possible I only went on these adventures in the first place just so that I *could* call, *could* text, *could* make her worry, make myself the centre of her world if only for those brief moments? The times I'd walked through deserted streets, ears pricked for footsteps, and called her so that she could know that this was what I was doing. At the time, I told myself I was giving her something more exciting than her dull, settled life. But I wasn't, and I didn't believe myself anyway. I was taking small and warped revenge. I knew this. I'd always known it. I'd ignored her texts, switched off the phone the night Gary had come into my house. But before that, I'd made sure to contact her to tell her exactly what I was about to do. *Look at me*, I had effectively said. *Worry about me. Think about me.*

Love me.

I sank again to my knees.

Gary crouched down beside me, his breath hot against my neck. 'Admit it, Pip. Admit it all. You'll feel so much better if you do.' He caressed my cheek and blew softly, once, into my eyes, forcing me to close them. 'All this sleeping around, all this drinking, all this fucking *loneliness*, Pip. It can end, don't you see? It can all end.' His knuckle caressed my cheek, over and over, as rough as a paw. 'But not with her. She can never love you like you love her. She can never love you like I can, and there's nothing you can do about that. You know this, Pippa. You always did. Lies. So many fucking lies. You're drowning in them. You can't breathe. Lift your head Pip – lift your face out of this poisonous lake.'

I opened my eyes but I did not turn to look at him. I wiped my nose with my sleeve. There was nowhere to hide from him. There was nothing I could hide *from* him. He knew everything about me, things I didn't know about myself, as if he'd taken a torch and shone it into every corner of my being, discovered all my secrets there, lined up like tombs in a vault.

'I'm going to *liberate* you.' He stood, cradled my head with his hand, pushed it to his belly, the hard line of his ribcage against my hair. 'I'm here to set you free, my love. This is why you need me. It's why you've always needed me. Men like Bobby can't save you. Marlena can't save you. They can't give you what you want. They'll never understand what you want. And they'll never make you the centre of their world.' He pushed my head away and brushed his lips against mine before staring brutal and black into my eyes. 'Only I can do that.'

'I…'

'Stand up.' He gestured at me with the gun, pointing it at Marlena. Another second and he was behind me. 'Stand up and tell your friend you love her and you're sorry for all the shit you've put her through. Look, she's waking up. Tell her.'

On aching legs, I staggered to my feet. Behind me, a rattle, like coins. I shifted my head, caught the angle of his elbow in my peripheral vision. He was attending to the gun. The rattle was bullets on the kitchen table. He scratched them up, dug into his pocket. Was he unloading the gun? I did not dare look around, not fully. A click. Yes, he had unloaded it, removed the danger now that he'd dispatched the male rival. He didn't need a gun to kill me. He had strangled a woman in cold blood.

Marlena was blinking, blinking, screwing up her eyes, blinking, focusing. She met my gaze and her dry lips pressed themselves together, seemed to want to smile. I thought of the terrible things I'd said to her, all the times I'd enjoyed her outrage at the stories I'd told her, bathed in her concern like a child whose mother brings them hot chocolate, rubs their little hands after a cold walk home, puts her hand to their brow when they're sick. I had wanted her to cherish me like that, like a child; she, who was so stable, who would never flip out, never abandon me. And yet I resented her for all of these things – for her safe, warm home, her stability.

And even as these thoughts ran through my mind, I think I knew that no matter what she did or had done for me, it had never been enough. It would never have been enough. She always returned and always would return to her family, to Steve and the children, to her parents, and, once home, would forget about me until my next crisis. And so I lurched forward to that next crisis, so that I could have her again, if only for a short time. Veiling myself in some fabricated rebellion, what I actually sought was danger, drama, shadows in the dead of night. *Look at me, Marlie. Save me. Love me. Look how drunk I am, look how helpless, kiss my forehead and put me to bed.* And as the years passed, never getting her completely to myself to the exclusion of everyone else, I had convinced myself that I resented her, resented everything she had even though I didn't want it, not really. I had never wanted it. It was her I wanted and yet didn't want, knew that even if one day I had her, really had her to myself, it would still never be enough, because no one was enough – no one had ever been. But still I loved her and still I hated her. It was just easier to foster hate than to carry on humiliating myself, to carry on resenting myself.

What a mess. What a fucking mess.

And Bill. Bill *had* loved me, more than anyone else. He had been mine alone. I had been his centre. But I had convinced myself that he wasn't enough, that what he did fell short, because it was easier to find him wanting than to look at myself. I had convinced myself that true love, or a *better* love, lay out there somewhere, when all the time I'd had it in my grasp, right in front of me. At least, I'd had as much as anyone ever gets: the raw material, the starter pack, the kit. But love doesn't exist on its own. It is not something you sit back and wait for. It requires input. Work. Faith.

What a waste. What a waste.

'Pippa,' Marlie croaked.

I ran my hand down her face, took her taped-up hands in my own filthy, bloody fingers.

'I'm so sorry, Marlie,' I said. 'I'm so sorry.'

She closed her eyes. A tear slid from each and rolled down the edges of her face. My head spun. I was weary, so weary.

A nudge on my shoulder.

'Here.' Gary put the gun into my slack grip. 'You've told her you love her. Now I'll tell you why you hate her. You're impossible, and you know it. Anyone who gets close to you turns away from you in the end. Little Miss Marlie here is all you've got left. Her and me.' He stepped half in front of me so that I could see both him up close and Marlena in the chair a little way behind. He stared at me, his eyes fathomless voids. The slick burn beneath my skin came stronger than ever, the feeling of being wholly electrified. 'You love her more than anyone else in this world. But she will never love you like you love her and it kills you. It kills you, Pippa, and it poisons you every fucking day. She has her kids, she has her husband. They are the centre. Not you, Pippa. Never you.'

Over and over he said the words. I held the gun in my hand. The repeating and repeating, the taunting playground rhythm, *never you, Pip, never you.* I looked away, beyond the square of his shoulder, to Marlie's brown eyes on mine, the eyes that had looked at me with such sympathy, eyes that had rejected me, judged me. *Stop it, Pip. Don't be silly.*

'Pip?' Her face crumpled in confusion.

'She will never love you as you love her,' came Gary's thick, educated voice. A voice in which he had trained himself to speak as he had educated his mind inside the walls of his stinking cell.

'Shut up,' I said – to whom I wasn't sure.

'You will never be the centre,' he whispered, and it was only then that I was aware of him moving, prowling cat-like behind me once again. 'And that is why you hate her. Your love is your hate.'

The blade of a knife at my throat, the vice of his hand on my shoulder. 'Now, my love. You need to end it. It's her or you now. Pull the trigger, Pip. Pull it now and we can be together at last.'

'I won't,' I whispered. I couldn't move. A line of sweat ran cool from my armpit down my side. A mind game, another mind game: *shoot your friend with an empty gun*. A symbolic act.

'You will.'

'I won't. Stop saying that.' *Shoot your friend with an empty gun.* Was it empty? Had he left one barrel loaded? Russian roulette? Was that the game?

'Oh, you will.'

'I won't.' A pressure against my neck. A pressure against my forefinger. 'I won't.' *Shoot your friend with an empty gun. Russian roulette.* 'I won't. I won't.'

'You will, Pippa.'

Shoot your friend. A symbolic act. Knife against your throat. She will never love you, not like you love her. Your mummy left you. Your daddy left you. Everyone turns away in the end. Shoot your friend.

'I. Won't.' Steel against my forefinger. Blade against my throat. My head spins. My vision blurs. I am weary, so, so weary. *She will never love you.* A dull, lisping thud.

'Oh, good girl.'

'No.'

Marlena. Jerking backward, slow and fast. Her eyes widen and close, disbelief and realisation, shock and peace. I turn the gun in my hand, look down at it, feel its weight in my black, grimy hand. *No. No, no, no.*

'Marlie!' I cry out. 'Marlie!'

She collapses forward, falls into my arms. I hold her to me. I hold her. She is mine. Mine at last.

CHAPTER TWENTY-TWO

PIPPA GATES: PRIVATE JOURNAL

Whenever I think of that moment, the moment I killed my best friend, my heart tightens. Though the pain is less now than it was. Gary told me later that he'd simply walked into her house and told her to get her car keys. I didn't believe him. I still don't. I think he inveigled his way in, asking after me. And from there, who knows. It was a shock to learn that she'd been home during the day, an even greater shock to discover that this was because she was on maternity leave. A third child, a little girl, and I didn't know. Hence the new people carrier. She hadn't texted to let me know about the baby. That hurt.

Gary said he'd left the baby in her car seat on the kitchen table. That's why I don't believe that she left without coercion, without violence. She would never leave her child. He drugged her, there in her home. Handy with a syringe, years of practice, underworld contacts. No problem for a man like him. The baby must have started crying eventually, alerted a neighbour. But by that time Gary would have been halfway here, long beyond copying my address from Marlie's phone into her satnav.

'I wanted to talk to you properly before she woke up,' he said days later, when he had deigned to speak to me again. 'I was going to explain everything, but you had a visitor, didn't you? Always making everything more complicated than it needs to be.'

I can't believe they haven't traced Marlena out here yet, that they wouldn't have spotted her car on CCTV or something.

Even accounting for sluggish bureaucracy and lack of resources, surely in the case of a missing person, especially a happily married working mother of three, they would find the means? It saddens me sometimes that the police didn't come to me as a matter of routine. I was her best friend after all. *They don't see each other anymore,* Steve will have told them, if my name even came up, which I doubt it did – why would it? *Haven't been in touch for a year or two now.* And of course her mobile phone will be long gone, thrown in the sea or something. Buried with her, perhaps.

But as my saviour from all of this, Mrs Danvers, reminds me: my job is not to worry about such things anymore. My job is to write, here at my desk. I have banished procrastination to that other country: the past. The outside world and its mundanities are not my concern. I must sit my scrawny ass down and do what I failed to do before Mrs Danvers saved me: follow up on the success of *Framed by Love* before it fades from public consciousness, whilst keeping the reality of my circumstances (the reality you're reading here and which will become ever more clear) strictly under wraps. The grisly truth behind *Framed by Love* and all that followed must never come out. If it does, if it has, then you'll know it, because you'll have seen it on the news and I'll most likely be, as we've discussed, dead.

I am not a betting woman. But if I were, I'd lay money on that.

As you have read, it turned out that the story I had written, contained within the actual pages of *Framed by Love*, was a fiction based not on a truth but on another fiction, which in its turn was like any fiction that ever was – part truth, part imagination, part extrapolation of that old fictional chestnut, the *what if?* scenario. Throw in a little subconscious, a nod to what the reader wants, maybe an anecdote overheard on a bus, a chance remark that sticks… whatever, the flotsam and jetsam of what makes a good yarn told over two hundred and fifty pages, give or take. Truth or lies? It's academic.

Talk to the author of the grisliest crime novels you can imagine and you might find an ex-cop, the indelible dirt of street life rimmed in brown crescents under his world-weary fingernails, or it's equally possible you'll find the kindest, funniest scone-baking cutie-pie, a rosy pink mouth in which butter wouldn't melt. Talk to the creator of a gigolo action-man spy and yes, you might meet a man in a tux who can unzip your dress with one hand whilst shooting a man dead with the other, or you might equally find yourself faced with some kindly pensioner living in a bungalow in Lyme Regis, happily married these past forty years, fifteen grandchildren and counting. Romance writer? Well, while I'm sure some romance writers live up to the popular image, dictating their stories from their chaises longues while draped head to toe in pink velour, burning through marriages like so much kindling, some may well have married their high-school sweetheart and be living out their lives in sugar-coated pastel shades of happy-ever-after. Or they could be like me: someone who wouldn't know love if it kicked them in the face wearing steel-capped boots.

The point is, who knows? Novel, blog post, Instagram, Twitter, Facebook. Whatever the fiction, whatever the story, you can never know who made it, or what lies behind it.

'Well done,' Gary said, while I watched, horrified, as he lunged forward and threw my best friend over his shoulder. 'We need to move. We have a lot more work to do yet.'

He whipped the gun from me and flicked it at the kitchen door, indicating that I should lead the way outside. His face was dark with mud, his sweater covered in blood and earth. In a trance, I went, caught between disbelief and the deepest of all human needs: to survive.

'Open the garage,' he said.

I obeyed.

He carried my beautiful Marlie into the barn and laid her on the ground. I winced, my shoulders braced at the sight of her on that cold stone floor. My Marlie. My best friend and, yes, the love of my life. Steve and the kids would be wondering where she was, because, just as Gary had said, she was the centre of their world, they the centre of hers. Her last sight was of me, my finger on the trigger, but her last waking thought will have been of them. They could not know, even now – in my now, that is – that they would never see her again. But if this comes out, they will. They will know already. Steve will have taken the call, identified the body. It will have been in the papers. Oh God, the thought of it. The Wiltshire Murders. My name alongside Gary's. But they will never think that I killed her. That I pulled the trigger and shot her in the heart. They will pin it all on him, unless… unless they read this. How strange – my posthumous journal will exonerate him of at least one crime. And I, I have redefined myself in act and word. *Author names herself as murderer.* Murderer trumps author in anyone's deck. I am no longer an author. I am a murderer.

Was.

Gary straddled Marlie's body, there on the concrete floor of the barn, and aimed the gun at her chest. Unable to bear it, I turned away, closed my eyes, heard that dull spitting sound, once, twice. He had not taken the bullets out of the gun. He had not emptied the gun but reloaded it. The urge to be sick came again, but I clamped my hand across my mouth and it subsided. But he was already wheeling the bike backward out of the garage.

'You'll have to drive the car,' he said. 'We need to be quick, but we'll have to be careful too. I'll lead the way. We'll take the back roads, avoid the cameras.'

'Where are we going?'

'We need to dump the car – Christ, what do you think, Pippa? Wake up! The bike we can bury or dump in a lake or something, but I can't dig a hole for a fucking car.'

'How will we get back?'

'If you try anything funny,' he said, ignoring me, 'I will fucking execute you, do you understand? You're in this with me now, Pippa. Where's your phone?'

'In my bedroom.'

'All right.' He glanced towards the upstairs windows, then at his watch. 'OK, so it's 2 a.m. It starts getting light at around seven. We have until then. Let's go.'

A feeling of dread lodged low and solid in my gut. But if I'm to be honest – and after all, that's what this journal is about – I would have to admit to other feelings too, no matter how difficult and unpalatable that might be for either of us. Because the fact is, reader, I was gripped. I can think of no other word for what I felt. I was utterly tuned in, turned on to what we were doing, to what I was doing. The shock was fading, quicker than I would ever have thought it would. If my heart pounded, which it absolutely did, it wasn't solely fear that accelerated my pulse. It was excitement, raw and intense, a kind of orgasm of the blood.

I waited, trembling, on the gravel in the dark, while he covered Marlie's body with the tarp.

'Come on,' he said, closing the barn door behind him. He stood close, his face in mine, his black eyes on mine. 'You're going to follow me. But listen to me now and listen well. I will be watching you. Every metre, every centimetre. I'll see the turn-offs before you do, I'll know they're there, and if I see you so much as swerve in their direction I will turn the bike around and catch you before you can change gear.' His mouth on my ear. 'Trust me, you don't want to do that. Do I make myself clear?'

'Yes,' I said. 'I won't.'

He jumped on the bike and led the way, the triangle of Bobby's leather jacket on his back, the back of his hair below the helmet, dancing fronds lit only by my headlights. I followed him through the night, my hands soldered white on the black leather of the steering wheel. The same thought revolved around my head, never leaving, never letting me go: everything he was doing, everything that had led him from that night in my kitchen to this moment now, out on these deserted roads, was for me. It had all been for me. I, no one else, was the centre, the epicentre, of his world.

We drove for about half an hour, maybe three quarters. Vaguely I was aware of street signs and roundabouts, but mostly I focused on Gary, on keeping the car on the road, on not driving it into a hedge. The sky lightened. I became aware that we had joined the main road, and then that we were heading for the airport; a little later, as we hit the smaller airport roads, that we were following signs for the long-stay car park.

Gary pulled up to the barrier. He took off his helmet, parked the bike to the side and got into the car.

'Move forward,' he said. 'Take a ticket from the machine.'

I did as I was told. Crawled across the great expanse of tarmac, row upon row of cars, dead dystopian hulks in the black night. At the last row, he indicated a free space. I parked, killed the engine and exhaled in a long, shuddering breath.

'My God,' I whispered, forehead to the steering wheel. 'What have we done?'

'Get out,' he said. 'Hurry up.'

'All right.'

'Have you got your parking ticket? And the car key?'

I nodded.

'Give them to me.'

He too got out. He was wearing Bobby's biking gloves, though I could not remember having seen them or having seen Gary pick them up. He shoved the ticket into his jeans pocket and handed me another ticket, stamped with an earlier time: 17.36. This he told me to place on Marlena's dashboard. I did as I was told. He locked the car and thrust the key into his pocket along with the now-redundant ticket. 'Come on.'

I followed him back to the bike. He closed the visor. 'Jump on the back.'

Automatic as a robot, I climbed on behind him, felt his thin torso beneath the thick leather of the jacket, smelled the oil of his hair, the patchouli on his skin. He started up the engine. I noticed he kept his head down, clearly not taking any risks. There were no cameras that I could see. Or maybe I never looked. My memory of that evening is imprecise, its sounds muffled, its colours muddy. I can remember the smell of oil, the greasy thickness of Bobby's leather jacket on the palms of my hands.

We came to the short-stay car park, this time a multistorey. Again he took a ticket from the machine, and we climbed to the third floor before stopping at a beaten-up but rather lovely navy Saab.

I got off the bike. He handed me a ticket and lifted his visor, but only a little.

'Get in and follow me. No tricks.'

I nodded.

He dug in his pocket and produced a twenty-pound note.

'You need this to get out.'

'If only.'

I could tell by the crinkle in his eyes that he was smiling, but it was a moment, nothing more, before his gaze blackened once again. 'No tricks.'

'I get it.' I looked miserably at the key in my hand. I like to think now that in that moment some cloudy awareness of where he was going with all this was beginning to dawn. We were heading to the source, I thought. To where all this began.

A little over forty minutes later, we arrived back at the farm. My watch said 3.57 a.m. As soon as the engine died, I burst into tears.

The car door opened with a loud rusty squeak.

'Get out,' he said.

I was shivering. I stood. The shivers became shakes. He put his arm around me and marched me, shuddering violently now, to the farmhouse.

In the hallway, he stopped and said only, 'Basement.'

I sniffed, wiped the tears from my face with my sleeves and opened the door to the cellar. Behind it was a pull cord for the strip light, which flickered and chimed into stark white life. I had only been down here once, the day I moved in. I had been too scared to go down again.

'Please, Gary,' I whispered.

He said nothing, just pressed his hand between my shoulder blades.

Fearing he might push me down the stairs, I moved. I took the steps one by one, blinking against the glare of the strip light, snivelling, my hand tight on the cold metal banister. A smell of damp, of concrete, of dust.

I reached the bottom and entered the stark, cold space. On the floor, against the far wall, were tins of paint – drips long dried against their sides in the faded colours of the farmhouse walls. There was a length of dirty white cloth – a ground sheet or something. A dilapidated shelf unit by the tiny window at the top of the cellar wall had rusted almost entirely to brown; it held nothing but an old pair of men's work boots and a flimsy plastic toolbox, open, with nothing in it. I was still weeping, I realised.

'Gary,' I said, my voice a croak.

I turned to face him, but before I could take anything in, he grabbed my hand and yanked my arm round to my back, spinning me round to face the paint tins and the junk once again. I heard the rip of tape, felt the stickiness of it on my wrist before my other arm was yanked behind me and taped to the first. A hard shove at my back sent me falling to the floor. I managed to stagger, enough not to hit my face. My ankles then, dragged behind me, until I lay prone, the hard floor cold, gritty against my cheek. The rip of the tape. My legs pulled at, my ankles bound.

'Not my mouth,' I whimpered. 'There's no one to hear me, Gary. Please.'

He ripped another section of tape; I closed my eyes as he pressed it over my lips. He stood, turned and walked away.

Please don't go, I thought. *Don't leave me here.*

But he was already at the foot of the stairs. He was not looking at me.

'Where are you going?' I tried to say, but of course my words were no more than muffled noise.

He continued, his boots scuffing the concrete steps.

I groaned. Sweat sprang up on my skin. I tried to sit up but could not.

Don't go, I thought. *Don't go.*

He stopped, as if he'd heard my thoughts, glanced at me and shook his head. Saying nothing, he kept climbing towards the cellar door. The door closed. A moment later, it opened again, and a thick blanket landed at my head. Another moment, a click, darkness thick as petrol. The bang of the door. The rattle of the lock. Then silence. Blackness. Solitude.

Blog post: PippaGatesAuthor
#thiswritinglife
Find me on:
Instagram: @GatesPip
Twitter: @PipGatesWrites
Facebook: Pippa Gates Author

I seem to be in a melancholy mood today, I'm sorry. Mrs D has just told me that Marlena of all people has gone AWOL, what is it, three weeks ago now? It's in our former local paper. And with Bobby Wilson missing too, it just all feels a little close to home. I barely knew Bobby, of course – I said hello to him in the shop, but that's all. Marlena, though, is another matter. I just really feel for Steve and the kids. Where the hell could she have got to? Apparently she'd been suffering with postnatal depression, as she had with her first two children. According to the papers, there's no sign of the car, no note, nothing. It was a shock to read that they'd had another child, I have to say. A little girl, three months old. Marlena had been at home on maternity leave. No one saw her go, nor anyone call at the house. The police found the baby in a car seat on the kitchen table, come to no harm, thank God.

I'd had no idea she'd had postnatal depression with the other two. I would have known that, being her best friend. Wouldn't I?

According to reports, there's no trace of her phone. That would suggest she's either left it somewhere or lost it. She'll be all right. She'll turn up. Probably just needed some space.

I always told her to come and see me out here whenever she wanted, take a break from her manic domestic life. I should call Steve, I really should. But he and I were never close. And since moving out here, I guess I feel I'm not part of their lives anymore. Sometimes, when you move away, that's a weight you must bear.

As for Tessa Nichols, Bobby's fiancée, she must be breaking her heart. His motorbike gone was the thing she first noticed, according to the report, poor girl. All the local places have been scoured. There was CCTV footage of him at Bristol Airport, but they searched the car park and found nothing. They're saying he's made a break for it, gone travelling. But poor Tessa even so. I feel for her, so much, and I think she'd be surprised by that. Sometimes I think it's a shame that we can't let strangers know that we're thinking about them. In this case it's with deep sympathy, but we hide other things too, don't we, out of fear? Admiration is a good example. We think we might come across as weird or creepy or just plain mad. And, of course, we hide love, if we think that by confessing it we will lose the object of that love. Sometimes we have to keep love secret. What is it they say? The most romantic love is the one that cannot be.

I am learning, of course, through the lovely emails and Facebook and Twitter messages, and sometimes even the handwritten letters my agent passes on to me, that there are those of you out there who love *Framed by Love* and cannot wait for the next book. That is a comfort and an inspiration. And so, dear readers, I must write! It is to you and for you that I say toodle-oo! TTFN. *Hasta la vista*, babies!

CHAPTER TWENTY-THREE

PIPPA GATES: PRIVATE JOURNAL

The past creeps up, a shadow ever lengthening as the sun sets on this grimy tale.

The author, me, incarcerated both in this moment of my story, before my salvation, and there, with you as you read these words spoken by the lips of my ghost. A prison, a farm basement – not much to choose between them, not really.

And so, dear reader, my country idyll was brutally destroyed. My lover and my best friend dead, my tormentor become my jailor. Yes, they were dark days, my darkest ever, before Mrs D saved me, before I allowed myself to *be* saved.

The day after my abduction – is it still abduction if you get locked in your own home? – I woke stiff and shivering in the foetal position on the concrete floor. My skin was sticky with a mix of tears and dried dust, the concrete rough against my face. At the sound of the basement door opening and closing, I realised that I'd been woken by the key in the lock. I was so cold. I could not believe I had slept at all.

By my watch, it was 7 a.m. A faint smell of bacon. Coffee. I dragged myself upright. My muscles, my very bones groaned in pain, a thick phlegmy taste in my mouth and throat. I blinked against the thin dawn light filtering through the filthy window high up on the wall. Down the steps came the thud of boots. The aroma of food intensified.

'Gary,' I tried to say but of course could not.

By degrees, he transformed in my line of vision: black lace-up boots, then denim-clad legs, then headless hoody man, and finally, fully formed adult male. I saw that he was carrying a tray with what looked like food and a cup of something hot. He did not look at me. So garrulous the day before, today he was mute.

He walked towards me, taking his time. In front of me, he bent over and laid the tray on the floor. On the tray was a white plate. On the plate were two sausages, two rashers of bacon, two fried eggs, two rounds of buttered toast and a mound of baked beans. Hot coffee steamed in a floral china mug I recognised. Saliva pooled in my mouth. My stomach let out a loud gurgle. The urge to remove the tape from my mouth was unbearable. And I needed to pee.

He squatted a moment, analysed me as if I were a casualty in A&E and he the doctor assessing the damage. In one swift movement he reached for me with his bony fingers and whipped the tape from my mouth. I yelped at the sharp pain, resolving as I did so never to do that again, never to give him the satisfaction. A second later, my lips stung, wet and slick; a trickle ran down my chin. I edged out my tongue, tasted the metallic tang of blood. I licked at it, but it came thickly, ran down my chin. The bastard had whipped half the skin off my lips.

But he wasn't looking at me. He had already stood and was now at my back. He must have had a knife, the same knife he'd held to my throat, I guessed, because he cut the tape from my wrists with one swift slice. I snatched my hands away, brought them round, rubbed at my chafed wrists, which were red, puckered with the marks from the tape. All the while, I licked at my lips, could only imagine what I must look like with blood all over my mouth and chin: some mad carnivorous beast, some half-human cannibal locked in the cellar.

He stalked back round me, stopped, crouched quickly, in that lithe, lean, panther-like way he had, then took the knife to my ankles. I gasped with relief, flexed my feet, rolled them round to loosen the stiffness in the joints. I longed for a soft chair, a soft bed, a shower to wash the sticky grit from my skin, the grim smell of the night and its sweat, blood and earth.

I pictured Marlena in the barn, covered in the old tarp. She would be cold, I thought. Blue and rigid. Marbling slowly, turning to stone. It could not be. And yet it was. And here *I* was, a prisoner, a murderer, a madwoman.

Lips pressed tight, Gary nodded at the food.

'Gary,' I tried to say, my voice dry as dust.

Finally, he looked at my face. His eyes narrowed in disgust. 'Oh Jesus Christ.'

A woman broken. An animal. Grubby, exhausted and bloody. I attempted to lick and wipe the mess from my chin, but it smeared together with the dust and the soil, and then my hands too were brownish and crimson, sticky – a cold stink of iron.

He stamped away, huffing and puffing, as if my bleeding were a great inconvenience, and returned minutes later, by which time the blood was trailing down my neck. He knelt in front of me and set a basin of water and a full kitchen roll on the ground. Brow furrowed in concentration, he tore off a wad, dipped it into the water then pressed it to my face. This he repeated, his inky eyes fixed on the task, until my mouth at least felt clean. I wanted to close my hand over his as he tended to me, to look him in the eye and say his name, but I did not.

'Eat,' he said, and stood.

'My hands.' A croak. 'Can I at least wash them? And I need to use…'

As if he hadn't heard a word, he crouched and retrieved the tray.

'No,' I croaked, my heart pumping. 'Don't take it.'

But he did take it, silently, his expression utterly neutral. I scrambled to my feet but immediately toppled over. My vision blackened. All strength in my legs had gone. To my horror, my bladder gave in, my jeans warm and wet.

'Come back,' I called hoarsely after him, forcing myself up again.

But he was at the top of the stairs, he was opening the basement door, he was closing the door, he was turning the key. My cooked breakfast, which I could still smell, had been withdrawn.

A punishment, then. For my rudeness. My ingratitude. For the words *at least*.

I sat down on the floor, panting, weeping, whimpering.

'Bastard,' I whispered. 'Bastard.'

I would have to be more careful. If I wanted to eat. If I wanted to live.

Silence. Meagre daylight from the grimy little window at the top of the wall.

I plunged my face into the basin of water. Wondered if I could drown myself, whether I had the will to keep my mouth and nose submerged until this wretched life left me. There was nothing in it now of any meaning. Gary Hughes was the only living person I had left. A sadist, a psychopath, a murderer. A jailer. *My* jailer.

How different this version of him was from the man in my kitchen, that sinister but thrilling presence I had found, I realised, terrifying and electrifying and revolting and irresistible. I drew my face from the water, listened to the drips fall from my chin into the water: plop, plop, plop. With the remaining bloody water solution, I rubbed my face and hands clean as best I could, letting drops trickle into my mouth. The water clouded with blood and earth. It was not fit to drink, but if it was filth, at least it was my own filth. Finally, I sat in the bowl as best I could and soaked the crotch of my jeans. I knew the water would turn cold as it dried, but it was all the dignity I could salvage.

I lay on the frigid floor and shivered, pulled the blanket over me and curled up.

No sooner had I closed my eyes than Marlena fell towards me, her brown eyes rolling back in her head. The shots: one, two. Her body laid out on the hard barn floor, still, cold, marbling by degrees. Her lovely eyes closed. Marlena under the tarp. Marlena sucking a mojito through a straw, laughing. Marlena with her coat over her pyjamas, no make-up, shadows under her eyes. *Are you drunk or mad?*

I was beyond mad. If I'd wanted her to look my way, why couldn't I have told her a joke, like a normal person? Sent her a funny text, cooked her dinner, called round for a cup of fucking coffee? No, I had to throw myself to the floor like a child, a toddler having a tantrum in the middle of a store: *Look at me, look how I suffer, feel sorry for me. Love me. Put me me me at the centre.*

Marlena falling towards me, her head in my filthy hands.

I must have fallen asleep again, because when Gary returned, it was midday. I was woken by the key in the lock.

He was carrying a black leather bag with a neat handle, a little like an old-fashioned vet's case. He set it on the floor and surveyed the room a moment, his eyes slits of concentration. He looked so clean, that scrubbed look I had first noticed, but as he walked past me I noticed that he smelled good, of better soap, *my* soap, of drier towels. He was thicker-set, too. His job in a restaurant kitchen had laid a layer of meat on his scraggy bones. He was still wearing Bill's clothes, though, which was disconcerting.

After a few seconds, he pushed the shelf unit away from the window – a loud scraping, enough to make your fingernails drop out. I watched, my fingers hovering over my thick, scabbed lips. He took out an electric drill, screws fatter than any I'd ever seen, and various bits and pieces. I'm not going to give you all the details since this isn't a DIY manual, but suffice to say, with deafening noise and dust but no words at all, he attached a metal panel, about thirty centimetres square, to the cellar floor. To that panel he attached a chain, and to that chain he attached a cuff, and to that cuff… yes, you've guessed it, he attached me.

'Gary,' I said gently. 'You don't need to do this. Let's talk. We can talk about this.'

He jutted out his stubbled cleft chin and brought air through his nose like a racehorse – undiluted, undisguised disdain. I wondered when and how he would kill me, what his reasons were for delaying it. He had killed baby starlings, ritualistically. Lined them up beneath a tea towel. Perhaps he would end my life in some ceremony only he understood. Perhaps he would lie me next to Marlie, our hands arranged upon our chests, just so, beneath the tarp. I wondered who could possibly rescue me. Who would miss me? Bobby would have saved me, but he had killed Bobby, put him in the cold ground. Marlie would have… oh God, Marlie, my beautiful best friend. There was no one, no one I could think of who would even notice I had gone. My editor, Jackie, perhaps. Morgan, my agent. Or Julie, my wacky and brilliant PR manager. Straws, all three of them, and I had no way of reaching out to clutch them. My deadline had been extended to take account of the ridiculous success of *Framed by Love*, and then the house move; the manuscript was not due in for six months. It would be weeks before they thought of me, months even. And by then I would be dead.

He left. I stared after him, my ankle chained to the floor. Once he'd gone, I wrenched myself to my feet and made myself walk, round and round, assessing the diameter of my tiny circle of freedom. I had stopped weeping, at least, and my mouth had stopped bleeding, but I was weak with hunger and desperate for a shower. And now, writing this, I wonder if that can be true. Could I have been calm enough to have thought of matters so mundane as food and cleanliness, faced as I was with imminent death or lifelong incarceration? Yet I did have those thoughts. Which makes me think that I must have believed, in some deep part of me, that he would not kill me, that he would have done that by now, and that at some point I would be rescued.

How arrogant of me.

Time passed. Gary had not locked the door, but of course, now I could not reach it.

He returned about twenty minutes later, again with a tray. I almost shouted with glee. The smell of coffee drifted into my nostrils, sent fresh tears to my eyes.

'Thank you,' I simpered. 'Oh, Gary, thank you so much.'

He gave no more than a twitch of his lips really, but it was something. I'm ashamed to say I longed for more – for him to smile, say something to me.

He had brought me crushed avocados on toast, a boiled egg cut into quarters, a tomato sliced and drizzled with green olive oil, tiny boulders of salt. There was a glass of water and another cup of coffee.

Glancing up at him for permission, I drank the entire glass of water and felt it trickle through me, cold and fresh as a mountain stream. I could have drunk another three glasses but said nothing for fear of angering him and risking him taking the food away a second time. I ate. The sticky traces of dirt on my hands and face bothered me, but I was so hungry, and at least he had provided a knife and fork. I eyed both, but they were no use as weapons, not against him, or anyone for that matter.

I finished every scrap. I would, I think now, have eaten it with my hands. I would have plunged my face into it like a farm animal.

'That was delicious,' I said, in some mad pastiche of a normal mealtime in a normal life. 'Thank you.'

He slid the tray away from me. My God, I wished he would talk. I would have cried with relief for one blast of his ridiculous vocabulary, for one of his know-it-all theories.

'I need the loo,' I said.

He nodded and walked away, up the stairs: thud, thud, thud. I thought he was going to fetch the key for my ankle chain, but he returned moments later with a bucket and a toilet roll. My chest sank in dismay. I was about to make a smart remark but thought better of it. He had taken so much away from me, but there was more, much more he could take.

He placed the bucket on the floor and pulled the roll of tape from the back of his baggy jeans.

'Not the tape,' I said, shaking my head, but he was already pinching it between his finger and thumb.

Rip. He lunged forward, pushed the tape across my mouth. It was as if I hadn't spoken, as if I hadn't bled out earlier like a shotgun victim, as if, in fact, I wasn't human to him at all. He took the end of the tape again and twisted. I pushed my wrists together and held them up, the gesture almost a supplication. He smiled and tore another strip, strapped my wrists together in front of my chest. A butcher, I thought, tying the trotters of a pig bound for the hook.

He met my eyes. I tried to plead with him with mine, but there was nothing behind his expression, nothing at all. Without smiling, frowning, without speaking, he turned away from me. All I could do was watch him, the man, the jeans, the boots on the stone steps. A moment more of light. Then semi-darkness, the remains of daylight straining through the tiny window at the top of my cell wall.

Minutes. Hours. It is difficult to pee into a bucket with your hands taped together. Small mercy that my legs had their independence, I suppose, although I still managed to wet my sock. Minutes. Hours. His footsteps above me, the chink of keys, internal doors opening and closing, the back door opening and closing, the car engine, tyres on gravel. Was Marlena in the boot? I wondered. But then why leave the earth next to Bobby's grave?

For the second time, I peed in the bucket, tried not to think about what would happen when the solids worked their way through. I dozed, fitfully. The light dimmed, brightened – clouds passing before the sun, dimmer, brighter, the day zigzagging down towards darkness.

At the sound of his car returning, my heart battered. It was dark by then; I could barely make out the walls, the base of the steps. I reckoned it was late afternoon, early evening. I stood, jumped from foot to foot. He was back, at last, and – this is as hard to admit to as it is to explain, even to myself – at his return, I felt something very like joy.

The cellar door opened; the strip light flickered into white light. I closed my eyes against its glare. There was a pause. The grinding squeak of the back door again, the crunch, crunch of his boots on the gravel, a cold blast of air whipping down the stairs. Then a groan, as if he were exerting himself in some way. A bang.

'Fuck,' he muttered.

Another groan. I couldn't see to the top of the steps, hidden as they were by the beginnings of a plasterboard wall the last owner of the house must have started and given up on. But then he appeared, descending backward, his hands cupped beneath a cardboard box that appeared to be bigger than him. He was inhaling and exhaling deeply. I could tell with each movement that the box was heavy but could not tell what it might hold.

Once at the bottom of the steps, he manoeuvred the box around the base and dragged it across the floor towards me. It was a couple of metres long, I guessed, there or thereabouts, and about twenty centimetres across. Planks of wood, possibly.

'Christ,' he muttered, then, 'Christ's sake.' Words not addressed to me, but at least they were words, audible words.

I scanned the box for a label, but there was nothing. It looked like it might contain flat-pack furniture, but I could not be sure. He was already clomping back up the stairs.

I waited. A while later, I heard him huffing and puffing again. This time when he appeared, he was wrestling an object covered in plastic, and this, yes, this I recognised. With a sinking, stone-in-my-gut feeling, I knew immediately what I was looking at.

A mattress.

From under the tape, I protested – a ridiculous, manic hum.

Without blinking the merest acknowledgement, he took his knife from his back pocket and scored the edges of the box. He pulled the packaging away with his strong, rough hands. There was no denying the implication of the mattress now that I could see the rest: quite clearly, the sides of a frame. For a bed.

My bed.

CHAPTER TWENTY-FOUR

A further three trips out to the car and back again. Once he had what he needed, he peeled the tape from my mouth – carefully this time, although the blood came thickly again; he handed me a wad of the loo roll to staunch it. Then he took his flick knife from his back pocket and slit my wrist tape with the deft precision of a chef. Still he addressed not one word to me. I asked him questions – where had he been? Was he really going to make me sleep down here again? Couldn't we talk about this? – but eventually I felt tears of rejection welling, heard my voice crack, so I shut my mouth and said nothing more, only watched, helpless, as he built my bed in front of me.

He worked with quick hands, strength and skill, pausing only to pull his sweater over his head, releasing a whiff of fresh sweat, a flash of the now slightly thicker roped torso I remembered from the night of our impromptu dinner party *à deux*, not so long ago, so very long ago. His T-shirt had been grey that night, laundered to a non-colour. Now, he wore a white one, which looked new. His new white T-shirts, I thought. He had told me about them in such detail when he'd spun his cock-and-bull Dickensian yarn there in the low-lit warmth of my kitchen. He had fed me what I wanted to hear. I had claimed to want to know his story, but I hadn't, not really. He had given me the laundered version I wanted, the soft, bleeding-heart-liberal version, the grit no more than a tasteful crumb, nothing too heavy, nothing too corrosive. As with so many things, he'd known what I really wanted long before I did.

He bit on a screw, his face intense, focused. When he moved, he did so with accuracy and speed, the way predators do. The high whizz of the electric screwdriver. Illogically, I closed my eyes, screwed up my nose against the din. He barely glanced at the instructions, and watching him, I could not help but think of Bill, bent over our IKEA wardrobe, his flustered brow, the air filled with expletives, his palpable sense of inadequacy when it came to tasks of this type. How I had rolled my eyes and offered, instead of help and encouragement, only sarcasm and undermining comments, once asking if I should call Steve.

'He knows how to do this stuff,' I had said.

What a cow I was. Really.

Outside, the sky was deep blue. The air smelled of sawdust, of concrete, of my own urine. I was so thirsty. He must be too, I thought, but I had resolved not to say anything in case he took it as a complaint.

When confronted by madness, survival depends on playing along.

The frame built, he grappled with the mattress and threw it on, then ran the blade of the knife deftly over the plastic, which he pulled away like so much flimsy clothing. And then he was gone again, and back, a workman's vacuum cleaner held loosely in one hand as if it were no more than a handbag. He plugged it in and vacuumed the entire place. The everyday domesticity of the sight in the context of what was swiftly transforming into my prison cell was beyond surreal. I half expected him to jab at me with the vacuum attachment for a joke, as Bill used to do. But his face betrayed nothing at all: no trace of the arrogance and mischief of that first night, not a hint of that old fire and fear and thrill.

He shut down the vacuum cleaner, but before I could ask him anything, he was away again, his boots loud and brisk on the stairs, as if he were working against the clock.

He returned with plastic bags stuffed with something soft. Bedding. Of course. He pulled out a duvet, a pillow and some bed linen. The bedding was not new, but the covers were still in their packets. I wondered how much he had packed before he came to find me, how much he had been out and bought today. I thought about his car at the airport, ready, waiting, part of his big plan. The boot had been full, perhaps, full of what he would need when he, in his mind, moved in with me. I was beginning to piece it together, I see now. I was filling in the blanks, reaching erroneous conclusions, getting everything jumbled. He must have hoodwinked Marlie as he had me, I thought at one point. He had gone to her place of work. He had turned up in the car park at the station and won her over. He'd pretended to be on his way to see me, flattered her into giving him a lift. He'd pounced on her as she unlocked the car door, slipped into the passenger seat before she had the chance to protest, as he had done to me.

All wrong. He had kidnapped her in her own home, in broad daylight, and left her baby to cry. She had been his ticket to find me. She had been the only witness to his continued pursuit of me. And then... and then once he'd killed Bobby, an unexpected inconvenience, Marlie, my beautiful Marlie, was all that remained between him and the woman he believed to be the love of his life: me.

The tiny window on the cellar wall was flat black now. My stomach growled. Gary made up the bed with the rigour of a marine. And then he was beside me and, without a word, was unlocking my ankle chain. He stood, dug into his pocket and drew out the gun.

I nodded. 'I get it,' I said. 'No tricks.'

'Shower,' he said. 'You stink.'

I almost wept with gratitude. The twenty-first century, the West. No one, *no one* went without running water for more than twenty-four hours, unless they were a down-and-out. He pushed me ahead, up the stairs. The jab of the gun in the small of my back.

Once in the bathroom, he closed the loo seat and sat down. There was a long moment before it dawned on me that he was not leaving. It was a choice of strip or stay filthy. I turned away from him and undressed as best I could, trying to retain some dignity. In the warped framework of Gary and me, this, I supposed, passed for a striptease. I peeped at him over my shoulder. But he wasn't looking at me. He was seemingly lost in contemplation of his gun, which lay flat between his legs, on his lap. And yes, the metaphor was all too obvious. My striptease had apparently left him unmoved. He wasn't even glancing at me. He was indifferent, bored. Flaccid.

Did he not want to look at me? Did he not desire me?

The pig.

In the cubicle, I soaped and rinsed myself twice, washed my hair twice, conscious of not knowing when I would next be allowed to get clean. My exit prompted the same bored indifference as my undressing. I reached for the towel since he made no move to pass it to me.

Once I'd covered myself, he gestured with the gun and a brief nod towards the door. I understood that I was to head to my bedroom here on the first floor, presumably to get dressed.

'Gary.' I tucked the towel into itself around my chest, attempting a smile, at which I felt my lips crack, moisten with fresh blood. 'We don't have to do it like this,' I said, scrabbling for a few sheets of loo roll to dab my bleeding mouth, moving then towards my bedroom. 'I get it. I've pissed you off.' I looked towards the window, casually, as if searching for the right words. 'I'm not going to try and fight you, I—'

I lunged for the gun, hoping to surprise him. I don't know if I'd got as far as intending to turn the weapon on him, I don't know what I was thinking beyond getting out, getting the hell away from him. Whatever, it was a mistake. He caught my wrist and twisted my arm behind me before I had a chance to berate myself for my own rash idiocy. I felt a hard crack on the back of my head.

*

I woke up, groggy, blinking against dusty, weak light. Above me were footsteps – heavy, purposeful. Cracked ceiling. Smell of cold. My head ached. I was in the cellar. Soft firmness, blissful beneath me. Crisp, clean bed linen. New brushed cotton against my skin: cream cotton pyjamas I had never seen before, a floral design running in vertical vines, wooden buttons – like a little girl's pyjamas. I rolled onto my side, felt a sharp metallic dig in my ankle. A heaviness. I threw back the covers. My ankle was chained to the floor. He had moved the bed so that I could sleep like this: chained like an animal, a dog, a lunatic.

The madwoman – not in the attic, but the cellar.

When? When had he done this? I must have been out cold. That's right, I had lunged for the gun. The crack on the back of my head. He must have knocked me out, carried me down here and, not content with locking me in, chained me up in my bed. Pyjamas. He had dressed me. Touched me.

Rage fired in my guts.

The bastard. What did he think I was? What was going on in his mind? We belonged together, that was what he professed to believe… but in what way? One of us chained up in a fucking cell? The other pacing about like a jailer? Was this his view of a *relationship*?

I had feared for my life. But now, for the first time, I felt afraid for how the rest of my life would be now. For ever.

I had to get out. I had to escape – but to what? Bobby dead in the grounds of this farmhouse, Marlie too. Two dead people. One killed by Gary. The other… by me.

I squinted up at the grubby rectangle of glass. Rapunzel's window, I thought. In reverse. Too high for me to reach in here; outside it was at ground level, and yet no one would think to look through.

The bareness of the room hit me. Three metres, maybe four across, and maybe five or six in length. The rusty shelf unit had gone, yes, he had taken that. And the paint tins. How hard he had worked, dogged and unrelenting as a plough horse. I wondered what he had done with Bobby's motorbike. I wondered how I could overpower him, make my escape on it. There was a chance they would never find the bodies. Never find me.

But even if the bodies remained undiscovered, the crimes we had committed unsolved, what would my life be like now, outside this farmhouse, out there in the world? If I called the police, he would tell them I'd murdered Marlena. He would have evidence against me, I was sure. If I didn't call the police, he would simply hunt me down and bring me back kicking and biting to my basement, subdued, tamed. The life of a fugitive was all I could see ahead, always looking over my shoulder, no access to my bank account, no way of contacting anyone in case he traced me, sleeping on the street even, or an inmate in some grim institution surrounded by gurning, predatory women off their heads on smack.

Fuck that.

But anything would be better than this airless, lonely hell, wouldn't it? Wouldn't it be better to take my chances, plead kidnap, mental and physical abuse? I considered the bed a moment, the only piece of furniture in this bleak, miserable space. It was too far from the window; the window too small for me to squeeze through. I could push the bed across the floor, I thought, force the window open and cry for help.

To whom? There was no one here. No one for miles. That was the whole point of here. It was what I had chosen: freedom from other people and their complications, their wayward emotional demands, their failure to recognise mine.

I thought about Tessa, Bobby's fiancée. She would be at home, too worried to go to work, waiting for him to come back, weeping with fear and dread and loneliness. Perhaps she thought he'd taken off, as he said he wanted to. Better that than the truth – or was it? I wasn't sure. Perhaps it was better for her to know he was dead. At least then she could hold on to the mistaken belief that he loved her, provided our affair didn't come out. Oh, but poor Bobby – so alive, so full of a force that seemed to pulse in every cell of him, his careless, beautiful nakedness, the strong triangle of his back... He was in the ground now, a broken angel buried in damp and filthy earth. Rot would have already begun its process of decay. Tessa would know none of this yet. I hoped she never would. She would never have to suffer the horrific and eternal juxtaposition of these two images: her lover alive and her lover dead, so utterly irreconcilable, so utterly inextricable.

I had to think about these things. I alone. It was worse for me, I thought. Much worse.

Twenty-four hours had passed. Tessa would have called the police by now. But there was nothing, nothing at all to bring them here to the farm. My relationship with Bobby had been clandestine, the whole point being to keep his presence here a secret. His motorbike would never have been spotted from the road. There were no other farms overlooking this one from the back. And so in this deception lay both my chance of escaping justice at the hands of the law and also my doom, my own private prison sentence here in this basement. If the police didn't come here, they would never find Bobby and arrest us for double murder. But equally, if they didn't come here, they would never find me. A great fan of irony, as I'm sure you're by now aware, I was nonetheless unamused by this rather ironic turn of events. No, dear reader, I didn't find it funny in the slightest.

The smell of bacon drifted down the cellar steps. In response, my stomach growled. I had not eaten since... Christ, I had not eaten since yesterday morning. And where normally I would need to pee, my abdomen lay flat between my hips, my bladder all but empty. Dehydration. Starvation. The realisation dried my mouth, hollowed my insides. I clutched at my concave belly and brought my knees up to meet it. Hunger, this would be the next torture. Of course. Yesterday it was the silent treatment. Today would be starvation made all the more intense by the taunting smells of my captor's cooked breakfast.

Bastard. I hated him. How I hated him.

The rattle of the lock. Bacon. Sausages, possibly, my God. Coffee. Toast. Water pooled in my mouth. I licked my lips, tasted blood on the scabs that had dried overnight. I dragged myself to a sitting position, groaned, pushed my face into my hands. Tears welled in my eyes, threatened to burst their banks. But I would not weep. I would not weep in front of him. If he offered me breakfast I would say *no thanks.* I would not allow him the satisfaction of laughing in my face and taking it away. I would not allow him to taunt me.

His boots on the stairs. I could not bring myself to look at him, but even as I avoided all sight of him, I knew he would pick up how acutely aware of his every move I was, how my every sense located him on its radar.

'Pippa,' he said.

He had crossed the cellar and was now standing in front of me. He smelled of soap, of aftershave or cologne. I realised he no longer smelled of cigarettes. He had stopped smoking, then. Which, along with living out here in the fresh air, explained his improved complexion.

'You need to eat.' He paused a moment before lowering the tray onto my lap. There was a full cooked breakfast: a glory of pink, white, yellow, caramel browns on a white plate, a cup of steaming filter coffee and, judging by its acid vibrancy, what looked like freshly squeezed orange juice. There was a small vase in which stood a single pink marguerite.

I met his blue eyes and saw what looked teasingly like kindness. Affection, even – the kind of softening you find in the eyes of someone you have fought with, someone you love.

He smiled – his teeth were pale cream, not as discoloured as they had been. He had definitely stopped smoking then, possibly invested in some decent toothpaste.

'Eat it before it gets cold,' he said. 'I'll leave you to it. Mine's upstairs. I have stuff to do.'

He walked away. Boots on stone steps.

You could bring yours down, couldn't you? This was what I wanted to say, the words I forced myself not to utter. *We could eat together, couldn't we? Would that be so bad?*

Don't ask me why. I could not have answered then, and I cannot answer now.

I ate like… well, like the starving prisoner I was, ramming huge mouthfuls down my gullet, barely chewing, having to stop when my throat blocked and gave me an indigestive pain in my chest. I glugged the fresh juice, wolfed yet more food – sausages, black pudding, scrambled eggs, toast. I ate like a beast… well, a beast that's got the hang of cutlery.

This was before I was saved, of course. It was pre-routine, pre-manners, pre-salvation at the hands of Mrs Danvers. Though of course I didn't know anything about being saved, nor what form that would take, not then.

I lay back on my bed, moaning with the outward-pushing pressure of overindulgence, my stomach a tight, round hump. I didn't care. I lay and waited for the discomfort to subside, and at the thought of that, another thought surfaced. What went in would have to come out. What then? Was this whole gourmet brunch thing not kindness but instead another ruse, designed only to cause me further humiliation? I could already feel the coffee and the juice making themselves known in a sudden need to urinate – the solids would not be far behind.

With his customary and prescient sense of timing, Gary returned.

'I need to pee,' I said.

'Use the bucket.'

'Jesus, Gary,' I said. 'Can't you just unchain me and let me go upstairs? I'm not going to go anywhere. I know I wouldn't get far.'

He left. At the top of the stairs, he paused. A moment later, the strip light flickered on, coating everything in its harsh white glare. Then the door, the key in the lock, followed by loneliness, howling loneliness, stark and grey and hard as the concrete floor, white and cold as the light.

I listened. Footsteps. The creak of the back door. The slam of the back door. Gravel crunching under boots, fading. He was going towards the barn.

Was Marlie still there? She would be cold now. Rigid as stone. Mottled. Marbled.

My God.

I used the bucket, cursing when a trickle of urine ran down my leg, wetting the pyjama bottoms a little where I had been forced to bunch them around one ankle. It was not escape I wanted in that moment. I wanted to kill Gary, slowly and painfully, but only after finding some way to humiliate him right back. I wanted… I wanted to pee on him. I wanted to defecate on him. There. I am dead, I don't care what you think about that. Looking back, I think those thoughts came to me because my existence had become no more than wanting to be fed, to eliminate. There was nothing else; I was bound up with my own bodily functions, my survival. I was a murderer. I was an animal.

I curled up on the bed and wept softly. And yet when I think about that moment, it seems to me I wasn't scared. My faith that he wouldn't kill me had returned; perhaps hope that someone would save me, eventually, if I just played along. That I could say Gary had killed Marlena, not me. The thought that he wished to keep me alive like this was perhaps more terrifying than death by pistol, but it wasn't terror I felt at the prospect; it was something more akin to depression: resignation, maybe, or maybe something worse, a weight of knowledge that here I would stay, possibly for the rest of my life, and no one, no one at all, would miss me.

I woke dry-mouthed and stiff around the shoulders. The light in the little window was dim, and I figured it was probably mid afternoon. That meagre rectangle had become my vague timepiece. I peed again in the bucket. Whatever else I needed to expel was refusing to budge, at least for now. I didn't blame it. I'm no supermodel, but we all have our limits on the terms for which we're prepared to get out of bed. Clearly, where my colon was concerned, a cold bucket with no flush option was a deal-breaker, and, yes, you'd have to be a writer to compare a supermodel and her unwillingness to get out of bed to the contents of your bowels and their refusal to make their exit. The way my mind works amuses me sometimes. Sometimes it is all that separates me from despair.

The strip light still shone its cruel white light. I thought of asking Gary for a lamp, maybe some books, and smiled at my own insane optimism. He had known he would be out all day. That was why he had left the light on. It seemed we had progressed from no talking to minimal talking, from no food to food, from no light to light. It was as if he'd planned my enclosure, made of it an experiment. I was his lab rat.

But where was he? What was he doing?

I made myself stand. I hobbled – chain clanking like the bloody ghost of Marley – as far as the window and back to the bed, back to the window, back to the bed, over and over until the window darkened to purple and my legs ached.

I should record the days, I thought. Was this day two or day three? It didn't matter, there were no tools to scratch a tally on the wall. I laughed aloud. Day two or three and already I thought I was Robinson Crusoe.

I lay down on the bed and stared at the line between the ceiling and the top of the wall, stared at the strip light, closed my eyes, made kaleidoscopes, all the time chanting to myself: *Where has he gone? Nobody knows. When's he coming home? Nobody knows. Who's going to find me? NOBODY KNOWS.* I have no idea how many times I closed and opened my eyes, how many times I repeated this pathetic refrain that didn't even scan, but it was enough, in that darkening solitude, to feel the first shimmers, the first dizzying loops... of madness.

CHAPTER TWENTY-FIVE

Pippa Gates: private journal

'Wake up.'

I opened my eyes. Gary's face loomed over mine. 'What time is it?' My voice was little more than a croak.

'It's half past four.'

'What?' I croaked. 'Today?'

'Yes, today. Afternoon.' He waited until I had pulled myself upright then handed me a mug of tea. With a feeling that was at least a distant cousin of euphoria, I noticed that in his other hand he held a second mug. He sat down. On a chair that had not been there earlier.

'New chair?' I said.

'It was in the garage.'

A moment passed. I tried to sip my tea, but it was too hot. Gary looked about him before returning his gaze to me.

'I'll get more furniture tomorrow,' he said. 'I had to go for food today.'

I resisted the obvious temptation to ask him what he thought this was, this conversation we were having about furniture while drinking our tea, me in an ankle chain – not, I might add, of the fine silver-charm variety – with a bucket of my own piss at my feet. Instead, I nodded, the flashing fire beneath my skin so strong in that moment that I wondered if it had ever gone away or whether it was always there and only now in this moment of

calm could I feel it. Now, of course I know that it was him. That
burning was – was always – him.

'I'll need your help later,' he said.

Marlie, I thought. Had to be.

'I've taken care of your friend.' He sipped his tea. Mind reader.

I noticed that his fingernails were rimmed with black dirt, and
that the same dirt darkened the crevices in his hands. His face too
was muddy where he must have wiped at it. The more I looked,
the more I saw. There were brown smears on the knees of his jeans.
So. This was where he had been for most of the day. Putting my
best friend in the ground and covering her in earth.

Tears welled. I closed my eyes against them.

'Where?' I said, no more than a whisper.

'With your other friend. It made sense.'

I nodded, and tears spilled out and ran down my face, blotted
on the bloody tissue at my mouth.

'There's bags of stones in the garage,' he went on, impassive.
'Cobbles, I'd call them. Smooth but big, you know? About as big
as fists.' He held his bunched hand out in front of him, twisted
it this way and that before dropping it back to his lap. 'Maybe a
little bigger. Must have been planning to build a wall or something,
whoever lived here before. There's twenty bags or so. I found them
behind the old feeding troughs.' He sipped his tea.

'Yes,' I said carefully. 'They had plans for a campsite, the
previous owners.'

'I was thinking we could bring those troughs to the front, fill
them with some decent earth. Bit of compost, plant some cyclamens or geraniums – something colourful. I saw that done in a
magazine. Very effective, and those troughs cost hundreds to buy.'

I made myself look at him. 'Sounds good.'

He took another swig and blinked, a moment of reflection in
this grotesque parody of an old-married-couple conversation we
were having. And that's the thing about insanity. It presents as just

the opposite. Here he was, sitting on a chair, sipping tea in a calm moment after a hard day's digging, talking about cyclamens and geraniums and design ideas for the farm with his… his what? What did he think I was right now? His *wife*? What did he imagine he was doing, here, now, having this cosy late-afternoon chat? Next he would be suggesting we visit the garden centre, maybe afterwards take in a tea room, order some fucking scones.

'What do you need me to help with?' I kept my voice level. It was important, I felt, not to break this illusion he had going. If I ruined it, he might become angry. And if he got angry, he would leave.

He drained his mug and stood. 'Maybe it would be better to do it tomorrow, but I was thinking we could build a cairn on that patch of land. In the upper field, you know?'

'A cairn? Is that like a pile of stones?'

He nodded. That was why he had said about the cobbles.

'I've decided to call this place Cairn Farm. A cairn is a landmark that signifies an achievement of some kind, the arrival at a summit usually. I think it's fitting. And it seems like the right place to build it. It's the highest point on our land.'

Our land.

'All right,' I continued, emboldened, possibly by disbelief. 'You mean, where we… where Bobby and Marlie are? As, what, a memorial? Something to commemorate them?'

'I was thinking more to hide the disturbance in the turf. You know, in case anyone decides to visit.'

I stood, straightened up until I was looking down at the top of his greasy hair. 'Who would visit us, Gary? Neighbours? Friends? Are you expecting someone? What are we going to do, throw an at-home?'

At the sarcasm in my voice, his torso stiffened. It was no more than an infinitesimal shift in his shoulders, but I saw and felt it as if it were a violent shudder.

'I don't like your tone, Pippa.'

I sat back down immediately. 'Sorry. I had cramp in my leg. It's gone now. I was just wondering if you'd invited anyone over, that's all.'

He appeared to relax. 'I like the idea of a commemorative cairn,' he said. 'Let's build it tomorrow.' He stood, withdrawing the mug from my hands. 'It'll do you good to get some fresh air.'

He took the stairs slowly while I listened to his every step. At the top, he paused.

'Dinner's at eight,' he called down. 'Do you like prawns?'

'Yes,' I called up.

The light went off. Darkness: the punishment for my minor infraction.

At precisely 8 p.m., the door opened, the light came on. I was in bed. It was the only way to stay warm in that freezing basement. For the last fifteen, twenty minutes I had suffered the wafting aromas of garlic and chilli, the sweet, beachy smell of prawns searing in a frying pan. And now here he was, standing in front of me. Ryan Marks. Gary Hughes. He had showered and changed. He smelled good – of my orange and ginger soap, but of cooking too. He wore a loose white shirt I hadn't seen before and dark denim jeans, his black belt with the bronze buckle. His hair was pushed back, and he had shaved close. The outdoors had improved his colour. Food had made his cheeks less hollow. It occurred to me that everything he had bought, he must have done with my bank card. He had found my PIN – of course he had.

I sat up on the edge of the bed. He placed the tray in my lap. His fingernails were scrubbed clean, no trace of earth left. On the tray was a deep white plate of pasta butterflies with finely shredded courgette, fat pink prawns, burnt orange flecks of chilli, verdant chopped flat parsley and fine yellow curls of lemon zest. To one side, white wine sweated in a tumbler.

'This looks incredible,' I said.

'*Farfalle alla zucchine e gamberi*,' he said. 'It is.'

He walked back towards the stairs.

'Gary?' I said.

He stopped.

'Don't you want to eat with me?'

He sighed. 'All in good time, Pip.'

At the top of the stairs, he stopped again. 'Eat up. You'll need your strength for later.'

After dinner, he collected my plate and glass and left me once again. I slept.

'Wake up.' Gary was unlocking my ankle. 'More work to do.'

'What time is it?'

'Two.'

'In the morning?'

'Yes. Get up.' He threw a pile of clothes at me: a thick sweater, jeans, boots.

I blinked. 'What are we doing?'

'We have to get rid of the bike. There's a lake. It's not far.'

He meant Blagdon or Chew Valley, I was pretty sure. I'd seen that there were lakes when I'd first studied the map, had taken a drive out that way to get my bearings before putting my offer in on the farm. Blagdon was the nearer.

'No tricks,' he said, handing me the keys to the Saab.

'No tricks.'

I followed him. On the passenger seat was a tartan blanket I didn't recognise, an overcoat, a dark grey towel and what looked like a knitted black hat. It occurred to me only then, following him that second time, that if any rural CCTV did pick him up, they would think he was Bobby; indeed, Tessa would identify him as Bobby, dressed as he was in Bobby's helmet and jacket.

Turn-offs came and went. I watched their white signposts slide away, become small in the rear-view mirror.

As I had predicted, we drove towards Blagdon Lake. Once near, he took a right, a road called Park Lane. I followed. A little further down, we stopped at a quaint low-roofed Tudor-style hut on the shore.

I parked up, got out of the car. Ahead, at the water's edge, Gary was already wheeling the bike into the lake. I watched in silence. He pushed forward, the water reaching his knees, his thighs, his chest. He walked on, as if through nothing but air. A moment later, his feet came up, his head dipping below the surface. The surface calmed. I caught my breath.

'Gary?' I called out.

I eyed the car. If I jumped in now, he would not catch me. I could drive away. Surely he wouldn't catch me. Not on foot.

A splash. He resurfaced. I had not moved. And then he was walking out, his hair and face and clothes dripping. The time to act had flashed and gone. Too late now, too late. The moon slid from behind a cloud, lighting the pearls of water on his skin. He was no more than a metre away, half a metre. He was at my shoulder. He passed by, heading for the Saab. He opened the passenger-side door and pulled the towel from the seat, towelling himself as dry as he could before putting on the coat, grabbing the blanket and hat from the seat.

'Let's go.' He put on the hat, wrapped the blanket around his shoulders. It was November. He must have been freezing, though his teeth didn't chatter; he didn't shiver.

I got in and drove him home.

'What was that hut?' I said.

'Fishing Lodge,' he replied. 'I disabled the CCTV earlier today. That's why we had to do it tonight. I didn't want the bike in the garage. Too risky.'

I nodded, as if that was perfectly reasonable. 'Do you think we'll get away with it?'

'Yes,' he said simply.

After a moment, he shifted his body towards me. I could feel his gaze, almost see him out of the corner of my eye. I focused on the road.

'But I'll tell you this,' he said. 'If we don't, I'll put a bullet through your head and then one through mine. I'm not going back inside. I'm never going back. And I'll never let them take you away from me.'

Blog post: PippaGatesAuthor
#thiswritinglife
Find me on:
Instagram: @GatesPip
Twitter: @PipGatesWrites
Facebook: Pippa Gates Author

Sometimes, when I'm writing, I find it a great comfort to hear footsteps above me, the rhythm of someone else's day as they pace around; the clunk of the back door, the *bock-bock* of the chickens as they compete around their feed, the chink of china plates as they're arranged on the dresser, the louder, metallic clang of the pans going on to the S hooks that hang from the metal rod above the Aga. Later, I'll listen for the popping of tyres on gravel, the faintest smell of exhaust trailing in through my little office window. The house will fall silent then, and sometimes I'll think about getting out and about, though I never do. After all that hard work, Mrs Danvers would be so disappointed if I didn't meet my word count.

Often, I check the clock on my computer and, depending on the time, calculate how long it will be until my next break. Now, for example it's 10 a.m., so I know that in forty-five minutes, it will be coffee time and that I will be able to have a fifteen-minute chat. It is by far the best way to work, the only way to write. I'm allowed half an hour for my blog post, which I always do first. My blog is my warm-up exercise for the writing itself. Every evening after dinner I catch up with my readers and any correspondence I may have, post my Instagram pictures and reply to tweets and emails. If there is a lot to do in that regard, Mrs D is really quite flexible, as long as it doesn't interfere with television time.

Routine is everything, yes, but it doesn't do to be too rigid!

CHAPTER TWENTY-SIX

The smell of cooked breakfast. Light in the little window. Day three or four. As long as I kept a loose track, I would be OK. I hoped that soon I would be able to ask him for a pencil and paper. The cellar was freezing. I wondered when I would be able to broach the subject of a heater. I got up and managed to pee in the bucket without wetting my pyjama trouser leg (still no sign of anything more serious, though I can honestly say that if ever constipation were a positive, it was then).

A few minutes later, Gary came thudding down the stone steps with my breakfast on a tray: full English, freshly squeezed orange juice, fresh coffee, flower in a vase.

'Good morning, Pip,' he said.

'Good morning, Gary.'

He walked back towards the stairs.

'Thank you,' I called after him.

'Don't mention it.'

'Gary?' The clomp of his boots stopped halfway up the stairs – my cue that it was OK to speak. 'Have we any plans today?'

'I'll be out for most of the morning,' he said. 'I need to pick up a few things. There's a house clearance in Weston-super-Mare.'

'All right,' I said. 'What time will you be back?'

'Not sure.'

He left. I watched him disappear by degrees behind the plasterboard wall, listened to his boots on the stairs, the creak of the door, his footsteps above me. I ate my breakfast alone, pictured him eating his at the kitchen table. A little while later, the back door opened and closed, his footsteps crunched on the gravel. The growl of the engine, the rumble of the tyres rolling past the little window at the top of the cellar wall.

Then silence.

I lay back on the bed and exhaled heavily. I tried to sing a pop song to myself but couldn't remember the words. I sang a few scales, up and down, louder and louder. I shouted the alphabet to the ceiling. I got up, hoofed my way through a mangled version of a Beyoncé song, threw some dodgy shapes in my PJs, dance moves that bore a closer resemblance to the extras in the 'Thriller' video than to any of Destiny's Child – though I might add that this was no fault of the ankle chain. Undeterred, I danced until my body warmed up and my forehead grew damp with sweat. I ran out of inspiration, fell back on to the bed, got under the covers. I stared at the grey ceiling, the ragged crack that ran from the wall nearest the stairs to the strip light. I closed my eyes.

Moments later, my eyes still closed, someone said hello, soft, into my mind's ear. And then there she was, a distinguished-looking old lady, her papery hand shaking mine, her thin silver hair pinned back in a comb, the teary film of old age shining on her haloed grey eyes. Arcus senilis.

'Hello,' she said. 'I'm Daisy Philips.'

'Hello,' I replied, apprehensive, sitting in a wing-backed chair opposite her, noting that she was sitting in a chair of the same style and that the light was amber and warm, and I could smell butter melting into toasted teacakes. In the distance, brass-band music played on a scratchy record player; woolly figures moved in my peripheral vision. Where were we? The smell of mince. Of Dettol.

'We're in the Grange Retirement Home,' Daisy said. 'I was jilted at the altar. Many years ago now. I don't know his name yet. I don't know much more than that, I'm afraid.'

My guts flipped. My skin tingled. My hair follicles lifted. I reached over for the touch of her warm, papery hand, held it in mine as in the background the music crackled under its stylus.

'Tell me about that,' I said.

She spoke, her voice wavering but only as a flag trembles in the breeze, its post firm in its foundations, its fabric strong. I held her hand and let her meander, backtrack, reinvent, complicate... but always in her own voice, this tentative and lovely well-spoken burr. The hands gave me the thin forearms, the shallow curve of her upper back gave me the bird-like dip of her neck...

Out of the fog she came, pulling with her Bing, whose name she knew by now; Bing young and old, herself young and old, then the communal area of her residence, its pastel colours, then a tea room in Weston-super-Mare – upholstered chairs with bronze-coloured frames, muted, like photos in a developing tray, images yet to fill up, solidify.

And then nothing.

I opened my eyes and sat up, desperate for pen and paper, consciously trying to hold the whole thing in my mind.

Where was Gary? I had to get him to bring me something to write on, to write with.

I stood and paced back and forth from the bed to the wall. A story had come to me almost fully formed, now, in this unimaginable circumstance. Now, when I was trapped, with no hope of escape and no clue as to what would await me if I did. I had been free before, in my past life, to think of a story, but nothing had come. I had not had the time nor the space, I realised, with everything that had been going on. I had made excuses. But there in the basement, in the solitude of my cell, with no internet, no email, no company, no obligation and no responsibility – no excuses – a character had approached me unbidden, from nothing. Yes, she had come from exactly that: nothing. There was nothing in my life, and it was into this void that Daisy had wandered, a little bent, a little hesitant, but crystallising all the while. She had not come before. There had not been room.

For the second time, Gary had inadvertently brought me inspiration.

I attempted to work, mentally, on the raw material my subconscious had offered up to me, to impose the beginnings of some shape. I had always wanted to write something set in the past, in a time when people wrote letters, kept their emotions hidden instead of splashing them all over afternoon confessional shows or shouting about them on Facebook. A time when people didn't swear and those who did were vulgar. This would be a novel set in both the past and the present.

By the time I heard the Saab on the driveway, I was frantic. I would have scratched notes into the floor if I could have, cut my finger and written with my own blood. I knew that if I didn't write it down, it would dissipate, ephemeral as smoke, into the air.

The back door swung open, clattered against the outer wall. The door to the basement creaked. I walked, clanking, towards the stairs, to the limit of my chain, leant as near to the stairwell as I could.

'Hi, Gary,' I called out.

A roar of exertion, the bump of something heavy. Why didn't he ask me for help? I wondered. Not like I could run away, unless I battered him round the head and left him unconscious, and I was hardly going to do that with a tray, an empty coffee cup or a plate.

Another roar, the scrape of heavy furniture at the top of the stairs. His heels appeared from behind the half-wall, the corner of something, an unmistakable piece of furniture that filled me with dread and delight.

A scratched dark-wood surround, corners scuffed pale, framing a mottled green leather top, a gold vine running around the edge. It was about twenty centimetres deep and there were three drawers running across the length. He lugged it, step by step, to the bottom.

'Let me help,' I said, once he was near enough. I bent and took the edge. It was heavier than I'd thought. He circled around with the other edge before laying it on the floor. A brief nod of thanks and he was clomping up the stairs once more. Two more trips and he had carried down two columns of drawers.

'Lift that end,' he said.

I did as I was told. He put the first set of drawers underneath and I rested the desk on the top. I moved to the other end and lifted that, and between us we adjusted the heavy top until it sat correctly on its two sets of drawers. We pushed the whole back a little until it was just below the window.

'It's a desk,' I said. No shit.

But he was halfway up the stairs again. I walked to the chair he had brought down the day before and carried it over to the desk, positioning it as if to work there. I drew it back, sat on it, pulled it forward. The chain reached just far enough to allow me to sit comfortably, but, I realised, not far enough to allow me to climb on the desk and reach the window.

His footsteps behind me.

'Here,' he said, placing my laptop in front of me.

Pen and paper, I thought. Keyboard and screen.

'There's no internet on it,' he said, walking away. 'I'll bring you something to eat.'

At the bottom of the stairs, he paused, looked over at me, a smile playing on his lips as he added, 'Now, earn your keep.'

Once he'd gone, I switched on the computer. It was as he had said: stripped of access to the internet – no Google, no email, nothing. I opened Word, started a new document and wrote:

Pushing Up Daisy by Pippa Gates

It was a working title, nothing more. It was a rather sick play, obviously, on the phrase 'pushing up daisies', meaning six feet under, a dark joke relating to the characters' advanced ages. I remembered a short story I'd written in my twenties about a group of pensioners who start a writing group. It was called 'The Almost Dead Poets' Society'. I can see now that as titles go it did perhaps lack compassion. I knew it was only for my own purposes – something to stick at the top, a name for the document. But we have to start somewhere, don't we? That's life. Acorns, oak trees, et cetera.

Underneath the title I wrote – since that is all writing is, one word after another, a sentence, another sentence, until faded pictures step forth from the fog, step forth in all their flaws and complications… Here comes Daisy… here she comes… look… do you see her?

Daisy Philips stared out of the French windows of her room, watching a robin peck at the grass. Jab jab jab. She leant forward, dabbing with a Kleenex at her forever-watering old grey eyes. Jab jab jab. That robin wasn't giving up. It looked around, twitching left and right, as if to search for help, and then, finding none, discovering perhaps in that moment that we are, all of us, our own only reliable resource in this life, jabbed once, twice, three times more before pausing a moment, a worm dark and lithe in its determined little beak, and flying away.

A knock came at the door, and a moment later, Susannah's face appeared.

'Daisy, love?'

'Yes, dear?'

Susannah stepped inside, her blue nurse's uniform bulging at the bosom, a wisp of black hair falling from her hairpin. She smiled.

'There's a new boy here this week,' she began. 'Says he thinks he knows you.'

'Oh yes?' Daisy thought for a moment. She had, years before, returned to her maiden name, Philips; James, her married name, the cause of memories best forgotten. Whoever it was, then, must know her from a very long time ago.

'Yes,' said Susannah. 'Bing Davies. Ring any bells?'

Bells indeed, Daisy thought. Church bells, as cacophonous in her mind as they had been that fateful day. Bing Davies. Yes, he did know her from before, from a very long time ago indeed.

She tipped her chin and fixed the young nurse with a steely gaze. 'I'm afraid you'll have to tell Mr Davies that I am unavailable. I have nothing to say to him. Nothing whatsoever.'

I sat back. The writing was more marker pen than quill just at the moment, but it was a start. And with that start, I was back. Pippa Gates, author. There was something in that act that didn't escape me then and it doesn't now, and it is this: I had only written my second book because of Gary, and the same would, I knew, be true of my third. For all the violence subdued beneath his surface, for all the murderousness that formed the very core of him and which I had witnessed with my own eyes, for all that he had me chained like a beast to the basement floor in my own home, two of my friends dead and buried in the neighbouring field – for all this, without him, I was adrift.

CHAPTER TWENTY-SEVEN

PIPPA GATES: PRIVATE JOURNAL

Gary brought me my supper, for which I had been pining like a Bisto kid on the 5:2 diet. The aromas had drifted downstairs – spices, heat, warmth. Chicken tikka masala with steamed rice, raita and mango chutney. A half-pint of lager. A small spray of fuchsias in a vase on the tray. The curry was delicious, the eating of it at the desk more civilised than on my lap, even if it was lonely as hell and afterwards all I wanted to do was drink more beer and talk to someone about my work.

When, after dinner, he came to collect the tray, I sat bolt upright in my chair.

'Dinner was unbelievable,' I said. 'You're an amazing cook.'

'Thank you.' He picked up the tray.

'I've written something,' I said, wanting to detain him, wanting to *please* him, and was filled with pride when he rewarded me with a smile.

'Good,' he said. 'Good work.'

Bolstered, I wrote through the evening, until my eyes and back became sore. I reached five thousand words, a personal record, though let's face it, there was nothing else to do. This was 'Write a Novel in a Month' on acid. I lay on my bed under that white strip light, closed my eyes and saw the kaleidoscope imprint of its glare. I had begun to feel stale and grubby again. My stomach had begun to stick out and to ache. I longed to clean my teeth, to get some air.

At eleven, the cellar door opened and my chest swelled with the hope that he would let me go upstairs and use the bathroom. I would be super-friendly, I thought. Suggest a walk around the grounds. We could maybe share a cigarette outside by the barn.

But he did not come down.

'Light off,' he said.

A moment later, I was in blackness thick as cloth.

'Sit up.'

I blinked against daylight, did as I was told, and to my surprise, he unlocked the chain at my ankle.

'You can use the bathroom.' He took the handle of the bucket and stood up in front of me. 'It's 7 a.m. I'll take you up in the mornings and at lunch, tea and in the evening. Anything else you need, there's the bucket. In the mornings, from now on, you can shower, as long as you behave.'

'Thank you,' I said, meaning it. The hot, flashing feeling beneath my skin returned in a blaze. But I wasn't afraid, not exactly. Apprehensive, perhaps.

He nodded towards the stairs. 'Ladies first.'

Ignoring the thick irony in his voice, I led the way up into the farmhouse. The stone steps pressed cold on the soles of my feet. I wondered if at some point, perhaps in a few days, I could ask for some slippers.

Upstairs, the house smelled clean – of lemon Flash and polish, and as I neared the bathroom, I caught the aggressive base notes of bleach. The bathroom shone – the taps brilliant, as if they'd been buffed. There were two towels I hadn't seen before on the radiator: one green, one blue. Two smaller towels lay over the side of the bath: one green, one blue.

'Yours are the green towels,' he said, leaving aside the fact that the blue were clearly his, that this was some kind of crazy *Mr & Mrs* show we were now playing out.

I turned to face him, expecting him to sit and guard me as he had done the last time. But he made no move to come in. He stood in the doorway, one hand on the handle.

'Has there been anything on the news?' I asked.

'You've been good,' he said, as if I hadn't spoken. He met my eye. 'I'll be right outside. If you lock the door, I'll kill you. If you try and get out of the window, I'll kill you.'

I nodded. 'I understand. No tricks.'

He closed the door.

I showered, blissed out by my beloved Italian clementine soap. I ran a razor over my legs, ran my hand after it, loving the silken feel of my skin. I had made a lot of money from *Framed by Love*, it was true. But of all the luxuries I could now afford – the house in the country, my jazzy jeep, pretty much whatever clothes I wanted – there was no greater feeling of wealth than this, here, the luscious stream of hot water, the soap bubbles sliding down from my shoulders to my shins, the shampoo trailing from my hair down the length of my back. I was groaning, I realised, lost in the sensuousness of this most mundane of daily pleasures.

'I'm done,' I called tentatively once I'd wrapped myself in the larger towel, made a turban of the smaller one.

He threw open the door, his smile less sinister, more wolfish. 'Sounded like you had someone in there with you.'

I laughed in surprise. It was a long time since he'd made any kind of joke.

'If you go into your bedroom,' he said, 'I've prepared your outfit.'

'Thanks,' I said. 'Thank you.'

On the bed was a black velour jogging suit, some new green and coral Nike trainers. I knew there was little point in protesting but decided to risk a quip.

'Very *Desperate Housewives*,' I said, and added in an American accent, 'I guess that's what you call a leisure suit, huh?'

No response. Nothing but the whisper of metaphorical tumbleweed.

'You can't write if you feel constrained,' he said. 'You need a full belly, plenty of water and loose-fitting clothing.'

'All right.'

The door closed and I was alone in the strange familiarity of my bedroom. The bed was neatly made. The covers and sheets were mine, though they were not the bedding I had last used – when Bobby was alive. Closing my eyes against the memory of that, I bent my face to the pillow and sniffed. Soap, patchouli oil. Something else, beneath, something human.

Gary.

He slept here. Of course he did. I lifted the pillow, expecting perhaps to find my nightie there, thinking that perhaps he would press it to his face at night. But there was nothing, nothing at all.

I threw down the towel and dressed. Judging by the old pants and bras in my bedside cabinet, at least he hadn't bought me new underwear.

I glanced at my little pile of books: Zadie, Hilary, my ridiculous self.

'What do you reckon, Hils?' I said to the copy of *Wolf Hall*. 'Do you think he'd go for big cotton pants? Or Victoria's Secret? Maybe something crotchless from Ann Summers? So the bitch scribe can multitask while she knocks out a novel? Eh, Hilary? What d'you think?'

I was crying, I realised. Sobbing without effort as the tears rolled out unnoticed. I was pulling on the trousers, the hooded top. God, they were comfy. Holy shit, they were soft. Dangerous clothes. There might be no going back. I would become woman-in-a-leisure-suit, queen of the elasticated waist, a sloth in expensive activewear. In the full-length mirror I caught my reflection, a timely signpost that there would be, there had to be, a going back: to tailored clothes, to make-up, to haircut and colour. Jesus, I was pale, my eyes black with shadows, my hair dye faded, my roots peppered. I looked drawn, haunted, the veins in my neck like cables. And the leisure suit. I looked like a poster girl for cheery suburban low-grade insanity. But then, I had just been chatting to Hilary Mantel, had I not? Yes, I thought, taking in my strange appearance: I looked mad.

Perhaps I was.

The next day, Gary brought me my breakfast before I had visited the bathroom.

'This is not the routine, but I need you to help me with that job,' he said. 'You can use the loo after you've eaten.'

'OK.' I had no idea what he meant. The breakfast was glorious. I had thought about asking if I could have a break from the full English, and with his customary psychic ability, he had brought me muesli with milk, a little Greek yoghurt, some runny honey.

'Is it local?' I asked, hoping to detain him at least for a couple of minutes. 'The honey?'

He shook his head. 'Too soon for smaller shops,' he said. 'It's been nearly a week but we need to keep a low profile.'

No danger, I thought. Living in a cellar was pretty much the last word in low profile. Any lower would be an actual grave.

'What is it we're doing?'

But he was already clomping up the stairs. I ate in silence. At least now I had my story to think about. That would be company of sorts. I could process the words I had written the day before. I hoped Gary wouldn't make me help him for too long. I was itching to get back to Daisy and Bing.

After breakfast, he came back down the stairs and threw some of my old jeans and a sweatshirt on the bed.

'Get dressed.' He crouched to unlock my ankle. 'Come upstairs when you're ready.'

'We're going out?' I could not hide the excitement in my voice.

'Only to the field. Don't wet your pants.'

Upstairs – that's to say the ground floor – he was waiting in the hallway. He handed me my coat and some thick work gloves. In silence, he opened the back door and stepped out. The sky was vast. I blinked against its light. The air tasted like clean cold water. I closed my eyes and gulped it.

'Come on,' he said.

In the garage, he picked up a bag of cobbles.

'Is this for the cairn? I thought you'd done that?'

'I've been busy.' He placed the bag into the cradle of my arms.

My knees sagged; pain shot through my arms. I gasped, leant back, tried to readjust the weight against my torso.

'It's too heavy,' he said.

'No, it's fine.'

'It's too heavy.'

In the end, Gary took four bags to the upper field, one after the other. I waited for him in the gravel car park outside the barn, watching his figure draw closer as he marched down the hill, recede as he staggered back up with more rocks. He was blowing at his forehead, the sweat pouring down the sides of his face by the end, but he did it without a break. He was still very slim, but his slimness belied an incredible strength. He could probably lift me above his head without a thought.

At the burial site, we built the cairn cobble by cobble, the base perhaps half a metre in diameter. Twice Gary had to go back and fetch another bag. While we worked, I told him all about my new idea, how the story would progress. He listened, properly listened, as Bill never had. He even chipped in ideas, helped with Bing's backstory.

'I was thinking they could fall in love somewhere around here,' I said.

He placed the final cobble on the mound.

'The White Horse,' he said. 'Though that might be too obvious.'

'No. No, that would work.'

We stood back, hands on hips, like some kind of crazy parody of a batty but harmless country couple.

'It's actually really lovely,' I said. 'It's a feature.'

He peered at me and shook his head. 'You're so nuts.'

'I'm thirsty is what I am. I could murder a cup of tea.'

'Me too.' He checked his watch. 'And then your shower. And then work.'

'All right.' I smiled.

'All right.'

Over the days that followed, Gary and I fell into a routine. It had started patchily, with all we had to do. But once the work of murder and the disposal of the evidence was over, we settled. Up at 7 a.m., shower, breakfast at 8 a.m., brisk walk, down to the cellar for me, work on the farmhouse and its grounds for him. Coffee at 10.45 a.m. Cup of tea at midday, lunch at 1 p.m. Tea at 5 p.m. Finish at 6 p.m.

By week two, this was our day. Gary cooked, washed my clothes, ran errands, did the grocery shopping. He had got my debit-card number from my phone, he said. I had listed it under 'card'. He teased me about that. From his trips out, he brought trinkets: my porcelain dancers, a lamp, some sheepskin slippers, and, finally, an oil heater. By day, I heard him cook, mend things, paint, and it comforted me to know he was there, to hear those noises.

I have no access to the news here, nor even the television, and there is freedom in that. Because a kind of freedom is what I have. I'm imprisoned, sure. But what working person alive can tell you that they are not imprisoned in their place of work? All right, there are no ankle chains in an office, no constant underlying threat of execution, but it's not as if anyone can simply down tools and walk out, is it? No one has that kind of freedom. Not without repercussions. I will concede that my own potential repercussions were extreme, but that's only a matter of scale. And I think by the end of the second week, my thought processes had taken me further than I ever would have imagined. And they were reflections that would prove fundamental to my ultimate liberation. Because a mere fortnight after we buried Bobby and Marlena, a little over a week ago, in fact, the transformation from the old Pippa to Pippa Gates, author and media creation, was complete.

I was saved.

CHAPTER TWENTY-EIGHT

My epiphany came much more quickly than I believe is usual in these situations, which further confirms my theory that my imprisonment began not three weeks but over two years ago, on that night, when Ryan Marks, as I knew him, knocked at my suburban door. That was the night I signed myself over to him. That was the night I allowed him to take me prisoner.

As for my less metaphorical and more actual imprisonment, here at Cairn Farm, that's when my journey towards enlightenment really began in earnest. That's when it stepped up a gear or three, as they say. Over the days that followed the building of the cairn, Gary woke me each morning at 7 a.m. and took me upstairs to use the bathroom (you will be relieved, though not as relieved as I was, to know that my digestive system did return to normal) and to take a shower. Evenings, I would talk through my work in progress with him; he would make suggestions, conduct research trips for me, take photographs.

The rest is as I have detailed, the timings non-negotiable.

Such is the requirement of art. I was beginning to accept this, although my salvation was not yet complete.

One day, four or five days ago, I think, Gary came home from an errand with three gifts, gifts that would combine to win me my freedom. The first two he had bought as he bought everything – with my debit card. The third, well, the third was something money could not buy. Reader, we are approaching the moment when all of my past that you have read here creeps up to join my present. When it arrives, you will finally be up to speed and have a better understanding of my recent life. Which will, by the time you read this, of course be over.

It was 4 p.m. when I heard the Saab roll up the driveway. I knew I wouldn't see Gary for an hour, since it wasn't tea time until five. I continued working. I was writing the emotional scene of Bing's apology to Daisy, and I have to admit, I had become a little tearful myself. I was disturbed from my work by what I thought was a squeaking sound – a piece of equipment that needed lubricating, perhaps, one of Gary's power tools. But I could hear Gary's voice too, and it sounded as if he were talking to a child. This disturbed me more, and my thoughts turned immediately to his criminal insanity, a side of him I was finding increasingly easy to block from my mind, but which I had not forgotten. Had he taken a child? Had he extended this warped game of man and wife we were playing and decided to start a *family*?

My fears increased a little before 5 p.m. when I heard the clomp of his boots on the stairs. He was talking, his voice high and soft, almost effeminate.

'It's OK,' he was saying. 'It's OK, little girl. Let's go and see Mummy.'

My insides turned over. My God, it was as I had dreaded. He had taken a child from some poor, distracted mother outside Asda or something and had brought the little girl here to be our daughter. Possibly to live here in the cellar with me. This might answer the question of why we had not become intimate. This in turn made sense of his indifference towards me in the bathroom the time I took a shower in front of him, his dressing of me in girlish brushed-cotton pyjamas by night and loose clothing by day, his keeping of me in the cellar, as far as possible from his bed.

'Gary?' I called out.

His boots clomped slowly. He was taking the stairs one at a time.

'Gary, who's with you?'

'You'll see,' he said, and then, clearly not to me, 'She'll see, won't she? Won't she, Frieda?'

I stared as he emerged from behind the half-wall. And that was when I saw the ball of wriggling golden fur under his arm.

'This is Frieda,' he said, letting her down.

Tail wagging, the golden retriever puppy drove her nose around the concrete floor like a vacuum cleaner.

I shrieked and stood up at my desk. I ran after her, but she took fright and darted into the corner of the cellar. My chain stopped me short, and I almost fell.

'Come here,' I cooed. 'Come here, Frieda.' My eyes filled with tears and I glanced at Gary.

It was a second, no more, but I caught him. He had not been staring at the puppy but at me. And his eyes shone with an expression I recognised immediately: pure, fathomless, helpless love. I had only ever seen that expression once before. For all that my mother had been jealous of my father with regard to me, my father had never once looked at me like Gary had just now. He had only ever looked like that at my mother.

Gary hated me. He loved me.

I hated him. I...

'She's beautiful,' I managed to say, crying now. 'Is she ours?'

He shrugged, inspected his shoes. 'I bought her, so...'

This too was something new – this abashed version of Gary, this little boy who wanted only to please me.

'Thank you,' I sobbed.

'We can walk her in the mornings. I'll walk her further afield while you work. We can take pictures of her. I need to talk to you about that. She'll be good for your social-media profile. Apparently dogs get a lot of likes.'

I bit my lip. It was a crushing blow. He had not bought the dog for me alone, but for some marketing ploy to make him rich, to keep him in the style to which he had become accustomed.

'Don't take that the wrong way,' he said, reading me as plainly as ever. 'I bought her to keep you company. She won't talk, so you can still work with her here, and if I walk her for an hour or so, she can snooze by your side and help you stay calm. But I have been thinking about how to improve your social-media profile, and on the way home, I realised that Frieda will be a star in her own right.'

I opened my mouth to speak, but he was walking towards the stairs.

'Don't go,' I said.

'Hold on,' he replied, holding up a forefinger. 'I've got something else. Wait there.'

He returned moments later with a supermarket-type cardboard box. I sat on the bed so that he could deliver the box onto my lap. But Frieda, until that moment uninterested, seemed to sense that here was something that risked stealing my attention away from her, and jumped onto the bed, where she began nuzzling into the folds of velour at my waist and making the cutest little crying sounds.

'Oh my God, she's adorable,' I said with childlike glee.

He sat beside me. He had never sat on the bed before, and at his warmth, at his proximity, more tears trickled from my eyes. Together we fussed over the puppy, our little Frieda, our hands touching at moments before he reached over me and scooped her up in his arms. She wriggled in his grip. Seconds passed while he fumbled to keep hold of her. He set her down on the floor, tickled her ears. He was leaning across my lap, the thin nape of his neck so near, vulnerable, deeply tanned. I found myself wanting to place the flat of my hand there. I felt that my touch would calm him, and me.

He sat up, glanced at me, meeting my eye. 'Are you all right? Your face is flushed.'

'I'm fine,' I said, clapping my hand to my cheek.

'I found a second-hand bookshop in Weston-super-Mare,' he said after a moment, with the air of someone changing the subject. 'Thought you could do with some reading material. I can order whatever you need, but this is just for, you know, pleasure.' He picked up the box and placed it in my lap.

'Thank you so much,' I said, feeling my face grow hotter still. I looked through the collection, fingering their spines one by one. '*Madame Bovary*,' I said. 'Always wanted to read that... *Jane Eyre*, gosh, they had all the classics, didn't they?' I continued through, at last pulling out the one I knew I would read first. '*Rebecca*,' I said. 'Daphne du Maurier.' I leant into him, kissed him on the cheek. 'My favourite.'

The keen reader in you will have spotted that I haven't mentioned the third gift. That came later and, as I have said, was not something money could buy, nor paper wrap in its folds.

The third gift was my physical freedom.

Later that night, I was saved.

I had eaten my evening meal (lamb chops, wilted spinach and pommes boulangères for those of you with culinary interests, served with a 175ml glass of room-temperature Bourgogne). I had made my customary trip to the bathroom and changed into my brushed-cotton pyjamas and the sheepskin slippers that Gary had bought the week before. He had secured my ankle chain and left me for the night. I didn't know where the puppy was, but I assumed he had bought a bed for her and that she was probably in the kitchen.

I was sitting on my bed reading *Rebecca* by the yellow light of my lamp when I heard the basement door open. A flare of panic rose inside me. My heart quickened, and I felt the flash of fire I had learned to accept now as simply part of my new physical make-up. Gary coming down the stairs at 11 p.m. was not part of the routine. I was so used to the schedule by then that for a moment I thought it might be someone else.

'Gary?' I called.

No boots clomped on the stairs. When he rounded the half-wall, I saw that he was wearing blue cotton pyjamas with white piping around the edge and sheepskin slippers like mine. I had never seen him in his night attire, and the intimacy of the sight took me aback. He had parted his hair at the side and combed it strangely, tucked it behind his ears. Light and shadow chiselled his slim face, made dark pools of his eyes. Under one arm he carried a teddy bear and his gait was hesitant, his gaze shy.

A little boy ready for bed.

And I, I thought, a little girl.

'Gary, are you OK?'

He was staring directly at me, in the intense way he had when we had first met. The dark blue of his irises had deepened to almost black, though not the same black eyes as when he had arrived here and held me at gunpoint. They had lost their brutality.

I was shaking, I realised. The book dropped to the floor.

'Ryan?' I tried.

'My name is Gary,' he said quietly, so quietly. 'And I am not a window maker. I have committed murder. I am criminally insane.'

I closed my eyes a moment and nodded. A whimper escaped me.

'I know,' I said. 'You know I do.'

'Yet you're still here.'

His hands fell to his sides. The teddy bear dropped onto my lap. In his other hand, I saw the gun. This was it. My final moment on this earth. I would be ushered out of my life in some bizarre, ritualistic performance of ruined childhood. I had kissed his cheek earlier, when we were sitting together on the bed. Whatever crazy courtship this had been, whatever game of surrender, it was over now. Just as I had signed and begun some contract that first night on my suburban doorstep, something told me that the chaste kiss I had given him was its consummation and its end. To bring me to that point, he had dehumanised me, brutalised me, humiliated me. I hated him, and yes, if you're wondering, I did by then love him.

Of course I fucking did.

'Why didn't you just tell me the truth?' I asked. 'That first night.'

He sighed. 'I wanted to. I started to. But you were a nice girl living in a nice house leading a nice life writing your nice books and teaching in your nice school. You didn't want my story, did you? Not really. I read the blurb for your first book. I understood what you wanted. You wanted a different story. You wanted something that wouldn't upset anyone. You wanted romance. So that's what I gave you. You still want it, just not that kind. Only you and I know what romance really means. What love really means.'

He knelt in front of me and put the gun to his head.

'Gary, don't,' I cried out. 'Don't do that.'

'On the news, they said they'd found the car,' he said. 'My prints will be on it, my DNA. I'm not going to prison again, Pip. I can't go back.' His finger paled against the trigger.

'Gary,' I whimpered. 'Listen to me. Listen. I'm not a nice girl. Yes, I was living a nice life, but it bored me – you know it did. That's what you identified that night. I was bored out of my mind. And you scared me witless, you know that, that night you came into my house. I was absolutely terrified.' I raised my palms to him, made myself keep talking. 'But I have never felt so alive. You were right, my love. I signed a contract with you that night. I signed it seconds after we met. And not a moment has gone by since then that I haven't thought of you. The book, everything I've done, it's all been about you. It's all been *for* you. And everything you've done has been about me, hasn't it? Hasn't it, Gary?'

His hand shook, his finger still white around the knuckle. Two tears escaped from the corners of his eyes, and all the while he did not lift those black irises from me. I was all there was for him. I was all that was keeping him from killing himself, all that he had to live for. I knew it then as I had always known it. I was the heart of his matter, the eye of his storm, the centre of his world.

'I know why you gave me *Rebecca*,' I continued when it was clear he couldn't speak for emotion. 'Gary? I knew the moment I saw it. The way you know things about me without me having to say. That's love, isn't it? That's real devotion. You're my Mrs Danvers, aren't you?'

He nodded. 'I want you to call me that. Will you call me that?'

'Of course I will, my love. Anything you want.'

'So I'm your Mrs Danvers?'

'Yes, my love. Of course.'

The colour returned to his forefinger. His grip on the gun had relaxed. Slowly he lowered his hand, and a moment later he collapsed, his head falling into my lap. His shoulders shook. I laid my hand on his warm neck.

'Shh,' I said. 'Don't cry.'

I don't know how long we stayed like that. Half an hour, perhaps, maybe a little longer. He stopped crying and the two of us became still. Outside, an owl hooted; in the distance, a car on the B road.

Eventually Gary lifted his head, wiped his face with his rough, bony hands. Artist's hands, I thought. Long, sensitive fingers, clean nails, his silver Celtic rings. His little-boy pyjamas: how incongruous, how apposite. He was my terrifying, dangerous man. He was my little boy, my broken little boy.

'I'm letting you go,' he said.

My chest swelled. My breath shuddered as I exhaled.

He was unlocking the chain. Gently he took my ankle and ran his thumb over it.

'Is it sore?' he asked.

'Not so much now,' I said. 'Thing is not to pull against it.'

He nodded; studied my foot for a moment. 'Can you do something for me?'

I nodded. 'Anything. You know that.'

He sat on the bed and held out his foot. 'Put the ankle chain on me, will you?'

'What?'

'Put the ankle chain on me.' His black eyes held mine. 'I want you to lock me up.'

CHAPTER TWENTY-NINE

PIPPA GATES: PRIVATE JOURNAL

I closed the basement door behind me. Gary had told me to lock it too, and I did, leaving the key in. I looked around the hallway, breathless. The kitchen door was closed. Frieda must be asleep in there, I thought. I could take her with me.

I was free. Completely free.

I could take Frieda or not, pack a case or not, run out to the road in my pyjamas and coat, reach the nearest payphone and call the police. Gary could not pursue me. He could not threaten me or hold me prisoner anymore. I would tell the police that Gary Hughes had stalked me for two years, had followed me here and killed my lover, Bobby, and… yes, my best friend too; by now, my fingerprints would have long been wiped from the gun, and even if there were some small trace, I could easily say that he had made me hold it, made me take part in his wicked games. I could tell them he'd forced me to hold it to my own head – yes, yes, that was what I would tell them. If they found my prints on the car, so what? I could just tell them the truth, that he had made me drive with him to dispose of Marlie's car; how I had driven, fraught and weeping and afraid, how I had tried to escape but he had caught up, had driven me off the road and made me understand that no matter what I did, it was useless.

Get out, Pippa.

I ran upstairs, tore the pyjamas from my body. I was panting by now, my breath ragged, my chest burning. I scanned the room.

My mobile phone must be somewhere, but I couldn't see it. My cash card too – I would need that if I wanted to get further than the end of the driveway. In the top drawer of my bedside cabinet I found two brand-new packs of five plain white cotton knickers, my size but as deep-fitting as a little girl's. I shivered. Weird. Beyond weird. In the second drawer I found six bras – again, all brand new, all my size, all white and very plain in design – and four vests, again like a child's, and all white. In the third, two packs of five plain black ankle socks, still on their plastic hooks; three pairs of black tights, still in their packets.

'Jesus.' Nausea rising, I pulled on underwear, scouted about for a holdall. 'What do you need a bag for?' I hissed at myself, rummaging in the bottom of the wardrobe, finding only shoes, rows of them, all new, all my size: walking shoes, trainers, leather boots, sandals, mules. Then, on the left-hand side, larger walking shoes, trainers, boots – his?

'Just get the fuck dressed,' I whispered. 'Run, you stupid cow.'

My gaze fell on the clothes hanging above, and my chest tightened into a screwed-up little ball. Skirts, dresses, coats, jackets, all new, all neutral, all size twelve – black, burgundy, navy, camel. It took me another second to realise that in one half hung ladies' clothes, in the other, men's. The difference in style was minimal – simple tailoring, clean lines, plain colours. His and hers. It seemed he wanted us to dress as if, even in our clothes, we were a match.

Breath shuddering as I exhaled, I opened the third wardrobe door. Four compartments, in which sweaters sat in columns, folded with expert care, as in a clothes store. The bottom two sections were apparently his, the top two mine. In one compartment, cashmere; in the other, cotton. Four of each, all crew neck – burgundy, navy, black, cream. What were we going to be, twins?

My breath caught. I ran over to the chest of drawers, having more than a strong idea by then what I would find – and yes, exactly that: T-shirts, long-sleeved T-shirts, trousers, jeans, one drawer dedicated to him, two to me. All new, all my size, all folded to perfection. I found some jeans – dark blue Levi's – and put them on. They were a little tight. I pulled my hair into a ponytail, slipped on the trainers that Gary had given me – had bought for me, rather, with my own money. Here was some bizarre reversal, I thought, of traditional gender roles – wife a slave to earning money, husband cooks and cleans and facilitates career. Wife becomes too busy then too useless to buy own shoes, own pants… parent–child relationship ensues. Next he'd be sending my father a birthday card over in Phuket because I couldn't be trusted to remember, making me look at sofa catalogues while I was trying to watch the match.

Get out, Pippa.

I pulled on a long-sleeved top, a black cashmere sweater. Downstairs, I unhooked my parka coat, found my gloves, scarf and hat in the neatly arranged box next to the shoe rack. It was chilly now with the heating off for the night. I ran into the kitchen, thinking – thinking what? Water, possibly, that I would take water. On the floor, his leather vet's-style case gaped, displaying what I took to be pens, biros of some kind. Slowly, I crouched and pulled the bag open. I inhaled. My chest expanded; my hand flew to my neck. Not pens, but syringes, and tiny pouches of silver foil in transparent bags… drugs. Heroin? I sat on the floor, head in my hands.

'Shit,' I said. 'Shit.'

He was still using. He was a functioning drug addict. I had no idea how that worked – had only seen it on television. He must time his doses, I thought. Perhaps that was why he was so strict about routine, why I had to work in the cellar. Yes, of course. That was it. But now *he* was in the cellar. How long before he started to shake, to sweat, to climb the walls?

A whine and a scratch from the utility room. I opened the door and Frieda yapped, jumped up at me, her tail waving like a windscreen wiper. I fussed her, told her to shush, carried her back into the kitchen. A computer I didn't recognise was on the table. Gary's laptop, presumably. It was open. I pressed the space bar and it fired into life.

And there in the silver moonlit kitchen, I stood squinting, reading, muttering in breathless half-asked questions, as what little sense of reality I had left dropped away.

Blog post: PippaGatesAuthor
#thiswritinglife
Find me on:
Instagram: @GatesPip
Twitter: @PipGatesWrites
Facebook: Pippa Gates Author

Tonight, here at Cairn Farm, Mrs Danvers is making a chicken casserole, perfect for the winter's evening chill...

My eyes skimmed frantically over the words...

... longed-for flakes of snow... nettles glittering with frost...

What?

... Ice has the power to transform ... this stinging weed becomes the most innocent sugared confection... Jack Frost's handi-work... mulled wine and log fires...

Blog post? A blog? I didn't have a blog. What the hell *was* this?

I scrolled through, reading entries in fevered snatches. Our idealised life together, our trips out, our love. The trip to the White Horse that we never went on, the rewriting of our reasons to go to Blagdon Lake, even concerned references to Bobby and Marlena, their disappearances... my God, the audacity.

What hideous *sugared confection* of my life was *this*?

Mrs Danvers… the nickname…

He had written all of this. He had left it open for me to see. There were tens of entries… the night sky, trips to Weston-super-Mare, conversations we had never had. He had started it days after he'd got here. Or before? Time had melted away these last weeks, become nothing more than daily routine, moments written in coffee breaks and tea breaks and showers and meals. But he knew. Back then, even in the blood and terror of those first days, he had called himself Mrs Danvers. When he found the book, of course he bought it, wanting me to understand his devotion. When had he bought the book? Before he came to Wiltshire? Hadn't I said I loved du Maurier that first night? It was possible. It was all possible. The clothes in the wardrobe, the laptop left here where I could see it… who knew when he'd begun to plan his campaign? Probably from the moment he knew I'd left London… before… Was it possible that he knew before I did that I *would* go? Had it been so inevitable? Had I been so predictable? *Tout vient à qui sait attendre.* Always waiting. From that first night, that first foot on my doorstep. And just when I thought I'd been clever, gone one step ahead, he was further along still. There was nothing, nothing I could keep from him. He knew me better that I knew myself. No wonder he could write this blog, pass himself off as some oxygenated, sweetened version of me – but stylistically me all the same – while I stayed locked in the cellar.

Something buzzed. A phone. I spun around, eyes darting. Next to the toaster, an iPhone was charging. Mine. I hadn't seen it for months. I lunged for it, snatched it from the cable. A text.

Next few weeks sounds fabulous, Pip. Well done, that's speedy work. J x

By now trembling, I opened the phone, accessed the thread.

Hi Jackie. Wi-Fi a bit patchy here as usual but just to let you know, I'll have the first draft done in the next few weeks. It's going really well. Take care. Pippa

The phone fell from my hands, bounced off my foot and onto the floor. Immediately I picked it up, the coloured logos of Instagram, Twitter, Facebook shining up at me. I hadn't used them since Gary got here. But even as the thought formed, I knew I had.

He had.

I opened Instagram. Seventy-three likes. Today's picture: Frieda, with the caption, *Picked up this little girlie today. I'll never get any work done now!* There were five or six heart emojis. The next picture I had posted was a beach. Apparently I had been there a couple of days ago. *Bracing stroll on Weston-super-Mare sands this morning! Fresh air is good for you!* I scrolled through – the lakes, the beach, my statue… my lovely statue of Bing and Daisy dancing in the life they never had: *Look what Mrs D brought me today! I will use this for inspiration!*

This life. This sugared confection. *My* life. *My* sugared confection.

Gary Hughes. Mrs Danvers.

Like a parent giving a young child the illusion of choice, he had offered me the books, knowing I would pick *Rebecca*, knowing that I would read it again for comfort and see the parallels, and that when he asked for his pet name, I would agree. He even knew I would like it because it was the name of a woman, not a man; that this would appeal to some core of mischief and desire to obfuscate deep within me. He knew that later – tonight, in fact – I would find this blog and realise that he had been writing my life, my other life, my public life for months. Why else leave it out on the table? The clothes he knew I would find tonight and not before, as evidence of his devotion, of his vision for our future together.

He had orchestrated this whole thing – including my chaining him up in my own cellar.

'Fuck,' I whispered, feeling the hard kitchen chair against the backs of my thighs.

Frieda nuzzled into my shin. I petted her soft head.

'Fuck,' I whispered. 'Holy fucking fuck.'

I didn't need to see any more. The tweets, the Instagram and Facebook – Frieda would be all over my feeds today, another glittering, frosted-icing moment in my other life: the beach, the tea rooms, the statue, all with the cutesy captions, the lame jokes, a whole persona created for my readers while I sat stinking in the cellar, chained to the floor, a murderer, an accomplice, a prisoner. Everything that had happened, here in my real life, had barely dented the surface of this public face. My sugared confection had proceeded, unhindered, without me.

I pocketed the phone, clipped Frieda to her lead. The car keys were in a bowl on the windowsill – casual, as if left there by a spouse. I grabbed them and headed out – to salvation. To freedom. To the police.

The night was full of stars. Frieda panted happily in the passenger seat; tyres popped on the gravel. I turned the car around and rolled towards the driveway. From the bottom of the farmhouse wall, a dull amber glow shone through the tiny window. He was in there, in that cell, lying in his bed, awaiting his shakes and hallucinations, his heebie-jeebies and his fate. Gun by his side, his intention, I knew without the merest shadow of doubt, to shoot himself the moment he glimpsed the blue flashing light, heard the *wow-wow* of the police siren. He was sending me out to call them, to direct them to him. He had made me chain him to the bed so that even if he wanted to flee, he could not. He had saved me by unlocking my chains, then saved himself from his own inclination to run by securing that lock once again. He had made absolutely certain that his only choice when the police came was death.

I drove past that small amber glow. The tyres crunched, the engine murmured, but not loud enough to drown out Gary's words as they teemed into my mind like rain, words from years ago, uttered to a different me, in my former home, his hand around my neck.

Lies, Pip. His grip tightening, my head against the wall. *Lying is for others, not you. Lying's for the boys and girls who give you what you don't want. Lying's for your weaker self, in your bars and your restaurants, the you that pretends to care what wine goes with what, pretends you want someone to explain it to you, pretends to laugh at jokes that make you sick while you wonder how much longer you have to sit there and look at the designer lighting bouncing off his white teeth, his over-groomed stubble, his fake-prescription glasses, or whether you have the nerve to stand up, to throw down your linen napkin and say 'Your conversation is of no interest me, you are of no interest to me and I want you to shut up.'*

Lying is for when you eat your minute steak, your hand-rolled sushi, your al dente farfalle, and pretend not to wonder whether he's going to pick up the bill, whether he's going to pretend he's a gentleman for long enough to get you into bed and whether in the midst of yet another dreary fuck you will close your eyes and try to imagine someone else, someone more exciting, and when that fails, fake it just long enough so it can stop and you can creep out into the dark night on the excuse of a day at work tomorrow and hobble home while you text a polite version of 'If I see you again I'll slash my own damn wrists and save myself the long, slow death of one more evening with you.'

Lies, Pippa. It's how you keep going. It's how you survive. But we can do more than survive. We can live. Stay with me, Pippa.

I had given my first book to this man, as a gift. I had signed it, using his fountain pen, there on the threshold of my home, a threshold he had breached, utterly, as surely as he had breached every wall, door and room of me.

We belong together, I had written, egged on by him.

I had driven him to his hostel.

I had answered his texts.

I had never blocked his number.

I had never called the police.

I had alienated my best friend for him.

I had killed my best friend for him.

I had helped him bury my lover, built a monument of cobble-stones over him and Marlena.

And I thought about how, when we made the cairn, Gary had left me quite alone and untethered. He had left me on the gravel at the back of the farm while he lugged the stones to the top of the furthest field, a distance of at least a hundred metres. And there I had stood, in the open air, the driveway but metres from me, the B road at the end. There I had stood, listening for cars. I'd even looked up into that vast, woolly overcast sky, fancying that I might see a paraglider or a light aircraft of some sort. I had stood and listened and looked.

But I had not moved.

I loved him, had done from the first evening he came to my door. Hadn't I just told him that, seconds before he handed me my freedom? And he had loved me, did love me, more than his own life. He had catered for my every need. He had been the instigator of my best work. And just minutes ago, he had given me my life in exchange for his. He had given me all the power. The power to destroy him. There was no denying it. I was the absolute centre of his world. No one, no one had ever loved me as much. No one could.

I stopped the car, engaged reverse.

CHAPTER THIRTY

PIPPA GATES: PRIVATE JOURNAL

And this is where we come full circle. The story of how I was saved. How Mrs Danvers brought me to the light, to the purest, deepest love. How I come to be here, chained to my desk, as I have joked, and you perhaps thought at first that I meant metaphorically when actually I have a metal cuff around my lower leg attached to a metal plate bolted to the floor. Perhaps now the decision to write my posthumous journal is a little clearer. I simply had to record the events that brought me to this pass, otherwise how will anyone make sense of finding me here in the cellar, the bodies in the field? How would they even *find* the bodies in the field?

Scratch that. There's a fucking cairn there, for God's sake.

So.

Perhaps now, in your now – that is, my past to your present – you will realise that here, in my imprisonment, I am free; do you see that, there in your now? Do you see how free I am? Mrs Danvers has *liberated* me. No cooking, no cleaning, no social media, no emails, no accounts, no DIY, no shopping, no friends, no socialising. I could go on, but I'm sure you get the gist.

All I have to do is write. And he takes care of the rest.

He does this for me because he loves me more than any other living being, more than anyone has ever loved anyone else. He is my Mrs Danvers. And if I am dead, then surely I am his Rebecca.

There is freedom in imprisonment. There is freedom in routine. It is 9.45 a.m. The sun is up and I have almost finished my journal for today, almost finished the first draft of my novel. It is rough as old boots, but even so – three weeks has to be a record. Through the tiny window, the sun shines a weak yellow light. At 10.45 a.m., he will bring morning coffee with something home-baked; at midday, a cup of tea to keep me going until lunch at one, which I will eat while reading my morning's work. He anticipates, is able to anticipate, my every need as he has always anticipated my every thought. Because he knows me, you see. Has known me from the first night he met me. I wasn't ready to accept it, but I understand it now.

If you're reading this, it's possible by now that Mrs D has read it too. I intend to share this with him one day. I want to give it to him to read and say, look, my darling, here is the story of our love. Perhaps he will let me publish it. Perhaps he already has. Perhaps, as I have said, I am dead.

But to return to my routine, the root of my new-found sanity and success: at 8 p.m., provided of course that I have written a sufficient word count, Mrs D unlocks me and together we have dinner upstairs in our cute country kitchen. His restaurant training means he can perform the most impressive culinary miracles pretty much every evening. He has fitted a walk-in larder cupboard in the corner of the kitchen, complete with a mobile internal carousel – it really is terrific, like something off a lifestyle show. Sometimes, after dinner, we take a stroll up past the commemorative cairn, neither of us voicing what is to be found beneath, what we did on that darkest of nights, what ultimately sealed a deal we had signed long, long before.

And in case you think this a clear case of yet another woman abused by a more powerful man, I must add this: the terms of our deal are more equal than you might at first think. At night, I accompany my own Mrs D down into this very cellar, you see. He likes me to clean his teeth for him first and brush his hair and help him button up his cotton pyjamas. He likes me to put the chain around his ankle and lock it. He likes me to pull the covers over him and kiss his forehead and wish him goodnight.

'Goodnight, Gary, my love,' I whisper before climbing the cold stone steps. 'Lights off now.'

'OK, Pip,' he replies.

I pull the cord. The cellar goes black.

Some nights he begs me to return, shouts and clanks his chain. Some nights, he bangs his fists against the wall and cries expletives, barks orders: *get down here and unlock me right now.*

But I never do. That would be an abuse of trust, a very particular trust understood by us alone. What was it he said that first night? If you want love, find someone whose madness is compatible with your own. Where there is repulsion, there is attraction; where there is hate, there is love, and so on. I didn't listen. I didn't want to. Caught up as I was in my own ideas about romance.

I understand what he meant now, and I'm sure you do too. In fact, I will ask you directly: in what way are you mad, dear reader? Is your other half the right mad for you? Look at them and tell me, are you sure?

But I can hear you niggling away, there in your now. You think I can't hear, but I can, through some psychic sense, some warp in the space–time continuum. Surely if I am safe, you're saying, then I must be bored, right? Surely no matter how much devotion he shows me, it will never be enough – that's what you're thinking, isn't it? Judging by what you've read, what I've confessed to you in these pages: the woman who could never get beyond love's first flush, the woman who lost her husband and her best friend to her insatiable need to be the epicentre of their world… the woman who can never have enough love…

So why him? Why is he enough?

I'll tell you. This one last thing. Come close. Listen. I know that at any moment, he could execute me just as he did Bobby, and that poor woman in Norfolk all those years ago. I know that he would do it without hesitation. He has that power. I gave him that power. Think about it – it isn't just the time I waited while he carried rocks up the field; what about when I drove to the airport? You're telling me I couldn't have turned off somewhere, driven as fast as the car would go, at least tried to escape? What about when he wheeled the bike into the water, when I watched him disappear under the shining surface of the lake? I could have made a dash for it then, but I did not. I did not move. And before that, when he first locked me in the cellar, if you flip back, you'll see that I didn't even try the door. I heard him go out, I could have at least struggled up the steps. There were tins of paint, heavy enough to bash against the rusty old lock. Maybe it would have been too difficult, I don't know. But I didn't even try, did I? And years ago, I let him into my home, aware of his potent danger, aware that he could murder me there where I stood. I drank with him, ate with him, smoked with him, defended him to my late best friend, never once called the police when his behaviour became invasive, his language sinister.

He has a gun in his pocket. He is in charge of my care, of my survival, whether I'm fed, warm and clean or starving, cold and filthy. He has the power to destroy me every single day. And every night, I have the same power over him. He is chained up and locked away in the basement. I can leave. I can take the car and drive to the police station and tell them everything, knowing that he will kill himself the moment they arrive. I have his permission to do that.

Because that's what love is, isn't it? It's not flowers or cards or breakfast in bed; it's not trips to the theatre, a Michelin-star restaurant, a sports car with a bow tied around its bright titanium carcass. No. Gary was right; he was always right, don't you see? Love is no more than the compatibility of madness. Love is no less than the handing-over of the power to destroy from one human being to another. Love is saying, here, now you can annihilate me. Go ahead. That's love. That's real love, isn't it? Can you, dear reader, tell me any different? Can you really argue that your loved one does not have that power over you? They might not carry a gun, they might not chain you up, but they can cheat on you, stop loving you, abandon you, belittle you, humiliate you, leave you broken and bewildered, left to disentangle what you thought you knew of them from what you have come in that sudden and shocking moment to know.

This is why we have to be so very careful about who we love.

But wait. The gravel is rumbling. Someone is driving up to the farm. It can't be Mrs D, because I can hear his footsteps upstairs. The noise is getting closer, the popping of gravel under the tyres. It's 10.12 a.m. Gary's footsteps quicken on the kitchen floor above me. Through the tiny window comes a flash of blue light, the discordant slide of a lazy siren.

The cellar door opens. That's not right, not right at all. It's only 10.14 a.m. It's not time for coffee yet. Something

CHAPTER THIRTY-ONE

LETTER FROM THE EDITOR

Thank you for buying *The Proposal* by the late P. K. Gates.

This book is an unusual thing, I suppose, which is why I felt that some clarification might be useful.

The Proposal is less a novel, perhaps, than an amalgamation of excerpts from Pippa's complete private journal, which forms the bulk of the book; extracts from her novel, *Second Chance* (known to you in these pages by its working title, *Pushing Up Daisy*), published posthumously in February this year; blog posts written by her partner, Gary Hughes; and of course, audio excerpts of Hughes' verbal testimony taken from the cassette found in his second-hand Dictaphone. I edited and compiled these excerpts to produce what you have read here in these pages.

As Pippa herself pointed out, if you purchased *The Proposal* after reading the news coverage relating to the Wiltshire Murders, you will know such details as were reported in the press. However, I believe it is necessary to add at least a summary of them here for anyone unfamiliar with the actual events. Most of Pippa's account corresponds with the facts, with a few notable exceptions. And of course, her account is fuller and more personal.

Police traced Hughes to Pippa Gates's Wiltshire farmhouse after a Ford Galaxy was reported abandoned at Bristol Airport long-stay car park and found to belong to missing woman Marlena Morton. Traces of DNA in the vehicle matched that of Hughes, who was linked to Pippa after police interviewed Marlena Morton's husband. Mr Steven Morton explained that Gates had become obsessed with an ex-offender and door-to-door salesman, and had based her novel, *Framed by Love*, on him. According to Morton, Pippa regularly gave Hughes lifts back to his hostel and sent him texts that were, if not affectionate, then amiable in nature. The phone evidence was later corroborated upon the discovery of Gates's mobile in the kitchen of her home. Morton also told police that his wife, Marlena, had fallen out with Pippa on Christmas Day after Pippa arrived at the Morton family home bearing a Christmas card from Mr Hughes, explaining that he was waiting outside and asking if he could be included in the family's festive celebrations. When Marlena refused, Pippa left their home in a rage. The two women had no further contact until Pippa notified Marlena of her change of address.

Ms Gates was found dead from a bullet wound to the head in the basement of her Wiltshire farmhouse and in the arms of her captor, Gary Hughes, also pronounced dead at the scene, also from a bullet wound to the head. It was established that Hughes had shot first Pippa and then himself after becoming aware of a police car on the property. Pippa had been chained by the ankle to a secure galvanised steel panel bolted to the cellar floor. The key to the ankle chain was discovered in the drawer of her desk, where it would have been in easy reach.

The body of local shop owner Robert Wilson was discovered buried under a pile of cobbles in the top right-hand corner of the upper field at Cairn Farm, known to the locals as Smith's Farm, after the former owner of fifty-three years. The police inquiry found that Hughes murdered Wilson before taking Ms Gates prisoner in her own home and holding her captive in the basement for a period of six weeks. However, there was evidence of the most mundane cohabitation: toothbrushes and towels in the bathroom, crockery in the dishwasher, DNA evidence from both Pippa Gates and Gary Hughes in the bed. And of course, there was the journal in which Pippa confessed to killing her friend, Marlena Morton.

Marlena Morton was found in a box room on the second floor of the farmhouse, in a state of heroin dependency. She had sustained significant bruising to the chest and three fractured ribs. Unknowingly, Pippa Gates had shot her friend with a rubber bullet, which the police concluded was placed in the gun by Hughes. Hughes then fired two further bullets into the barn floor before doping Ms Morton without Ms Gates's knowledge and carrying her to the second-floor bedroom of Cairn Farm, where he kept her fed and sedated. He did not at any time make Pippa aware of this hoax, and this was believed to be further evidence of his intention to manipulate his victim and send her beyond the realms of sanity.

Ms Morton, after a period of trauma counselling and rehabilitation in a private hospital in south London, was reunited with her children and has now returned to work. She has made no comment at any time on this case. What is interesting is that, despite her survival, the events at Cairn Farm have always been referred to as the Wiltshire Murders – plural. Which to me at least suggests that, in the collective public mind, intention was more important than the crime itself.

And so to the book. We knew that fans of Pippa Gates would be expecting another romance novel, so it was decided to use her initials, P. K., instead of her full Christian name, as befits what have become the traditions of the psychological thriller. And a psychological thriller is undoubtedly what this is, categorised by the well-known tropes of the genre: a sinister presence, a predator, murder, a twist – even, it must be said, a slightly unreliable female narrator. However, I feel sure that Pippa, as I knew her, would have been amused to realise that, as a writer of much-loved romance novels herself, she had effectively written a psychological thriller, yes, but one that upheld the equally well-known conceits of popular romance: girl meets boy, girl doesn't like boy, girl believes love lies elsewhere only to realise that love is in fact to be found with the boy she met at the start.

Such a profoundly sad take on that most heart-warming and beloved of literary genres, isn't it?

Personally, I would never have believed Pippa capable of such a journal. While her ability to stick to her deadlines was questionable, she was always pleasant to deal with and had a lively sense of humour. Her three novels, *Fight for Your Love, Framed by Love* and *Second Chance*, are warm and sincere, funny and achingly romantic, and I had always assumed that she knew the joy of finding true love just as her wonderful heroines did.

The opposite was true, it seems. Much has been made in the more salacious press of her bisexuality and promiscuity, but what appeared to matter to her most was neither male nor female, stranger nor friend but, as she put it, *the time-worn comfort of flesh on flesh, hearts beating if not as one then at least as two in close proximity.* Her love for her best friend, Marlena, is not clear, but it is my opinion that it was not clear to Pippa either. She did make a clumsy pass while drunk, but it is entirely possible that in the moment it was merely physical closeness that she craved – she wanted, simply, to be held. She seemed, to me at least, always to be searching for not sex, but love, in whatever form, wherever and with whomever she could find it.

What is also interesting is that where her Tinder date was recounted in some detail, her sexual encounters with her lovers, Bobby and Sarah, were less explicit, and any account of her sexual relationship with Gary Hughes was conspicuous by its absence – which seems to me to be uncharacteristically coy. This may suggest that her desire to divulge every last detail about her life – to the point of including her toilet habits while held prisoner – decreased as her perceived level of, in her mind, true connection with another human being increased. As if, in the end, she found something she valued highly enough to keep entirely for herself, a small and precious remnant of her life she chose to keep private. But as Pippa herself has said in these pages, it is erroneous and even dangerous to assume anything about the writer on the basis of the novel.

This book, however, is different in that it is mostly autofiction, so can, I believe, give some insight into the author as a person. Reading these pages, a troubling picture emerges of someone whose view of love was tainted by the trauma experienced when, aged six, she discovered her mother's body after she had taken an overdose. Her father's inability to cope no doubt left an indelible mark, as did his gradual retreat into himself and his ultimate callous abandonment of her just as she entered early adulthood. Her parents were so bound up in their own pain, they unwittingly caused hers.

Of course, her views on love could have been vastly altered due to Stockholm syndrome, a condition much discussed in the column inches surrounding this case, which so fascinated the nation. She had, at the end, undoubtedly been brainwashed and had fallen for her captor, Gary Hughes. Whatever spell he cast on her, whatever caused her to obsess over him, to write a book she believed was an adaptation of his true life story, began long before she was taken prisoner.

As for Hughes, what led him to trace her to the wilds of Wiltshire and kill off all possible competition for her love, make her believe she had murdered her best friend, imprison her in the cellar and keep her like a pet only to have her do the same for him, in some grotesque re-enactment of his own deeply dysfunctional childhood, appears to have been but the last stage in their increasingly insane affair, a process that, she acknowledges, started that night in June when he arrived at her door selling cleaning products. Who was obsessed by whom, who was captive and who was captor, will remain a mystery buried with these most messed-up of star-crossed lovers. Indeed, she made mention of

Romeo and Juliet as the model of perfect love, a love that ends in death before it has to face any of the difficulties real life throws at us. How apt, then, that shortly after professing their love, she and Hughes should die in each other's arms. Pippa Gates and Gary Hughes destroyed one another, which I suppose makes this, in a way only they could understand, a story of true love.

As Pippa herself said: *Love is no less than the handing-over of the power to destroy from one human being to another. Love is saying, here, now you can annihilate me. Go ahead. That's love. That's real love, isn't it? Can you, dear reader, tell me any different?*

Thank you for reading *The Proposal*.

Jackie West

All materials are published here with permission from the author's father, inheritor of her Wiltshire estate.

A LETTER FROM
S.E. LYNES

Dear Reader,

Thank you so much for taking the time to read *The Proposal*; I am delighted that you did and hope you enjoyed it. I very much hope you will want to read my next book too. If you'd like to be the first to hear about my new releases, you can sign up using the link below:

www.bookouture.com/se-lynes

The Proposal was inspired by an article by Alain de Botton in *The New York Times* entitled 'Why You Will Marry the Wrong Person', which I once posted on Facebook and my other half commented: *Cheers*. But it was actually positing the theory that romantic compatibility lies in one person's insanities complementing their partner's. 'In a wiser, more self-aware society than our own,' de Botton wrote, 'a standard question on any early dinner date would be: "And how are you crazy?"'

This fascinated me. On a mundane level, we could talk about opposites attracting or one half of a couple becoming stressed about different things than the other half. *Jack Sprat could eat no fat, his wife could eat no lean…* But I wanted to explore this idea through the psychological thriller, which meant blowing oxygen into it until it exploded. In *The Proposal*, Pippa and Gary are, in terms of their madness, a perfect match. And the result is dark, disastrous and deadly.

I also found in *The Spectator* a review of a book called *That's Disgusting* by Rachel Herz. The book proposes ideas surrounding repulsion and attraction – it is there that I found the example of Ecuadorean *chicha*. So into the pot went that too.

I had to find a way of making Ryan fascinating to Pippa, despite the fact that when he arrives on her doorstep, he is physically repulsive due to poor clothing, limited facilities and bad diet. The above theories gave me his opening conversation and clues into his motivations. He has educated himself in a kind of vacuum – prison – and cannot wait to find someone willing to listen to his new-found knowledge. Pippa's keen interest in him is an unexpected and delightful surprise. His way of engaging her is different to anyone else she has met. In addition, as an ex-offender, he is, in her mind, full of latent menace, and this excites her.

Halfway through the book, I realised I was writing a psychological thriller that was taking shape as a romantic novel. Pippa, then, had to be a romance writer but one whose ideas about love I could subvert for my dastardly purposes. I can't remember when Mrs Danvers arrived in the mix, but once I had the nickname, I knew I had to keep the gender hidden until later in the book. Pippa thus became attracted to both genders, which fitted perfectly with her insatiable desire for love, wherever and however she could find it. And by then, the book had me in its gnarled and nasty claws. I could not stop working on it and seeing just how dark and crazy these characters could become.

If you enjoyed *The Proposal*, I would be so grateful if you could spare a couple of minutes to write a review. It only needs to be a line or two – in fact, the best reviews often are! – and I would really appreciate it. I am always happy to chat or answer questions via my Twitter account and Facebook author page if you wish to get in touch. Writing can be a lonely business, so when a reader reaches out and tells me my work has stayed with them or that they loved it, I am truly delighted. I have loved making new friends online through my first novel, *Valentina*, through my second and third, *Mother* and *The Pact*, and hope to make yet more with *The Proposal*.

Best wishes,
Susie

 @selynesauthor

SE Lynes Author

ACKNOWLEDGEMENTS

Firstly, as ever, I want to thank my editor, Jenny Geras, whose laser-sharp skills and lightness of touch mean that my stories are better but still very much mine. All the team at Bookouture work so hard to make these books happen and to ensure that people know about them, so I would like to thank Kim Nash, Noelle Holton, Lauren Finger, Jane 'eagle-eye' Selley, and all the team.

As ever, I need to thank my other half, Paul, whose madness is compatible with my own but who isn't a murderer, thank goodness. Not so far as I know, anyway. Thank you for continuing to talk me down from my various ledges and allowing me to talk you down from yours. Thanks to my kids, who drive me mad but for whom I would walk over hot coals in bare feet – the usual mum stuff.

I want to thank my friends who have read and continue to read my work even though it isn't homework nor any sort of condition for my love. My writing group, Hope, Robin, Cat, Sam... who don't meet as often as we should now, but whose advice is always invaluable, and who were there at the conception of *The Proposal* and seemed to think it was a goer.

Huge love and thanks to the readers who review and to the amazing bloggers out there, who support us authors by reading and raving about our books. You all rock and I owe all of you a pint.

Finally, as ever, massive love and thanks go to my mum, Cath Ball, who has read *The Proposal* in about four different versions, under various titles (*The Knock at the Door*, *The Salesman*), and who is my first trusted reader and invaluable adviser.